FIRST DAWN

BOOK ONE OF THE LOST MILLENNIUM

MIKE MOSCOE

ACE BOOKS, NEW YORK

This book is an Ace original edition,
and has never been previously published.

FIRST DAWN

An Ace Book / published by arrangement with
the author

PRINTING HISTORY
Ace edition / December 1996

The Putnam Berkley World Wide Web site address is
http://www.berkley.com/berkley

Make sure to check out PB Plug, the science fiction/fantasy
newsletter, at http://www.pbplug.com

ISBN: 0-441-00392-3

ACE®
Ace Books are published by The Berkley Publishing Group,
200 Madison Avenue, New York, NY 10016.
ACE and the "A" design are trademarks
belonging to Charter Communications, Inc.

FIRST DAWN

Lieutenant Launa O'Brian.

Captain Jack Walking Bear.

They are the first time travelers, guinea pigs in an experiment that cannot fail. From a future nearly destroyed by plague, they must travel thousands of years into the past to the dawn of civilization. Among tribes of primitive hunters, they will trace a fatal chain of events—and alter history to save humanity from itself.

BOOK ONE IN

THE LOST MILLENNIUM SERIES

DEDICATED TO ELLEN

The best friend, story problem solver and
lover a writer could ask for,
who didn't complain about sharing the hot tub
with Launa and Jack for five years.
And never seems to have regretted giving me
that college course bulletin eight years ago,
with the fiction writing course circled.

ACKNOWLEDGMENTS

LIKE MANY FIRST novelists, I owe a debt of gratitude to a lot of people. Debts are always paid.

A special thanks to the folks of Sheila Simonson's "Fiction Writing Class" at Clark College. It may have taken them three years to hammer the basics into me, but we never gave up on anyone. Mary Rosenblum and so many other writers gave me the graduate course.

The gang at work was special. They kept me honest, making sure my characters fought, and if necessary, died right. Merv's eagle eye always spotted what others missed.

Thanks, Stan, for buying the stories that kept my spirits up, and the words flowing.

They usually don't get mentioned, but I want to express special appreciation to all those editors and agents who took the time to read and reject the earlier incarnations of this story. Your thoughtful notes were bright beacons in the education of this writer and the direction of this story.

Riane Eisler, the late Dr. Mariju Gimbutas, Dr. Colin Renfrew, and many others whose works fill a bookcase in my study, held up a candle to the remnants of the Old Europeans. What I saw there sent chills down my back and my imagination roaming. Still, the world of River Bend and Tall Oaks is my own responsibility, patched together from years of rummaging libraries and watching the ever present Kurgans and Old Europeans around me today.

Lastly, thank you, Ginjer and Jennifer and the crew at Ace and the Donald Maass Agency for bringing Launa and Jack, Lasa and Kaul, and the galloping hordes to life on these pages.

ONE

COLD RAKED LAUNA'S bare skin, but it was the fear clutching her heart that made her shiver. Beside her in the darkness, Star nickered and yanked on his primitive halter. When Launa asked what would happen if one of the animals bolted from the energy capsule, the scientists shrugged. They had built the time transport, but that didn't mean they understood it.

Launa pulled down hard on her horse's reins and stroked his neck. The nervous shuffle of his hooves slowed. At her feet, the dogs whined, but stayed huddled together around her ankles, sharing their comfort—and warmth.

In the pitch dark, Launa could hear Captain Jack Walking Bear soothing his mount and the pack horse. By all rights Jack should have been her commanding officer. But nothing had been right since she had been summoned from an afternoon class at West Point two months ago and offered lieutenant's bars and a mission beyond strange.

This afternoon, the President of the United States had given the orders for the Neolithic Military Advisory Group to *her*. All her life, Launa had dreamed of command. She never expected to get it like this.

Launa drew in a quick breath, and coughed. Even the bitter cold could not cover the stink of ozone. The copper knife at her side began vibrating, taking up the hum in the time transport bubble that had started low, but was quickly rising in pitch. Seeping into her bones, it threatened to tear her apart. *Was this what happened to Muffin? Had the dog's flesh been shattered into molecules and strewn across a millennium?*

After the test run with the dog, the time machine hadn't focused on any year more recent than A.D. 1000. Jack's and her temporal jump had better work. There was no more time for the Livermore team to get it right; their world was under a death sentence. Fear rose again in her throat. *Thinking like that doesn't help a mission, Lieutenant.* She ordered her mind to empty.

How much longer? In the rush to leave, she hadn't asked how long it would take to go six thousand years and halfway around the world. She clenched her teeth—to stop their chattering and hold in her courage. A vision of her frozen body dropping into some paleolithic swamp flooded her mind. As if sharing her nightmare, Star yanked on his halter, dragging her out of herself. She pulled his head close to her bare breasts and stroked his muzzle. "We can make it, fellow." With a shudder, her breath left her. "We have to."

Launa gulped in air. The acrid stench was less severe. She blinked; the black slid to gray. A moment later, they floated in an ebony sky full of unblinking stars. Candy-colored clouds drifted below them.

Now might be her only chance for aerial reconnaissance; Launa whipped her head around. Gulping back nausea, she tried to see everything within the curved horizon. She spotted blue sea and white-capped mountains framing a rolling plain laced with streams. To one side, the world disappeared into shadow; on the other, a dazzling sun dawned.

Then, with an eagerness Launa only half appreciated, the capsule swooped toward the earth. *Where will the energy bubble leave us?* They had to be above ground. But too much of a drop and their horses, loaded with everything they had from the twenty-first century, would break their legs in the fall.

The mad dive slowed. The air almost smelled normal. The

energy bubble shimmered, sparkling with a rainbow of hues. When it paled, Launa stuck her hand through it. Warm air!

"Let's go." Launa found herself echoing the Colonel. *Well, there were a few things about Dad worth imitating.* She stepped off on her left foot—by The Book—leading the horse and dogs. Her first pace came down hard, as on concrete. Her second step crunched grass. Beside her, Jack was already pulling his horses forward, into their new world.

Busy with her horse, Launa dropped the dogs' leashes. Frieda, the German shepherd, launched herself into exploring. Mist, a Border collie, tried herding a dozen butterflies. Jack let Alert off her leash. The attack dog, a Great Dane about the size of some Viking castles, lumbered along beside Jack, eyes vigilant for anything, living out her name.

Launa broke off a wildflower and tossed it where they had been. The flower disappeared into the shimmering.

"They'll know we've arrived." Launa paused, then added, "And where to send reinforcements." *If any support is available.*

Jack nodded and looked around. "Wherever *here* is."

To Launa, it looked like Eden. Ripe grasses covered the plain, bending at the first hint of a breeze. Wildflowers, some up to her horse's shoulder, scented the air. Mist stopped to sniff a clump of yellow blossoms and sneezed. Launa allowed herself a chuckle, and glanced up. Birds of every hue shared a pastel sky with their first dawn in this new and ancient world. Beautiful. *But remember, kid, even Eden had a snake.* The Colonel had taught her well to look past the first glance.

She finished her three-sixty at the same time Jack did. The vista was innocent of humanity. They could be when and where they were supposed to be—four thousand and something B.C., near the mouth of the Danube River. Then again, places where they'd trained in Wyoming had looked just like this.

The sandals and briefs the anthropologists had copied from the art of the goddess worshipers were the wrong uniform for a hike through tall grass. When she turned to Jack, he was already pulling two pairs of leather boots from Big Red's pack.

That was a good start for them. In any rational situation, Jack would be giving *her* orders. But they were targeted for a culture where women led. When the President gave Launa their orders, Jack had stood at attention, like a good soldier. Still, Launa wondered how a combat veteran would feel about taking orders from a woman who a few months ago had been a West Point cadet studying for finals. Their practice at cooperative command during their training had been anything but successful.

It took a moment to pull on boots. She would have added elk skin leggings, but her pair had burned in the sneak attack that wrecked their training site. She'd lost a lot of gear, and friends.

Would the President have ordered a long shot like us if he'd had more time and a machine that gave him more choices? But the plague left no one with time, and Judith had always insisted the neolith was the best hope for rationalizing human history. The President had gone along with Judith. Launa and Jack had gone with what they could grab.

Jack produced two wide-brimmed hats and grinned. "Maria thought we might need some shade."

Launa settled the gentle Mexican cook's gift on her head. She could feel Maria's wide arms hugging her; it almost soothed the edginess in Launa's gut.

Jack did another three-sixty. "Where to?"

Part of Launa wanted to burrow into the ground, have a good cry. Every rational fiber in her body screamed there was no way they could win a war lost six thousand years before they were born. Judith was dreaming if she thought two people could nudge history out of the destructive path that led to a dead twenty-first century into some peaceful, cooperative alternative. But Launa had never quit anything, and now was no time to start.

With a measured breath, Second Lieutenant Launa O'Brian of the United States Army straightened her shoulders. Drawing herself up to her full five feet four, she issued the mission's first order—sort of. Pointing at the lone tree standing above the nearest rise, she said, "On the way down, I spotted a stream on the other side of that hill. If we camp under the tree, we can keep the landing site under surveillance. We'll see any support or message"—or recall—"they send. In the meantime, we do as little as possible to impact things here."

"And we'd have a water source." Jack pointed at the empty water skins. "I wanted all the tools and trade goods the horses could carry. I didn't waste any lift on consumables."

Launa nodded her agreement. She also relaxed a tad. They had cooperated on their first decision just like Old Europeans; Judith would be proud. The anthropologist insisted the goddess worshipers made all their decisions in cooperative partnership. That was something Launa wanted to see.

Jack led off for the hill.

The walk and the sun grew hot. Sweat dripped into Launa's eyes. She hoped her sunscreen was as waterproof as the label claimed; she only had two tubes. Their equipment was supposed to be just what was available locally. Judith had been adamant; no students of hers would play gods to primitives. Still, Launa had hidden a few things in their packs without asking the permission of the President's old college professor. *She'll never know.*

Launa licked her lips. "Damn, I forgot Chapstick."

Jack chuckled as he shook his head. "Grandfather would say, 'Walk the green fields. Feed your eyes on the blue sky. Let your heart turn its back on worries. Forget about dime store potions.'"

Launa swallowed a hot rejoinder. She hated it when Jack started quoting his Apache grandfather. She knew damn well Jack grew up in L.A. with his stepfather. Except for a half dozen summers with his grandfather, his background was no more Indian than hers. But Jack threw in a lot of his grandfather's sayings; they added a flavor to his facade. Launa wondered if she'd ever find out what was Jack and what was just show.

As she avoided Jack, her eyes took in her new world. Despite the messenger, Grandfather's advice might be worth taking. Mist played with a bird; Frieda took off after a rabbit, but quickly gave it up. Both trotted back to join Alert. She strode, unruffled, ahead of Jack.

Tongue hanging out, Mist beamed happily. Launa envied the collie her enjoyment. Maybe Jack's relaxed outlook wasn't so bad. *It would be great not to worry, not to spend every second planning options. How does Jack do it? Maybe he doesn't, but I sure can't see the worry behind those dark eyes.*

"I think we got company." Jack's words put a brake on her thoughts. Heart racing, Launa looked where Jack pointed—the solitary elm they were walking toward. The sun glared off the baked dirt around it, but beneath its wide branches was darkness. In that dark, something moved.

Launa squinted, tried to focus, but heat shimmers distorted the air. "Animals?" she hoped.

"Could be," Jack agreed.

Launa silently cursed the rules that left her without a pair of binoculars. Then she shrugged. "I had hoped we'd have a while before we made contact with the locals, like after we heard something from up-time, but we're going to make contact with them sooner or later."

With a soldier's resignation, she kept walking.

"Should we get out the bows?" Jack's voice was even—a good executive officer going down the checklist.

A quick "no" jumped to Launa's lips, but she swallowed it. Judith had taught her a process for decision-making, and it was time to use it. First, get agreement on the facts. "Bows are a projectile weapon, useful for attritioning an enemy crossing a killing ground." *Damn, I sound like a West Point lecture.* She hoped Jack didn't take it wrong. A glance at him showed his face a soldier's mask. She went on.

"We don't have any official targets we can kill at three hundred meters. Besides, if they're goddess worshipers, they shouldn't be dangerous and we don't want to show off our longbow. Assuming Judith and Brent were right about these folks."

Jack blinked twice. "You trust the anthropologists?"

The question surprised Launa. During training, Jack had

never openly doubted the two scholars. Oh, he questioned them plenty, driving them to give him plain answers when they would have preferred scholarly suppositions. Launa knew Judith and Brent had done the best they could—from dusty relics.

She shrugged. "Growing up Army, I met plenty of people who didn't fit their society's norm. Let's not take any chances we can avoid. Now, knives are merely tools." Grinning, Launa pulled the copper knife from her belt—and hid it in her boot.

Jack gave her an approving nod and switched his knife to a boot. Then he retrieved two more knives from Windrider's pack. "These are bronze. They may be a bit ahead of their time, but . . ." He shrugged, and Launa put the backup in her other boot.

Figures broke from the tree, dust rising behind them. It was hard to make out their numbers. One thing was clear. They were mounted.

"Oh shit, Kurgans." Launa spat the word. Here were the horse raiders they had come to stop.

"If we're in the right place and time." Jack pursed his lips.

"And if the locals haven't traded for horses," Launa finished muddying up the tactical picture.

"Do we fight?" Jack asked.

A void yawned open in Launa's gut. The lost hopes of billions sucked that emptiness into hard vacuum. Launa willed the chasm closed, ignored it as she centered her mind on the approaching riders.

She had orders. She snorted; they said nothing about Kurgan horsemen fifteen minutes into the mission. She'd spent the last month getting ready for this moment; nothing prepared her for this. She had five minutes to make the most important decisions of her life, maybe of all history—and she would have to wing it.

Launa fell back on her West Point training, methodically ticking off issues, searching for a strategy. "We don't know for sure where or when we are. We don't know who these people are. We can't start killing people before we know the situation."

"Yep," Jack said, adding nothing.

Frustration coiled around Launa like a killing snake. "We're not supposed to muck with history while there's still a chance they might find a cure for the plague. Hell, one of those guys could be my grandfather, a couple hundred times removed. We start killing people, and I might pop like a soap bubble." Launa didn't know whether to take that last one seriously or not. Since she'd volunteered for this lash-up, she was never sure where reality ended and fantasy began.

Jack grinned. "There are advantages to being half Apache, paleface." Then he sobered. "What do we do?" He glanced over his shoulders at their horses. "We're too loaded to run, and I'm not dumping this load of tools for Kurgans to paw over."

Jack turned back to the approaching riders and squinted, as if to see ten minutes into the future. "Tactical situation sucks." He waved at a stretch of grass that was only ankle-high. "I suggest we meet our new neighbors over there."

Launa nodded and, as she led the way, knew she had one more decision to make. "Jack, it doesn't look like I'll be talking to women any time soon."

"Yeah."

"If we're dealing with men, a man should do the talking. I think you should take the command."

"Yeah." Jack didn't even shrug.

Damn. Jack's gone into strong silent mode. Didn't he learn anything from Judith? But that was Jack. One of these days, Launa was going to find a club big enough to crack the shell he wrapped around himself. Or maybe his head. Launa put that thought aside. She had enough problems today.

We were supposed to meet a bunch of farmers and talk their women leaders into resisting the horsemen. Instead we run into horsemen. What the hell is going on here? The chasm was gaping open again. Launa held her gut together with her fingertips. Then Jack's actions got her full attention.

He pulled the leather scabbards and quivers from the horses' packs and dropped them into the high grass. "If we

let people get close, our longbows are worthless. I don't
want Kurgans seeing them."

*So much for all that practice, but Jack was right; start
thinking in real time, girl.* Launa pulled two quarterstaffs
from Star's pack and tossed one to Jack. "These'll be good
close in."

"Yeah." Jack caught the staff without looking at her.
They'd reached the field; he whistled in the dogs. "I'll hold
the horses. You keep the dogs. They don't much like
strangers."

Launa didn't much like the dogs. Moving from post to
post, she'd never had so much as a pet goldfish. Now Jack
expected her to keep that Great Dane under control. The
bitch outweighed her! Jack put the attack dog on a leash
while Launa collared the other two.

As he handed her Alert's leash, his eyes were on the incoming horsemen. "Take the dogs and stand behind the
horses."

Launa struggled to keep the dogs from tangling her in
their leashes. She opened her mouth, but before she got a
word out, Jack turned to face the horsemen. *Damn it. We're
supposed to be cooperating here, Jack. Understand the concept. I can't do it from the back of the line.* But The Book
said you don't question orders in the face of the enemy.
Launa went where she was sent.

Alert surprised her; the highly trained attack dog obeyed
her, even sat when ordered. *Good thing I remember the few
commands they taught me.* The other two dogs were a handful.

Launa took station behind but to the right of the horses.
With luck, she could give Jack some support from there. It
also gave her a clear view of the ten approaching riders.

Each led one or two spare mounts. They all wore boots,
leggings, and open vests. Stone heads tipped their ten- to
twelve-foot-long lances. Square wooden quivers holding a
few arrows and a short bow swung from the belts at each of
their waists. Their hair was brown, red, blond like hers,
pulled back in one or several plaited tails. Launa found her-

self checking noses and mouths. Did any of them look like the Colonel?

The rider immediately behind the leader held a pole with the bleached skull of a wolf lashed to its top. Judith said many animals were sacred to the goddess; she'd never mentioned the wolf. These folks didn't look like the goddess's type.

The riders halted fifteen feet out from Jack when the leader shouted something. Launa had spent hours with Judith and Brent trying to figure out what proto-Indo-European might sound like; she didn't have a clue to what he said.

Jack moved his quarterstaff to his left hand and raised his right. For a long moment, nothing happened.

Then the leader brought his right foot over his horse's neck and gracefully slid from his mount. He tossed his lance to the totem bearer and strutted toward Jack. Slapping Jack on the shoulder, he went straight to Big Red. The horse shied, but laden and on leading reins could not escape the man's attention.

Big Red rolled his eyes even as the horseman tried to soothe him. The leader did manage to get a good look at the horse's teeth. Launa didn't need a translation to catch the approval in the horseman's tone. Big Red had an admirer.

Alert growled low beside Launa. While the leader held her attention, three riders had edged around her. One of them now dismounted and swaggered toward Launa.

"Jack, I have a problem over here."

"Launa, we're outnumbered. Let's keep things smooth."

Launa pulled Frieda and Mist in tighter.

Most of the riders had dismounted. They milled around the three horses Jack held on tight reins, examining the knots on the packs and moving the blankets to see what was inside. Two men now stood in front of Launa, alternately frowning at the dogs and leering at her. Men had undressed her with their eyes before. It was easier to take when she had more on.

"Jack, I don't like the way this situation is developing."

"Neither do I, Lieutenant."

"Yessir," Launa answered and stiffened to attention, her

alertness going up a notch. *So Jack's ready to start soldiering.* Maybe that was why she spotted the rapid motion.

A large war club hung from the leader's belt. He turned away from Jack. Then, bringing his club up from his hip, he swung around, back at Jack.

"Jack!" Launa screamed. Someone grabbed her from behind, knocking her hat over her eyes.

Launa let go of the dogs' leashes. "Attack!" she screamed as she stomped on her attacker's insole—*My boots are tougher than yours, jerk.* She grabbed an arm and flipped him over her shoulder. Her hat went one way as he went the other.

The Kurgan landed with a *whoomp* and a shocked look on his face. A second later Launa's knife was out of her boot and in his throat. She took a second to glance around while her startled assailant convulsed in death.

Jack was down; the Great Dane charged his attacker. The leader bestrode Jack, about to bring his club down on Jack's skull when Alert took the Kurgan in the throat. Blood gushed.

Launa didn't have time to watch someone else's fight. She yanked her knife loose. Her next would-be attacker stood immobile, wide eyes locked on his companion. Launa made a swipe at him, leaving a gash along his chest. He turned and ran.

Launa took two steps in pursuit—and missed a lance jab to her back. She whirled; the bastard sat on his horse, grinning. He made another thrust. Launa sidestepped as she grabbed the shaft, then yanked hard. In a second, she had the lance. *Someday you boys are going to learn respect for women.* She was glad they hadn't yet.

Flipping the lance around, Launa nicked the horse's ear. It reared and shied sideways. The horseman kept his seat, but at the price of ignoring Launa. As the horse bucked, the rider pitched forward. She drove the lance into him.

Gasping for breath, Launa glanced around. The only Kurgans near her were dead or running. She snatched up a fallen lance and caught the halter of the nearest horse. Grabbing a handful of mane, Launa swung herself onto its back and paused for a second to recapture situational awareness.

Jack lay under a pile of bodies. The leader, Alert, and another Kurgan were on top of him. *Oh my God! I'm it. It's just me.*

Three Kurgans were stringing bows; it was time to leave.

With a war whoop, Launa lowered her lance and charged. Warriors and horses scattered out of her way like pigeons. She let them.

Once clear of the Kurgans, Launa rode for the ridge and the tree. A glance under her shoulder showed two riders giving chase. Launa urged her horse for more speed.

In the shade of the tree, she paused to let her winded mount catch its breath. *What I'd give for an M-16.* She had a three-minute lead on her two pursuers, but they had spare mounts and already hers was tiring.

Three Kurgans had finished rounding up most of the mounts she had scattered, as well as Launa's own heavily laden horses. It would take them a while to join her pursuit, but they were coming to the party. A single rider still chased a few strays.

Launa turned her attention to her own problem—escape. In the valley before her was a wood. She kicked her mount to a run. Once among the trees, she'd have a better chance. Maybe these steppe-raised bastards wouldn't follow.

As her mount reluctantly responded to her urging, Launa half laughed. She'd killed two men and hadn't disappeared. *Hope my luck holds.* Then again, being all alone, six thousand years from her birth, with a mission almost beyond comprehension, she'd need a lot more luck than she'd had so far today.

TWO

JACK CAME FROM blackness to the feel of a dog licking his face. His head was a throbbing agony. He took a breath; it came in a half gasp and smelled of grass and flowers—and blood. Jack froze, listening for any movement, any sound. All he heard was a dog panting.

An ice age came and went as Jack waited for a lance jab. None came. Jack wished he had a chip off one of those glaciers for his head. He risked opening an eye.

Frieda whimpered and sat back on her haunches. Still not moving, Jack took in all he could see. Grass and a dog. Something heavy lay across his legs. He risked moving his head a smidge. The Kurgan leader lay across him, his throat ripped out. Alert was on top of him, three lances and an arrow in her. Beyond her sprawled another body, its face mangled.

Remind me to write a "Thank you" to Alert's trainer.

Trusting Frieda for warning, Jack shoved the bodies off and sat up. He searched his surroundings as his fingers gingerly explored his head. He'd expected some kind of fight. Launa's shout had warned him enough to flinch. Maria's hat and the hair he'd grown in the last few months must have helped too. He had been conscious when he hit the ground, trying to figure out how to use feigned unconsciousness to his best advantage. Then Alert arrived. Sometime in that brawl he had gone from faking it to being out cold.

Using a discarded lance, Jack pulled himself to his feet. Where Launa had been were two dead Kurgans. That kid had done better in a brawl than he had. So much for the folks who thought she was too green. "Maybe I ought to let her take charge whether we're talking to women or men." Then again, he'd been point; his response time had been a tad shorter than hers.

Getting back to business. Jack did the cold arithmetic. Subtract Launa's two and the two Alert had taken care of, and there were still six horse thieves around here somewhere.

He spotted one; a lone rider chased three scattered horses. Matters may have gotten confusing enough for these guys to lose track of their horses, but they would never leave without them. A warrior had been assigned to collect the strays.

Jack put a clump of tall flowers between him and the cleanup man while he finished searching the horizon. Three riders and a dozen horses topped the rise near the lone tree. Three of the horses carried packs and moved at a walk.

Those horses belonged to Jack. He wanted them back, and his gear. *No question who's a legitimate target now. If it's on a horse, it's dead meat.* "Now, how to make 'em dead."

An inventory of the weapons on the dead Kurgans didn't help. He quickly dismissed the lances and club. The bows were no better. Short and simple, they were good for maybe fifty meters. Jack needed something with a long reach and that he'd practiced with. "How far back did I dump the longbows?"

The tall grass turned out to be as good a hiding spot as Jack had wanted when he dumped the bows and a lot better than he needed at the moment. He kept low, despite waves of dizziness. The grass slashed him until his arms and legs bled. The sun and bugs added to his pain. And every minute or so, Jack risked checking on the Kurgan wrangler. He wasn't having any better luck collecting the strays than Jack was having finding something to kill him with.

After five frantic minutes, Jack stumbled on a quiver. *Well, the rest have got to be around here somewhere.* A long minute later, he found a bow scabbard. As he strung it, he spotted the rest of his weapons. Quickly collecting them, Jack considered his problem—how to kill a man and steal some horses. In Wyoming, he and Launa had practiced on targets up to three hundred meters out.

Yeah. But they weren't armed and moving, Bearman. How you going to get this bastard in solid range? Jack glanced over his shoulder at where the vultures were already circling. *Those bodies still had their weapons load.* Unless there was a taboo against stripping the newly dead, someone was coming back. Jack knew who. He began to low walk back to the bodies.

The cleanup man had caught two of the horses. When he had the third, he headed for the site of the recent unpleasantness.

Jack hid in the grass until the Kurgan was sixty meters out, then stood up. Their eyes met. Without a moment's reflection, the rider lowered his lance and charged.

Jack put an arrow into his chest.

The warrior didn't even flinch, but kept coming.

Jack aimed higher, for the head—and missed. He put his third arrow into the guy's upper chest. The Kurgan's lance was aiming straight for Jack's heart.

Jack dropped and rolled across the horse's path. The lance point started to follow, then faltered. As the horse veered away from Jack, the Kurgan slid from his mount.

Knife in hand, Jack raced for the fallen man, then dropped and rolled again as the rider brought his lance up, trying to impale Jack. Once inside the lance's reach, Jack batted it aside and slid down beside his wounded foe. The man hissed something as he grabbed for the stone knife in his belt.

"You guys don't know when to quit, do you?" Jack growled and slashed the man's throat. Blood spurting, the Kurgan's hands and feet flailed out. Jack took a slap to the mouth as he scooted back.

Turning his back on the dying man, Jack stood up; he'd seen enough blood in Iraq. He'd also seen plenty of men standing in line to surrender. This horseman had fought to his last gasp. *Different war. Hope they're not all hard cases like this one.*

Jack whistled up Mist, and sent her to chase in a mount. The dog's unfamiliar scent quickly drove a horse within

Jack's grasp. Once mounted, he easily caught the other three.

Ready to leave, Jack surveyed the battlefield. *Five down. Five to go.* He glanced at his enemy, now shivering in final convulsions. He ought to retrieve the long arrows sticking out of him. Jack had four quivers; Launa needed him now. He could take care of security later.

Jack pulled his horse's head around, kicked the animal, and galloped for the rise the horsemen had vanished over. The dogs would follow on their own. Switching to a fresh mount in the shade of the tree, Jack studied the shallow valley that lay ahead of him. A tree-lined stream made gentle turns from a grove half a mile below the tree. The riders he was following had dismounted halfway down the valley, in front of a large wood.

Jack grinned. Launa had probably gone to ground there. "You bastards are in trouble. Never pick a fight with that woman in trees."

It was time to weigh options. Confusion was on his side now; they didn't expect trouble, at least from someone riding these horses. *Let's help them stay dumb.* Swinging a quiver at his waist like a Kurgan, and hiding his longbow by holding it beside his lance, Jack kicked his fresh mount to a run.

Jack's targets—they were no longer human beings— made camp at the edge of the woods. He approached at a gallop. Two tended the horses, while the third fed a fire and began lashing several lances together.

They ignored Jack until his first arrow took one of the horse-tenders full in the chest. That one's cry brought heads up. Jack's second arrow missed as the fire-maker bolted for the trees. His third arrow also missed. Shooting from horseback was no way to hit evading targets. Jack lowered his lance, aiming for the last man racing for the woods.

The man was good. As Jack pounded up behind him, the Kurgan dodged away. But he lost his footing and went down.

Jack kept the lance aimed at the guy's back. The flint head sank into its target. Jack held the haft loose, letting the lance slip through his hand, then let go as the lance tried to bash him in the back of the head. Lances were a one-shot weapon without stirrups. Quickly, Jack yanked hard on his reins and swerved to avoid the trees. Putting distance between himself and any archer who might be hiding in the forest, Jack considered what he had done, and what was left.

Two Kurgans were down. Jack had regained control of his twenty-first century resources and acquired those of a small Kurgan horse patrol. Not a bad afternoon's work. *If I find Launa alive and can stay alive myself.*

Seven targets down, three to go. The odds were getting better.

Jack dismounted beside the Kurgan his first arrow had hit. Though wounded, the man had tried to string a bow and return Jack's fire. Blood pooled around him; Jack had hit an artery.

The second Kurgan moaned. Jack went to him. Pulling the lance from his back, Jack rolled him over. Eyes glazed in shock stared at Jack. The chest wound sucked air, and the man half coughed, half choked. He mumbled something; it might have been a curse or a prayer. Jack opened his neck as a grace and stood back while death took him.

Frieda and Mist arrived, and Jack turned back to his situation. His three Arabian-quarter horse crosses had been unburdened and let to graze. They towered above the local mounts. Jack waved Mist out into the pasture to keep the horses together.

Frieda sniffed around the camp, then growled and headed for the edge of the woods. She paused there, waiting.

Jack checked his knives, collected his bow and quiver. Launa was in there somewhere, trailed by men who wanted her dead. Six thousand years from now, Jack had sent Launa into the woods angry and naked for what he thought was a survival hike. Two days later he'd picked up a very mad woman who, barehanded, had killed a gunman with an AK-47. Jack had sworn he'd never underestimate Launa again. And he'd gladly given her the command—given it to her before she broke his male chauvinistic neck taking it.

Jack walked into the woods. This time he would help his partner.

THREE

LAUNA WAS MAD, madder than hell. They had briefed her. They had trained her. They gave her a bow and copper knives instead of something really useful, like an M-16. They had also told her to go easy on changing things until the powers that be were sure they really wanted history remodeled. Like the Kurgans had given her a choice. Fuck them one and all.

Launa kicked her horse for more speed; it struggled to a gallop. There was no way to outrace her anger—or her fear. She was supposed to meet women leaders of egalitarian communities. Instead, she'd run into an overbearing, hyped-on-testosterone war chief. *So much for Judith and Brent's briefings. They haven't gotten one thing right. Now what am I supposed to do?*

Stay alive. She answered her own question, and centered herself on that answer. *Forget what should have been, girl. Concentrate on what is.*

Her lead was down to two minutes when she took a game path into the green darkness. "Damn, what I'd give for a sniper rifle, or even a bow. 'A trooper should never be without her weapons,'" she recited, repeating the old sergeant's lecture.

Things don't always go by The Book, Launa answered herself. Then she laughed, a bitter cackle. "Guns don't kill people. People kill people. Let's see what we can do about killing some really deserving bastards."

Leaning low over her mount's neck to avoid limbs, Launa guided her horse down a series of game trails, more to confuse her pursuit than accomplish anything. One path led into the stream, and she went there. Most of the bank was reeds and mud. She stayed in the water until a more rocky bank offered an out.

Launa let her horse take a quick drink while she paused to listen for her pursuers. Nothing. She'd had enough of running. "I don't need a bow for an ambush, just a weapon." She had lost track of the copper knife she had used to kill the first Kurgan. She fingered the bronze backup Jack had given her. A rocky bank in Wyoming had confused a guy with more gun than sense. Why not do it again?

She urged her horse up the bank, then stopped. Carefully, she backed the horse into the stream. Pausing again, Launa studied the trail she had left. It wasn't much of one, and it was confused. Good.

She kicked her mount; spray flew as it started down the stream again. Launa grabbed an overhanging twig within sight of her false exit and broke it. Before she had gone too far, she also guided her horse through some tall grass. Any joker on her trail would be sure she was somewhere ahead.

A graveled stretch of bank offered her the second exit she wanted. She took it, careful again to leave only a hint of a trail. This time she did not backtrack. After a hundred feet, she slid from her mount. Slapping the horse's rump, she sent it on its way, encouraged by a few well-placed pebbles.

Hardly glancing at her surroundings, Launa headed back up stream, looking for the trail she'd started to take the first time. The brush beneath the tree canopy was sparse; in the cool light she could usually make out the stream to her left. But she needn't have worried about missing her goal.

Where she'd first left the water, two horsemen rested their mounts and argued loudly. One pointed into the woods. The other pointed downstream. They got louder. *Maybe they'll save me the trouble and kill each other.*

Finally, one kicked his horse and splashed downstream.

The other shouted something after him, then urged his mount up the bank Launa had backed down a few minutes earlier.

Launa spotted a broad-leafed bush near the trail and went to ground beneath it, keeping a careful eye on the Kurgan. He didn't look all that comfortable under the trees; his eyes kept searching the limbs above him. So long as he kept looking up for trouble, Launa's plan just might work.

As the horseman rode past her, Launa tossed a rock at the horse's front feet. It recoiled. The rider pulled tight on the reins. The noise of Launa bursting from the bush added to the animal's confusion. Launa reached around the Kurgan's back and slashed open his belly before he knew she was there.

Again, Launa felt how easy a knife sliced human flesh. The rider started at the pain—and struck at Launa with the butt of his lance.

Launa fended off the blow as she fled. She had killed the man, but he could still kill her. Twisting through trees, she put a large trunk between them, then turned to face the dying man. He struggled with his horse, refusing even with a death wound to let it master him. Still, he took a moment to hurl his lance at Launa before his weakness forced him to slide from his seat. Riderless, the horse bolted down the path.

Launa retrieved the lance. Slowly, she approached the man who would have killed her. He screamed something, whether at her or to her other pursuer she could not tell. Driving the lance through his throat silenced him.

Launa stared down at the body as it went rigid, then passed into convulsions. He had wanted her dead. Launa started shaking; her knees gave way and she collapsed in a heap.

How many had she killed in what—two days? Three here and one, maybe two up-time. Each had wanted her dead. Each had died in her stead. How long could she stay one step ahead of the dying? All her life she'd wanted to be a soldier. Never had she dreamed it would be like this.

Movement in the brush startled her. Something crawled quickly away. *You're losing it, girl. If you're smart, you'll leave too.* Leaning on the lance for support, Launa stumbled back to the stream. Cold water washed blood from her arms and hot emotions from her face.

She was the hunted; there were five more like that one. She had no time for feelings. Launa put her game face back on. Anything that had ever been soft she stuffed into the empty cave where her heart had been. Slowly, her fingers played along the edge of her knife.

Think, Lieutenant, think. How long before the slower group catches up with the two who raced after her? Unknown. Here and now the odds were one on one. The Kurgan could wait for the rest to arrive; she had to find him now.

Knife in hand, Launa went looking for her death trap. Mouth dry, hardly breathing, she walked the game paths, carefully measuring each step. She moved through the trees as silent as a shadow, slowly working her way back to the path where she had left the stream.

The trees were thinner here. Through the underbrush, she could see the glare of the steppe. There was movement on the prairie. A horse grazed. Launa paused, her back against a tree. There were several horses out there: the brown she had ridden, the black whose rider she had killed—and a third.

So the other Kurgan's gone to ground. Where?

A rush of noise came from behind her. *Someone's not being very careful.* Launa dove for a bush; it hid her not a moment too soon.

A man in Kurgan garb pelted down the trail, running as if whatever hell he feared was right behind him. Fifty feet past Launa, he tripped. As he sprawled into the leaves, another man in leather vest and breechclout leaped from a tree. A stone knife flashed for a moment—and stopped inches from the foolish runner's throat. The fleeing Kurgan had stumbled into the trap meant for Launa.

Who is this new guy? What's going on? Launa's rush of questions froze as something cold touched her thigh. Slowly, Launa looked down.

Frieda's big eyes looked silently back at her. *What's Frieda doing here?* Launa snapped her attention back to the two Kurgans. They talked rapidly, throwing worried glances back the way the runner had come. Launa bet more than a dog had chased that last guy. Maybe she wasn't alone.

An arrow whizzed past Launa's ear and buried itself in a tree between the two warriors—a longbow's arrow. Launa's pursuer dropped, only to appear a second later with a bow, arrow nocked. He let fly.

Allowing herself a hint of a grin, Launa ducked behind her tree. A moment later, his arrow thudded home.

"Not even close," she heard Jack taunt.

"You're alive," she half whispered.

"Thanks to you and Alert."

Launa wanted to scream, dance a jig, hug Jack. *I'm not alone! Jack's still here to guard my back.* Instead, she edged around the tree to check the Kurgans; both had hunkered down.

A second arrow stuck a tree behind the archer.

"How many of these bastards do we have left?" Launa asked, barely keeping her voice steady.

"Just these two." Jack let another arrow fly. It splintered the bark of the tree the archer was hiding behind.

Either arrow or splinters drew blood, because the Kurgan's arm was bleeding when he sent a second arrow their way. Launa didn't hear that one hit anything.

"The quivers I've captured never had more than four arrows. Maybe we can shoot him dry," Jack suggested.

The dumb one who had run into the other Kurgan's trap stuck his head around his tree, shouting and waving. Jack let an arrow fly, but dumbo was behind the tree when it whizzed by. The archer did the same, and Jack missed him too.

"Looks like they're trying to shoot you dry, Captain."

"You want to try edging around them?" Jack asked.

"No way. The archer might get me when I got closer. Even if I did get in a knife fight with one, the other'd be right there. Think up something better."

"Standoff," was all he answered.

Several minutes passed with Kurgans playing peek-a-boo

and Jack not shooting. The horsemen stopped risking themselves. Launa could hear them talking. *What next?*

The Kurgan archer stepped out from behind his tree. Knife brandished in his right hand, his bow was unstrung in his left.

"Looks like they want us to come out and fight like men. Let's see how they handle this," she shouted as she stepped into the open.

If the Kurgan had gone for an arrow, Launa would have been behind her tree before he could hit her. He didn't.

Both Kurgans waved their knives, made obscene gestures, and shouted what she guessed were more of the same. Launa returned the compliments. Inside, she could almost feel the click as something snapped. She'd had enough of cool control. She was sick of people who wanted to kill her, tired of caution and logic and thinking things through. She wanted to kill someone, drive a knife in a man's belly and watch his eyes as he felt his heart gush. She screamed back at them, throwing the words sergeants only used when they thought the officers' brats weren't around.

I'm going crazy, part of her thought, but she no longer cared. When she came up for air, she glanced back at Jack. "You going to hide behind that tree forever? I'll kill those bastards myself."

"Maybe I ought to let you try." Jack sounded maddeningly calm as he stepped from behind his tree, strung bow in one hand, arrow in the other. His eyes locked with hers, holding her, keeping her from dashing down the trail and throwing herself at the men she hated.

"Frieda. Stay," Jack ordered; then, in the same deadly soft voice, he said, "Launa. Walk behind me," as he slowly paced off the distance to her.

I'm not your bitch, Launa thought, but swallowed the retort. Jack's voice was the Colonel's, hard with generations of command. She'd learned not to take it from the Colonel; she damn sure wasn't going to take it from Jack. "I've killed three of these bastards already," Launa glowered.

"Yes, you have," Jack agreed, his words low. "But if you don't start soldiering, Lieutenant, you'll make a stupid mistake and get splattered all over. When I clean up the mess, I won't find an ounce of brains." Jack's eyes fixed Launa, pinned her to a tree like a butterfly to a mat. He walked past her.

"You're a professional," he said without looking back. "Start acting like one."

Launa couldn't have felt the slap harder if Jack had hit her. She'd been hyperventilating; she held her breath, clenched her fists until they shook. *He's right, damn it. I'm not here to knife people. We've got an army to raise and a war to win.*

Launa took a slow breath and put the knife back in her boot. Running her sweaty hands through her hair, she felt the warmth in her face and cheeks. Firmly, she set her jaw and paced her breathing. Control was back. She had a man to kill.

As Jack neared the two men, they backed down the game path toward the prairie. Launa nodded; here was something she and the Kurgans agreed on. For a stand-up fight, she favored an open field. Spotting a fallen branch, Launa picked it up and whittled away the worst rough edges. She struck the ground; it bent but didn't break. "Good quarterstaff," she muttered.

"See one for me?" Jack hadn't taken his eyes off the retreating Kurgans.

"No."

"Don't worry, I should be able to take the archer without too much trouble."

"He's the tough one."

"Yeah."

They reached the open steppe. The archer dropped his bow and the Kurgans spread out. When they spotted Launa's staff, they leered and jerked their hips at her. Her temper flashed; then she remembered to laugh and brought the pole up from her hips. "I got as much equipment as you got," she growled.

"Expect they'll fight dirty," Jack observed aloud as he turned toward the archer.

"Don't worry. They can't kick me in the balls," Launa said as she turned to face her man.

The Kurgan grinned, weaving the air with his knife, promising how he would cut her apart. Launa grinned back. "Show me what you got."

They circled. From the corner of her eye, Launa knew Jack was doing the same with his foe, but she had no attention to spare. Only her skill lay between that knife and her death.

The man feinted at her. She gave ground. He laughed. Launa tried to look weak and fearful; it didn't take much of an effort. The warrior crouched low. In a flash he grabbed a handful of the yellow dirt and threw it in Launa's face.

She'd expected that, and gave more ground, pirouetting away from him. *Look, ma, those ballet lessons finally came in handy.* In a second she was facing her foe, the dust cloud safely off to the side. "You can do better than that," she chided him.

He shouted a retort—and lunged for her. Launa brought her staff down, smashing his knife hand, then swung the other end at his head. The Kurgan hit the ground with a scream and Launa drove the end of the stick into his back, then danced away quickly as he rolled over, trying to trap her staff with his body.

Well out of his reach, Launa hung on her staff, gasping for breath, while the man slowly got to his feet. Her knees wobbled. *I'm living on adrenaline. God, let there be some left.*

The Kurgan was none too steady on his feet, either. He held his knife in his left hand now. Launa switched her hold on the staff, now right hand high. The man approached her more cautiously this time.

Now it was Launa who feinted and he who gave ground. First she made to swing at his knife hand. He pulled it back. Then she aimed for his head and he retreated farther. She feinted for his head a third time, and carried through on her blow, whirling around in a full circle. This time she let the staff slip through her hands. It became a long club, aimed at her opponent's feet.

Startled, he jumped it, then half stumbled, half lunged for

her. Launa did another full turn, taking a step away from him and converting her club back into a quarterstaff. Facing him again, she brought it down where she expected his knife hand to be. It was. He screamed and dropped his weapon. Then screamed again as Launa smashed the other end of her staff against his head.

He collapsed in the dirt, hands fluttering in confusion, like a baby.

Dredging up her last drop of strength, Launa dropped her hand to her boot and grabbed her knife. A second later, she slashed his throat. He did not have time to cry out.

Gasping for breath, Launa stumbled away from her dying enemy. She sprawled in the dirt beside him, watching numbly as the blood spurting from his neck slowed to a drip.

Somewhere she heard grunts. It took her a moment to remember she wasn't fighting alone.

She used the pole to drag herself to her feet. Jack's fight was still going. Leaning heavily on her staff, Launa headed for the two. She should help her partner—but how?

"What's taking you so long, Captain?"

"This son of a bitch is good."

Whether the Kurgan saw an opening in Jack's defense, or feared Launa would use the bow to shoot him down, the man dropped his knife and lunged at Jack, overpowering his guard. They went down in a knot, the horseman using both of his hands to force Jack's knife against its wielder.

Jack's left hand slammed up into the Kurgan's jaw once, twice. The third time, the warrior groaned and rolled away from Jack. But Jack's knife flew out of his hand to land at Launa's feet. She stared at it blankly. *If I reach for it, I'll keel over.*

The Kurgan crawled toward the knife. Jack half lunged, half fell on top of him. With one hand pulling the Kurgan's beard left, Jack yanked the warrior's pigtail right once, then again. With a crack, the fight ended; the Kurgan lay limp beneath Jack.

Jack rolled off the man, but made no effort to get up. "I hope . . . every day in this place . . . ain't like this one."

Launa collapsed beside Jack.

FOUR

JACK LAY ON his back, gasping in air that reeked of blood and shit—someone else's. It could have been his. *You knew the risk when you volunteered.* Jack grimaced; he was no cadet. He'd read his orders. *Why don't the cold words on paper ever say what they really mean?*

Don't just lie there like some damn reservation Indian, Jack could hear his stepfather chide. *Get up, do something.* Jack hated the old bastard, but it *was* time to get moving. Above him, the buzzards already circled, hungry for the leavings from what he and Launa had done. *Now there is one hell of a woman.* With an effort, Jack got to his feet.

"Want a hand up, soldier?" he asked.

Launa shook her head, using her staff to lever herself up. She'd almost made it to her knees before she shrugged and reached for his hand. "I'm pretty spent."

In the two months Jack had known this woman, she had never accepted anyone's help. He offered a joke along with his hand. "I didn't think I could get up either, but one of those buzzards looks like it thinks I'm lunch."

He got a weak smile from her, but as soon as Launa was up, she was all business. "What do we do with the losers?"

"We better strip the bodies. This has to look like an intramural disagreement—Kurgans killing Kurgans."

Launa hobbled over to loot her kill. Jack stuffed his man's

stone blade in his own belt, then rolled him out of his leather vest and pulled off his boots and pants.

Launa followed suit. "Did they mutilate the bodies?"

"Don't know," Jack answered. "The buzzards'll take care of the evidence quick enough."

"If there's not another horde of these guys over the next ridge." Launa scowled.

"If there is, we got the horsepower to stay ahead of them."

"You captured their horses!" Launa, eager once more, snapped her head around to face Jack.

"Mist is guarding twenty horses at their empty camp."

"Damn good!"

They took their time retracing their steps through the woods. First, they retrieved all the long arrows at the fire-fight, then stripped the body at Launa's ambush. Back at camp, Mist was as happy to see them as Launa was to see the spare mounts. They stripped more bodies and dumped the loot beside the still-smoldering fire.

Lying next to it were four lances lashed together in a square, dropped by the Kurgan Jack's arrow had missed. Launa studied it for a second, then all color drained from her face.

Slipping her right hand into the leather rope at one corner, she reached across. It was a painful stretch. There were ties at each corner.

Jack growled deep in his throat; death wasn't something that just happened around Kurgans. Killing was play for them, and Launa would have been their toy. There were a few moments in a soldier's life that made all the training and drill worthwhile—killing these sons of bitches was one of them.

Launa dropped the rack like it was a snake, then stooped to pick it up again. Her eyes slowly roved the plain, dotted with grazing horses. "Now we have horses. Here's wood for pack racks. And the leather." She grabbed a pair of leggings and slashed it with her knife. "Let's spread our gear out light on a batch of packhorses so we're always faster than what's behind us."

"Yeah." Jack gave her five as she stood up.

The sun was starting down the sky when all their gear, modern and captured, was packed onto a dozen horses. Launa looked askance as Jack bundled up their loot. "I can understand boots and bows, but filthy britches?"

Jack chose his words carefully; Launa's temper had been working overtime today. "I want to study this stuff. In this campaign, intelligence on the opposition will be where we find it."

Launa shrugged, swung herself up on Star, and led out a string of horses. Jack finished tying down the last load, and followed her with his own.

"Head for the tree," Launa shouted. "I want to keep our jump site under surveillance."

The trip back was uneventful; they stopped twice. At the first pause they dropped a six-point buck that ignored humans at two hundred paces—a fatal mistake. Jack promised himself not to make the same mistake in this new-old world.

Their second stop was at the small grove within sight of the tree. They gathered wood, filled their water skins, and found a tiny waterfall cascading into a small pond. For a moment Jack thought Launa might dive in, but she turned away and they rode up the hill in silence.

No words were needed as they unloaded their gear, strung up the deer carcass, and set the horses to grazing. Jack felt something almost solemn as they laid out their bedrolls across from each other. He would dig the fire pit between them. He was about to start when his eyes were drawn to the scene of the morning's encounter. Vultures circled above the site.

"I used three arrows down there to kill a horseman." He held an arrow from their longbow next to a local make; theirs was twice as long. "We got to retrieve our calling cards."

Launa blew out a long breath, as if this day would never end. Jack was about to suggest they do it tomorrow, but she was already jogging out to get Star. "Let's get it over with," she called back. "Who knows what we'll do tomorrow?"

It was a ten-minute ride to the killing ground. Most of the scavengers still circled, but one or two early birds were already at their feast. When Jack dismounted, they flapped off, complaining the whole time—and quickly settled back down again.

Jack pulled the two arrows from the lancer who had charged him and stripped the body. A quick scan of the grassy plain was enough to settle the question of searching for the arrow that missed. It had been tough enough finding the quivers and scabbards he had dropped; hunting for one stray arrow was hopeless.

Which brought him back to the two Kurgans Alert had killed—and Alert's body. As Jack rolled the leader who'd clubbed him out of his bloody clothes, his eyes were held by the lances in Alert's side. *If the dog hadn't been the center of their attention, those would have been in me.* A shiver went down Jack's back, twisted his gut, and turned his legs to water; he collapsed to his knees. *Oh, God, if Launa hadn't gotten them chasing her . . .*

He glanced around for Launa; her dead enemies had been stripped and she had remounted. She was carefully looking anywhere but at him.

Jack took two deep breaths and prepared to get on with the day. Alert deserved a soldier's burial. Jack was considering the hardness of the ground and the softness of the copper tools he had when the thunder rolled over them.

Jack whipped his head around. It was blue sky from horizon to horizon. *And there were two peals in that thunder—a sonic boom.*

Jack searched the sky above them. A thousand feet up, a streamer twisted on the breeze. Launa was already chasing it when he threw himself on Windrider and took off too.

INTERLUDE

JUDITH LEE RESTED her eyes on the wilted wildflower. Everyone in the bunker was thirsty, but no one would rob their talisman of its water. This message-bearer from Launa and Jack had been the focus of their lives since it popped into being in the space the two soldiers had vacated. That gift had kept the Livermore lab crew going.

Judith leaned her head against the cool, unpainted concrete wall. Through it she could hear the pounding begin anew as the mob tried to batter their way into the bunker. Did they really think a cure for the plague was in here?

"What do you think it will be like when Launa and Jack start changing history?"

Judith turned to stare at Brent Lynch. Was he so sure they'd picked the right place, the right moment in time for the kids' drop point? There were so many sites that nobody had dug into, so many questions. Judith had been fearless, arguing her point with a cocktail in her hand at faculty parties; no one could prove her wrong. What had Launa actually found? Maybe we should have had a committee review all the competing opinions. *Right, and Launa would be sitting here beside me, waiting for that committee to make up its mind while the world died.*

Beside her, Brent rambled on in the innocence that eighty-year-olds brought to second youth. Listening to him distracted Judith from the voices ripping her heart apart; she listened.

"What will it feel like when the world starts to change? Will we go to sleep one night and wake up in a different world? Or will we see it happening? Maybe the picture will waver a bit, like the way they do people on commercials. In a blink, my bow tie will change to a sedate long one. Next moment my sandals will be oxfords with gleaming polish. I will dearly hate becoming stuffy."

Despite it all, Judith smiled. "My dear Brent. No matter what Launa and Jack do, you will always be your own wonderful self, a sixties hippie born twenty years too soon."

Brent shook his head. "Will I even be born? My mother was a Donut Dolly when father met her behind the lines in the Great War. Would they even have met in a world without war?"

Judith could not tell if Brent was serious or not, but his mournful ruminating beat watching what little news was still coming in. On the wall across from her, someone had taped up the faxes showing the virus that was killing the world.

Oh, the joys of modern technology. Any two-bit country with a strongman who thought the gods had anointed him to rule the world could have its own gene lab to splice together anything he damn well ordered.

At first the plague seemed only an old flu virus everyone would catch but few would die of. But embedded in this bug was Hepatitis E. Once the lungs were involved with the flu, the hepatitis attacked the liver. Normally, Hepatitis E was a slow mover that drugs could cure.

But not this one. Stitched into the hepatitis was a fragment of the AIDS virus—the DNA code that made AIDS reproduce with frantic speed. Now liver functions were destroyed in days, not months, and no miracle drug could stop it. *What did we do to deserve this?*

Judith knew the answer. Cholera and AIDS had ravaged Africa and South America, killing tens of millions. Little had been done, and among the survivors were those willing to sell their scarred souls to a charismatic madman.

Now the attack aimed at Europe was spreading around the globe. Billions were dying and nothing could be done.

Judith twisted where she sat on the floor, putting the faxes out of sight, facing Brent. "Why don't we write down our memories? That way, we can read them when we've changed. I could even sketch you."

"A sketch might work, but what's the good of writing? Do you write in Latin letters or cuneiform?"

Judith threw up her hands. The old scholar could be such a bother. "You can write yours in both, and throw in Linear A and hieroglyphics to boot, a real Rosetta stone."

"Assuming paper has been invented."

Judith couldn't help herself. Brent's glum face made her laugh. It was the first laugh she'd had since her old friend, the Chair of the Joint Chiefs, invited Judith into her nightmare project. "You always said the world would be a better place if your Old Europeans had run it. Want to find out?"

Judith had ended hundreds of lectures with that question—never expecting an answer. Now she prayed she was right in so many of the things she had so casually tossed off. To take her mind off her sins, she headed for the command console to rummage up some paper.

The lights dimmed. Dr. Milo looked up from his work, the despair of the brilliant engineer who can't quite make his pet work adding lead to his dark eyes. "We lost another generator. I'm afraid the accumulators are giving up more energy than they're acquiring." He looked down. Gauges reflected in his thick glasses. "We have enough electricity to send a few grams. Would you compose a message?"

Judith found a thin piece of paper and hastened to fashion some words. *How do you report the end of the world? How do you tell a young woman you've dumped all history on her shoulders?* The modern U.S. Army had plenty of combat-ready women, but Judith had held out for someone like Launa, young, eager, not so thoroughly trained that she'd try to fit an old answer to a new question. Launa had been everything Judith had hoped for. *Now to tell her so.*

Judith wrote.

Done, she read it through quickly and handed it to the

Time Transport Director. "Can you get this to Launa, and not some other Launa . . . or . . . I mean . . ." Judith gave up trying to put into words the slippery eel that time had become to her.

Dr. Milo's laugh came out half snort, half cough. Beside him, Dr. Harrison looked up and nervously pushed her glasses back up her long nose. "Next door, six of the greatest mathematicians are at work. They've shut down their computers to save power, but they're still flailing away at what we're doing here with chalkboards and slide rules."

"They shocked the scientific community when they said the math would allow for time travel, faster than light, too." Dr. Milo seemed to be talking half to himself as his fingers moved over the keys of his control panel. "But none of those number dreamers was any less surprised when Harrison's instruments showed power arriving before we turned it on."

The two experimental physicists shared a smile; the tall, slender woman united by memories with the short, pudgy man. Together they'd given birth to a contraption just in time for it to become humanity's last hope.

"Did we send Launa and Jack back in history or off to some other time line, or are they creating their own?" Here was Judith's nightmare, that all she was doing was for nothing.

Dr. Harrison shrugged. "The mathematicians have no idea, or rather the six of them have a dozen different theories, none of which we have time to test." Harrison's hand gestured, its sweep taking in the entire hardware-crammed room. "It seems to work, therefore we do it." Then the woman's eyes locked with Judith's. "Did we send them where they can do the most good?"

So this was their nightmare, too. Judith drew herself up and faced them squarely. "For six million years, humanoids in general and for three hundred thousand years *Homo sapiens sapiens* in particular lived together. When we lived off the land, and especially when we started farming, cooperation gave us life. Isolation was death. That's what's in our genes.

"Then some joker tamed the horse, and it all went to hell.

What one guy can tame, someone stronger can take. And the limited havoc one small bunch of walking crazies could do got huge when that crew could cross country at the speed of a horse."

Judith paused for a breath, prayed that the sparkle in the two scientists' eyes was hope from her words, not the dying gleam of their instruments.

"We've put Launa and Jack down in front of the first wave of power-hungry horsemen." *I hope. Don't let them see the fear.* "Launa and Jack are soldiers. Soldiers buy time. Launa and Jack have to buy time for the farmers to figure out a way to bring the horse peacefully into their cooperative culture. I know they can do it." Judith was glad neither of the two in front of her asked how. In the end, the answer to that most pressing question would be left to Launa and people Judith would never meet.

Dr. Milo reached for the message in Judith's hand. She gave it to him; he glanced through it quickly. "Once the message is sent, we'll open the bunker. I'm dying for a drink of water."

Judith's daughter lived a mile from the lab. It would be nice to see her one last time.

The CIA man who had cared for the horses they brought from Wyoming stuffed the message inside a tube from an empty roll of toilet paper, then wrapped a length of tissue around it.

"This'll unravel as it falls. They'll see it for miles. Used this once for a message drop in Iraq." His grim face cracked a smile as he put the message on the X that marked the energy capsule's pickup point.

"I'm aiming for the same time and place as last time, just a bit higher," Dr. Milo mumbled. "It's bad enough trying to shoot for where the Earth was six thousand years ago, and Romania at that. I hope they haven't made any major changes in the history flow. Power is fluctuating badly. Here goes nothing."

With a soft pop, the message disappeared.

FIVE

LAUNA FIXED HER eyes on the streaming paper. It was high and moving toward the tree no faster than Star could walk. Jack caught up with her. Neither spoke.

The paper drifted along. Only when it sank below five hundred feet did it get serious about falling. They trotted after it and were at the foot of the ridge before it got low. Jack reached up with his bow, caught it, and dismounted to give it to her.

Launa slipped from Star's back. She was proud of herself; her hands were steady as she accepted the message. She pulled a green buckslip from a tube and held it for both of them to read.

After the first words, Launa lost it. She crumpled the note in a fist as her gut went empty, breath exploding from her. Beside her, Jack stood wooden still, ashen-faced.

Gritting her teeth, Launa forced herself to smooth the message back out. Slowly she read the last words she would ever receive from home. She blocked the message with her hand, moving it to reveal a line at a time, forcing her eyes to take it in piece by horrible piece, not racing ahead, not refusing to go forward.

YOUR MISSION IS GO   YOUR MISSION IS GO
It is a week since we sent you. Plague stalks the planet.

No place is safe. Panic is everywhere. The California power grid collapsed on the first day. We could not recharge our accumulators to reinforce you. We expect a mob to break into the bunker any time. We are destroying the machine.

YOUR MISSION IS GO   YOUR MISSION IS GO

Maria said "Go with God." The Admiral said "Godspeed." I can't think of anything historic to say. But the words of my little daughter keep repeating in my head. "Make the hurt go away. Make it better."

YOUR MISSION IS GO   You can do it

Launa folded the message to hide the words. It was done. She and Jack were on their own.

Since the day she'd been called from class and asked how she would defend a Neolithic village from horse raiders, she had known it might come to this. Still, every night she'd wrapped her hope away, sure the great men of the world weren't stupid, confident the Army was doing what it did best—preparing for contingencies that would never happen. Now they had happened.

The hope in her heart flamed out, a cold, dead ember. Launa ripped the message in half once, twice, three times. Each tear of the paper ripped at her heart. The void that had threatened to swallow her this morning yawned open. Everyone she'd ever known, everything she'd ever wanted to be, to have, was gone. Nothing would ever be. The bastards had done it. Bastards like the ones who had tried to kill her today had killed everyone six thousand years later.

Tears threatened to flood her eyes. Launa hated tears. She fell to her knees, her fingers clawing at herself. She found a knife, one of the long Kurgan flint daggers. Slowly she brought it up, turned it, let the sunlight play across it. The shadows were dark as old blood—her blood. They wanted her dead. It would be so easy to bury the dagger in her own gut, to end the waiting for death.

"Damn it!" she screamed. "I killed you bastards!" She plunged the dagger into the dirt. It glanced off a rock, sending sparks flying. Launa yanked the blade from the ground, flipped it in her hand, and slammed it sideways against the rock. More sparks flew, but the flint blade was unscathed.

Groping through her tears, Launa found another rock and perched the knife between the two. Grabbing a third, she slammed it down, shattering the blade. "Damn you all to hell!" she screamed, the worst curse the nuns had forbidden her.

"You murdered and raped. What you couldn't understand, you wasted. Those who wouldn't bend, you butchered." She pulled a second knife, a third, a fourth from her belt, and screamed at each as she shattered it.

When her belt was empty, she looked up at Jack. His dark eyes were deep; what was going on behind them showed nowhere on his face. Launa waited for the words that would cut her down to the rank of private. He said nothing as he pulled a Kurgan dagger from his belt and dropped it beside her. Without a word, she shattered the blade, and then the three more he dropped one by one. There were no more curses within her.

When the last knife was broken, Launa collapsed in the dust and let the racking sobs take her.

A million years later, Jack took her arm and gently pulled her to her feet. "Come on. We'd better get back to camp," he said as he half led, half carried her up the hill.

"I'm sorry, Jack," Launa whimpered. "I'm losing it. I don't mean to. I'm sorry."

"Don't be. I tried the other way. Trust me, your way is better."

Tears streaming down her face made mud of the dust she'd foundered in. Launa eyed Jack, wordlessly begging him to go on, tell her how this undisciplined breakdown could be better than anything.

Jack pursed his lips. "I knew a woman once."

Launa knew Jack had been married. Before the jump, that was all she had needed to know. Now she listened.

Jack sighed, his unfocused eyes centered on the tree at the top of the ridge as they slowly hiked toward it. "I met her the summer of my third year at the Point. I was doing two weeks at what was left of the Presidio. First evening, I wandered down to Fisherman's Wharf. And we bumped into each other."

Jack shook his head. "I don't know what she saw in me, but next day, there she was outside the gate, waiting for me. We spent evenings exploring San Francisco. She knew every nook and cranny. She was in her third year at Berkeley, studying literature, but really, she majored in life."

Star had been following Launa; now he nuzzled her. She put an arm around the horse's neck, grateful for the support. Jack talked on, his words meandering, as if over familiar and pleasant ground. "I wasn't good at writing letters, but for her, I wrote. All my senior year, I expected a letter telling me I was old stuff. It didn't come. Fort Lewis had a light infantry brigade. That was the closest I could get to Frisco. She talked her folks into grad work in Seattle."

Jack paused, and Launa blinked away old tears to study him. He pursed his lips as he eyed his bow. "They warn you that you're married to your first platoon. You'll spend every waking moment with your team. God, they were right. I was two hours from Seattle, and she might as well have been on the moon. I made it up maybe once a month. We were going nowhere, and I told her so. Her answer was, 'Do we get married this weekend or next?' God, what a woman!" Jack let out a long breath.

"She got a job teaching, which helped. Tacoma's no place to live on a second louie's pay. It must have helped fill the time, too. I was working sixteen-hour days. I told her it wouldn't be forever. Once the platoon taught me everything it could, I'd get a staff job. Then there'd be time for us." Jack choked on the last words.

Jack's quiet talk of Army life, marriage, and family soothed Launa. Those had been her dreams for as long as she could remember. They wouldn't come easy, but she would have them. Now they never would be. Loss had been in Jack's last words. Launa waited for him to go on. When he did, his words came in a rush.

"The baby was born when I made first lieutenant. I got my orders for battalion staff a couple of months later. I worked late that Friday night, cleaning up. Called about midnight asking for a ride. She piled in the car with the little one and headed down to get me. The police report said that was about the same time a welder weaved out of a bar and got in her truck. How could anybody be so drunk she couldn't tell which side of an interstate she's driving on? Her big pickup came around a curve and took our little car apart. They didn't have a chance."

Tears were streaming down Jack's face as they reached the camp. "I sat dry-eyed through the funeral, too empty to hurt. Days went by. Weeks. My knife, my pistol developed a sudden allure. I'd be stroking them and couldn't remember picking them up. It would have been scary if I'd been able to feel anything. One morning the knife and ammunition were gone.

"A month after the funeral my new battalion CO came by, asked me to go fishing that weekend. Saturday night, around the fire, he told me what it was like watching cancer kill his oldest boy. I couldn't cry for my wife and kid, but I cried for his. And then I cried for all of them. Sandie, Sam, Grandfather, my dad. Finally, I cried for all of them." Gently, Jack pushed her down onto her bedroll.

"That Monday, my sergeant brought back the knife and ammo. Didn't say a word, but I knew what it felt like to have someone care, care enough to fight death for me." Jack looked down at her. "Go ahead and cry, cry for all of them."

Launa settled herself cross-legged on her blanket. New tears began to flow. First for two people who had meant so much to this quiet man. She could weep for a woman and a boy she had never met, without fear that the void would swallow her. Then she wept for Judith and Brent, for Maria and all the people who had put her here, struggling to find a way to save them all, call them back from death. She wept.

The air was growing cold; she gathered her blanket around herself. Her teeth began to chatter. Between sobs, she looked up again at Jack. He searched out the spare blanket and settled it around her. "I'm so cold, Jack." She opened the blankets and he slipped into them with her.

His body was a furnace; where she rested against him, the cold fled. His strong hands rubbed warmth back into her freezing arms and legs. Once his fingers grazed a breast. The fire of that touch shot through her. He did not brush there again, and she did not invite him.

She was lost, lost in tears, lost in memories, and slowly, lost in the returning warmth of human touch. She let herself sink down to lie on her bedroll, let her mind spin empty away from the horrors of the day. Somehow she slept.

Jack sighed; the tears had come again. Sandie and Sam were an old pain; he had thought all those tears shed. It was good that there were still a few left—there was nothing else up-time worth crying for. Maybe he'd done too good a job of letting nothing and no one get near him. Maybe he hadn't. His finger still tingled where it had brushed Launa's breast. *Damn, this is getting complicated.*

Like any gray haired duenna, Judith had collared him one afternoon about his "intentions toward Launa." He had quoted the policy on senior officers striking up relationships with juniors.

Judith snorted. "The Uniform Code of Military Justice wasn't written six thousand years ago, and it won't fit there."

Jack had excused himself; he had a class on copper smelting or something. Anything to avoid a part of himself he had put on ice since Sandie's death. Ice that had begun to melt the first time he saw a certain young female cadet.

Jack shifted where he sat, trying to keep from pressing his growing need against Launa. A soft snore told him he need not have bothered; she was asleep. Good.

He slipped out of the blankets and paced off the short distance to the crest of the hill. He was a soldier with a mission, and he'd better not forget that.

To the east, the last remnants of the sunset darkened. Yesterday he and Launa had practiced their archery as the sun sank over California. A guard had found them; they were needed in the bunker. As Jack collected his arrows, a windmill died on the hills above the lab at Livermore, priced out of the energy market by cheap oil. In the bunker he watched a world begin down the path to death. Jack shook his head, shaking away yesterday's ghosts.

It's time to soldier, Bearman. Jack searched the plain for any sign of life, then turned and did the same to the valley. No smoke, no fire. The dogs circled the grazing horses, keeping them together. The stallions sniffed around the mares. The ladies clearly were uninterested.

The stallions were also checking each other out. The three modern mounts had already worked the kinks out of their relationship. A couple of the local stallions were learning the hard way that there was a new pecking order in the herd tonight. Both dogs were pregnant, and would be the mothers of many. The horses were male and in time, Jack would breed them, creating a new line, but that was a way off. He hadn't been around horses in a while, and the refresher course hadn't gone quite as planned. The afternoon it was scheduled he'd been fighting for his life instead. Time had run out for a lot of things.

Jack stretched, and found his need still there. He glanced at Launa. The two of them were alive. Despite everything two worlds had thrown at them, they lived. The power of that filled Jack, made him hungry to send it coursing into a woman. He hadn't felt this overwhelmed by need since . . .

He pushed away the memory, and the urge. He was a soldier. So was Launa. They had a job to do, or die trying. Six months from now, that job wouldn't be any easier if his partner was heavy with child. He headed for his bedroll.

Again he did a three-sixty. Nothing. The dogs and horses would let him know if anything worried them. With just the two of them, they couldn't post a night watch. That *was* why he brought the dogs.

Jack yawned as he settled down across the unlit fire from Launa. The night was getting chilly, and his single blanket wasn't going to be much help. He could start the fire, but it sure as hell wouldn't bring anything good to them.

Launa's teeth began to chatter again. Jack picked up his blanket and laid it over her, then worked his way under the covers back to where he had been when she fell asleep. He turned his back to her. *We're just two soldiers, sharing warmth.*

SIX

KANTOM SHIVERED. COLD in the dim first light. Still, he raised his long-bladed knife to greet the Sun. It would not be right for it to see the firstborn of the Mighty Man of the Stormy Mountain Clan standing afraid in its morning rays—even if that son was only seeing his thirteenth summer.

Kantom tightened his grip on the flint knife. His father had given him the long blade of a man the morning Kantom rode out of camp with Uncle Perto and the other warriors of the Hungry Wolf Band. "Please, dagger, make me hard like you," he prayed.

For three hands of days, the riders had seen only endless grass, tall and green. This would be good pasture for the horses of the Stormy Mountain. They had ridden as in a dream.

Too young to be counted among Uncle Perto's ten warriors, still Kantom and Toman had laughed with the warriors' joy. Then Toman shot a deer, but his arrow had not brought it down. Unwilling to return with no meat and no arrow, Kantom had kicked his horse to the chase.

For two days they had tracked it, Toman whining that they should give the deer to the wolves and ride after the warriors. Kantom would not. The first songs about Mighty Arakk's son would not be for women to laugh at.

They had found the deer at last—and wolves had brought

it down. Again Toman begged to flee, but Kantom would hear no such words. He fought the wolves for their dinner, and the pelt of one who had been slow learning to fear the long blade of a man of the Horse People was now rolled up beside Kantom's horse blanket. The women would cure it.

The Sun rose, a red eye to peer deep into his heart. Kantom smiled. "Light my way today, Father. I will find the trail of ten warriors. Hungry Wolves riding in new land will leave a trail of feasting that even a little girl could follow."

His confidence regained with the warmth of the Sun, Kantom turned to rouse the still-sleeping Toman. This rich new land held nothing that two young warriors of the Stormy Mountain could not slice with their blades.

SEVEN

LAUNA CAME AWAKE as her first dawn in this land lit the horizon. It was warm beneath the blankets with Jack at her back. For the last two months, she'd kept her distance from him, like a good junior officer. What about today?

Judith had been so maddeningly calm in the private lecture she gave Launa on "marrying in" or "marrying out." "If you and Jack become a couple, you'll strengthen your ties with each other and the mission. That's good. If you and Jack select local people, you'll strengthen your ties to the community. That could be just as good. Why not let nature take its course?"

Launa had reminded the white-haired anthropologist of the Defense Department's strong rules against fraternizing.

"Do you really think those apply?" Judith had answered, her green eyes twinkling.

Lying in Jack's warmth, Launa wasn't as sure as she had been. *They haven't written The Book on what we're doing.*

Launa had grown up with friends who figured there was no tomorrow, so you better grab what you can today. Launa had lived for tomorrow—when she got to West Point, when she got her first platoon. Yesterday, she'd come face to face with tomorrow. She and Jack would have to make it with their own two hands. Jack's hands had felt awfully good last night.

Launa rolled over and stroked his broad shoulders. "Good morning," she whispered.

He rolled away from her like she'd dropped ice down his back. "Morning, skipper. I'll start a fire." He left her two of the blankets, but held the third tight around his middle as he produced flint and iron.

So much for touching back. Launa shrugged as she wrapped a blanket around herself. *Sandie and Sam. Jack hadn't named them until the last moment. Even now, they mean that much to him. Will I ever matter that much to a man?* Launa threw the blankets aside. "Let me get the fire going. You cut us some breakfast off that deer we killed yesterday."

The meal passed in silence. Jack was rubbing grease on his arms when he finally looked at her. "What do we do today?"

"There's bound to be some decent people in this world. Let's find 'em."

Jack nodded. "I'll start packing."

The loot bothered Launa. "I don't want to try explaining this junk to Kurgans or Old Europeans before I've learned a word of their bloody language. I say we burn it now."

"Then we better find out what we can." Jack answered, and scattered the booty around them on the ground. Launa sat down beside him. He inched away from her, but not enough that they couldn't work together. Other than the knives she'd smashed, there was little to help them match these people against any Brent or Judith had told them about.

But the clothes seemed to intrigue Jack. He held up two vests. "These ought to be decorated with beads, religious symbols." He tossed them back with the rest. "Nothing. Either these people don't know boo about art, or something is wrong."

Launa examined a vest closely. The Colonel's wife had seen that her daughter took at least one course in sewing. "There are holes here, as if threads had been ripped out. They're old." Launa stared hard at the outline made by the stitching. "You can see where the leather's a bit less weatherbeaten. It looks like a triangle. Wonder what that meant."

Jack studied the vest. "I see what you mean." He checked two more. "These don't have anything."

Launa fingered one of them. "They're newer. It's as if somebody fell on hard times and had to sell off their finery. Anything they made new was done cheap."

"Could be younger sons going a-conquering. That's where William got most of his knights for the conquest of England."

Launa shook her head. "Don't push the intelligence too far. Ten riders is not an invasion. All we know is that a handful of warriors were down on their luck." *And had worse luck when they ran into us.*

"Okay," Jack agreed, "but if they'd been successful raiding lately, they'd be wearing their loot. Maybe the war hasn't started yet?"

"Would be nice to think so."

Launa tossed the vests on the fire. Smoke rose to drift away on the light breeze. Her eyes followed it. If only destroying the Kurgan threat were as easy as burning a few clothes.

Dawn was long past when the last of the booty was burned. Launa scowled as she rubbed away more of the gritty mud from last night. "I need a bath." She raised an eyebrow in Jack's direction, offering to share the tub with him. Maybe more.

"I'll stand guard," was all she got for an answer.

Why's this guy such a hard case all of a sudden? Launa shrugged. "I thought that was what the dogs were for."

Jack didn't answer.

The grove with the waterfall and pond was less than half a mile away; several horses grazed closer to it than they were. Launa picked up a pair of bows and quivers and handed one set to Jack. "Come on. Get Frieda. Leave Mist with the horses."

Jack took his bow and followed her.

The brisk walk was enough to put Launa in a light sweat. She was really looking forward to a bath by the time they reached the shady woods. Standing on the sand at the pond's edge, Launa made a number of decisions, but only voiced one. "I'm going to wash my hair." She turned to face Jack as she wiggled out of her briefs. "Come on, Frieda will warn us."

"No, I'll stand guard." Jack fixed his eyes on his bow as he strung it, but the briefs they had been issued were thin. Launa didn't miss his reaction to seeing her naked.

With a shrug, she waded into the water. It was cool, bracing. A couple of strokes brought her to the waterfall. It was hardly taller than she was, but the water pouring over her quickly washed the grit and mud from her skin. She stood directly under it, let it cascade down on her, cleansing the dirt and grime of a horrible day from her hair. But it was not just her body that was coming clean.

The sun sparkled on the trembling waters. The water sang its song. Birds and insects melded into the serenade. Launa's soul wanted to join in, make it a four-part harmony.

All her life, she had gone swimming when things were bad, the Colonel drinking too much, the folks fighting. She had found solace in water's embrace. Once again, the water stroked her, healed her. But the nearness of death, the emptiness that had gnawed at her soul, now filled her with a hunger. Coming alive as she had never been before, Launa wanted another human's touch.

She breaststroked back to where Jack stood his post—guarding against nothing. "The water's great. Come on in."

Jack scanned around the pond, looked everywhere but at her. "I will, after you're finished." Frieda danced happily around the beach, sniffing, yelping, being very doggie.

"Damn it, Jack, if there was anything wrong, Frieda would let us know. Let's take care of a bit of personal hygiene, trooper."

With a wry grin, Jack took one more look around, then set his bow on an overhanging bank. Keeping his back to her, he slipped out of his briefs, then turned and was a blur as he made a dash for the water and dove in. Launa laughed and swam in pursuit.

For the next few minutes, they swam, chastely covered by

water that shimmered and foamed around them—but water that caressed every inch of Launa's body and left her more hungry for a human touch.

"Let me wash your back," Launa finally offered. "Maria said sand could be almost as good as soap."

Jack shook his head, water droplets flying through shadow and light, but said, "Yes."

He settled on a rock in a half foot of water. Launa gently rubbed sand on his back, then splashed water to wash the sand off. Then did it again. After a few minutes, she found herself just rubbing his back.

"I'll give you one year to stop that," Jack moaned softly. "You feel wonderful."

"It feels good just to touch you," Launa whispered, kissing the back of his neck.

Jack turned; his arms went around her. "Launa, I want you. I think I've wanted you since the first time I saw you."

"You've got me, Jack."

He shook his head. "Six months from now, will we have a home? Will we be in any shape to be raising kids?"

Launa put her head back and laughed. "So that's why you've been outrunning me." She surrounded Jack's face with her hands, let her fingers caress away the concern she saw. "They put three years' worth of birth control implants in me before we jumped. Give us three years and we'll be ready for anything."

In an instant, Launa was on her back in the water, Jack's lips on hers, softly asking. She answered with fire.

For a long moment, their lips consumed them, but Jack's fingers had already found her breast. The water had hardened them, the air had softened them. Now, they hardened again as Jack's touch lit fires around them. His lips traveled down her throat, inflaming her as they went.

Launa's back bowed. Her arms flayed out, paddling her toward the beach, drawing her out of the water, leaving more of her exposed to Jack. When she could stand it no more, she rolled over, putting Jack on his back. Her hands went to his raging hunger. She wanted him. Now.

On the bank, Frieda growled an alarm.

EIGHT

NOT DARING TO move her head, Launa hunted out of the corner of her eye for the German shepherd. The dog stood, legs splayed, hair bristling. Frieda's eyes were locked on something directly across the pond.

Launa slid off Jack, her hand wandering down his belly to what was rapidly shrinking. He settled deeper into the water, hiding his sudden disinterest. "What have we got?" was the sweet nothing he whispered in her ear as he kissed it to keep up appearances.

"Give me a second." As she rested her head on his chest, fingers playing in the hair of his belly, her eyes slowly tracked over every inch of the far bank. Nothing. Inside her, a mix of hormones fit to eat through tank armor rose in her stomach. She struggled to keep up appearances, to keep breakfast down, to spot anything.

On her third sweep, something caught her eye directly across the pond, forty feet away. "I think I see a man."

"Just one?"

"That's what I said."

"Armed?"

Launa hesitated. She wasn't even sure she had a target. The wind blew; a branch waved; sunlight played across her target. "He's got a spear, carried underhand for thrusting."

"Anyone else?"

"I told you, I only see one," she snapped.

"Wonder how long the pervert's been watching?" Jack might have carried off the attempt at humor, but his voice broke. "What do you want to do?"

What Launa wanted to do was kill somebody, quick, with lots of blood. *You can't kill everyone you run into. That's not the mission. Is it time to gamble, girl?* "He's not moving."

Everything in her ached for action, but she held herself on a tight leash. If the guy so much as flinched, she would go for Jack's bow—but he didn't move.

The stranger stood, frozen in place. His eyes moved, quickly sweeping the pond, always coming back to Launa. Judith said subsistence hunters had to be stealthy to eat. Well, this guy was good; he'd gotten too damn close. Maybe Judith had finally gotten something right.

The man wore a leather vest, tied shut, unlike the open vests of the horsemen. His leggings were a patchwork of different skins, almost like camouflage. Everything was different from the dead Kurgans. Had Launa found a hunter, or was this how the well-off Kurgan made his fashion statement?

The cool of the water was getting to her. It was time to act. "Jack, I'm going to stand up and treat this guy like a long-lost relative. I want you to slowly collect the dog and go get what's left of yesterday's kill."

"Not the bow?"

"Right."

"Launa, it'll take me a good ten minutes."

"Damn it, Jack, I can dodge his spear at this range. If he charges, I'll have the bow in a second and he'll be dead the next. I know how to run a risk assessment. Now, are you going to get me that meat, or do I use your head for an offering?"

"Okay." Jack rested a hand on her shoulder. Launa almost shoved it aside. "Tell me when to move. I just hope you have better luck making friends than I did."

"Right," Launa tried to get her temper under control. *Will I have to argue every command with you, Jack?*

She took a deep breath. "Now."

Launa stood and took a step deeper into the water. She raised her right hand in greeting. "Hello." *Right, like he's going to understand me. But there's more to communicating than words.*

Behind her, she could hear Jack's measured tread as he left the pond. He softly called Frieda, and a moment later broke into a run. In front of her, the man did not move, even when Jack whistled for a horse. *He'll be back in a lot less than ten minutes.* Launa raised both hands. "Greetings."

The stranger sidestepped from behind the bush, still holding the spear low. Launa studied the man.

He was shorter than she, probably a little over five feet. A leather sweat band held his black hair out of his face, letting it hang free to his shoulders; his beard showed streaks of gray and had been trimmed to a few inches. The belt that held up his breechcloth was woven from different shades of leather. Two rabbits swinging from his belt showed his success at the hunt.

The hunter did another eyeball search of the pond area, then returned to her.

Launa hardly breathed. *What have I gotten myself into, standing alone and naked in the middle of a pond? I'm crazy.* With the horsemen, a suit of plate armor wouldn't have been enough clothes. This man was different; his eyes met hers evenly. It wasn't as if he ignored the rest of her. She had seen his glance flicker over her, just as she had studied every inch of him. Still, his eyes returned to hers, as if to see her soul through them—as if that part of her alone mattered.

Taelon, who walked first among the Badger People, backed out of the bush that sheltered him and eyed the woman across the pond. Clearly, she was unarmed and harmless. Clearly, she was welcoming him. Just as clearly, he did not understand a word she spoke.

The man who had been with her quickly left the water. Taelon had spotted the bow and quiver on the bank. If the strange man stooped for the bow, Taelon would run. The man walked past it, out toward the plain where horses grazed.

Taelon's eyes saw what lay before him, but his heart could make nothing of it. The trail led too many ways.

Farther down the valley, he had passed a night camp of Horse People. He had also passed scavengers feasting on five dead horsemen. Their clothing and weapons had been taken, as was the custom, but not their heads. Strange.

Beyond the trees, many horses grazed. Yet a woman rode with this man. And when they talked among themselves, she said much more than a woman of the Horse People would. It seemed, at the end, that it was she who told the man what to do. Very strange.

Taelon stared into her eyes. They were blue, not the dark brown of a hunter's. *What path do you walk?*

The man returned with a deer carcass. The woman seemed to offer it to Taelon as the man held it out.

Slowly, Taelon trod the path around the pond, but his eyes never left the pair. Always he knew where he would run if these two suddenly grew the teeth of wolves or the claws of bears.

The woman turned her back on Taelon and walked slowly from the water. At the edge, she slipped into clothes that no woman of the Horse People would wear; they covered almost nothing, and were not leather! Too much here; Taelon's heart urged flight. *But the hunting is best where the land is new and full.*

Taelon rested on his spear. Again the woman offered the deer meat with a sweep of her hand. The man placed it halfway between them, then pulled on clothes much like the woman's. Never taking his eyes from her, Taelon moved forward and stooped to sniff the meat. It was good. The People would eat well when he returned.

Launa was surprised at the wave of relief that swept over her at Jack's return. But she only started breathing again when the hunter sniffed the friendship offering and smiled. "I think the worst is over."

Jack slowly picked up his bow and unstrung it. "Judith had pictures of the goddess, most of them naked."

"I must have looked like Venus."

"You'll need to put on a few pounds to pass for the local one." Jack's grin destroyed the insult. Launa started to slug him, then thought better; the stranger's eyes never left them.

Returning his arrow to the quiver, Jack nodded at the man. "I'll say one thing, this fellow looks more interested in running than bashing me in the head. I like that in a guy."

Right, but is that just a hunter's caution, or does this fellow have a reason to fear horsemen? Launa added that to the long list of questions she wouldn't answer today.

Slowly, the man got to his feet. He put the fist of his right hand on his chest and spoke. "Taelon."

Launa repeated the motions. "Launa."

Jack did the same, then added under his breath. "Have we introduced ourselves, or screwed up a thank-you?"

Launa wanted to throttle Jack and his sense of humor. Then she spotted the warning. What she *knew* she knew was more dangerous than what she was still checking for accuracy. This was one assumption she could test; she pointed at the stranger. "Taelon." Then her companion, "Jack." Then herself, "Launa."

The stranger followed suit, naming each.

Jack grinned. "Score one for our language expert."

"Nuts. Learning names is a long way from learning a language, but at least we wouldn't be shouting, 'Hey you.' "

Taelon picked up the carcass, hefted it over his shoulder, and glanced around as if to say "Where to?"

Launa motioned for him to follow her. When they stepped from the trees, Taelon took in the horses with a glance. There was no surprise in it. *How much of us did this guy check out before we noticed him, or he let us notice?* "Jack, we can't ride and this guy walk. I think we ought to give away a horse."

Jack hesitated only a moment before trotting out to select a middling-size stallion; Launa presented the gift. In a blink, Taelon dropped the deer. The horse was a bit nervous, but the hunter patiently won it over. Once it settled down, Taelon swung himself up with an easy grace.

Jack's words belied the smile he talked through. "For a hunter, this guy sure knows his horseflesh."

Launa had started to relax. *For once, things are going smoothly.* Jack's words came like a flash of lightning, showing her the cliff she was inches short of walking off. As her mind spun through the void, her eyes took in the hunter, then suddenly found a focus. "Jack, check his feet. They're as big as mine in combat boots. Those calluses must be an inch thick. He's a walker, not a rider."

Jack rubbed his chin. "Yeah," he nodded, "but how come he knows horses?"

"You tell me and we'll both know," Launa let the sour bile in her stomach gush through her words. "When's the next satellite pass? Think it'll tell us anything?"

Jack snorted.

Taelon kicked the horse and guided it toward Launa. He wasn't nearly as steady in his seat as the Kurgans who had chased her yesterday. She loaded the deer carcass across his mount, then whistled for Star. Mounted, they quickly trotted uphill to the camp.

Which brought them back to the dogs as well. Jack had both on leashes and tied to the tree, and their complaints could be heard halfway down the hill. Launa didn't want to declare the hunter "friend," but they couldn't afford to have someone constantly holding the dogs. She decided to risk it.

Mist took to the hunter without difficulty, or maybe she just wanted to get back out on the steppe, shepherding the horses. Frieda was another matter.

With a low growl she circled the hunter. Taelon stood rigid but never took his eyes from the dog. Launa suspected the hunter had stared down wolves before. In the end, Frieda returned to her guard position, watching the camp in general—and Taelon in particular.

Jack started loading equipment, and, after making sure Frieda would not take offense, Taelon added a helping hand. They got into a rhythm, Launa bringing sacks and pack racks, Taelon and Jack mounting them and lashing the gear to the horses. Between them the work went quickly.

Launa glanced over what was left of their camp as the men loaded the last of the baggage. She headed for their bedding. As she pulled the blankets apart, her "pillow" fell out. She didn't remember putting the small leather sack there when they made camp yesterday. There was a lot about yesterday she didn't remember, or want to.

Launa stooped to pick up the soft white leather bag. She fingered the markings on it, wondering what they said, if they were Native American or Mexican. She didn't know, and hadn't had time to ask Maria.

Launa held the sack out of sight of the men and let its contents pour into her hands. The second lieutenant's bar came first. All her life, Launa had worked for that simple rank insignia. She'd worn it once, to take the President's orders. Jack had spotted her removing it from her uniform when they changed into what little they wore for the time jump. He hadn't objected, so Launa brought a keepsake on this crazy mission.

But the book that slid out of the sack next was no symbol. Launa had grown up Army; she could identify any combat vehicle or aircraft in a second, but she was doing good to tell a rose from a tulip. Now, plant identification would decide if she ate regularly. When the CIA program manager send Launa off to an old Mexican cook, Launa had been a bit skeptical.

One trip to a native plant reserve showed Launa how wrong she could be. Maria was a botanical gold mine. Learning from the woman was like drinking from a fire hydrant. Launa got so much, but much more washed over her.

And there was more to Maria. She fed Launa, in body, in mind—in soul. The first morning's breakfast had included a hug that made up for the twenty years of fidgeting distance around the O'Brian house. As the days went by with Maria, it was all Launa could do not to lie down, roll over like one of the dogs, and beg the woman to scratch her belly. Launa had never felt like that around anyone before.

And when all hell broke loose, and the team was desperately rummaging through the wreckage for enough gear to get on the next plane to Livermore, the cook had wound her way past the gun-toting guards to bring a moment's calm to Launa. "You have much more to learn, little one, but no more time." Maria, whose security clearance wasn't supposed to extend past the kitchen and certainly not to the coming end of the world, dismissed it with a gentle shake of her head. "This will help where you are going." The old Mexican put the leather bag in the young soldier's hands.

When Launa wanted a reason to keep going, it wasn't her mother or the Colonel she thought of, nor even the President of the United States. It was Maria. Maria, and all the Marias of the world, deserved something better.

Launa opened the thick, weathered book, as she had on that distant, yet-to-be day. *"The Pharmacology of Herbs*, 1902, Philadelphia" stared back at her. The very title tasked Launa. There was much in it, so much she didn't know.

Launa closed the book with a snap. *Study can wait, kid. Break's over. Let's do it.* Sliding the book back in the sack, she turned to face the men.

Beside Big Red, Jack stooped to pick up the last sack. Launa tossed the blankets to him, and he stuffed them in and started lashing it to the horse's rack.

Launa strode toward Star, quickly tying a water skin to the sack with the book, then slinging the pair across her horse. As she mounted, she dismissed the vacant camp with the same quick glance so many houses had gotten in her wandering army life.

Astride Star, Launa pulled Maria's hat down tight and set her jaw as her eyes swept the land before her. Somewhere out there was Maria's future. "Okay, Taelon, where to?" She reinforced her question by waving her arm in a circle.

NINE

KANTOM OF THE Stormy Mountain Clan sat his horse as he studied the valley before him. He had found the trail of Perto's warriors, not too far from their last camp. It had been easy to follow. To his left, the smoke of a fire drifted on the light breeze. But the trail led straight ahead.

Toman nudged him as he pointed at the smoke. "Uncle Perto must have slept late this morning. If we ride quickly, we can catch up with him."

Kantom shoved back. "My father says to always let a trail tell its own tale. Look, warbirds gather." Ahead, where the tracks led, black birds circled and settled to feast.

"They're probably just after the leftovers from an old camp," Toman whined, but Kantom heard in his voice the submission of the weak to the stronger. He let his mouth form the hard grin he had seen his father wear at moments of such victory.

"We go." Kantom pointed straight ahead.

"I hope we're not late for supper" was his companion's only response as he kicked his horse and followed Kantom at a trot into the valley.

It was approaching noon when they rode among the warbirds. It was not the whitened bones of a deer that the birds fought over, but Cento and Devon. An arrow had killed one warrior, a lance in the back the other.

Toman slid from his mount to stand, tears flowing, keening a woman's wailing in his high pitched, still-boy voice.

Kantom wanted to race from this death, but he was Arakk's son. He ran from nothing. Carefully he searched the dust, letting it tell him of the battle. It said little, too little. These warriors had been taken by surprise; there had been no real fight here. Was that why no heads had been taken? But these men were strong warriors. Any man of the Horse People would be proud to have one of these skulls dangling from his saddle blanket.

Beside Devon were boot prints like none Kantom had seen before. Those boots were also beside Cento. Where they went into the woods, they also came out again, this time with another pair like them. Kantom circled the camp, hunting for where the horses left. The trail was easy; a hand of hands of horses being led on one, maybe two, strings were easy to find.

They would be easy to follow. "Come, Toman. We go."

TEN

JACK'S NECK FELT whiplashed at the speed with which Launa went from vulnerable kid to goddamn general calling the shots, and no thank you, mister, for your opinion. Somewhere in between they'd run a near miss of becoming lovers—and that near miss was still tearing Jack's gut apart. He didn't know who she was from moment to moment, and he wasn't too sure who he was either.

And now there was Taelon. *Who is this guy?*

As the hunter led out, Jack dropped back, letting Launa take the lead. That also put her next to Taelon. *Is that smart, letting an unknown get that close? Remember yesterday, kid.*

But it was Jack's head that ached, not hers. And it was her body he wanted to make love to. Jack shook his head; what had he told himself last night? We're just soldiers with a job to do. *Okay, Bearman, shut up and soldier.* But keeping a soldier's interval had been a lot easier before he held her in his arms. *Damn.*

Taelon led them downstream at a pace that seemed to increase as he got more comfortable riding, more comfortable a hell of a lot faster than any new rider should. Jack spent his time doing three-sixties, trying to spot anything that looked dangerous before it got close. He saw no threat.

He did notice that Taelon quickly crossed the stream and stayed to the left of it. The tall trees along the watercourse gave them cover from anyone's view on the other side of the valley, but the hunter rode far enough from the trees to stay out of bowshot range. The guy was careful, something Jack liked. What he didn't like was not knowing why Taelon was so cautious.

Jack wondered how the hunter would react to dead horsemen. Was it coincidence that they were well out on the plains when they passed two very dead Kurgans feeding buzzards? Jack spotted the black birds; Taelon never looked that way.

Jack also spotted the horses they'd left behind yesterday. With Launa's permission, he wrangled them back into the herd. The whole time Taelon managed to look everywhere except at the bodies. *He has to know.*

With Launa ordering breaks every hour to switch horses, the trip down the valley took what was left of the morning. Where the stream flowed into a river, Taelon forded it and led them west. They crossed more small rivers, skirted a marsh, then cut across a wide stretch of grassland. The sun was halfway down the sky when Taelon turned and followed a tree line. Suddenly, the hunter slipped from his mount and jogged into the woods.

Jack surveyed the tactical situation and did not like what he saw. They were in short bow range of woods he couldn't see nearly far enough into. Jack wanted clear fire lanes; he pointed his mount back onto the prairie toward a shallow depression.

"Jack, what's the problem?"

He slid from his horse and began stringing his bow while avoiding Launa's eyes. "No problem. I just want a little distance in my fire lanes."

"Jack, there's nothing to worry about."

He rubbed gingerly at his skull. "Yeah."

"Jack, these people are different. Did you see what Taelon did for me last break? I was pulling at my oily hair and he showed me a plant with roots like soap. One of those Kurgans yesterday wouldn't have cared about a woman. This guy does."

Jack let out a slow breath. Was Launa being dumb, or was

that the kind of intelligence they would have to trust this trip out? *Damn!* "Okay, we do it your way."

"Thank you, Jack." Launa's voice dripped sarcasm like a colonel's. Before Jack could say anything more, a babble of voices from the woods got his attention.

"Let's get the dogs leashed," Launa ordered. "I'll take Mist." Jack was just tying a rope onto Frieda's collar when Taelon led a collection of men and women from the woods.

Like him, they were short and dark. The women wore everything from full-length leather dresses to short skirts of leather or woven reeds to practically nothing. Jack spotted a few cases that dispensed with the "practically."

It was the same with the men. Some wore britches and vests like Taelon. Others settled for just breechcloths—and a few settled for nothing.

Beside him, Launa swallowed hard. "Oh my God. What would the Colonel's wife say?" But she walked forward to meet her new allies, carefully looking them in the eye.

Jack studied the mob with a scowl and a churning gut. Once again, he was outnumbered and up to his ears in un-knowns. And from the looks of matters, neither female nor male was in charge. No bows were visible. Jack would have preferred to know where the projectile weapons were. He glanced at the feet of the approaching people; everybody's were the size of boondockers. There had been no horses where he and Launa now pastured theirs. *Okay, you're not Kurgans, but who the hell are you?*

Taelon offloaded the deer carcass to a young man who hefted it on his shoulders and headed back up the trail. Three women trailed him, talking happily. Jack could imagine them swapping recipes. He smiled—and immediately went back on guard.

Taelon was unloading the other horses. Jack did not want people handling his gear. He could not afford to have his tools pilfered, especially the bronze ones.

Jack dropped Frieda's leash, stepping down firmly on it as he half drew his bow and pointed it in the general direction of Taelon. "Launa, stop them. Our gear doesn't go any-where."

People stared quizzically at Jack.

"Don't be ridiculous; they're just helping."

"We damn near got killed last time. Launa, we're out-numbered. Let's not get in the same mess."

"I can't negotiate with the locals with a dog on my hands. Here." Launa slammed Mist's rope into Jack's right hand. He couldn't aim the bow and hold a dog that was happily trying to follow Launa. Then Frieda took off in the opposite direction. Jack dropped his bow and grabbed for both leashes as the dogs entangled him in a web.

"Sit, damn you, sit." They stared up at him, big eyes dumb and wondering. Jack glanced at the crowd.

Launa stood beside Taelon, pointing at a spot far enough from the trees to be out of bowshot. "We'll make camp there." She took a load and led the way through the mob to drop it where she wanted. Taelon shrugged, handed the next load to a young man, and pointed him toward Launa. The porter laughed at whatever Taelon said and brought his burden straight to her.

In a few minutes, with the help of several men, their gear lay in a circle around Launa. "Okay, Jack, now what do we do?"

Most of the people were disappearing down the wooded path. Taelon waited, a woman at his side. Jack gritted his teeth, tried to shake off his fear, wondered if he should. He fell back on Judith's advice—ask a question. "What do you want to do?"

Launa stood, legs apart, arms folded across her chest. "I'm glad we're finally making decisions like partners, Jack. This unilateral bullshit has to stop."

Jack scratched his head and winced. It still hurt where he'd nearly been brained.

"Jack, these folks are not Kurgans. We treat them different and they'll treat us different."

Jack gritted his teeth. He'd learned to trust his instincts. If you could not trust your gut in combat, you got dead or went crazy. Then again, the last few days his gut had been going in so many directions, it was hard to tell what was real and what was background noise. But Launa was right; risk was the name of this mission. "What do you have in mind?"

"Let's keep together and follow Taelon. You take a bow. We both take quarterstaffs." Launa let out a long breath. Was it exasperation with him, or did she feel the tension too?

"Okay," Jack agreed. "The dogs can raise a ruckus if anyone messes with our gear." Jack let the German shepherd off her leash. "Frieda, guard. Mist." The Border collie looked at him, about as dangerous as a hamster. "Oh, hell. Stay girl, stay." Then Jack added, half to himself, "Frieda better do as good a job of guarding the gear as she did of guarding us this morning."

Launa marched off. Maybe she hadn't heard.

Jack unstrung his bow and swung quiver and scabbard across his shoulder before he followed her.

The hunter studied them for several moments, then introduced the woman beside him as Tuam and led them into the woods. There was little underbrush beneath the trees, and most of the trunks were too small for an archer to hide behind. Jack let a nervous breath out, trying to relax. Fifty feet down the path, it opened on a field and Jack got his first look at a Paleolithic village. There were no huts like Brent had told them to expect. Lean-tos around the wood's edge seemed the only protection from the weather.

Taelon stopped with Jack and Launa where the deer was being hacked apart. Chunks of the deer and several smaller animals were tossed into a clay pot. "Pottery." Excitement was in Launa's voice. "The hunter-gatherers are not supposed to have pottery."

Jack scrubbed at his beard to hide his face from Launa; she had a short temper and enough reasons to be mad at him today. She'd spent extra time with Judith, like a 4.0 cadet boning for exams. *Well, we're smack dab in the middle of the test, and it looks like Judith is flunking.* Jack loved the old scholar, but he had had his doubts. A soldier learned to expect surprises; Launa had better get used to it.

Taelon handed Jack a deer antler. Pointing at a section of ground, he made digging motions. Jack nodded. "I think I'm digging a fire pit."

Taelon's woman took Launa's hand and led her toward the woods. When Launa balked, Tuam picked up a stick and waved it. Jack stiffened; his quarterstaff came up on guard. *If the woman hits Launa . . .*

Then Launa waved him off. "I'm collecting firewood with Tuam."

"I thought you didn't want us separated."

"We improvise. You dig the fire pit. I gather wood. Keep your head up, but let's go along. Okay?"

Jack didn't like having one plan dropped so fast. He surveyed his surroundings; nobody was around. He heard dim shouts and other noises from the tree line on the other side of the clearing. *Improvise, soldier. Improvise.* Jack reached for the antler.

Calm down, he told himself. *Just because that woman can switch gears faster than a ten-speed is no reason to get riled. And it wasn't her fault you got interrupted this morning.* He'd had the day to drain those juices out. How much of his edginess this afternoon was his gut still doing flip-flops? *Men got hormones too.*

Jack threw himself into his work.

ELEVEN

KANTOM RODE HIS pony slowly, his eyes sweeping the ground. He paused often to lift his head and search the steppe around him. Whoever had rode this trail before him kept out of bow range of the woods, but close enough to hide there. Did they not love the open steppe with the Sun shining down upon them? What kind of men had killed two warriors of the Hungry Wolf? Such men Kantom wanted to see, if at a distance.

The trail led past the butchering of a deer and up a hill to a tree. The tree was a problem. Two people, maybe three, had made camp here, but the tracks followed many paths. Many horse strings went down the hill to the steppe before them. One string led back the way they had come. Droppings were fresh; the horses had still been here this morning.

"Kantom," Toman called from the shade of the tree. "More warbirds circle."

Kantom searched in the dust. There were many tracks, and they led in both directions. He followed those strange boots to join Toman. They had come up the hill from the steppe, and he followed them down. What he found filled him with wordless rage.

In the dust, cast aside like some moss tainted with woman's blood, lay the shattered pieces of warrior blades.

Kantom threw his head back, cried to the Sun. "What sacrilege can this be?"

He looked down at the broken shards, anger turning his heart to fire-hardened flint. "Who did this?" He glowered at Toman. The other boy stared back, wide-eyed and silent.

Kantom studied the dust, demanding it tell its tale to him. He could make out knee prints, and caked mud. *The one who did this cried like a woman!* Kantom forced his heart to accept what his eyes told it.

Slowly Kantom knelt to pick up the shattered blades and put them in his medicine bag. There was not enough room. He studied the knife hilts. One wore the face of the angry wolf.

"Perto's knife," Toman whispered. "Somewhere the warbirds feast on strong Perto?"

"Yes." Kantom stood and strode to his mount. "And we will find him. Then, we will avenge him."

"Just the two of us," Toman squeaked, pale as an old woman who never left her master's tent.

Kantom made no answer as he mounted and kicked his pony toward where the warbirds gathered. There was wisdom in Toman's words, even if they were the words of a coward. How often had Arakk told his son that a Mighty Man was not only strong in arm, but strong in cunning, like the fox. Should the small kit seek revenge with its own teeth, or run to the wise gray fox, who could bring hands of hands of lances?

Kantom did not know what path to follow. First he would use his eyes, feast them on all there was to see. Then he would choose a path for his horse.

TWELVE

JACK DUG IN the soft ground with a will; this was something he could put his back into. Here at least was one place he could see results. Beside Jack, Taelon set a leisurely pace, digging for a while, resting for a while. It made for easy though dirty work; Taelon was quickly down to his loincloth.

When they finished the pit, Taelon called an elderly woman from one of the lean-tos. She brought a clay-lined gourd and a bundle. Arranging moss, twigs, and punk in the pit, she used a stick of green wood to lift a glowing ember from the gourd.

With the fire started, Taelon motioned Jack to follow him. Jack retrieved his weapons and headed downstream. At an inviting pool, the hunter stripped and splashed in. Jack shed his briefs and joined him. It felt good to wash off the sweat of the day and the dirt from the digging.

Others who had been fishing joined them, and not just to soak. People splashed each other and got splashed back. It reminded Jack of a beach party he'd gone to as a kid, one of his few good memories of L.A.

Taelon was not exempt from the water fights; he gave as well as he got. Jack could not picture the Kurgan leader who had tried to take his head off trading splashes with a ten-year-old girl. Launa was right; these folks were different.

Jack began to relax, to let the day's tensions wash off. The laughter and playful fun softened the hardness of yesterday's killer and left something gentle in their wake. Jack couldn't recall the last time he'd let himself just enjoy a moment.

He didn't totally forget the mission. He set about learning the word for water. *That shouldn't be too hard.*

It was. Every time he asked, he got a different word. As much as he hated to, he'd have to leave the language to Launa. Her personnel folder said she picked up German, Spanish, and Arabic when her folks had been stationed overseas.

Taelon washed his breechcloth and didn't bother putting it back on. Most of the other people did their laundry and showed no inclination to wear their wet clothes.

Jack checked the flax weave of his briefs; it probably would not take too many washes. He rinsed them gently. When they returned to the fire, he had his thrown over his shoulder like everyone else. Low branches make good clotheslines.

Launa was just coming back with a final armful of wood. She dropped it, then followed Tuam toward the river.

"Go on," Jack quipped. "The water's fine."

He got a scowl for his reminder of the morning's swim.

The fire was a bed of glowing embers; a ceramic pot rested beside the pit. Stones were heating in the embers. As he watched, a cook pulled one from the fire and dumped it, hissing, into the stew. Another cook used a different pair of sticks to fish out a cold rock.

Launa returned from bathing wearing her briefs. Jack raised an eyebrow, which she ignored. *Where's that friendly woman I ran into this morning?*

As the evening dusk thickened, the people gathered in a circle around the fire. Jack did a quick census. Twenty adults, three or four of them showing gray. Fifteen to twenty kids. Those were harder to count; they never stayed still.

Taelon cleared his throat, and even the kids grew quiet. The hunter began a story. Jack understood nothing, but the hunter's posture and tone of voice were those of the ageless storyteller. Jack leaned back to enjoy the sound of the story, the cool of the air, the fragrance of the evening.

Jack snapped out of his warm, fuzzy feelings when Taelon went through what looked like the motions of riding a horse. *Is he telling about this morning?* Nothing Taelon had done before seemed to match today's events. *Damn, what I'd give for a translation.* He glanced at Launa. She was intent on the storyteller.

When Taelon finished, supper was served. First baked fish, garnished with berries and roots. The venison stew was next. It was thick with barley, wheat, and lentils and was served in individual wooden bowls for Jack, Launa, Taelon, and Tuam. Others used leaves to scoop out the lukewarm broth.

"Where'd they get the pot, or the grains?" Launa whispered.

"Tell me and we'll both know." Jack felt like he was putting together an immense jigsaw puzzle. Except most of the pieces weren't on the table yet. And the next section just might kill him. His eyes wandered to the faces around the fire. Everywhere was the contentment he'd seen among his grandfather's people after a hard day of honest work. Could he trust that experience? *The Apache were a deadly race off the reservation.*

Inconspicuously, Jack checked his boots. The knives were in easy reach. The quarterstaff was beside him, as were his bow and quiver. If it came to a fight, he'd do the best he could.

When dinner was finished, the entertainment continued. A woman and a man came forward. As she sang, he beat a slow rhythm using two hollow reeds, varying meter and tone. He made the notes lower or higher by hitting the reeds together in different places. The song felt funny and scary and sad at different times; the reed accompaniment was always right.

The music was so simple, yet so right. Jack let it unkink the tension his back held from the day.

Dancers followed. This time several older men and woman produced drums. Two young couples went through a wild series of steps, twirls, and leaps that beat any aerobic workout Jack had ever seen. He grinned to himself; he didn't understand what the dance said, but he knew what it meant. Like most dances kids did, it showed their elders just how out of shape the older people were.

But Taelon and Tuam answered the challenge. They and another middle-aged couple jumped to their feet. The circle made room for them. First one foursome, then the next did their best to outdo each other.

Jack wondered how long this could go on. Each group tried again and again to kick higher, leap farther, throw one or another higher into the air. *Somebody's going to get hurt.*

At that moment, one of the old drummers threw his stick in the air. The rest followed his lead. The beat died.

The dancers came to a halt. Laughing breathlessly, the eight joined in a monstrous hug. The onlookers cheered. The dancers pounded each other on the back and collapsed in a pile.

When the laughter settled down, two women began to sing. Their voices rose and fell together in a way that left Jack haunted and excited all at the same time.

The dancers lay where they had dropped. As the song went on, Taelon began massaging Tuam's legs. Other dancers and those around the circle followed him.

Jack reached for Launa's feet. Slowly he ran his hands down one leg, using his thumbs to work the muscles of her foot. He drew a pleasured sigh as his reward.

Around him, the men continued their ministrations, expanding the scope of their efforts higher up the women's legs. The women smiled and made themselves more accessible. The song changed. It had to be bawdy from the way they sang it and the way the men joined in the refrains. Jack prepared to do as a Roman in Rome.

Launa took matters differently. Flushed, she grabbed her quarterstaff and rushed for the path that led to their packs. Her departure drew bewildered stares, but she did not look back. Taelon and Tuam exchanged questioning frowns. Jack, embarrassed, and now the odd man out, collected his gear, nodded in what he hoped was a respectful way to Taelon, and followed Launa down the path.

Taelon watched the strangers go. His heart was troubled by the path they walked. He remembered again the bodies of the five horsemen, dead in battle, but no trophy heads taken.

Taelon also remembered the talk late at night around the campfire last autumn at the gathering of the hunter clans.

The families who hunted to the east had been troubled. And Taelon knew the strange ways of the Horse People.

And Jack this afternoon had drawn his bow. His were the eyes of a man who could kill another. *What path do the People walk when wolf and gray wolf hunt, Dear Goddess?*

Tuam nudged him. Just because the two strangers did not play was no reason for him not to. Taelon turned his attention back to Tuam.

Jack found Launa wrapped tightly in her blanket. "Mind telling me what's going on?"

"I'm sorry, Jack. I didn't come prepared for an orgy."

"I don't think these folks considered it an orgy. Did you see the looks you got when you busted out of there? You're not helping us get along with these people."

"And your pulling that bow stunt this afternoon didn't help matters one bit either."

"I was worried."

"And I'm not your toy."

Jack bit his tongue. Launa was within her rights. Maybe if he hadn't gotten his motor all revved up this morning, he'd be as slow as she was in adjusting to local customs. He waited for her to say something else, but she just pulled her blanket tighter.

Jack settled into his bedroll a safe distance from Launa. The night was warm; he wouldn't find her rolled up against his back in the morning. Lying on his back Jack watched the familiar stars. Then he checked for the polestar. Polaris had wandered from the north. Some important things had changed quite a bit.

First light brought Jack awake. His blankets held no warmth but his own. He stretched and sat up.

Across from him, Launa sat, staring into the morning sky. "I'm sorry about last night."

Jack lay back. "Launa, I'm not one of those men who doesn't know that no means no."

"Yes, but I've always prided myself on sending consistent signals. I sure didn't do that yesterday."

Jack could agree with that, but he kept his mouth shut.

"What was it like, growing up in L.A.?"

Jack's head swam at the speed this conversation was making turns. "I guess it was like growing up anywhere else."

"Growing up Army is like growing up nowhere else. I watched TV shows when the Colonel or his wife weren't home. Did kids really behave like that?"

"No." Jack remembered a few nights. "Well, not normally."

"That was never normal for us. The Bill of Rights doesn't exist inside the perimeter fence. And if you screw up, it's not just you, it's your old man's neck in the noose too. Swimsuit styles were set by the post commander's wife."

Launa faced Jack. "Just once, I took a school friend to the pool and wore one of her suits. General's wife saw us. The Colonel was on the carpet the next day, and she got the lifeguard fired for not throwing us out." Launa scowled. "I never wore anything that skimpy again until they issued us these outfits."

"You're kidding." Jack knew she wasn't, but the words leaked out. Considering the ribald talk in mess, he had a hard time believing officers would treat their own kids like that. *On second thought, hypocrisy wasn't mentioned in the code.*

"Captain, I've never even smoked pot. You don't risk the Colonel's career. Not that it mattered. What does matter is that yesterday, at the pond, I wanted you. Then we showed up here, and everywhere I look, it's a hippie convention. All that's missing is the pot smoke. And there's something else."

"What?"

"I don't know." Launa stood up, scanned the horizon. "There's something I can't put my finger on. Something wrong."

"Sure it's not just the change in customs?"

Launa shot him a nasty glare. "No, I am not letting their uniform of the day, or lack thereof, throw me."

Jack chose his next words carefully. "I had planned to spend my day with Taelon. You want me to stay close to you instead?"

"No. These people are safe. Naked. But safe." Launa grinned wryly.

Jack tossed off his blanket. "Keep your boots on—and your knives in them. We'll make it through." Jack wanted to give Launa a hug. He skipped it.

As they walked the path back into camp, Jack was careful to keep a proper military interval between them.

THIRTEEN

JACK AND LAUNA joined the tribe's breakfast of dried fish and berries. The fish was hard as nails; the berries softened it a bit. No one minded; they were all headed for the river.

Jack followed Taelon and got a fishing lesson quite different from the one his CO gave him in the Washington Cascades. The spears, nets, and weirs weren't fancy, but people put them to good use. Some spears had an added stick to eliminate the location distortion of a fish under water.

No matter how a fish was taken, each one was personally thanked. Jack didn't understand a word, but he didn't need to; the reverence showed through the language barrier. These folks gave the goddess a lot more than a quick grace before dinner.

The morning went quickly, and it was well into the afternoon when Launa appeared on the bank. "Jack let's go hunting."

Jack had just finished saying a thank-you, in English, to a fish he'd speared. He held it up. "Fishing's pretty good."

"Soldier," Launa snapped, "let's go hunting."

Jack tossed his spear to a young woman who'd helped him get the hang of fishing. *Come to think of it, a lot of the young women had been very helpful this morning. That couldn't be pissing Launa off.* Maybe it was.

Launa didn't wait, but quick-marched across the camp.

She grabbed a bow and was mounted before Jack caught up. He got his gear, but Launa was halfway across the meadow before he was mounted. *What's got into that woman?*

He galloped after her, but they were on the prairie before he caught up. She rode for a herd of red deer. They were a kilometer away before she slowed Star to a walk.

"You wanted to talk," Jack reminded her.

"Let's get supper." She dismounted and strung her bow. Jack followed suit; an archer was much more accurate without a horse under him. They paced off the range until it was down to two hundred meters. "The ten-point buck," Launa said.

They drew and released together. The stag looked up as Jack's arrow hit him. His hind legs collapsed. He struggled to regain his footing, then, with a final bugle, foundered.

Launa's arrow had missed.

Something really is bothering her! "We've got dinner. Now, what is it?"

"Have you figured anything out about the language?"

"Nope. I can't even ask for a drink of water."

"Actually, the language is easy." Launa was in her lecture mode; Jack settled in for a long wait. "They're speaking something a bit like Navaho and German."

"Say again?"

"They aren't actually talking Navaho or German. It's just that their minds work the way Judith said they did. Water isn't just water. They tell you all about it and merge the modifiers into one word, like German."

Jack nodded. "So I got a different word every time."

"Right. Water in midstream, and the water by the shore, and water flowing through your hands are all different words. Did you spot the one syllable that was the same each time?"

"No." Launa still hadn't said anything, but the way she wasn't saying it sent a chill down Jack's spine. *Get on with it, woman. Even an Indian's only so patient.*

"The root sound is *ah*. That's what the Hittites will call it. The Latin word is *aqua*."

"Those are Indo-European languages." Jack did not need a language degree to know that meant trouble. Big trouble.

"Right." Launa's breath left her in a half sigh, half groan. "Other words like south, east, summer, even horse, sound familiar. I don't know what to make of it." The nervous way she held her bow told him she did, but couldn't say it. If the Kurgans had already conquered this area, the two soldiers were too late to fight, much less win a war.

"Oh, God." Jack's knees went weak as his head seemed to spin off his neck. Slowly he made himself tick off the options—neither of them good. "We're either behind enemy lines, or way off our target time." Jack didn't like losing—especially being counted out before he had a turn at bat.

They trudged toward the fallen deer.

"What do we do now?" Launa breathed the empty words.

A good part of Jack wanted to collapse in the dust and bawl, frozen with terror and overloaded by the odds. They reached the deer. Jack staring down at it, mind too hammered to switch from walking to butchering. In his head, he heard his stepdad. "Yeah, just sit there in the sun like some reservation Indian. You'll never amount to anything."

Jack hated his stepfather. The Apache were good people; they had led the pony soldiers a hard chase. It had taken the might of the United States Army to bring them to the reservation. And it had taken whiskey to kill them. Jack clenched his fist; he was damned if he'd accept defeat until the last ball was thrown. If defeat was all he had, he'd take it on as a warrior.

"Lieutenant. We've been here two days. We don't know anything for sure. We started a reconnaissance; let's finish it." He held up two fingers, ticked off his choices. "If the invasion has begun, we find the main line of resistance and join the fight. If the war is already lost, we incite rebellion." He shook his fist at the sky. "We came here to change things, and I don't quit until they kill me."

Launa watched him with cold, measuring eyes. *If she laughs off my dramatics, we're lost.* Then her face split into a she-tiger's grin. "You better learn the language, then."

They slung the buck on Big Red and tied it down. The

cooks at camp could butcher it. As they were crossing the
meadow toward camp, Jack signaled Launa to halt.

"Did you understand anything the horsemen said?"

"I was too busy running or killing 'em, Jack."

"I just wondered."

"So do I. It hasn't been easy getting the handle I've gotten so far on the hunters' language. I can't remember a word
the horsemen babbled before they started swinging."

Jack also had trouble remembering, and it wasn't just the
knock on his head. No one relished the memory of killing
another person hand to hand. At least not the man Jack
wanted to be. He urged his horse to a walk. All the un-
knowns they faced lodged in his gut, leaving him empty for
more than venison stew.

What the cooks did that night with their deer did not help.
Liver, kidneys, everything went into the pot. Launa started
looking a bit green when the brain and eyes were added, but
Jack's stomach did a final flip when the genitals were tossed
in.

"I respectfully request permission of my commanding officer to cut us some steaks. I don't give a damn what the locals think of our skipping out on their stew."

Launa sighed. "It's either that or order in pizza. I don't
think even Domino's delivers here."

The laugh they shared felt good.

They excused themselves after supper and before the
singing began. Launa laid her bedroll on one side of the circle made by their gear; Jack settled himself on the other.
They were back to soldiering. Friendly soldiers, but soldiers
with a mission. Jack could accept that. They had enough
problems without complicating the command structure with
hormones.

Over the next few days they learned a lot. This was a fishing camp for a clan that ranged the rivers and woods; their
winter camp lay farther downriver.

Launa bubbled with excitement the evening her language
skills finally let her ask about the pot. "They got the pottery
from a group of farmers. When the rains stayed late last
year, these hunters helped the farmers do the plowing and

planting. They also did some of the harvesting last fall. The farmers gave them a share of the crop and the pots to store it in."

Launa was in full flight as she spread her bedroll. "That's how Judith said it happened. Not confrontation but cooperation. Not the way the modern Europeans treated the Indians, but a rational way. There's room enough for all."

"What about the horsemen?" Jack asked.

Launa deflated. "I don't know. When I ask about horsemen, I think I'm getting answers about us. These people can't separate one group from another. Everyone seems to be the same."

Jack settled into his blanket. They had been warned about that. It wasn't just finding the words but knowing what they meant. During their second week at the ranch, Brent had outlined what they knew of the proto-Indo-European dictionary. It had left Launa puzzled. "How do Jack and I tell the goddess worshipers 'To arms, to arms, the redcoats are coming'?"

"I haven't the foggiest," Brent had said for about the thousandth time that day. "Verbs like 'to be' and 'to come' were already in the invaders' tongue. They didn't borrow them from the Old Europeans, so we don't know what they were. But the real problem is finding someone fool enough to take up arms."

Jack had agreed with that. "Mom told me how Dad felt when someone spat on him after his first Vietnam tour. Grandfather wondered what he got for going to war against the Japanese. Why fight?"

"Right," Brent agreed. "To raise an army, you must think like them. These people are not dumb, just different. Let me explain." He fiddled with his computer; then the large screen on the briefing room wall lit up. Two women in flowing gowns stood beside a nude man who held a plow by its yoke pole.

"Found it the first time," Brent said, congratulating himself. His control of the data on his computer was rarely so good. "This is a vase painting showing the goddess giving man the plow."

"But there are two women," Jack observed.

"Different manifestations of the Great Goddess," Judith answered. "Note his penis." It was draped across the pole.

Launa frowned. "It's bent at the same angle as the plowshare."

"Right," Brent said with a grin. "They haven't studied biology, but they know if you plow the ground, it is more fertile."

"And if you plow the women, they are too," Judith finished, with her usual flair for the profane. "Their handle on cause and effect is not tied to scientific proof, but they've got it."

Jack had begun to understand. "I see the problem. If I say 'The Kurgan is the enemy,' it'll be vague for the Old Europeans by its very exactness. But, if I say 'The Kurgan is a river in flood, destroying all before it,' they'll understand."

"That's it." Judith beamed. "Let your Indian blood speak."

"But the problem's bigger." Launa spoke slowly. "The flood is a natural part of the world. The goddess sends it for good and bad. You just have to accept it. If the Kurgans are like a flood, won't the Old Europeans think of them the same way?"

Brent and Judith had nodded slowly. Now Jack was living with the problem. Somehow, he and Launa would have to help these people see the Kurgans and themselves in a very different light.

Beside him, Frieda got to her feet, ears forward, a low growl in her throat. "Trouble, girl." Jack came out of his blanket, knife in hand. Beside him, Launa was up, armed and ready.

"What do you think it is?" she asked.

"Don't know."

FOURTEEN

KANTOM WATCHED THE two as they came out of the woods, babbling together. It had taken him long to find them. The trail had led through rivers and plains. He'd lost it many times, but always he found it again. He had to. The sights of the first day burned in his heart.

Warriors dead. Ten warriors dead. Killed in honorable combat, but not one of the heads honorably taken. Kantom searched for a word to name anyone so lacking in a manly heart. There was nothing in the Horse People's tongue for such a man.

And now Kantom had found them, a man and a woman surrounded by Perto's horses. But the strangeness of the two made him pause. She wore almost nothing! What warrior would not grab what was so open to him? Any father or husband or brother would have to fight many men to keep his honor. The man dressed no different from her. What manner of people were these? Kantom closed his eyes, prayed to the Great Sun that these demons would vanish from his sight.

The two people were still there when he looked again. Kantom drew his knife from his belt and began to crawl through the woods. Toman pulled urgently on his elbow. When Kantom looked back, the other was shaking his head. He held up his hands, all ten fingers spread, and shook them.

"Two hands of warriors they killed. Ten," Toman whispered.

"And I will cut their throats as they sleep. We will ride back to our fathers with many horses. We cannot let strangers take clan horses."

"Your father said use our eyes, not our knives. When a Mighty Man says that, I obey." Toman crawled toward the horses.

Kantom snorted; he had heard his father's words. But his father also bragged that he did not lead the clan because he did what gray heads told him. A man knows when to strike like a snake. Kantom crawled forward.

Darkness drew closer around him, hiding him, but making it harder to see where he put his hand, his foot. He was close enough to see that the two had wrapped themselves in blankets when a twig snapped. He froze.

From the camp came a wolf's rumble. Suddenly, a bundle he had taken for baggage was bristling fur on four legs. The two, fast as any warrior, were out of the blankets, heads searching. Kantom knew he had only a second to choose life or death.

In a flurry of leaves and twigs, he spun around, and, running low, dashed for the horses. Toman was already mounted, holding Runs-like-the-Wind. As Kantom threw himself on his pony, Toman whispered, "I told you so."

"I am not done with those two," Kantom growled back as he kicked his horse for speed. They raced for the open steppe. *Even the wolves obey these demons! How could Perto of the Hungry Wolf warriors stand against his own totem? Father, let your ears hear my words.*

FIFTEEN

"WHAT WAS THAT all about?" Launa asked, eyeing the woods.

Jack shook his head. "I don't know. Animals, kids? I wouldn't turn Frieda loose on it. Might be a skunk."

"Whatever it was, it's gone." Launa settled back in her bedroll, but now she faced in that direction.

"Tomorrow night, I'll picket the horses in close."

"Good" was Launa's only response.

Near noon the next day, people dropped their fishing gear at shouts from upstream and ran off in that direction, talking too fast for Jack to catch anything. He checked his knives and went looking for Launa. He found her with Tuam.

"What's going on?" Jack didn't like this.

"What path do the people walk?" Launa asked Tuam. Jack did not understand the hunter woman's answer. Neither did Launa; she asked again. This time Tuam spoke very slowly and mimed as she did. Jack focused his attention upstream.

It was a long minute before Launa spoke. "Jack, I think they've spotted traders. I'm not sure. That's my best guess."

"Traders?" Jack turned.

"Right, people who give you things and you give them things." Launa handed a stone to Tuam. She held it up, studied it, grinned, and gave Launa a stone in return. "It looks like some kind of trading to me. What's your guess?"

"I'll take your word for it."

At that moment, a small parade arrived back in camp. Three men led a tiny horse or donkey. They were short and dark-haired like the hunters; one of them wore a linen breechcloth.

"They've got woven cloth!" Launa yelped.

"They've also got a horse," Jack growled.

But the hunters and new arrivals couldn't have been more friendly. The hunters relieved the traders of the large woven sacks they carried. The traders seemed glad for the help, but they kept their spears, which they used as walking staffs.

Once in camp, the man in linen arranged the sales show. The youngest man untied the roll on the donkey's back and spread out a reed mat dyed in a flamboyant pattern. As the traders pulled items from sacks, they held them up for all to see, and laid them out on the rug. Most of their merchandise stayed in the sacks.

"Interesting," Launa observed. "Now I see why folks were grabbing for our bags the first day. They took us for traders."

Jack nodded. "We had enough sacks. We confused them, and they scared me." Knowledge did not ease the tension knotting the back of his neck. *Where'd they get the damn horse?*

"I wonder who these people are?" Jack mused.

"I don't know, but I mean to find out. Traveling with traders might be just the cover we need."

Taelon broke away from the crowd around the traders and strode toward Jack. "Will you hunt today for Suno as you hunted for the People of the Badger?"

Jack pointed at the trader in linen. "Suno?"

Taelon nodded.

"Let's get several deer," Launa said. "If we're leaving soon, I'd like to leave behind plenty of meat."

Each led a string of two horses as they galloped out. They had just bagged their fourth deer, and the herd was bounding away, when Jack heard yells. His head came up as he nocked another arrow. Charging into the fleeing herd were two horsemen. Bows out, they brought down a deer of their own.

"Where'd those bastards come from?" Jack asked nobody.

"Let's wait and see," Launa said beside him. "The traders have a horse. Let's not go ballistic."

Jack shrugged. "You keep an eye on your friends. I'll load this deer." Launa kept her arrow nocked.

Jack was tying down the kill when the two horsemen trotted up. A small doe lay across the horse in front of a boy with flaming red hair. The other boy's hair was blond, almost white; neither sported a beard. Their britches and vests were the same as those of the ten dead Kurgans, but their long wooden poles had no flint points. *Just kids out to see the world. Why'd you have to stumble into mine?* Jack picked up his bow and nocked an arrow.

Launa raised her hand. "The Goddess walk with you."

The pair did not answer, but spoke rapidly to each other. The red-haired boy pointed his pole at Launa. They both laughed.

"You getting any of this?" Jack asked.

"Not a damn thing."

"Does it sound right?"

"I can't tell. They haven't said enough."

The boys trotted toward Jack. As Red passed, he brought his slender rod down, as if to touch Jack. The soldier knocked it aside. Red kicked his mount and the two kids raced away.

"What was that all about?" Launa asked.

"Showoff tried to count coup on me, or something. Some Indians got more credit for touching an enemy than killing him."

"Not a smart way to win a war," Launa concluded. "What do we do about those two?"

"Keep our eyes peeled. They might have been our problem last night. I expect we'll hear from them again." Jack rubbed his beard. Could he afford to have anyone, even kids, spying on them? "I don't know what I'll do about them."

"Jack, this close to Taelon's camp I don't want dead bodies to start showing up. The neighbors might talk, and these are the best neighbors I've ever had. Taelon must have seen at least some of the ones we killed before. Now if two more show up . . ."

"Yeah." Jack gave the kids one more check—they hadn't slowed down—and pointed his horse toward camp. It would make a soldier's life a lot easier if bad guys wore uniforms and evil empires sent declarations of war. But mankind had taken a couple of thousand years to figure that out. And he and Launa were here to make that discovery unnecessary.

The cooks were delighted with the wealth of food. Two extra fires were lit to smoke the meat, but Taelon looked sad. "Each must walk the path we see. I see a different path for you. Suno is a good trader to share a path with."

Jack clasped the hunter's shoulders. "But I see a path that will bring me back many times to share a fire with you."

Taelon pulled Jack into a powerful hug.

The honor of the first story that night went to Nak, the eldest of the traders. He sang of journeys from the mountains that touched the sky to the bitter waters where the sun rose.

After supper, Taelon stood up. "I have a gift for the hunter who has fed us so well." From a sack, he drew out a belt, woven like his own, of many different colored leather cords. He tied it around Jack's middle.

Tuam pulled a short leather skirt from the same bag and tied it around Launa. The soldier grinned like Jack had never seen her grin. But when the songs began, and the hunter couples began getting close, Launa was up, excusing herself. Jack looked around the fire; there were several pairs of batting eyelashes, which the traders quickly responded to.

He followed Launa.

SIXTEEN

THE NEXT MORNING, standing beside the fire pit he'd dug with his own hands, Jack felt regret at a leave taking for the first time in his life. He'd never been one for long good-byes; no one he'd ever cared about had lingered long enough for one. Not Sandie. Not Grandfather. Not the father he'd never known. *It's time to go, let's go,* was his usual attitude. The traders were ready to hit the trail; the hunters apparently had little Suno wanted.

But today Jack was in no hurry to leave the People of the Badger. He'd come to feel safe among them. It was a feeling he'd almost forgot. *Don't kid yourself, Bearman. You've got a lot to do before you and Launa will ever be safe.*

Still, Jack lingered until Taelon gave him a hug that threatened to crack ribs. Tuam's hug for Launa was no less dangerous—and Launa hugged right back. Was it Jack's imagination, or was that army brat just as reluctant to move on?

As the two women separated, Tuam whispered, "Go with the Goddess."

Launa answered, "And know her ways."

Jack had no idea what way that might be.

Launa paused as they rounded up their horses. "Think we'd miss a couple more?"

Jack did not give the question a second thought. "Let me

give a stallion to Taelon. You give a mare to Tuam." Jack picked one of the middling mares and a short but solid-looking stallion. The hunters would have good breeding stock.

Taelon was stunned. "What can we give you?" he stammered.

"The Goddess will whisper to your heart," Launa said.

Suno stood aside, shaking his head like a used car dealer watching someone else's stock drive off the lot unpaid for. Jack's stepdad had known a lot of used car salesmen. Jack hadn't found one he liked.

Launa offered Suno the loan of several packhorses. The trader seemed glad enough to be rid of his burden for a while. He balked, however, at riding a horse.

Launa shrugged. "If they walk, we walk. We can't be looking imperial around these folks."

By mid-morning, Launa was eating her words—and Jack was glad of it. "How can someone with such short legs walk so fast for so long?" Launa grumbled as she mounted Star.

Even at the pace Suno set, he was a nonstop talker. Over the morning, they learned quite a bit more about the language and their travel mates. Suno was on his fifth trip, peddling goods from the great forest where the sun rose to the great mountains where it set. Nak was a singer. Jack wondered if the proper translation should have been bard. Arlo was Suno's son, making the trip for the first time.

The day went quickly. With the evening's halt, Suno started ordering them how to set up camp. Jack didn't like his idea of a campsite. The fire pit was too close to the trees; fields of fire for the bows were too short.

"Didn't Judith say these folks made decisions cooperatively? This guy needs a lesson."

Launa's eyes measured the same problems Jack saw; then she shrugged. "He's spent more time on the road around here than we have. We do it his way."

Suno and Launa hunted up firewood while Arlo foraged for grains and vegetables. Nak and Jack were assigned to dig the fire pit. The sod was strongly rooted, and digging with an antler was hard work. Jack used his bronze knife to make the going easier. Nak eyed Jack's long blade. On the trader's belt hung a knife, its flint blade no more than an inch long. "Horseriders," the trader said, blending two words to make one.

Jack looked up, then quickly went back to digging. So Nak had a name for the horsemen. Here at least was a man who could distinguish the horsemen from the hunters. That would be something to talk over with Launa tonight.

After supper, the traders settled down to sing songs. None too sure what was on the agenda, Jack followed Launa to where their gear formed a circle and unrolled his blankets across from her. He settled in, then rolled over, propped himself on an elbow, and started a critique of the day. "Nak has a word for Kurgans: 'Horseriders.'"

Launa lay flat on her back and did not look his way. "Did you notice the necklace Suno has? Most of it is stone or wood carvings. But some of it looks like green copper."

"Metalworking. I wonder where he got it?"

Launa rolled over, away from him. "More questions. I'd like to have one or two answers."

Next morning, Jack fell back with Nak while Launa drew ahead with Suno and Arlo.

"Nak: horseriders, who are they?"

The singer's eyes narrowed. "You are horseriders."

"You have met other horseriders."

Nak nodded. "But they do not weave."

"Are there other ways Launa and I walk a different path?"

Nak looked hard at Jack; it was a while before he spoke. "The horseriders are not traders. Sometimes they take when they do not know other eyes see them. You two give too much and take too little." He glanced ahead to where Launa walked. "She speaks for you, as is proper." Nak shrugged. "You are not of the horseriders. But you are not of the People."

"Do the horseriders speak the words of the People?"

Nak shook his head. "We do not know the words that come from their mouths. They are strange."

Oh Launa, wait until we get time to talk. "Launa and I are horse people from far beyond the mountains where the sun sets. We are not like the horseriders of the rising sun."

"Maybe. But you do not play like the People play. You do not share our joy. You are strange, Jack, strange."

You don't know the half of it. Jack fell back farther. This reconnaissance was getting more interesting by the second.

After lunch, he invited Launa to hunt.

She was nonplussed. "And leave all our horses with these folks? My, you've gotten trusting. You and Nak have a good talk? Suno just yammers on and on. I can't get him to slow down. God, I miss Tuam."

"We need to talk about something Nak said. If we take a string of three or four horses, we can run 'em down."

The traders liked the idea of fresh meat. Jack and Launa were hardly out of sight before they spotted a large herd of red deer. As they approached them, Jack filled Launa in.

"So they do speak a different language," Jack finished.

"Damn" was all Launa said.

"Got any ideas?"

Launa was quiet for a long time. "Hold it." She reined Star in. "Brent talked about something like this. Some professor argued the technology of the Neolithic revolution was the most likely source for a new language. Judith didn't think much of it."

"That would sure explain what we're seeing." The tension that had gnawed at Jack since Launa dropped the bombshell about the language had let up; so why didn't Launa look happy?

She started to talk several times, but stopped, nothing said. Finally, she ran a hand through her hair. "Judith and Brent got into one of their anthropology arguments. I think the guy thought language was spread without an invasion."

Jack's gut knotted big time. "No invasion. How'd the cultural changes happen? You know, domination replacing co-operation? Nice people like Taelon's taken over by bastards like those that tried to kill us?"

"I don't know. I'm a soldier, goddamn it, Jack, not a professor. I didn't understand half of what those two said, but Brent talked about a 'Mafia option.' As soon as there was something worth stealing, some bastards decided they could get more by stealing than by making. And off they went."

"God damn," Jack whispered. "God damn! My stepdad used to bring home bastards like that. Grasping SOB's who could never have enough, and didn't care how they got more or who paid for it. I'll be damned if I'll let them win. This time, the first one who pokes his knife in someone else's belly gets his hand taken off by me."

"Any ideas how?"

Launa had Jack there. How do you stop something so basic to human history as greed? *You expecting everyone to be angels, Bearman?* "I don't have the foggiest idea," Jack finished, lame to even his own hearing.

Launa nodded, understanding in her eyes. "Well, at least we can go kill something."

They dropped the first deer that came in range.

Jack tied the carcass to Big Red. He would let the traders do the butchering and enjoy all the delicacies that turned his and Launa's stomachs.

"We have visitors," Launa whispered.

Jack looked where she pointed. Two riders rested on a hill three kilometers away. "How long they been there?"

"Not long. They rode up as I was doing a sweep."

"Look like the same two kids?"

Launa shook her head. "I'd need field glasses to tell."

Jack thought for a moment. "No way I could get at them."

"What do you think they're up to?"

Jack laughed. "They got no spare mounts. Wouldn't they love to ride back to their old man with a few of ours?"

"Horse raid."

"Probably tonight," Jack concluded.

That afternoon Launa talked Suno into an early stop so the horses could graze. Come night, Jack would picket them in close. He dug the fire pit farther from the trees, where it would give him some light around the horses. Worrying about the immediate problem didn't let him ignore the bigger one. Jack practically dug the fire pit himself; anything to get his muscles into something. While the traders delighted in the loaded stew, Jack and Launa ate quickly and went to their bedrolls.

Jack posted the dogs away from the horses and the fire,

then turned to Launa. "We can't stay up all night. If you'll keep a watch for an hour or two after sunset, I'll take care of the morning watch."

"How?"

"I can wake myself up well before first light."

"Okay." Launa spoke with the skepticism of one who lived by an alarm clock. Grandfather had taught Jack to awaken early to use the predawn cool before the desert heat stole the day.

Still, Jack could not sleep. *What if there is no fight, no war with an enemy you can put an arrow in? What if it's just stepdad and his buddies getting together for a night of rape and pillage? How do you stop the bastards from getting started—and pounding the people who cooperate into pulp or slavery?*

Jack dreamed about home that night, L.A. invaded by screaming Iraqi soldiers all wearing his stepdad's face. It had the small benefit of being a new twist on his two worst nightmares.

He came awake in the moonlight. Without moving, he listened. The dogs were quiet. One of the horses moved, but not enough to qualify as nervousness.

Jack reached for a captured bow. *What do you do?* These are just kids, out doing what their grownups brag about. *You ready to kill a kid? A kid about the age Sam would be now?* Jack shivered. He didn't know.

Jack searched the plain. Nothing moved in the moonlight. The kids would come through the trees. Jack headed for the horse line. Mist came to dog his footsteps.

He found a decent-sized tree near the horses and melted into its trunk, the dog at his feet. He didn't have long to wait.

Jack's first warning came when the woods got quiet. He spotted them as they edged out of the trees a good fifty meters from him. They paused for a moment to mount, and Jack made his decision.

Kantom smiled as he mounted. He had waited all night for this moment. His father had bragged that raiding was best just before first light. Arakk would be proud of his son.

An arrow thumped into the ground in front of him.

"What was that?" Toman squeaked.

"An arrow," Kantom tried to growl as he frantically looked for the archer, but his voice broke.

"They are night demons!" Toman whispered the woman's tale.

An arrow whizzed between them to thud into a tree.

Toman wheeled his horse, aimed it for the hills, and kicked it desperately. Still unable to see their tormentor and send an arrow to drink the demon's blood, Kantom turned and followed. Mighty Arakk would be near. He would bring many lances.

"I'm not a bastard," Jack whispered to himself as he watched the boys head for the nearest ridge. "But you're not stealing my horses. The bastards are not going to win this one." When the kids crested the rise a good three klicks out, they hadn't slowed down. With a tiny grain of hope that he and Launa would make everything different this time, he reposted Mist and went back to his bedroll.

"We have any trouble last night?" Launa asked as she stretched and shoved her blanket aside.

"A little about two hours back. We won't see them again. Kids didn't take too well to being bracketed by arrows."

"You let them see the longbow's range!"

"No, Launa, I used a short bow. They just ran."

Launa looked at him, a bit of a grin at the edges of her mouth. "And you let them."

"They were just kids."

The day went fast; they saw nothing of the kids. Suno expected to arrive at River Bend the next day, so Jack and Launa went hunting again and the traders got to eat the stew they relished. Jack hoped two deer would be enough. It was mid-afternoon the next day when the trader called a halt.

"River Bend is on the other side of that hill."

Thick columns of smoke rose straight up into the calm air above the ridge.

SEVENTEEN

FOR A SPLIT second, Launa just stared at the smoke; then training took over. She could feel the adrenaline rush as she yanked her horses around and got them back under the protective cover of the river's tree line. *So this is what it feels like.* With a tight grin, Launa grabbed her bow and strung it even as she searched the ground before her for any sign of danger.

Beside her, without a word spoken, Jack went through the same drill. No orders were needed; from the looks of things, this was what they'd come for.

A grassy plain rolled away in front of them. To their left, a gentle rise, covered here and there with woods, crested at about two hundred feet. Cottonwood and birch shrouded the stream they had just crossed as it disappeared around the hill. Within sight, nothing moved.

The traders had followed the horses into the shade of the trees. Suno talked loudly, his arms flying as fast as his words. Launa tuned him out.

"What do you think?" she asked Jack.

"Doesn't look like a single house fire. Brent said he'd put us down close to the first town the Kurgans burned. Maybe he did." A shiver shook Jack; he grinned like a thoroughbred at the starting gate. "I recommend we don't go round that bend until we know what's over the rise."

"Agreed," Launa said. *This is crazy. Any minute now*

someone could try to kill us, or we could be killing them, and it feels good. Compared with the dread of being at the wrong place or time or situation, Launa would gladly take this.

She turned to the traders. "Suno, take my words to your heart. What becoming could that be?" The indefinite in this language was still a bitch for Launa.

The trader shrugged. "Towns sometimes take fire. Poor trading for a while."

The Book said it was time to start issuing orders. Still, this was a cooperative command. Besides, Launa wasn't all that sure what orders to give. She turned to Jack. "Shall we stash our gear here?"

For a moment Jack considered, then shook his head. "This could be a false alarm. Even if it isn't, we can't leave our packs unguarded. A detachment might stumble on our extra weapons and tools, and then there'd be hell to pay." Jack pursed his lips as he studied what little cover the hill offered. "It'll be rough keeping our horses to cover, but I recommend we accept the risk of moving everything up that hill."

Launa agreed. "But let's leave the unloaded horses and the dogs down here." She turned to Suno. "We would see what lies in the next valley from yonder hill. Will you come after us?"

Suno shrugged and stepped out into the sunlight. The others started to follow him.

"No, no. Stop." Launa grabbed Suno and then ran out of words. How do you explain cover to someone who lacks the concept of being shot at? She settled for a simple, "Follow after me."

Jack went down to the pack animals, dropping off all the consumables but three water bags and one basket of bread. As he cut loose the spare mounts and picketed them, Suno started to say something, but the look on Jack's face froze him cold.

The advance up the hill was tense. Jack led the way, keeping to cover as much as possible. Still, more often than Launa liked, they and their ten horses were out in the open.

It took a long hour to get near the crest of the ridge. A hundred meters short of it, they tied the horses in a small copse. The traders exchanged puzzled glances.

Launa and Jack covered the final distance to the crest at a

low crouch. Using a tree for cover, they peered into the valley. Suno followed them, shaking his head.

The first sight of the valley froze Launa's blood.

Jack took one quick glance, grabbed Suno, and yanked him down. The man yelled his indignation, but Jack's hand was already over his mouth. He held the trader's face within the cover of the tree, pointed him at the town, and said one word. "Look."

It was terrible enough for Launa. What did it look like to a man who had never known war?

They were three or four kilometers from a fair-sized town nestled in the middle of a wide valley. The river snaked behind it, its lazy waters hidden by lush green trees. Neatly laid-out fields stretched from the town until they opened on pastureland at the foot of the hill they watched from. It must have been idyllic when the sun rose this morning.

It was not now.

Halfway down the hill to their right, three men lay sprawled in blood. Two raiders now watched the sheep. They leaned on lances as their horses cropped the grass. There were six horses. Launa hunted for the others. Beneath a tree there lay another person. It must be a woman. Three of the raiders held her down while the other . . .

Without thought, Launa reached for an arrow. Jack's hand was on hers in an instant. Curtly, he shook his head. A shiver went through Launa as the struggle began for her soul.

A soldier defends the helpless—that was the very reason she breathed. Still, a soldier isn't stupid; The Book says you calculate your risks carefully. What were the odds she could take out those six without getting every bad guy in the valley down her throat? *Damn slim.*

Launa squeezed her eyes shut, willed back the tears. *This is what you came for. What were you expecting, girl? Now let's get down to some serious soldiering, none of this bang-bang, shoot-'em-up shit.* Using a hand to shade her eyes, and to block the view of what was happening close downhill, Launa studied the situation.

The town had no walls, no defenses at all. Scattered homes blazed; as she watched, another took fire, adding its dark smoke to the thickening pall. Hundreds of horses grazed on the crops. On the outskirts of town, scores of bodies lay where they had fallen. People had come out to meet the Horse People, just as they would have come to greet Suno's traders. They had been slaughtered.

In front of those bodies, six men sat their horses. Before them lay a pile. Launa knew it for trophy heads even before a man rode out from town and tossed two more on it.

Kantom held the totem of the Stormy Mountain Clan high. Ahead of him, his father talked with Shokin, Mighty Man of the Stalwart Shield Clan. Beside Kantom was Shokin's totem-bearer as well as that of the Broad Sky Clan. Kantom tried not to tremble in the power of such company.

"We have lived with no blood between us and these people for many years," Shokin said.

"Should the Horse People spend each other's blood when these animals could not even stand against boys?" Arakk answered.

Toman galloped out from the burning town. With a whoop, he slung two heads onto the pile before the Mighty Men. "I honor you," Toman called as he brought his horse to a halt before them.

Kantom watched the heads as they rolled off the pile. The first to come to rest was a child's, hardly more than a baby. The second one tumbled off to land upside down facing the first. It was a woman's—the mother?

Toman cantered over to pause beside Kantom, wiped at the blood on his arm, and said, "You are missing much fun. I am a man now. I have taken heads, I have bedded a woman. Too bad you have to stay out here."

Kantom wanted to ask his friend if the woman had a knife like the woman in the horse camp Toman had run away from, but it was not the place of the totem-bearer to speak. Kantom looked straight ahead at his father's back.

Toman laughed. "After the Eagle Sacrifice tonight, find me. I will save a woman for you."

•　•　•

Hardly able to breathe, Launa finished her sweep of the town with a glance downhill. A lance to the breast had brutally ended the rape.

Beside her, Jack shivered. "Damn! I'd give my right nut for a platoon of light infantry. These sons of bitches got no security. One squad of good soldiers could blow them away." His harsh whisper, venting his own impotence, absolved Launa from some of the guilt of an idle bystander.

A nicker drew Launa's attention to their rear. The traders were pulling their packs from the horses that had carried them. Quickly, the two troopers slipped downhill.

Suno nervously shouldered his baggage. "There will be no trading here. We will not come back for many summers."

Launa's mouth dropped open. Was pillage just a business downturn? Where did this guy think he was going? Launa felt her temper tripping out. *It's not this man you're mad at. It's the bastards over the hill.* With her hands tight fists, the soldier softened her voice.

"Will you"—Launa searched for a word like "alert" or "warn"—"tell the People of the Badger what you have seen?" "Tell" seemed so inadequate, but it would have to do.

"What have I seen?" Vacant eyes wandered back to the crest of the hill. "My heart can hold nothing from this day."

Launa grabbed him by the shoulders. It was bad enough that Suno wasn't volunteering to join a rescue team, but this yellow running funk . . . She barely checked the urge to shake him until he rattled, until he saw good sense. Then she froze.

From the corner of her eye she saw Nak's hand go for his knife. As Jack's spear came down, Arlo lowered his.

Dear God, is the slaughter over the hill going to suck us in too? Launa chose her words as if a world depended on them. It might.

"Suno. Tell the people that this town was burned. Its people were hunted like deer, speared like fish, with no offering made to their spirits. Tell the people what the horsemen did here."

Nak's hand came away from his knife. His eyes grew wide as they shifted from Suno to Launa, then to the smoke.

"Nak, go see. Both of you, go with Jack. See. Let your hearts tell you what your eyes see here."

Jack raised his spear, motioning Nak to come. The singer came, as did Arlo. Like Jack, they stooped as they approached the tree. For several long minutes their heads swept back and forth. Their faces were ashen when they returned. They said nothing as they picked up their packs and fell in behind Suno.

The others trudged off in silence, but Nak turned. "Never have my ears heard in song what my eyes saw. The story of what happened here cannot be told at feasts or when wares are laid out for trade. I do not know where I will find words for this song." He brought his fist to his heart. "But the spirits of those people deserve that their story be told, and I will sing it."

Launa took the copper knife from her belt and held it out to Nak, hilt first. "This I trade you for that song. Take this knife and sing of what your eyes drank here."

Nak accepted the knife, then turned and trailed off.

Jack dismissed them with a curt shake of his head, half disappointment, half good riddance. Launa headed back to the observation post; Jack followed. Meticulously they quartered the valley, looking for evidence of survivors. They found none. Launa squatted beside Jack, trying to will away the sickness she felt—sickness at what she saw, at what she could not stop. Too wired to sit still another second, she backed away from the crest. "Our horses need water. I'll take them to the stream and collect the rest."

Jack helped her stash the baggage in the draw. "All those bastards seem focused on the town, but be careful," he told Launa as he patted Windrider good-bye.

She couldn't stop her hands from trembling as she guided Star from cover to cover. Now she tasted terror, a poison that soaked every muscle in her, robbing strength, clouding her thoughts like one of the Colonel's weekend drunks. However fast she scanned from one end of her horizon to the other, she couldn't search fast enough for the enemy that lurked just out of view, ready to rape and butcher her. Trying to look in every direction at once, she realized she was seeing nothing.

Launa reined Star to a halt. Gritting her teeth until her head trembled, she took a long slow breath. *Don't lose it now, girl. You and Jack've spotted those bastards coming every time. Keep your eyes sharp and you'll spot them the next time, too.* Maybe she wasn't right, but the pep talk made her feel better.

At the stream, she doused the heat from her face as the horses and dogs drank their fill. The terror was gone, though not the caution, as she led twice as many animals up the hill. She picketed the horses in a shaded draw farther downhill from where they'd stopped before. It was cool, and there was some browse for the horses. There was peace in common drills well done. She figured it would last all of three seconds when she took her next look at River Bend.

Jack was still at the observation post.

"Anything happen?" Launa asked.

"Nothing fit for the six o'clock news," Jack answered, then wearily rubbed his eyes with open palms. Again they scanned the valley for any sign of people hiding in the brush. Nothing.

"Here's some dried fish." Launa unwrapped it.

"Thanks. I think I'm hungry." Jack accepted two pieces.

Launa took one. Her gut was knotted; she might never eat again. Still, there was a void in her chest where a heart might have been. Food was all she could offer it today. She nibbled around the edges of the fish.

Behind them, the setting sun turned the sky a sympathetic blood red, memorial to the town and its people. Before them, gathering shadows drew a shroud over butchery. Launa let a long sigh escape. A battle was so much easier to take when you could reach out and kill somebody.

"I hate this," she sighed. "Can't we do something?"

"You've done pretty good, Launa. There's nothing wrong with being a hard charger; you just have to know when to push and when to sit it out." Jack turned his gaze to where fires marked off the town. A scream pierced the gathering twilight. "I watched a lot of crap before they cut us loose on Iraq." He turned back. "Go ahead and tally up the butcher's bill, Lieutenant. We'll be back someday to collect."

Jack's words were spoken as a fact, a history that just hadn't been written. She liked the cold, deadly purpose in his eyes. If only she could be that cold.

He glanced at the town. "Maybe you did better than anyone could expect. Nak will sing this day from here to
Greece. People will know what happened because you got
the attention of the man who can do it. Yes, we may have
done better than we had any right to expect."

Launa was grateful for the praise. She *had* done some
good here. Maybe she had started to screw up, but she'd not
done so badly for her first trip to the elephant where she'd
had some choices. "It's not easy to know when to act."

"Yeah, the devil's in the timing."

"If we'd left Taelon's camp a day earlier, we'd be down
there." Launa swallowed hard on the thought.

"Yeah. You do your best and live with it. It and luck."

"Luck." Launa spat the word. The Colonel said fools waited
for luck. Men went out and made it with their own sweat.

Jack raised an eyebrow at her reaction. "Don't count luck
out. I wouldn't be here without it."

Launa said nothing.

Jack turned back to watch the town, but that didn't stop him
from talking. "I'd had it with my stepdad halfway through my
senior year. I didn't know what I wanted, just what I didn't.
Finishing high school wasn't in those plans. Day I showed up
to drop out and hit the road, I ran into Sergeant Rodrigo."

"Sergeant Rodrigo?" Launa didn't want him to stop.

"I was sitting in the cafeteria when the school's recruiter
walked up and said, 'Kid, I know you from somewhere?'
No, I tell him. 'What's your name?' I gave him my adopted
one. 'Shit, I would have sworn I knew you. Your old man
ever in the Army?'"

Launa glanced over the hill. Jack's voice had taken the
edge off the last two shrieks. It was better to listen to him.

"I said, 'Yes. My father died in Nam. His name was Bear,
Samuel Walking Bear.'" Even at the gates of hell, Jack put
pride in his real father's name. He'd never told Launa his
stepdad's.

"That old master sergeant started pumping my arm like it
was a sawed-off shotgun. 'Holy Mother of God, you're
Sam's boy. If the Captain hadn't been the coolest jungle rat
south of Fort Greeley, me, and a lot of those like us, would

have bought the farm that day. I heard tell the CO put him in for the Congressional Medal of Honor. I wouldn't know. They medevaced what was left of me and the docs had a hell of a time putting all the pieces back together again.'"

Jack paused. "No one ever told me how my father died. Strange what gets lost in the shuffle. But Rodrigo remembered. Dad smelled something wrong that spring. He said it was his Indian nose." *Always the Indian,* Launa thought, grimacing.

"By '72, it wasn't our war anymore, and it wasn't his job, but that didn't keep Dad from taking out a recon platoon. They found what he smelled outside An Loc. Lots of bad guys standing around, getting ready for the Easter offensive while the suits in Paris talked. Dad had what he wanted, but the platoon got caught on the way out, new guy tripped a mine. The NVA threw most of a battalion at them." Jack recounted the story crisply, like a briefer for some rear-area brass.

"Dad was on the horn, calling in the world until everything in range was working for them. In the end, he was calling it down on top of them." Jack paused. "That's what killed him. An artillery shell landed in his foxhole. Right on the damn hole."

Launa studied her fingers. If Suno hadn't been too scared of horses to ride one they'd be down there. Launa had killed ten Kurgans. A hundred might have been a bit much even for her. Timing. Luck. Maybe life did take more than your own two hands.

"The guy that set off the booby trap was a young Hispanic just out of AIT. Name of Rodrigo." Jack shook his head. "Dad's luck ran out with Rodrigo. My luck started when I met him."

Jack took a moment to continue. "I cut class that afternoon, not to drop out but run a check. My dad had gotten the CMH. The deadline for the Point was that day. We spent the afternoon filling out paperwork. I missed the quota for that year. Rodrigo said I was a sure thing for '90. I signed up for a year with the infantry. Had my appointment all set. My CO did me a favor, got me excused from beast barrack, I'd report 15 August."

That was a hot date, but Launa's brain wasn't thinking by the calendar any more. She had to run it through a couple of times before it connected. "What was your unit?"

Jack chuckled. "Twenty-fourth Mech."

"The first to Saudi."

"Yep. So much that year for college."

"At least you had the whole world in there supporting you."

"And grateful for every mother's son of them I was."

The words hit a raw nerve with Launa. "We didn't get much support today."

Now Jack scowled. "Not that I wanted those traders all fired up, but it would have been nice to see a little backbone. Still, it's good you've got a Paul Revere singing 'The red-coats are coming.' I just hope some people listen. "There may be a reason why people who never knew war didn't do so good when it came calling."

A shiver that had nothing to do with the cooling night air swept over Launa. "Taelon, Tuam, they'd never give up without a fight."

Jack let out a sigh. "I think so. Let's hope we're right."

There was nothing more to say as the moon rose higher and the stars came out. In the pitch dark, they could see nothing. Together, they slipped downhill and spread their bedrolls. Jack posted Mist with the horses, Frieda at his feet.

"Do you want to take the first watch?" Launa asked.

Jack rubbed his nose thoughtfully. "We can skip it to-night. Tomorrow we've got to be more alert than them." His head snapped back to the crest of the hill as another shriek shattered the night air. "Those bastards are having too much fun to go looking for trouble. The dogs will do for tonight, right, Frieda?"

The German shepherd growled as Launa nodded her agreement with Jack's plan. The decision felt good—and they'd made it as partners. Maybe with a little more prac-tice, they could do things Judith's way.

Launa rolled herself into her blankets, but shrieks held sleep at bay. When finally unconsciousness came, she traded a waking horror for the nightmares of what she would do when payback time came around.

EIGHTEEN

JACK AWOKE TO birds clicking; dawn had yet to brighten the horizon. Launa had tossed about and softly cried out in the night. Events were taking a heavy toll on the optimism of her young spirit. He had watched over her until she slipped into a deep sleep. She was still in it.

He splashed water on his face before heading for the observation post. There was just enough light to make out the ruin of the town. He thought he spotted movement. "Judith, would a pair of decent binoculars have been so bad?" More study, and he was sure people were coming out.

Four raiders guarded ten prisoners carrying jars. The slaves were roped together at the neck. Their stooped and shuffled gait told of the night they'd spent—except one. The last captive in line stood ramrod straight above victims and captors alike. Jack squinted to see that one better. The prisoner's carriage and step raised the short hairs on the back of his neck. For reasons he could not name, Jack felt a spark of excitement.

The party came to a crossroad; one path led upriver, the other down. The one who held Jack's attention said something, and the captive at the head of the line turned to their left—downriver. That earned both of them whacks from their captors' lances. They went down, dragging the entire line with them. The invaders started whipping everyone to urge them up. But when they started off again, it was to their left.

"Son of a bitch. No city dweller is dumb enough to draw water down stream. So why is this one headed that way?" Jack could think of several reasons, none good for the intruders. A hard, tight grin stretched his lips as Jack checked out cover to the river. He'd had enough of being a helpless bystander. His hands caressed his combat load: knife, spear, longbow, quiver. Without a decision, he chose action.

A glance at the copse that hid their camp drew a frown. "Damn." He raced downhill, knelt, and shook Launa. She came awake with a start and grabbed for her knife.

"The other side's coming awake. I want to get a closer look at a water detail. Stay close." She was still blinking away sleep as he dashed off, crouching low behind the hill crest.

A stand of trees got him across the crest without being highlighted against the skyline. Jack made it to a wooded draw, breaking cover only once and never breaking stride. The party was slow winding its way to the river; he observed another general collapse among the captives.

By the time he reached the river, shouts and cries from the group gave him enough noise to home on. He spotted a sandy shore in the middle of a bend and, suspecting that was their goal, sought cover fifty meters downstream.

Launa passed from a nightmare to reality in an instant. It took only a moment more for her to remember that reality and nightmare were the same. Still, in those few seconds, Jack was halfway to the crest of the ridge. Launa stifled a shout for Jack to slow down, come back. The Kurgans could afford to shout. Those who hid could not.

"Damn that idiot," Launa mumbled as she grabbed her gear and raced for the observation point. She tried to track Jack, but he was good at staying hid. Only once did she see him break cover. She searched the valley below. A small group was slowly making its way down a path toward the trees and the river. What had Jack said, a water detail?

"Goddamn it, Jack, we're supposed to be a team," Launa

growled. "Guess we were, when there was nothing to do."
She studied the ruins of the town; nothing moved. She
searched the woods around the valley, starting with the side
where Jack had disappeared, then sweeping around to the
left. Nothing moved.

"Well, what's good for the gander is fine by me. Let's see
if Jack needs any fire support." She was half up when Star's
whicker brought her up short.

"Thirsty, boy?" Launa swiped at her mouth, tasting frustration. "If Jack thinks he can dump all the household chores
on me while he runs around playing John Wayne, he's got a
few lessons to learn."

With a bitter glance at the trees that hid Jack, Launa
headed back to do what had to be done. In the morning
gloom, she rode quickly to the stream, more concerned with
time than security. She was back at the observation post in
less than an hour, ready to give Jack the lesson he'd earned.
He wasn't back.

Launa checked the woods downriver from the town, where
Jack probably was. Nothing. Next she made a complete
sweep of the hills and woods. Launa froze as she finished; a
tree limb moved.

It might have been the wind. It could have been an animal. Launa focused on a thicket to the left of her position.
Something definitely was coming uphill—toward her.

Stringing her bow, Launa waited, trying to assess what
she faced. Whoever it was, they were good at staying under
cover. She wasn't sure of her target count, but there seemed
to be at least four.

Launa considered her options. She couldn't risk a fight in
clear view of River Bend today anymore than she could yesterday; Jack had at least been right about that. The copse
hiding the horses was a good hundred meters down the hill
and had pretty clear fire lanes to the crest. If she had to face
four-to-one odds again, that seemed the best place for it.

Slowly Launa backed away from the tree. Collecting
everything from where they had slept, she double-timed to
the horse picket line, Frieda at her heels. Once under cover,
Launa laid out her most jagged arrows; each shot would

have to do the most damage. She would let the first target that came over the crest live, for the moment. With luck, she'd have lots of targets in the open when she announced her presence. *See what kind of luck I can make for myself.*

Of course, it might be Jack coming back from his little walk.

In the trees at the crest, a head appeared. Launa nocked her first arrow, but did not put tension to the long bow. A moment later, a second head appeared. "Too many people for Jack." Launa glanced down; she had five arrows laid out. "Now it gets dicey."

One of the heads crossed the ridge in a low crouch.

Jack did not have long to wait for the water party. A trail led from the trees to the beach, and they soon came down it.

All ten captives were female, naked, beaten, bloodied, bowed—except the last one. Jack sucked in his breath. Another time she would have been beautiful. Her raven hair fell full and straight to below her waist. Even now she walked with a dignity that drew his eyes. She was bloodied too; welts and bruises spoiled the golden tan of her skin. Still, the other nine women cast her furtive glances. Jack knew who was in charge here, even if the sloppy guards did not. When she croaked, "Go to the left," the head of the column swung upriver. It cost the lead a blow to the face, but raven hair got the downstream end.

The prisoners knelt in the water. As they filled their jugs, they took the moment to wash. Jack studied his enemy. The three wore the same breechcloth and vests as the first batch he and Launa had killed. Bows and arrows hung from a flat quiver on their belts. All carried lances.

The last guard who trailed out of the woods got Jack's full attention. It was the blond-haired boy who had dogged his and Launa's tracks. Jack had let him live last time, but he shook his head today. *You should have played soccer, kid.*

After the tall beauty finished cleaning herself, she stood, bent over her jug, and drew every male eye to her sex. "Oh shit! She can't be that stupid," Jack whispered. The lancer closest to her tossed off his quiver and lance and swaggered into the water. He was ready for more rape.

One of the others challenged him. The beast snarled a reply, his hand going to the hilt of his long knife. The others picked different victims. Jack watched as even the boy made a move on one of the women.

The beast turned his attention back to beauty. While he had been establishing the privileges of rank, she had been busy doing something. Whatever it was, her hair had obscured it from Jack.

The beast reached her. Hands fondled her butt, then slid to where her breasts dangled. She wiggled playfully, but when she turned to him, fury contorted her face.

The rope fell from her neck as her hand jerked the beast's knife from his belt and drove it deep into his gut. Twisting the knife, she pulled it from his chest, blood exploding over her. She ran for deep water, a scarlet demon from hell. Still dripping gore, she clamped the knife between her teeth and dove for the deep channel.

The other three stood dumbfounded, then bounded from the water for their bows. Their transition from rapists to bowmen did not go smoothly. The kid screamed as his bowstring twanged his engorged manhood. That spoiled the others' aim. Jack bit his lip to keep from laughing as three arrows went wide while beauty dove. These guys made the Three Stooges look competent.

Jack sobered quickly as he counted arrows; each had two or three more. They may have blown the first round, but they had plenty more chances to get her and they looked too angry to quit.

Apparently beauty had bagged the lead beast. While his body bobbed downstream, the three shouted at each other. Finally the blond kid was shoved toward the remaining nine captives. Waving his lance, he cowed the prisoners into a circle. The second raider was ordered across the river. He waded it gingerly. The last began a bowlegged strut downstream, his eyes fixed on the river and the bank. Cautiously, Jack began a measured withdrawal.

To shouts from both banks, beauty surfaced for air. An

arrow hit where she had been only moments after she dove again. Several more times she sounded, but no more arrows were wasted on her. The raiders worked their way downstream as fast as she could swim and the current would carry her. They could breathe regularly—she could not. Nature's laws were against her.

Jack soon measured the tempo of her surfacing for breath. Allowing for the intervals getting shorter, Jack could just about tell when and where she would come up for air. Unfortunately, so could the beasts. She surfaced early, just in time to hear a bow twang, and dove before the arrow caught her. She was losing. When it came time for her to surface the next time, she did not.

Jack searched the bank. The lancers did too, with the advantage that they were closer to the river. Suddenly, the beast on the far bank backed away from the river, waving and pointing.

Jack climbed a tree and did not like what he saw. A log reached out from his side of the river. Beauty's head rested on it as she gasped for breath. Reeds blocked her view of the bank, and he suspected she could not see the hand signals of the man on the far side. The new head beast, on the near bank, grinned as he arranged his lariat along his lance. He would catch this fish for gutting later.

Carefully, Jack wedged himself in the tree and drew two arrows. He checked their straightness and balance, then nocked one to his longbow as he tried to decide who was target one. His close target, having left his bow behind, was edging his way along the log, hidden by reeds from beauty. His far target, an arrow nocked, was slinking toward the river. Soon Jack would not have a good shot at him. That decided it.

Jack's first arrow carried true, burying itself in the far target's chest. He fell forward into the reeds, thrashed about, then stilled. But the soft *twang* of the bowstring drew the attention of both beast and beauty.

She followed the arrow's flight until it drew a scream; then, with a grin at Jack's tree, she began rolling the log.

Beast was a horseman raised. The deserts of the steppe

offered little chance for experience with water and its hazards. He lost his footing and went over. Two quick steps brought the lariat within beauty's grasp, and she pulled his lance to her. Twirling it quickly, she waited for him to surface. When he did, gasping for breath, she speared him through the heart, driving him under. When he stopped flailing, she pulled him up.

A stone knife flashed in the sun for a moment as she slit his throat. Pushing the still-bleeding body toward center stream, she relieved him of his knife and tossed it on the bank. The current quickly took him.

She stumbled from the water and paused, leaning on the lance, dripping water, gasping in air. The first beast's knife was still tightly clutched in her hand as her eyes locked on the tree that sheltered Jack. Cautiously, he let himself down. Then, with his palms spread wide open and keeping himself well out of reach of the lance, he stepped toward her. Her eyes locked on him; the lance stayed aimed at his heart.

"Who are you?"

"One who hunts the hunters of women and men."

The lance never wavered. "Your tongue twists our words but your belt is a hunter's belt."

Jack looked through the narrow eyes of a woman to a soul where trust was a cold, burnt ash. "Taelon of the Badger People put it into my hands. I fed his people well."

"With the bow that sends arrows far." She twisted, gazing across the river for a moment. The lance came down. "Come." The lance pointed upstream.

"We go." He pointed to the hill.

She shook her head. "I will not leave nine sisters of mine to those animals. If you will not come after me, I will go alone." Her eyes sparked fire.

"If you go alone, then you will die alone."

She waved the knife. "I have killed two." Anger and pride danced in her words.

"The Goddess smiled on you. When will she turn away?"

"I am Antia, daughter of She who Spoke for the Goddess in River Bend. Now I Speak for Her. You will come after me, you strange one. Are you no better than these horse-riders?"

Another headstrong woman with a temper to match. Are there any other kind? Jack gave in. "I will cut your sisters loose. You will follow after me." Jack cut Antia off when she opened her mouth to argue. "The Goddess has made me a hunter of men. You are no such hunter."

Her eyes flashed.

"You'll be one soon enough," Jack added, picking up the fallen quiver and bow. Quickly he made his way upriver with her in tow. Her woodcraft was bad; several times he shushed her, pointing to the twig she had snapped. When they got close to the target, Jack waved her to stand behind a tree. Antia obeyed him.

He paused twenty meters from the beach to get a good look at his target. The nine women squatted beneath a tree. They were tied in a ring. Jack wondered who had done the knot and how well. The blond kid strutted around them. Now and again his eyes wandered nervously downriver, searching for his comrades in rape. He carried his lance slung over one shoulder, occasionally waving it to threaten the captives. They looked pretty cowed, hardly in need of threats. Jack grinned; the boy was spooked.

Since the kid was dividing his time between the women and the river, Jack turned away, slipping through the woods to the edge of the trees. A quick check of the town and environs showed some small boys beginning to go among the ponies, but no real activity. It must have been quite a night. Had whiskey been invented yet? He hoped the bastards were hung over as hell. His rear secure, Jack worked his way down the path to the river.

He settled for a tree fifteen meters from his target. From there he had a good view. *I know you, kid. Once I let you live. I won't make that mistake twice.*

The next time the boy turned from the women to scan the river, Jack put an arrow through the back of his neck. The boy spun around, a stunned look on his face. He croaked something and made a weak jab at Jack with his lance. Jack batted it aside as he ran to finish with his knife what the arrow had begun.

Done, he turned to the women. They squatted in stoic silence. Then Antia burst among them, and there were quiet tears and hugs.

Jack put an arrow to his longbow and kept guard for a long minute before he turned to them. "We go now."

Antia nodded. "Yes, we go now." The discarded leather rope that had bound the women's necks lay on the ground. She picked it up, looping it around her waist, fashioning a belt like Taelon wore. Another woman policed up bows, quivers, lances, and knives. Cleo, Antia named her. The look on Cleo's face was as cold as the one on Antia's.

The two pushed the boy's body into the river, watching with hardened eyes as the current took it. Jack did a quick check, then led off at a trot. Antia and Cleo brought up the rear with their lances.

NINETEEN

THE TRIP UP the hill was slow. Several women could hardly walk; Jack took the time he needed to keep to cover. The sun was high when he slunk across the ridge crest. The observation post was empty.

Downhill in the thicket, their bedrolls were gone. Jack left Antia to settle the women and went hunting for Launa.

He slid into the draw and exhaled with relief. The horses weren't gone. So where was Launa? Looking around, he froze as the skin of his back felt the nick of a sharp edged weapon.

"Where the hell have you been, soldier?"

English never sounded so good. He pulled away, turned to face Launa's spear point. "You scared the shit out of me."

"Wasn't any fun watching you run off, either, soldier." Launa worked her way out of the bush she had hidden in. Prickles, sharp as her tongue, raked her skin. One scratch dripped blood. "Hope your luck held." She fixed him with hard eyes. Jack figured he better make this sound good.

"Before first light, four guards took ten women down to get water. The leader made a pass at one of them. She took offense and cut his heart out." Jack hoped to get a grin from Launa. He had to settle for a flinch in her glower.

"His henchmen took off after her. She killed another in the chase. I took out a third. Then she insisted I liberate the women. It's hard arguing with Antia, daughter of She who Spoke for the Goddess in River Bend."

"So you rescued the goddamn princess?"

Jack had expected a little more enthusiasm. "Looks like we've got our first ally."

"Lucky you," Launa said and turned away. Jack followed her gaze to stare into the biggest, saddest pair of brown eyes he'd ever seen. The small boy they belonged to might have been six, but his eyes were ancient with terror. His dirty hand was jammed in his mouth and he sucked on it like a baby. Launa stooped to pick him up and gave the child a reassuring hug.

"My catch wasn't as big as yours. Sisu wandered over the hill an hour after you left. There were four other shepherd boys, scared stiff and hiding in the trees."

"Think there are more?" Jack connected with more eyes hiding in the bush Launa had crawled out of.

She shrugged.

"I'll bring the women down here."

"You do that."

The words echoed in Launa's ears. "You do that." The Colonel's words. He'd used them to deflate her when she thought she had a great idea and he didn't. It was one of the things he did that she'd sworn, when she took her oath at the Point, she would never do. She would not soldier like her father.

But the SOB sure knew how to put a subordinate in his place. She'd been there often enough. *Maybe it's time to take a few lessons from the old man. You've got your first troops.*

"Okay, Jack," she muttered as she collected the boys, "if we can't do this as partners, let's see how you like the view from the bottom. Those women, turkey, are not looking for a man to tell them what to do," Launa snorted. He may have pulled off the coup, but it played right into her strong suit. The Colonel's wife would love it.

When Jack brought the women down to the horses, one of

them scooped up Sisu. Little brown eyes had someone in the world to hold on to. The rest found friends but no kin.

With Sisu handed off and Jack divvying out what food they had, Launa turned to her new recruits. Which was the one Jack had talked about? "Who is Antia?"

One of the lance-carrying women stepped forward. Launa should have known this was the woman who had drawn Jack's eye. Despite the cuts, welts, and bruises, she stood as if nature itself waited for her call. She also was a beauty, with melons for breasts that Launa would have killed for in high school. *Not military, kid.* Then Launa swallowed a scowl. *Think Jack would have put the mission at risk for a hag?*

Antia was talking. "This man says you are hunters of men?"

Launa rested her fists on her hips, tightened the muscles around her mouth and eyes, and let the old man talk. "We are hunters of those who hunt women."

"Can you make us such hunters?" The woman's hand swept the desolate survivors as if they were Caesar's Tenth Legion.

"It will take seasons of hard work."

Antia needed only a moment's thought. "I took seasons to learn to swim, but now I am as fast as a fish. There will be time to learn in Tall Oaks. Then, in season, we will harvest horseriders as we harvest grain." She clenched a fist.

Launa certainly hoped so, but that was years away and she had problems at the moment. She turned back to Jack. "Will the Kurgans hunt for the ones you killed?"

"I don't know, but I'd suggest we get the hell out of here. Fall back to wherever this Tall Oaks is. It's dangerous out here." Jack gave her one of his lopsided grins.

"A feeling we share," Launa growled, then turned back to Antia to lay the groundwork for a well-ordered withdrawal. "Let us load the horses and go to Tall Oaks."

Antia bowed her head in acquiescence and turned to another lance-carrying woman. "Cleo and I will help. We will all help."

That turned out to be a bit optimistic. About half the

women were too far gone to do much of anything. Three of the boys were big enough to turn to. None of the able-bodied had any idea how to mount a pack rack or tie it down. Jack started to teach them, but Launa cut him off.

"I want a spotter at the tree who knows what an attack formation looks like. I'll take care of the logistics, you take lookout." Jack tapped one of the more able-looking walking wounded for a runner and headed up the hill.

It took Launa the better part of an hour to get the packs loaded. Done, she checked each strap and knot. They looked like they'd hold—if she didn't run any races. Launa helped the three women who looked the worst mount the shortest horses she had and prepared to walk her tiny command out of here.

Jack came to see her off. "I will maintain contact."

Launa nodded.

Antia had been hanging close to Launa's elbow; now she stepped forward. "One of us will stay with you. Cleo knows the way to Tall Oaks."

Antia cut a length from the rope at her waist and tied it around Cleo as a belt, hanging one of the captured knives from it. They hugged; then Cleo went to stand beside Jack.

"By your permission, Lady, we will keep watch." Jack sprinkled English among his local words. "If pursuit develops, I'll send her to warn you. I'll wait until you've crossed the river, then follow. I should rejoin before you make camp."

Launa gave him the curt nod the Colonel would have; she'd gotten the chain of command back into some kind of shape. *It better stay that way, mister,* her unblinking eyes ordered. "If you get cut off, we will rally at last night's camp." That was as far as Launa could go to set up that crucial collection point. She had no idea what direction led to Tall Oaks.

Despite the tension between them, Launa was none too happy splitting her tiny command. But The Book said you don't withdraw from an enemy without leaving a detachment in contact. If she broke a basic rule like that, Jack would bust her back to private—and he'd be right. She wouldn't let that happen.

"I'll push on until almost dark. You and Cleo keep a spare horse so you can catch up fast." *Or outrun any pursuit.*

"Thanks. See you soon." Jack gave Launa a jaunty salute. She returned it like a general.

Launa kept her exhausted team in the trees for cover as they descended the hill. Each time she came to open ground, she checked the observation post. The first few times she could make out Jack and Cleo. After that, she just looked and if she got no wave-off, she went. Even wearing the Colonel's hard ass, she found herself gnawing her lip a lot.

Antia seemed to be everywhere, helping where she could, encouraging everyone by promising them the blood of the horsemen who had done this. But more often than not as they worked their way downhill, Launa found Antia close to her, watching her with unblinking eyes.

At the river, Launa ordered a break to drink. After gulping down her own water, she trotted back to the edge of the woods to inspect their trail.

Antia joined her. "You worry much."

"Yes." Launa hunted for words in the local language she could bend to cover a West Point education. "Worry is the path to respect for me. Worry and saving people."

"The way you brought us down the hill, always in trees. No one could see us," Antia observed.

"Yes."

Antia nodded. "That stopped men from hunting us. My eyes must see the way you see."

"With summers of practice, they will."

Launa finished her study of the trail; no pursuit visible. She also saw no evidence of Jack rejoining now that they had reached the river. *Damn it, he can't even follow his own orders.* "Let us move across the river, but stay close to the trees so we cannot be seen from the hill."

Without hesitation, Antia went to carry out her orders.

Jack didn't like splitting their tiny force, but Launa was on a slow burn after his wake-up call this morning and he wasn't about to argue. The situation had called for immediate action, but he hadn't known many CO's who'd have liked what he did. *A medal or a court-martial.* Well, he lucked out big-time. Still, he'd better give that woman a while to cool down.

Launa was right to order oversight on the bandits at River Bend. Fortunately, nothing much happened around town while Launa was retrograding. More kids came out to take care of the horses, but the elder bastards slept in.

Once Launa and Antia's task force disappeared into the woods along the stream, Jack got down to some serious thinking. What were the odds these bastards would throw out a screen, maybe overtake Launa? Unknown. What was the doctrine? Unknown. Maybe it was time to get to know his enemy.

The big picture was one confusing mess. First there was that ten-man patrol right after he and Launa got here. What were they up to? Those two kids—what had they reported when they got back? One of them was dead. What about the other?

The objective of this bunch was pretty obvious—or was it? Was this a raid or the start of conquest and colonization? Jack hadn't seen any dependents. Were they camped downriver or half a thousand klicks away? *God damn, what I'd give for some satellite imagery.*

Jack didn't even know what this bunch of bastards would do next—head for wherever this Tall Oaks was or go back home to brag? Watching for a while just might pay off. Jack took a swig from his water skin and settled in to watch what came next.

It was near noon and Launa was long gone when lancers went looking for the water detail—and they went upstream.

After noon, the plundered town awoke to shouts and screams. The raiders formed their horses into seven or eight herds. Jack suspected it was this bunch's tactical organization. Each herd probably represented a clan of twenty to forty warriors. Say one to two hundred combatants. He and Launa might have killed a dozen yesterday before they were very dead themselves. *Thank God for timing.*

The crack of whips drove a mob of people from the town. Where someone didn't move fast enough, a lance put a stop to their moving at all. Beside Jack, Cleo watched with a face that might as well have been marble. Jack wondered if she recognized anyone; he did not ask.

There must have been some division of the spoils, because the surviving townspeople were separated into eight groups that were herded after the horses. All the groups headed east for river crossings—all but one.

One war chief and his totem-carrier sat their mounts. Quickly twenty raiders cut out horses, put together their string of two or three, and joined him. He turned them west—and Jack got seriously worried.

No way could he let twenty bastards find Launa and her exhausted kids. She couldn't hope to outrun men born to the saddle. She certainly couldn't outfight them. It was up to Jack to keep them off her trail.

Jack glanced at Cleo. With her slashed and bruised groin and thighs, she was in no shape for a hard first ride. *If I take both the spare horses, I might have a chance to outrun those bastards. But will I ever find Tall Oaks?* One thing was sure. Slowed by Cleo, he wouldn't see sunset tonight.

"Cleo, bring the horses to me."

The woman glanced toward the draw, then back at the horsemen forming up in front of the burnt shell of her home. "Yes, I go."

TWENTY

TYMAN. STRONG ARM of the Swift Arrow Band, called his men to him. Quickly they collected a warrior's string of spare mounts and gathered around him. The young men would see that their slaves were taken to the women, and the boys would care for the rest of the horses. Tyman's blood ran hot and he had much to do.

While he was still calling greetings to each of the Swift Arrows, listening to boasts of what they had done yesterday, and shouting back promises of the brave deeds they would do if they followed his totem, old Givod rode close to his ear. "Arakk Red Beard rides our way. He does not look happy."

Tyman laughed, but ordered his warriors to rest their mounts behind him. As he turned to greet Arakk, he composed his face, eyes of a hawk, smile of a fox. The Mighty Man of the Stormy Mountain Clan liked to be named Bloody Beard, but he spent most of his time groveling in the dirt to other clan's Mighty Men. Let him grovel to a Strong Arm of the Clan like Tyman.

Behind Arakk trailed his son with the totem of the Clan. Arakk would not let Tyman forget to whom he spoke, but Tyman might well use young Kantom to his ends this day.

Tyman raised his hand. "Greetings, oh Mighty Man of the

Clan." Let him stew in no more honor than the totem demanded.

"Greetings, Strong Tyman." Arakk gave less honor than he got. "The Clan rides to the east today, yet the Swift Arrow warriors are behind, like women, not at the forefront with the men. Strange, my heart says."

"The Swift Arrows always ride in the fore. Let others crawl last like women carrying the beds of their masters."

Arakk's eyes burned, red as his beard. Beside Tyman, Givod leaned close to whisper, "That was not well said. The Clan has not grown so strong that brother can shed brother's blood."

Tyman turned on the Swift Arrows' advisor to the *quarlto* of elders, showed teeth, but Arakk had already walked his horse close. His loud voice carried to all of Tyman's warriors.

"Last night, an assembly of Mighty Men from all the Clans to the east recognized the might and strength of the Stormy Mountain Clan. Each band of warriors will have pastures of their own this winter. But we must ride the boundaries so no one's horses will cross them. So no warrior will have cause for blood between Clan and Clan, Band and Band."

Behind Tyman, he could hear warriors muttering in approval. Once again, Arakk the Snaked Tongue had gotten with words what he could not get with might. Arakk leaned near to Tyman's ear.

"If you will not ride to the east with me, should I look for another Strong Arm to lead the Swift Arrow Band?" Arakk smiled as his words cut like dull arrows into Tyman.

"Yes, I will stay at your side," Tyman hissed. "But the Great Sun may be very dark because we did not ride, every one of us, west today."

Arakk frowned, then waved the hand that held his horse's reins. "Speak on. My blood listens."

"My youngest son, Toman, does not ride among us today."

Arakk dismissed the words with a flick of his right hand. "You know young men. Their first victory. Let him wear down two or three women, then he will be back with a manly grin on his face."

Tyman snorted. "He went forth this morning with three older warriors and ten slaves to bring water for the slave pen. None have been seen since." He had Arakk's attention.

"Perto's Hungry Wolves slaughtered. Toman and your son Kantom bring a story of horseriders who are not Horse People. They last saw these strangers not two days' ride from here. Now, warriors are missing even from our victory celebration. I say lances should ride to the west. Besides, someone must seek out the next animal hovel that we may bring the blessing of the Great Sun's Open Sky to them also."

"Father," Kantom began, but Arakk silenced his son with a glance.

For a long moment, Arakk said nothing. *Is your heart finally ready to throw away a woman's skirt and put on a warrior's belt?* Tyman held the question on the tip of his tongue.

Then Arakk looked Tyman hard in the eye. "I have ridden too long and hard to skewer what is on my lance. I will take it now. Come, ride after me for one, maybe two hands of days. Then, I will give you the Clan totem, and as many warriors as choose may follow behind you."

Tyman smiled the smile of a fox, and slapped Arakk on the back. "I will ride with you."

Arakk laughed and led off. Tyman followed, but his thoughts were already on what would be in two hands of days. He did not want to ride behind the totem of the Clan. If the next town's men were no better warriors than these, Mighty Man Tyman would take its slaves and pastures for the Swift Arrow Clan.

TWENTY-ONE

JACK WAS STILL trying to come up with a ruse to distract the bastards when Cleo brought the horses up close to the tree. He'd take both spare mounts and leave the woman to find her way to Tall Oaks alone. If he could lose these jokers, he'd double back and pick up Launa's trail. Then again, that might not be so good an idea. He'd just have to make this one up as he went along.

Jack stood, careful to keep below the ridge line. A final glance back at River Bend froze him in place. The horsemen had changed direction again. Now everyone was headed east.

Thank God, or Goddess, as the case may be, Jack thought as he slipped down in the tree's cover to reassess the situation. The seven herds, escorted by bands of warriors, headed toward different river crossings. A hundred head took the ford the water detail had used.

As the last figure entered the tree line, Jack backed away from his post, helped Cleo mount, and set the fastest pace he could to join Launa. That turned out to be a lot slower than he wanted. Cleo's thighs and groin had been brutalized, and she clearly had never ridden before. It wasn't long before fresh blood stained her horse blanket. Jack slowed to a walk.

Launa's trail was easy to follow. Her twenty horses left a fairly easy track, and her choice was obvious after the first mile. Launa stayed to the shade of the trees, taking advantage of its cover at the cost of becoming predictable. Not a bad choice when you're the cheese at a rats' convention.

Jack didn't take any shortcuts either. With Cleo, he wasn't in any better shape to run than Launa. He bagged a deer that he hoped would not only be supper, but a peace offering. Still, when he found Launa late that afternoon, it looked like the only piece she wanted was out of his hide.

"Where the hell have you been, soldier? You were supposed to follow us immediately. If I'd run into trouble, I could have counted on maybe three people here in a fight, which is a shitpot more than the support I've gotten from you."

Jack had been chewed out in his time by some very good sergeants, and even a colonel or two. He didn't know where this young woman came by it, but she had the lingo down solid. Jack braced and gave the required answer. "Yes, ma'am."

Launa held him there, eyes locked. Neither blinked. "Jack, I can't afford to lose you." She paused, seemed about to say something, then changed her mind. "Did you see anything?"

"No evidence of a pursuit. One started to develop, twenty strong"—that got Launa's attention fast—"but it fizzled while I was still trying to figure out how to play bunny at a greyhound track." Jack grinned. "How's it been with you?"

Launa's attention was on Cleo as Antia and another woman helped her dismount. There was a lot of new blood. "We've got some folks that have been beat up on pretty bad, but I think you know what I've been up against. She must have slowed you down."

Jack averted his eyes. There was nothing sexual about Cleo's nakedness; the welts and blood made it ugly. No woman deserved a man around at a moment like this. Glad that Launa was done being a general for the moment and ready to be a human, Jack headed for the spare mount with the deer carcass. "I think we can risk a fire. We've got to get some food into these people."

"Yes, Jack, but I've got a bigger problem." That tone was back in Launa's voice.

Personally, Jack couldn't think of anything worse than this mess. He raised an eyebrow for a question mark and waited.

"I've driven a Mustang since I was sixteen. Ridden wherever the post had a riding stable since I was six. But I've never been around these animals when . . ." Launa was at a loss for words. Jack hadn't seen that in the two months he'd known her.

She took a breath and spat out. "Those damn horses want to make love, not war. And I can't do anything with them."

Jack knew it wasn't the right thing to do, but he threw back his head and laughed.

Launa's scowl took on the lethality of an artillery barrage.

"Okay, okay, I'm sorry," Jack said, words he knew would have no effect. "Let's go look at the horses. Where are they?"

She pointed across the stream and Jack stepped off in that direction, then halted. Launa had not followed.

"Antia, prepare supper. Start a fire with this." Launa pulled the pouch with flint, stone, and tinder from her belt and tossed it to the woman. "Now, we go."

On the other side of the creek, the land opened into steppe. Big Red was intent on covering a mare. Not too near them, one of the local stallions hobbled away, bleeding from the mouth. Closer to Jack, Star and another local were hammering at each other while the center of their affection cropped grass.

"How would an Indian handle this?" Launa's sarcasm would have sparked a nasty retort from Jack, but he was busy trying to answer just that question.

Jack blew out a long breath. "You're supposed to geld 'em when they're young. I don't think it would do any good to cut them now, and we'd lose too many to infection." *How had Grandfather handled this?* Jack had only been twelve the last summer he spent at the San Carlos reservation. Strange feelings had begun to stir inside him by then, but the ranch kept him so busy, there'd been no time to scratch any new itches. He chuckled. "So that's why he kept some of the stallions in their own corral."

"We don't have corrals, Jack."

"Yeah. Okay. Here's what we do. Move all the local stallions across the river, away from the mares."

"Tried, Jack. About mid-afternoon, all hell broke loose. One of the women in the worst shape was riding a mare. Suddenly, the stallion behind her was trying to climb right on with her. The boy riding the big stud couldn't do a damn thing with it. And when I rode over to help, Star jumped right in the middle of it with his own agenda. These halters they gave us aren't worth shit for horses that have their mind on other things. You do what you can. I want my convertible back."

Launa turned. "Damn, there's a lot of smoke coming off that fire. I'll take care of it. You see that we've got some horses to ride tomorrow."

Jack was glad to have Launa somewhere else. He had a problem he wasn't sure how to solve, and he didn't need her second-guessing every try he made. He'd been so sure he had his modern breeding program all figured out, and the neolith was making a shambles of it. He took a quick stock of his assets as he stomped toward his problem.

He had twelve local mares and ten stallions left after the three gifts to Taelon. He also had three moderns who were holding up their end of the program quite well. *So, what do you do, Bearman?* First, get the local stallions out of the picture. Then, keep the moderns from killing each other over the mares. It's easy. *Yeah.*

Jack glanced around to see what help he had. Mist was doing her thing, keeping the horses from wandering too far. *Not a good idea, girl.* Three of the shepherd boys sat under a tree, watching the horses. *Have you ever met a boy that didn't want to be a cowboy? Let's put those kids to work.*

Jack waved at the boys. They trotted over to him, but when he explained what he wanted them to do, their enthusiasm vanished.

"It is the season for the animals to play with the Goddess. These are big animals. Let them play," the oldest boy said.

"What's your name?"

"Soren."

"Well, Soren, we're going to make sure these horses play where we want them. You and I are of the people. The Goddess put the animals here for us. Now follow me." Jack's version of Genesis got blank stares, but Soren followed him, and the others trailed along. Jack sent one of them to get the loser to Big Red; that horse looked pretty well out of the gene pool for the moment. The one challenging Star was another matter.

Jack retrieved a horse blanket that had fallen off and, waving it, got Star and the challenger apart. When Jack made a grab for the other's reins, he half succeeded. He got the rope, but it broke and he came up empty-handed where the horse was concerned. The boys laughed as Jack sprawled in the dust.

"The buck likes to play with you almost as much as with the does," Soren shouted. Jack dusted himself off and whistled for Mist to help. A moment later he was retying the reins on his wayward stallion and giving it to the smallest boy.

"Take these across the river and let them graze near the camp. And bring back the doe that traveled with me and Cleo." *Thank goodness that one didn't come in season on the way here. We had problems enough.*

With four where he wanted them, Jack took off after the other six. Most of them were sniffing around the mares that hadn't yet ripened, apparently hoping to catch them before the two big moderns noticed. It was getting dark as Jack got the last of the local stallions where he wanted them. He stopped by the fire to see if any food was left. Launa had saved him a small steak.

"Will we have horses tomorrow?" she asked.

"Will we have any people in shape to travel?"

"They have to." Launa's voice allowed no alternative. "We have to put miles between us and the Kurgans. And we've got to find reinforcements for one hell of a fight. If Judith and Brent are right, this is just the opening shot of a very long, losing war."

Jack tried to chuckle, but it came out a snort. "We were

worried they'd dump us in the wrong place, or the wrong time, or they got the whole drill wrong. I guess the bastards stole more of the language than even Judith gave them credit for."

Launa didn't seem to hear him. "We're on target, now we make it happen."

Jack swallowed a bite of steak. *Here was one cadet who'd never worry about the fine points of scholarly debate again. The mission was all that mattered to her. But saying 'we make it happen' did not make it so.* The others had done their part and died. He and Launa had to stay alive and somehow mount a defense for all of Europe. Now Jack knew how a fox felt, pinned in the lights of an eighteen-wheeler as it barreled down on him.

Finishing the steak, he wiped his hands on his arms. "I'll bed down across the way with the mares and modern stallions."

"I'll stay with the women. The boys going to stay with you?"

"At least the three oldest."

"Tomorrow, I'll start teaching the women hand-to-hand with quarterstaffs. We're going to put up a fight the next time we see horsemen."

Resolve hardened each of Launa's words. Jack had been Army long enough to come up against the gap between resolution and accomplishment, but he gave her the answer she wanted to hear. "Yes, ma'am. Good night."

TWENTY-TWO

JACK AWOKE WELL before dawn, nervous about horsemen and none too well rested. The three boys and he had shared one blanket. As soon as one kid slipped into any kind of sleep, the nightmares would turn him into a groaning, twisting dervish. Jack had tried holding them, soothing their moans, but no one had slept very long.

Big Red looked ready for a run, and Jack could use some morning wind in his face to clear his thinking. He'd spotted several hills that might make good observation points. Yesterday he'd seen all the horsemen head east, but he wouldn't put it past some of them to change their minds.

The land was open and rolling, broken only occasionally by tree lines where a stream cut through the prairie. A mech division could move through it and Jack would never see it—except for its dust. *Remember the dust, Bearman. You don't have remote-controlled drones in this war, but don't ignore what you got.*

The air was morning crisp and sweet; Jack put his worries aside long enough to enjoy the gallop. Big Red showed his joy at being free of the baggage he usually lugged and ran, hardly touching foot to ground, resenting even the brief pauses Jack insisted upon at each of the knolls.

The ever present deer wandered across the plain, browsing watchfully. There might have even been a herd of wild cattle off toward the distant dawn, but there was no sign of a horse patrol. Jack felt pretty relaxed as he rode back to camp.

Eighty meters out, he brought Big Red to an abrupt halt; the camp looked empty. Only as he walked the horse in did women with bows step from behind trees and normal camp activities resume.

Launa was waiting for him with hands on hips. "Anything on a horse is a target, Captain. You didn't check out. Keep this up and I'll lose you to friendly fire."

Jack locked his face down like a good soldier. *She's got a point, and you could get it right in the chest.* "Yes, ma'am. Would you prefer to do the morning recon tomorrow?"

Launa quickly dismissed his question. "No. I'm staying with the women. You do it. Just let us know."

"Anything to eat? The boys will be hungry."

"We already fed them. You can get yourself something from what's left. I'll mount the women up in a bit on the local stallions. You take the boys and keep the mares downwind from us. Is there anything I can ride?"

"I can loan you a mare that's not in season yet."

"And I'll get off quick if some stud wants to ride her. Okay. How're you going to keep our moderns from fighting?"

"I'm dividing the mares into three harems. I'll keep 'em a mile apart. The stallions should stay to their own."

"Worth a try, but how can I combat-train the boys if they're always on their own?"

Jack shrugged; that was one Launa would have to solve for herself. As far as he was concerned, nothing was more important than covering the miles between what was left of River Bend and this Tall Oaks place. He grabbed a quick breakfast and went to execute Launa's orders for the day.

She broke camp a half hour later and started moving her small band down the right-hand side of the stream. Jack kept his horses to the left side.

Soren led out riding Big Red and laughing that he knew when to get off. A kid named Spido had Star under moderate control. Jack couldn't pronounce the name of the fellow on Windrider; he called him Ted. Jack cut out a mare for himself and another for Launa, then spent the morning riding circuit up and down the line, making sure the boys weren't in over their heads.

There was no problem when Windrider stopped the tag end of the column for a reproductive moment, but every time Big Red or Star decided on a love break, Jack had to halt the whole parade, then get it moving again.

He only had one bad scene that morning when he guessed wrong and put a pack saddle on Big Red's next amorous interest. It took a while to clean up the wreckage and collect their gear after that one. Launa was well ahead of him by noon, though Jack had bagged a pair of deer for supper.

The afternoon was half gone when his herds arrived at Launa's camp. She was all business when he reported in. "I want to pull you and your boys in for an hour or two of hand-to-hand training. Think you can leave the horses alone long enough for us to give these people a lesson on the gentle art of killing a man? I can't let our transportation dictate everything."

Jack suppressed a grimace. Someday Launa would find out that a lot of things dictated how a commander fought a battle. With luck, today wouldn't be a learning experience. "Mist can probably ride herd on them. I'll post her."

When Jack got back, Launa was using one of his bronze axes to trim a quarterstaff she'd cut. Most of the survivors already leaned on one.

"We are hunters of the horsemen." Antia allowed for no alternative as she waved her captured lance.

"Yes" came as a low growl from each survivor's throat.

Here was one batch Jack didn't need to tell "The redcoats are coming." The bastards had already come. *But it takes more than passion to make soldiers.*

Launa took her knife from her belt and held it high so the sun glittered off its edge. "I will make you hunters of those who hunt women."

"What will we hunt with?" Soren shattered the illusion of power with a good question. "I don't have a knife."

"Staffs."

"Walking sticks," the boy snorted. "We would hunt horsemen, not herd goats."

"Get a quarterstaff," Launa snapped over her shoulder at Jack.

He borrowed one from a woman—and turned to face Launa just in time. She came at him like a fury. Jack had known more than one sergeant to use these damn poles to work out their rage. He defended himself for all he was worth. After a few seconds, Launa slowed down, began telegraphing her blows a little. She pulled a thrust that could have broken his leg. Jack was grateful for the favor.

Awe showed in the eyes of the onlookers, whenever Jack had a moment to notice. Finally, Launa called, "Enough."

While Jack caught his breath, Launa faced the recruits. "I killed a man with this 'walking stick.' Would any of you take Jack's stick and stand against me?"

The survivors stared back. Soren had the good sense to keep his eyes on his toes. Launa paired the group off by height and in the next hour taught them the basics. Most of the kids were too far gone to put much back into their drill, but they made up for it with determination.

When Launa called a break, Jack mounted up for a quick check of the herds. The horses had wandered a bit, but he brought them back in. When he returned, Launa was introducing them to her favorite weapon. She'd dug up three slings. "Anyone know how to use this?"

All five of the boys and six of the women raised their hands, and one of them even had a sling for hunting small game. Grinning proudly, he twirled it over his head for Launa and hit a rock ten meters away with his pebble.

Launa tossed Jack one of their copies of a Roman auxiliary's sling. "Show 'em, Jack."

He collected a rock half as big as his hand. Stretching the leather thongs out so it would swing in an arc nearly as wide as he was tall, Jack built up plenty of momentum before he let fly. The bullet arched out nearly two hundred meters to demolish a sapling—a meter from the one he'd been aiming for. Jack wasn't about to admit to Launa he'd missed.

Soren picked up one of the captured bows. Pulling it as hard as he could and aiming high, he couldn't get the arrow past fifty meters.

The survivors turned to sling practice with a will.

TWENTY-THREE

LAUNA ALLOWED HERSELF a breather as Jack showed the team how to loft rocks farther and farther with their slings. When Soren complained again that they would never hit anything, Jack cut him off. "You do not hunt a rabbit, but a horseman. He is bigger and slower." That seemed to settle the matter.

Maybe Jack was learning. It had felt good to take him on with the quarterstaff. She could have busted his knee, and he knew it. The Colonel would rub it in over drinks at the "O" club tonight. How hard would she have to be on Jack?

Antia was again at Launa's elbow, like a shadow, watching, rarely speaking. At the moment, she looked like she had something on her mind. "Yes?" Launa offered an opening.

Antia frowned as she watched the slingers practice. "Jack's arrow hit a horseman farther away than the horseman's bow could. Farther than the stone flew. Why practice with stones?"

Launa tried to suppress a wince; the longbow was supposed to be their secret. She couldn't fault Jack for using it when a life was on the line, but she wanted at least one ace up her nonexistent sleeve. "Slings are better," she quickly answered.

Antia made a face. She wasn't buying it.

There was no use explaining how deadly Roman slingers

had been—would be. Launa picked up a rock. "Arrows take skill and time to make. Stones are easy to find." She pitched it to Antia.

Antia tossed the rock in the air and caught it with a grip that left her knuckles white. "The horsemen are many. We can find a stone for every one of them, and if the rock leaves them still breathing . . ." She grinned viciously and fingered her captured knife. Tossing down the stone, she joined the slingers at practice.

Launa watched the woman go. Antia was her ally—her first hope—but the smile on Antia's face left Launa cold. She'd seen that same face on the horsemen she'd killed.

After supper, quarterstaff practice brought their first casualty: skinned knuckles and a badly scraped shoulder. Some of the survivors were getting their strength back and their anger out. Practice halted as Jack applied first aid.

Launa kicked herself for not thinking about this before. "Could you make some real pugil-sticks? These kids have too much anger to practice with live weapons."

"Guess we'll have to."

Launa called the company together. "Let us have no more hurt while learning to be hunters of those who hunt. Jack will make sticks with a circle of willow branches to protect your hands, and pads of moss and leaves to protect the one you hit."

There were murmurs in the ranks as she spoke. When she finished—silence.

It was Soren again who stepped forward. "We are not babies to flinch from pain. We have seen the horseriders. They do not flinch from pain. They seek it, the way a woman seeks a lover." He glanced around the circle of survivors, finding plenty of support. "We will be hunters. We will endure what we must."

Launa took a deep breath; she'd known this moment would come. The pits of hell were open and ready for business. Here was what she'd come six thousand years to put a stop to—not just the Kurgans, but their worldview as well.

She let her breath out in a slow prayer. *Well, Judith, how do we do this?* Soren probably spoke for everyone. The horsemen won; they treasured pain. If you wanted to win, you did it their way. If that thought won, the Kurgans won, even if every last one of them died. *Lead with a question.*

"Is Jack a hunter of men? Am I?"

"Jack has killed horsemen."

Launa noted they gave credit only where they saw it was due. "The horsemen kill women. The horsemen seek pain. Jack kills horsemen. Jack does not seek pain. Are there two paths for those who would be killers of men?"

Soren's brows furrowed; then he nodded slowly. Around the circle, most heads bobbed agreement. Antia stood, unblinking, studying Launa. Launa would give much to know what went on in that woman's mind.

The boy stepped back into the ranks. "You will make us killers of horsemen."

Launa folded her arms, stilled her churning gut, and set her face to flint. "To kill horsemen, you must first learn to hunt horsemen. To hunt horsemen, you must live. There is pain enough learning those skills. For now, let no one seek what will come in time." She glanced at the darkening sky. "Let us seek sleep. You will all rise early tomorrow."

With murmurs from all and yawns from the younger ones, the group dispersed. Antia, Cleo, and Jack joined Launa.

Jack came up beside her. "You done good, soldier."

"We'll see," Launa shot back; a commander did not bask in a subordinate's opinion.

Antia cleared her throat. "Our hearts would hear more of this other path."

"Let us sit by the fire and talk of what is in our hearts."

They sat in silence, staring into ruddy coals. Launa saw images from Dante's hell, a hell she intended to quench before it burned these people to ash. Yet, she could not just lecture Antia like the Colonel would. Judith was right. These were intelligent people; they would have to find the path for themselves. Launa broke the silence the way Judith would.

"Do the horsemen honor the Goddess?"

Antia blinked. "Everyone does."

Cleo frowned at Launa. "All honor the Great Mother. We come from Her. We go to Her. Everyone honors Her."

Launa said nothing, just stared at Antia. Launa had grown up with the multiplicity of Catholic and Protestant, Jew, Moslem, Buddhist, and hundreds of variations. Antia had never confronted the possibility of variety in the infinite.

For several minutes Antia stared back at Launa. Then her eyes widened, and her face twisted into a study in disbelief and revulsion. "They do not. They do not honor the Goddess."

Launa waited as the full burden of Antia's loss and gain sank deep.

When Antia spoke again, her whisper was harsh, desert-dry of any emotion. "My mother spoke for the People. A man led the horseriders. My mother held out her hands to the Goddess. He raised up a knife to the sky." She turned to Cleo. "I do not know what they turn to, but it is not to the Goddess."

Eyes wide in shock, Cleo sidled away from Antia's heresy until she sat as far from anyone as she could without leaving the circle of flickering light. She stared at her friend, mouth open, but no words came.

Launa waited. By rights, she should have felt proud of herself. Here was a woman who knew the redcoats were coming. Here was a woman who had tasted the full horror of what that meant. But there was a timbre in Antia's voice, a way she held her hands. Launa shivered and stared deep into the fire. The embers were burning down to dust. *Have I burned a woman's heart into a cinder? What have I put in its stead?*

You didn't do it, honey, the Kurgans beat you to it. There was no comfort in the answer. Launa dusted her hands off. "These are hard words. Let us sleep. Maybe in our dreams the Goddess will whisper what is difficult to hear with waking ears."

Launa left the two women gazing into the fire. Jack headed for his camp. As Launa rolled into her blanket, Antia and Cleo began to talk in low whispers.

Next morning broke cloudy. Launa heard Jack ride out on his morning patrol as she got the fire going. She wanted her troops up early. "Rise and Shine" or any of the other more obscene Army wake-up calls had no translation into the tongue. Launa settled for "Harken. The sun rises." Little Sisu pointed out it hadn't, but Launa led her would-be soldiers in stretches and gentle calisthenics anyway.

"What is this?" Soren questioned between gasps.

"You want to be a soldier. Well, be a soldier." Launa didn't even try to translate, but the meaning got through. There were no more questions.

Actually, Launa was gentle on the survivors. When Jack returned from his patrol, she dropped little Sisu and the three women in the worst shape from P.T. and sent them to start breakfast. After the rest had gotten quarterstaffs, she reformed them in column behind her and Jack and started a morning run. Jogging along beside her, Jack quietly called cadence to set the pace. In a moment, the two of them were in step. To Launa's surprise, when she dropped back to check for stragglers, all eleven of her troopers were in step.

"Count cadence. Count!" she called.

Jack launched into a series of cadence calls in English. The natural rhythm of the people served them well. They caught the beat of the sung cadence and turned the exercise more into a dance than a run, at least the first half. Exhaustion set in by the middle of the run. Launa cut the pace to a brisk walk for the final quarter. She saw Jack fall back to walk beside Soren.

"Enough pain for you, son?"

"I thought . . . you said . . ." The boy ran out of air.

"Launa said there is pain enough in learning to soldier without adding what isn't needed. You'll do fine, boy."

Jack fell back to where Launa marched at the end of the column. "These kids are healthy, but the last few days took a lot out of them. I recommend an hour for breakfast. Turn some loose on target practice, while I take four to help me put together padded pugil-sticks. Then we split the squad in half. One team breaks camp, the other practices with the sticks."

"Sounds like a good order of the day to me. Post it." *Maybe Jack could be a decent subordinate.*

The morning went as planned. The company left camp when the sun was halfway to noon. Jack returned to his horses with the older boys, but Launa led her troop out like real cavalry, in pairs. Each woman carried her quarterstaff like a lance, at the ready. Even little Sisu, riding double behind Cleo, clutched a pole Jack had cut to his size.

When the sun was halfway down the sky, Launa called a halt. While Jack took Windrider out for a run that doubled as a search sweep, Launa put the survivors to practicing. Thus they spent every waking moment in practice and exercise, travel, or meals.

It was early in the fifth morning that Antia looked around, took her bearings, and pointed. "Tall Oaks is beyond that hill."

The sky was clear and blue above it.

TWENTY-FOUR

JACK WAS FINALLY getting the hang of these lovesick horses. They turned out to be easier to handle than his CO. Using some spare rawhide, he'd tied Big Red up behind one of the mares that was no longer interesting and in front of one that had yet to come in season. He had just enough spare rope to give Star the same treatment. So far today, he'd been able to keep Windrider under control. *Now, how do I keep Launa happy?*

She trotted into view, trailing a string of the local stallions. "We're here. Tall Oaks is over that hill."

Jack glanced where she pointed, and was relieved to see no smoke. He took a second to show off how he'd strung out the horses. "I think they'll stay on good behavior for a while."

"Good. Antia wants to march the survivors into Tall Oaks in formation. Nobody rides."

Jack didn't ask why. "Can you help me with the horses?"

"Yes."

The boys jogged off to join up. Jack strung the horses out, with the mares that were in the mood kept well downwind. By the time he and Launa joined Antia, she had the survivors in a column of twos with staffs held smartly at the ready across their chests. Antia and Cleo stood at the head of the line, horsemen's lances shouldered. On Antia's command, they stepped off together, Soren calling cadence. The rhythm was one of Jack's; the words were Soren's.

Launa called in the dogs; it took only a moment to put them on leashes. Ready to enter Tall Oaks, Launa squared her shoulders. "Now we make it happen."

In Jack's experience, it was a lot easier to say that than make it so, but he kept his thought to himself. He just hoped they didn't fall on their faces.

A half hour later they rounded the bend in the river and got their first view of a major town in their new world—one that wasn't dying. Jack studied it with a tactician's eye.

Like River Bend, Tall Oaks sat in the middle of a valley surrounded by lightly wooded hills. Fields stretched out from it in neatly ordered rectangles. Sheep and goats grazed the open meadows—not a horse was in sight.

The town was set back fifty meters from the river. It stretched about a kilometer along the bank and was not quite that wide. A broad avenue ran down its middle to a plaza at its center. The houses were wood with high-peaked, thatch roofs. Jack estimated three hundred plus homes.

Toward the center of town, there was some semblance of city planning. Houses along the main avenue faced the plaza. Others were laid out in side streets, five or six deep on each side. On the outskirts, however, houses were scattered at random. Spread out as it was, the place would be a nightmare to guard.

There were no walls; raiders on the hills could charge straight across open fields and be in the streets in a matter of minutes. Jack gave up any immediate plans to defend Tall Oaks.

As they got closer, he checked out the houses. Each sported a garden growing peas and lentils as well as a pit for refuse. Pigs seemed to be the primary employees of the local department of sanitation. They were doing okay; the town didn't smell too bad, and the flies were no worse than what Jack was getting used to.

Despite Antia's brisk pace, the troop picked up quite a following; Jack could hear "Traders" being shouted. The packs on their horses were attracting attention. Children, women with babies, pigs, old folks, and young men and women filled the road and slowed the parade. The people looked much like Taelon's hunters. On this warm day, clothes were informal and scant. There was no extra flesh on anyone, but no one looked starved.

Jack tried not to think of what a Kurgan battle group would do to these people.

He was so busy assessing the situation that he didn't pay enough attention to the dogs. When a small child toddled up to Frieda, Jack spotted his mistake just in time to yank the dog's leash. "Heel, Frieda."

That saved the kid's arm until a woman snatched her away.

"Great way to make friends," Launa observed dryly.

"You've got Mist. Want to swap?"

They didn't have a chance. Antia called a halt, and the party stopped right in the middle of the road. The townspeople backed away to give Antia and the survivors some room. Jack glanced over his shoulder, praying the horses would behave.

Maybe he should have parked them outside, but, unlike Humvees, horses eat things, and demolishing somebody's garden didn't look like a good introduction. Of course, taking a kid's arm off wasn't so good either. Silence brought Jack's attention back front. Then a woman got all his attention.

She was about five feet tall. Her short skirt showed a colorful pattern; the shawl hanging from her shoulders did not cover her full breasts. She didn't so much walk, as let the earth pass beneath her feet. The power in her bearing and carriage brought Jack to attention; this woman commanded.

Antia saluted the woman with an upraised hand. "Greetings, Lasa, who Speaks for the Goddess in Tall Oaks."

The woman nodded back as a man stepped from the crowd behind her. Without being told, Jack knew the two were together. Yet the fellow did not walk in any shadow. A stone knife dangled from his belt, the only thing he wore, and he grasped a shepherd's crook. The way it fit his hand told Jack its owner would be just as comfortable guiding a lamb with it as taking the head off a wolf.

The speaker for the goddess studied the survivors for a moment more, then stepped forward and opened her arms. "My heart knows you, Antia, daughter of my mother's sister. Come to me and tell us why you come so strangely before us."

Antia stood her ground and began to speak.

"Oh Lasa, Speaker for the Goddess,
harken your ears to the words of my heart.
We come not as maidens for your womanly greeting."

The speaker's hands dropped to her sides. Jack strongly suspected a speaker for the goddess was not often rebuffed. Antia did not give a moment's pause.

"We come not as maidens or mothers to greet you.
We come as women taken consort
by men not of our choosing.
We come as women who cut the heart from such a one."

In the shocked silence, the speaker's whisper came through loud and clear. "Who has done what you say?"

Antia turned to address the crowd.

"When the moon was last full,
it saw our people celebrate with stories, song, and dance.
When the moon was full, it set on our happy town.
When next the moon rose, our town was no more.
For with the rising of the sun,
we went out to greet the horsemen.
For with the rising of the sun,
we greeted the horsemen with happy words and smiles.
With the rising of the sun,
the horsemen greeted us with arrows and lances and
*   knives."*

Cleo raised aloft the lance, bow, and quiver of the horsemen. Antia did not slow her story.

"As the sun rose in the sky,
the horsemen hunted the People among our homes,
as if we were rabbits in the woods.
As the sun rose in the sky,

the horsemen gathered the People
as if we were grain in due season.
As the sun rose in the sky,
the horsemen slaughtered the People
as if we were fish in run.
The horsemen cut our men's throats
and cast the blood to the sky.
The horsemen snatched babes from mothers' breasts
and cast them into fires.
The horsemen put knives to maiden throats
and made them their consorts
with the blood of their fathers and brothers
as their wedding bed.
I was such a consort.
My friends were such consorts."

A shock wave rippled around the plaza. Antia paused in her oration for the murmuring to die down. Then she drew her knife, raised it high.

"With this knife,
I cut the heart from he who made himself a consort.
With this knife these eyes had watched him
cut the heart from kith and kin.
These eyes saw him cut the heads off kith and kin.
These eyes saw him slaughter kith and kin.
Slaughter the way of our kith and kin.
Slaughter our way.
Our People are dead.
Our town is dead.
We who stand before you are dead.
Our blood lies in the dirt with our kith and kin.
What flows in our arms, flows for only one purpose.
We live to hunt those who hunted our People.
We live to slaughter those who slaughtered our People.
We come to ask what you will do.

Antia turned back to the speaker and sat cross-legged in the dust. The headwoman's eyes went to the welts and scars on the young woman's thighs and groin. Lasa's mouth dropped open; her eyes grew wide. Several times she seemed about to speak, but stopped. Finally, she took several deep breaths.

"Let us all enter the Sanctuary of the Goddess. Let us share food and drink. Let our hearts mull upon what you have said. In all my years, or the years of my mother or her mother, we have never heard of deeds as you bring to our ears. Come, let us give you what we can."

Antia stood, pointing her lance at Launa and Jack. "Without those two, we would have died with our people. Our hearts treasure them as they treasure life. We give them to you."

Lasa studied the two soldiers for only a moment. "Let them enter into our assembly," she said and turned, leading the survivors into the town.

Which left Jack with a problem: how to get twenty-five horses and two dogs into whatever their assembly was. He strongly suspected the building would be a tight fit. Antia was waving for them to come. Beside him, Launa's head whipped back and forth, wanting to go, but stuck with the same problem.

"You go ahead," Jack said. "I'll park the car."

Launa's scowl showed no appreciation for his humor.

Suddenly, the man with the shepherd's crook was beside Jack. "I am Kaul, Speaker for the Bull and consort to Lasa who Speaks for the Goddess in Tall Oaks. Oh, Lady"—he nodded to Launa—"go with our consort and her sister Antia. I will go with your consort to care for these wonderful animals."

One of those "wonderful animals" tensed beside Jack, eyeing Kaul and his unprotected middle. Frieda had been getting more and more nervous, surrounded by all these strangers. She gave a warning growl and crouched, readying for something Jack suspected would not be appreciated. He hauled back hard on her leash, half lifting the dog off the ground. "Down, girl. Heel, Frieda."

Beside him, Launa gave the same commands to Mist. The dogs went down, heads between their paws. Mist was mournful at rejection, but Frieda eyed the man, still ready to lunge.

Jack scanned the scene—not a dog in sight. When had the dog been domesticated in Eastern Europe? He suspected he now had empirical proof it was later than this.

Sweet Mist saved them; she edged forward, crawling on all fours with that happy smile so natural to her breed. Kaul smiled back and, as Jack watched in amazement, held out his hand. Mist sniffed it, licked it, and wagged her tail. Launa showed him how to scratch behind the collie's ears, and Kaul was quickly rewarded with a belly which he knelt to scratch as well.

"Let me take this wolf," Kaul laughed. "It is fitting that a woman attend the Goddess when she is called." Jack suspected Mist was not the first wolf this man had stared down.

Gingerly, Launa handed Mist's leash to Kaul and hastened after the others. The women survivors followed the speaker toward the center of town, but the boys trotted back to Jack and Kaul. *What gives? Is Judith's wonderful Eden a women-only club?* Launa had been a handful lately. Was she going to get worse? "Were not the words of the speaker inviting us to the council?"

"Yes, and we will go after caring for the animals. Many words will have been said, and many words will remain to be said, but no words of destiny are ever spoken while the sun is high in the sky. We men need not rush forward only to sit and listen."

Jack grinned; you had to like a fellow who knew how to dodge long staff meetings. But the walk back the way they came quickly grew quiet. Jack found the shepherd eyeing him time and again.

"It is a strange path," Kaul spoke slowly, "that brings women of River Bend to us with a story beyond belief of what horseriders have done. Yet, they come to us and give into our hearts you"—Kaul glanced back at the horses trailing them—"who bring horses among us. It is strange to my eye."

Jack nodded, playing for time. This fellow probably was as good a hunter as Taelon. Whatever Jack said had better fit together or this guy would be all over him like a baying hound. "The horseriders who did these things came from the rising sun. We come from far to the west where the sun sets."

Kaul grunted and led Jack to a grove of tall oaks beside the river. "This will make a good camp. The horses may graze here. Down that path, they may drink and also cross the river to more pasture. Other horseriders have camped here before."

Other horseriders! Jack had a dozen questions, but Windrider picked that moment to mount a mare that had wandered within reach of him in the shuffle. It took Jack the next several minutes to separate male from female, local from modern. He sent Soren, Ted, and Mist with the local stallions down the road to the other, upwind, side of the river, then turned to getting the pack racks off the mare before one of his moderns tore it apart mounting her. It took another ten minutes to finish that and spread the modern harems out. Jack send Sisu and the other two boys to watch them and make sure the horses stayed away from the crops. By the time all that was done, Jack needed a breather and a drink.

Kaul had helped, but the process brought a pensive frown. "It is the season for the Bull to play with the Goddess. Yet you send some bulls away and . . ." Kaul's words came to a halt; his hands indicated the three harems.

Jack took a moment to station Frieda on a pile of baggage and ordered her to guard. *But who will guard the guard dog?* Things were getting complicated. Jack made sure he'd done everything he should do as he tried to figure out the best answer to Kaul's question. He headed for the river and that drink, motioning Kaul to follow.

Brent said to get people talking. With luck, they'd answer their own question, or maybe forget it. "You know the wisdom of the Bull and the Goddess?" Jack asked.

"Yes. If there are no bulls among the People or the animals, the Goddess does not bless them."

"How many bulls do you need among the pigs, the sheep?"

Kaul shrugged. "As many as the Goddess sends."

"Among the people I have traveled from, we have found that when you leave one strong bull in the herd, all the offspring are strong like that one."

"Among the People far to the west?"

Jack nodded.

"And what do the People far to the west do with the bulls who are not so strong?"

Jack glanced at the man, proudly naked beside him, and decided not to talk about gelding. "Most we eat." Jack stooped to take a drink and slow down the pace of this conversation.

Kaul lifted water in his hands and drank, but did not let up. "It is strange. Many traders have sung by our fires. They have traveled from the woods where the sun rises to where it sets into the bitter waters. They sing of horseriders on the green steppe. None have sung of horseriders where the sun sets."

Jack wished he knew what the right eye contact was here. If he looked Kaul in the eyes, was he being aggressive? If he glanced away, was he lying? He tried to do neither as he struggled to find something to say. Fib number one hadn't worked out, but Jack had no fallback position. He'd just have to hold where he was. "There is land beyond the bitter water. With a strong horse, you can ride around the water." Jack hoped that would keep the hunter off his trail for a little while.

Kaul said nothing as they returned to the camp. Frieda had settled down atop one pile of sacks, making a nest for herself. Still, she worried Jack. "The dog, ah, wolf will do no harm unless a stranger approaches. I fear one of your people . . ." Jack ran out of words and ended up scratching his head.

Kaul's glance took in the dog, and the people working in the fields beyond. "Yes, I do not know how it will be when the People meet the wolf that follows after you."

Kaul's eyes swept the valley before them. On the hill to their right a young man chased some goats out of the brush. Kaul called, and the youth began an easy lope toward them.

"He is Bomel, first son of She who Speaks for the Goddess. I will have him keep watch over our people and the horses while the dog keeps watch over your trade goods and the horses. Thus, no harm will come to anyone. That will be good."

Jack hoped so, but the strange way Kaul named the boy left him confused. "Bomel is your son?"

"No. Masin Spoke for the Bull in those days. He can no longer make Lasa fertile, so now I Speak for the Bull."

Kaul gave Bomel his instructions. The young man grinned at Jack and settled down to enjoy the afternoon in the shade of a tree a comfortable distance from Frieda.

The dog eyed him, then relaxed.

As Jack collected his scabbard, quiver, and spear, he went over what he'd learned so far. Everything looked okay; he'd seen nothing on his morning patrols. *Still, when a strong man goes armed, bastards tend to go the other way.* There was one thing Kaul had said that Jack had not followed up on.

"Other horseriders have camped here?"

"Young men, on pilgrimage with the Goddess."

"They told you that?"

Kaul chuckled. "We do not speak their words, or they ours, but why else would young ones walk the land?"

Jack would like an answer to that one. But if Kaul knew something of the Kurgans, maybe Jack could help him tell the difference between them, and him and Launa. What had Nak said, sometimes the horseriders took when they thought no one was looking? "The goddess gave over a deer to me this morning, and some is left from yesterday's meat. Can I give it to you?"

"With joy I will take it. The Goddess did not smile on me this morning when I hunted. Maybe She smiles on us through you."

Jack hoped so.

As they walked toward town, Jack saw only a few dozen people working in the fields. What kind of economy did these people have? "There are many people in the town and few in the fields?"

Kaul glanced at a couple hoeing. "Some worked yesterday's sun, others today's, others tomorrow's sun. When the seed is heavy, we all work, as we do when we put seed in the ground, but the Goddess does not ask more of us. Now the sun is hot. It is a good time to make a song or a dance. Is that not so?"

Jack nodded into the man's cheerful smile. "That is a good way." So subsistence farms did not need that much work. With no warlords, kings, or priests to think up public works, the people had time to spend with their art. It was a good life. And it had survived in River Bend for about five minutes after the horsemen rode over the hill. Jack headed for the town; it was time to talk about redcoats.

TWENTY-FIVE

EXCITEMENT GREW IN Jack as he followed Kaul toward the center of town. Judith had often wished she could see the Old Europeans in council. Now, he and Launa would.

The sanctuary of the goddess was a longhouse, stone at the east end and wood the rest of the way along its length. The roof was flatter than those of the houses that surrounded it. It had a wide, shaded veranda facing the plaza.

Kaul headed for the west end. There, a team of women and men cooks were busy baking bread and filling several stew pots.

"The Goddess sends us meat along with our friends," Kaul announced as he handed off his deer. Jack let two men take his load, then he waited.

"Yes," the speaker for the bull agreed, "we must join the women and listen for the words of the Goddess." Jack paused with Kaul for a moment at the door set in the middle of the long south wall of the longhouse so his eyes could adjust to the soft light filtered down from the rafters.

To his right, against the east wall, Lasa sat on a chair of wood and clay. At her feet, Launa perched on her heels trying for all the world to keep her back cadet-ramrod straight. *Relax, woman. You're at the Lady's right hand. We're doing pretty good.*

Rammed dirt platforms ran down both long sides of the

room to the door. The older women of the town sat there on benches. In the twenty-foot space between the two groups of women, the survivors now rested cross-legged on the floor, still in their orderly column of twos. To the left of the door, the older men of the town sat on the floor, facing Lasa. Kaul steered Jack toward a place in the front row.

Jack sat. An elderly woman was helped in. An older man arrived. The room was silent except for serving girls and boys passing among them offering water. Apparently, for the entire time he and Kaul had been taking care of the animals, nothing had happened. *Good God! What are these people waiting for?* When no one else waved for water, the youngsters settled behind the men to watch and learn. *Not a bad way to handle civic lessons.*

Jack waited for something to happen. Nothing did. Jack waited some more. Near the front, a gray-haired woman snored in her place on the bench; the two women beside her smiled and supported her. From somewhere behind Jack, a man began to snore.

Jack took the moment to study Lasa. She stared at the ranks of survivors, her face a blank. He'd seen the same stare on Suno as the trader grappled with and failed to face the slaughter in the valley. God help them all if Lasa could do no better.

In the back of Jack's skull, stepdad's voice was screaming for everybody to get off their duffs and do something. Jack's fingers ached for action. How long did these people have before a band of raiders came charging over the hill and did here what they had done at River Bend?

Jack slowed his breathing. Grandfather had taken him to meetings with tribal elders. They had gone long into the night, and Jack, at ten or eleven, had usually fallen asleep before much was said. Now he wished he'd stayed awake.

One thing was clear; this war belonged to these people. They were the ones who'd do the fighting and bleeding. He and Launa could be no more than advisers—advisers from a frantically busy world that had found its own path to death. *Besides, if you do something without Launa's permission, she'll land on you like a tank.* Jack settled in for as long a wait as it took.

When Lasa finally spoke, her voice was distant. "In our mother's time, people gathered together and chose to walk farther to the rising sun, seeking land for crops and herds. All know that land as River Bend."

Around the room, heads nodded agreement. The snores stopped. Jack saw the women rock the old one awake. He wondered how gentle the men were with their sleeper. Lasa settled her gaze on Antia. "You are People of our People. Your loss is our loss. Your mourning is our mourning."

Antia jumped to her feet. "Then hunt with us those who slaughtered our kin."

Her blunt words shocked the room back to silence.

After a long minute, a trembling, ancient voice spoke from one bench. "People do not slaughter People."

Nods and mumbles of agreement flowed around the room.

Antia waited until quiet settled again, then waved the lance in her hand. "But the horseriders slaughtered our People the way you would not slaughter animals, without prayers offered to the Goddess, without benefit. They kill and laugh."

"That cannot be!" A woman spoke as dismay flooded the hall.

An ancient woman at the head of the room struggled to stand. Bent and frail, she leaned heavily on a staff. "When once I spoke for the Goddess, our dreams never revealed deeds such as these. The words of Antia flutter around my heart like a hummingbird, but how can they settle down? No People of the Goddess could do such things." She sat to sounds of agreement.

Antia grounded her lance and leaned against it while talk rumbled around her. After some time, Antia began pounding the floor with the butt of her lance. Gradually, talk ceased.

"Do the horseriders walk the way of the Goddess, or do they walk another?" Her harsh whisper reverberated through the hall. "Are they of the Goddess, or are they of something else?"

The hall exploded. "What else could they be?" "Of course they are!" "All creatures are of the Goddess."

Jack hunkered down for several minutes while the babble level in the room was off the scale. Then he sought Launa's eyes; the snake was truly loose in paradise. The seeds Launa had planted in Antia beside the fire were in full bloom now. How would these people respond? Jack slowly looked around the room, trying to measure people he didn't know. Not just their lives, but all history, turned on what these people chose.

The uproar ceased when the elderly woman again dragged herself up on her staff. "I, Bellda, have spoken the words of the Goddess to you since many of you were children. You know Her wisdom. Everything comes from the Goddess: seed, sheep, daughter of my womb. To Her all returns with the hope of life anew. Like the seasons, She gives and takes. If you climb to the stars, She is there. If you go to meet the sun, She is there. There is no mountain high enough that you could escape Her." Bellda's bony finger swept the room. "To speak of anything else is, is . . . is not to speak at all." Exhausted, she slumped back down.

Beside Jack, the gray-haired man who had arrived late leveraged himself up. Heads around the room swung to focus on him. "As Masin, I am proud to be named your consort. I have heard you speak those words many times, and they have warmed my heart. Before the rising of this day's sun, my heart was gladdened by those words. But not now." He turned to the men.

"The eyes see what the heart does not understand. This young woman says a wild beast is loose upon us like no beast ever seen. When a bear comes to feast on our herds, we drive it away, or we kill it. When wolves come to feast on our herds, we drive them away or we kill them. It does us no good to say these horseriding beasts are not here. These people have seen them. Whether we say this beast is of the Goddess, or walks a strange path for the Goddess, or is stranger still, we say only words. This beast stalks us." He raised his fist. "We must speak of it. We must drive it away from the People—or kill it."

As the man sat, the room exploded in words. Jack grinned at Launa. Here was a man they could stand shoulder to shoulder with. Now, for a couple of hundred like him.

Over the next long hours, Jack tried to remember that feeling whenever he could. It was not easy. For every one who spoke like Masin, five or six took a different tack.

The debate twisted away in words that had no meaning for Jack. Time after time the same question was repeated. How could the Goddess allow such a thing as Antia spoke of to happen? Most of the townspeople seemed divided into three groups.

Many of them just gave an accepting shrug. Flood, fire, and famine destroyed towns. Survivors were welcome, but nobody had to do something about it. The way of the Goddess was clear to all from of old. Judith and Brent had been right; Jack couldn't just holler that the redcoats were next door.

The second group was no better. Most of them would not look Antia in the eye. They glanced away and mumbled doubts that what she said had even happened. This group was the hardest for Jack and the survivors to take. But it was just Antia's words against what any reasonable person "knew" to be impossible. How do you make people believe in the elephant when they've never seen one?

The third group was toughest for Jack to understand. A hunter sitting behind Jack said it most bluntly. "My spear has tasted the blood of bears and wolves. None doubt the strength of this heart. But my spear will never taste the blood of another man. Never. That is not the way of the Goddess."

His gut doing fifty revolutions a minute, Jack searched for the right word to throw into this bubbling cauldron. He came up empty—and kept his mouth shut. As time went by, Launa slumped down farther and farther in her place beside Lasa. Jack met her dejected eyes. Was there any word that they could say to change these people?

Shadows were deep and the rays of a low sun streamed through the door when Lasa stood. "The way of the Goddess is often hard to find. Today, the path is very confusing. Let us go to our evening meal and our beds. Maybe our dreams will show us a path for our feet."

Kaul stood. "Oh Lady, all the wise hearts of Tall Oaks are puzzled today. Let us send runners to the People beyond our fields that they may bring wisdom and share it with us. Where many hearts seek, a path may yet be found."

"Yes, wise Speaker for the Bull, your eyes are keen. Let runners be sent." So saying, Lasa stepped from her platform and was immediately mobbed by women from the benches. The men stood, talking among themselves, waiting for the women to file out. Launa, Antia, and the survivors huddled in the middle of the women's side of the longhouse, waiting for something to happen. Jack stayed at Kaul's elbow. *What do we do next?*

Kaul greeted many of the men by name, thanking them for their words of wisdom. Since the men Kaul thanked had spoken on every side of the issue, Jack was left wondering where Kaul was coming from. He suspected even Kaul didn't know. Jack's stomach rumbled.

Kaul turned to him. "You must be hungry. The stew will be ready soon; will you eat with Lasa and me?"

Launa came up beside Jack. "We have meat," she said.

"I've already given it to them," Jack whispered.

Launa seemed too distracted to answer that with anything more than a nod. They flowed with the press of the crowd through the door. Back at the west side of the longhouse, people milled about. Jack glanced around, remembering the joy of Taelon's hunters after a day of fishing. He found none of that here. People passed from group to group, talking among themselves, casting furtive glances toward the band of survivors which had formed a knot at one corner of the longhouse.

The survivors were not alone. Several young men talked earnestly with them. Jack dismissed them; naked young women would always have young men talking to them. Then he rethought himself. Young townswomen were mingling with the survivors, too. *The young feel each other's pain, even when the adults can't. It's their world ready to go up in smoke. And mine.*

Jack drifted with Launa to the edge of the clump of people that had Lasa for a center. "Understand anything?" he asked.

"Nothing new. They keep going over the same old stuff. Judith said these people cooperate in their decision-making. She said she envied me the chance to see them at work." Launa glanced back at Jack. "I don't think Judith had this in mind."

"This may be what blew it the first time around."

"But how do we change it?" Launa asked in an empty voice.

Kaul joined them. "I thank the Lady for the meat," he said to Launa. "Because of you our stew will be thick tonight."

Jack and Launa turned their attention to Kaul, who had redirected his attention from the survival of civilization to feeding his people without missing a beat. "My hunt was not the only one that went unblessed today. Most of the hunters returned empty. Without you, our stew would be little but corn."

"The goddess blesses who she will," Jack said, using Taelon's answer.

"I will hunt with tomorrow's sun. Will you run after me?"

Jack glanced at Launa. She gave him a quick nod. "With a glad heart," he told Kaul.

Launa's eyes measured the crowd. "Is all of Tall Oaks here to eat the stew?" Jack also wondered how big this burg was. How was it organized?

Kaul shook his head. "Many pots cook tonight. We sent some of your deer to others. Some sent meat to ours. But many tonight have come to our fire to listen to the stories you sing. Traders' songs are always full of strange things."

Jack worried his lip; no way could he sing of his travels like Nak. Launa filled the silence. "We have seen no stranger things than what we saw at River Bend, but our heart has no song for it."

"Yes," Kaul said as his eyes took the measure of his people. "Antia's song is a heavy one to bring to our fire, and it will leave little room for any other song or dance tonight."

The meal proved Kaul right; it was eaten in silence. As

soon as they finished, Antia marched the survivors out.
Launa and Jack followed them.

At the camp, a fire burned and someone had brought supper to Bomel and the boys. Jack suspected some local kid
had swapped a very good stew for riding lessons, but he
didn't ask. From somewhere, blankets had appeared. Launa
spread her bedroll among the survivors beside the fire. Jack
collected a blanket and crossed the river. There was more
room there, and the moderns with their harems now grazed
across that plain.

As Jack lay, waiting for sleep, he weighed the day. *We
have met our allies, and they are confused. And confusing.*

Nothing had been decided, for better or worse. Brent said
the next town upriver was burned early next spring. Did
Jack have nine months to get these people off the dime?
How much did he want to trust carbon dating and tree rings?
If the bastards rode in tomorrow, killing and burning, would
Brent's machines be any the wiser? There had to be some-
thing Jack could do to help these people make up their mind.
But what?

He fell asleep with that question circling around and
around, like a ball on a roulette wheel, unwilling to fall, un-
sure who would win and who would lose.

TWENTY-SIX

BY DAWN THE next morning, Jack was up to his ears in things Launa wanted done, all Priority One, all critical to the long-range survival of doomed humanity—or so she acted.

Teenagers had started filtering in from town as soon as there was light. Each recruit required a pole as long as they were tall. While Launa led everyone in P.T., Jack demolished a small copse of alders. He and Soren were bringing back two squads' worth of weapons when Kaul came down the path.

"The Goddess has blessed us with another sunrise."

Jack didn't know how to answer that, so he grabbed a captured bow and said, "Let us hunt with her."

Kaul stopped near Launa and waited for her to notice him. "Lasa's heart would be gladdened if you walked with her today."

Launa's smile and thank-you were a bit lame. Jack suspected the idealistic army brat was discovering the boring details of administering a campaign, details that never made it past a footnote in the history books.

Jack was glad for a day off. He expected to learn a lot from the hunter. *With luck, maybe we'll find an answer or two.*

They rounded the hill at a comfortable trot, then Kaul froze. After listening for a moment, the hunter began working his way into a thicket. Jack heard a gentle rustling, but could spot nothing. Then a deer lowered its head to nibble grass.

Kaul inched his way forward, standing stiff as a tree. Even when he got in range, the speaker did not reach for his bow. *My God, he's going to walk right up to the animal.* Jack had heard Indians claim they hunted that way. His grandfather had growled that a rifle and a bullet were much more dependable, but he hadn't answered when Jack asked if he'd ever done it.

Jack got ready to watch the show—and ruined it when he snapped a twig. As the deer bounded away, the hunter shrugged. "Aren't they beautiful? Oh, to run with their heart."

They worked their way around the hill, looking for any deer that wandered within shot of the thicket. There were plenty of deer, but all kept a good two hundred meters between themselves and the trees.

At noon Kaul shrugged. "I hope the Goddess has blessed other hunters. She has turned her back on us."

Jack remembered Taelon's praise for how the goddess showed Jack and Launa such blessings when they always returned with meat. Now was no time to be deserted by said goddess.

"Let us go back to our camp. Maybe we are not yet done with the day's hunt. The Goddess may yet smile on our path." *Of course, if he hunts with the longbow Launa will go ballistic, but who do you want pissed at you the most, a goddess or your CO?*

The goddess won—by a nose.

Launa watched Jack leave for the hunt with a scowl on her face and a bitch in her heart. *Why does he get to go kill little furry things and do some of that male bonding shit while I'm stuck with a lot of yammering women? Talk, talk, talk, that's all they did yesterday. They're as bad as Mom's bridge club.* That thought brought Launa up short.

Was she looking at these women through twentieth-century eyes? They sure had sat on their hands yesterday. But faced with the challenge Antia had dumped in their lap, who wouldn't? Mom's bunch might have moved from post to post every few years, but the world they made for themselves when they got to each one didn't change all that much.

Launa took a deep breath, dug the skirt Tuam had given her out of a bag, and pulled it on. As she started down the road to Tall Oaks, she settled Maria's hat solidly on her head. *How do you nudge a world toward change? What would Judith do? What would Maria do?* It made for a good cadence.

Launa headed for the longhouse, but she found Lasa well before she got there. The speaker for the goddess was squatting in the shade of a house, listening to two women argue.

"I gave Callen a large clay jar in exchange for her fixing my garden fence. The pigs got in and ate half of the garden. She should give me what grows in her garden this summer."

"When Callen fixes a fence, it will keep out any pig," the woman across from the first answered. "But Maro cannot tell wood from straw. All of Maro's fence was weak. I told her I wanted two jars to fix all of it. She only wanted one part of the fence fixed. The part I fixed did not let the pigs in."

Damn you, Jack! You go hunting, and I'm stuck listening to this. Lasa let Callen and Maro talk on. Launa wondered if anyone around here ever ran out of words. But when the speaker for the goddess stood, both women fell silent.

"In the name of the Goddess, Callen will keep the clay jar, for all know of her skill with wood. But it is not right for Maro and her children to go hungry. Half of what comes from Callen's garden will go to Maro, and half of what comes from Maro's garden will go to Callen. Let Callen learn now to come to the Goddess quickly when her heart sees an unfortunate path and not wait for the pigs to walk it."

Lasa shook the fence; the whole thing looked ready to fall apart. "The Goddess would have all fences strong between animals and food."

As the speaker for the goddess turned to leave, Launa fell in step with her. "Would the Goddess have strong fences between all animals and those they would prey upon?"

"Yes."

"I would build a strong fence between the animals who ride horses and the people they would prey upon."

"How?" The speaker shot back.

"With strong hearts and sharp arrows."

"The fences Callen builds let the animals live where the Goddess would have them live. Sharp arrows take the life blood from them. Can you build a wall like Callen?"

"Can Callen build a wall against a bear or wolf?"

"No."

Before Launa could press home her advantage, they were interrupted.

"Oh, trader, see what I have to offer you."

Lasa stopped to allow an old woman to hobble up to Launa. And Launa reminded herself not to gawk. The long woolen smock the woman wore was a work of art. Its weave was an intricate, colored pattern, but more, in the very texture of the cloth was a counterpattern of knots. The hours and skill that had gone into that dress left Launa in awe. Then Launa remembered she was the trader being asked to see something.

"Yes," Launa gulped. "I traveled with Suno from the bitter waters where the sun sets." Launa hoped she was getting the geography right. "But I am just learning to trade."

"Any trader would be happy to see what Marbon's heart and eye give birth to," Lasa smiled. "Look upon it."

Launa looked.

Marbon held up a small jar; an elaborate pattern had been incised onto its surface. Launa took it gently, held it up to the sunlight, and studied how the shadows played across its surface. "Beautiful."

The woman responded to the praise with a toothless grin. She held up a wooden spatula with grooves cut in its end. "This is how I make the pattern."

"That is nice." Launa was at a loss. What was Marbon trying to sell her, the jar, the grooved spatula, or the . . . the idea? "I was never with Suno when he traded for something like this." Launa glanced at the speaker.

Lasa laughed. "That fox would never let your eyes see such as this, but a trader brings more than what is in her pack. A wise trader carries words for the heart as well as shells."

Launa hoped she was carrying something Marbon

wanted. "Bring this to me when I spread the mat; I will give you much."

The woman nodded, but her eyes were on Launa—no, above Launa. "I have never seen a hat like that one. Its pattern is smooth, like water over rocks. Maybe if you let me look upon it when you spread your mat, we will trade even."

Taken aback, Launa nodded. The woman gave Launa another toothless grin and hobbled off, softly humming to herself.

"New trader, you did well."

As they continued their walk, Launa took another swing at what she really wanted to say. "You say a wise trader brings words." *Information sharing.*

"Yes."

"What would Tall Oaks trade for the words of life?"

"Some say they are words of death."

"Words cannot kill. Only horseriders' lances and arrows do that." Launa didn't miss a beat either.

They had gotten to the next street before Lasa answered, and a woman and man were hastening their way. "But if we take the blood of the horseriders, where will that blood go? You say these horseriders live with blood on their hands. I am not sure that I could."

When Lasa turned to hear another case, Launa settled in to pay close attention. The speaker for the goddess had invited her to share her day, and now Launa realized how much she wanted to meet these people. From dusty fragments, Judith had constructed an idea of them. *No, an ideal.* Now, Launa had a day to meet what she was trying to save.

The day went slow and fast. Lasa listened to arguments; more trades that hadn't quite gone as expected, a couple dividing up a household, a fellow who insisted he'd worked the fields yesterday, but his coworkers said he was shirking. That one was sent back to hoe under close supervision.

It wasn't just disputes that came to Lasa. Four young women wanted to show the speaker a new dance. A male choir had a song they'd just composed. It had something to do with women and wind and the two never blowing the same way twice. *Some things don't change.* Another woman was attempting a new weaving pattern.

At first these people seemed reticent around Launa, apparently afraid the trader might steal their ideas. Launa hung back in the shadows. Lasa gave them what little encouragement it took for them to talk, sing, dance, and they did.

There were other duties. Lasa decided which new pasture to open for the goats displaced by Launa's horses, and the headwoman approved the building of a new house. Through it all, Lasa kept good humor as Launa turned every situation into a metaphor for the question of life or death, the people or the horseriders.

As the sun sank toward late afternoon, Launa felt good about her day. She couldn't help but like these people. Oh, they were the mixed bag you'd expect anywhere, but the way Marbon reacted to Maria's hat had set something flowing warm and deep near Launa's heart. There were a lot of Marias in this town. Launa enjoyed herself—right up to the moment Jack and Kaul got back from hunting.

Kaul carried a small deer slung across his shoulders. Jack dragged a ten-point buck on a one-man travois. He carried his longbow.

Launa started in a beeline for her exasperating subordinate, but the crowd gathering around the men as they came up the avenue was as solid a fence as any ever built. Fuming, Launa followed in Lasa's wake to the longhouse.

As soon as the hunters turned their kills over to the duty cooks, Kaul began the story of how he and Jack had seen many deer, but been given none by the Goddess. Then Jack brought down a deer with a long flying arrow and Kaul had shot another as the deer fled past where he hid. Jack squatted beside Kaul, looking too damn pleased for Launa's money.

Lasa listened to the story, then whispered to Launa. "Your arrows fly very far."

"Sometimes," Launa nodded. *What the hell had Jack done?*

"Then you have something we would trade much for."

I bet. No way, lady. Launa threw Jack a glare that should have melted him in place. He returned it with that look he got when he'd traded his brains for rocks. *We'll see, buster. You've broken security and chucked the chain of command again.*

Other hunting stories followed Kaul's. The sun was low and the cool evening air carried the smells of a supper that was almost ready before Launa finally got Jack aside for what promised to be a significant social experience.

But before Launa could get a word out, a distraught young woman dashed up to Lasa. Launa forgot Jack as she tried to follow the breathless gush of words. She caught enough to know something was very wrong but no more. "What is happening?" Launa threw the words out, hardly expecting an answer.

A young woman touched her elbow. "A child has wandered. Corna, her mother, and the family have searched for her. If she is not found before dark, wolves or the cold may take her life before dawn. We must all go to hunt for her."

"Frieda?" Jack asked.

Launa prayed the German shepherd was as good a tracker as promised. "Right. Get her."

Jack took off running.

"Does the woman have a blanket or something the child has worn? Can she show us where she last saw her?" Launa asked.

The young woman nodded in puzzlement.

"Have you ever seen wolves as they sniff the ground?"

"Yes." The answer came slowly. Then, "Yes!" A light dawned in brown eyes.

"Our dogs can smell someone's footsteps. But everyone must wait here while Jack gets one. If too many people pass where the child has walked, even our dog will lose the smell of her steps."

"I am Brege, daughter of Lasa. I will carry your words to my mother." In a moment, the young woman was talking with Lasa. The speaker glanced at Launa, then frowned. Around Launa, people began to hustle toward the edge of town.

Lasa did not move. "Wait," she said and raised her hand. The people stopped; the mother of the child and an older couple rushed to confront Lasa. Launa did too.

"The sun is low," the older woman lashed out. "Darkness is near. Why do you do this?"

"You have searched with your eyes. These strangers offer a wolf's nose. Do you have a blanket the child has slept in?"

The mother nodded.

"Bring it here."

The young woman ran off, frantic.

The older woman studied the western sky. "You would send a wolf to find my first born granddaughter. Your heart is open to too much that is new," she hissed.

Brege rejoined Launa. "Hanna does not see as my mother does," she whispered. "May the Goddess smile on the wolf."

"Do you often lose children like this?" Launa let her mouth run as she tried to ignore the dread creeping through her. They were gambling for more than a toddler's life. *Where is Jack?*

"Yes. Many young women enjoyed their time with the goats and a young mother may still go after them. We usually find the children who wander, but the sun is so low this time."

Jack's arrival with the big German shepherd ended the conversation. The mother returned with a blanket only moments later and led off at a panicked run for the outskirts of town. Jack and Kaul followed her apace. The rest trailed at a slower tempo, many carrying torches.

As they walked, Launa tried to remember their short course on tracking. She hoped Jack, or at least Frieda, remembered more about this business. Time to prepare had been so short.

A shepherd stood at the edge of the meadows; he pointed and shouted. "The wolf led them out into the fields, then back toward the trees and the river."

Launa's gut took a lurch. If the child had fallen into the water, all was for nothing. The crowd seemed unable to make up its mind whether to wait or follow. Several people around the edge headed for the fields. "The people must stay here," Launa said.

A worried Lasa shook her head. "No one may tell another the path for her feet. Yet I will try." The speaker shouted to the crowd. As Hanna glared at Lasa, the people continued talking among themselves. The talk grew louder and more were choosing to join the search when there was a yap, a scream, and a "We found her!" bellow from Jack in English. "She's okay."

As Launa translated, Hanna took off at a run. The man with her grabbed a torch and followed. Lasa followed them with her eyes. The worry lines that furrowed her forehead told Launa how much she had gambled. Launa and Brege stayed with the speaker as the crowd returned to the town and supper.

"Why did you"—Launa could not find a word for trust—"let the wolf use its nose rather than let the people hunt with their eyes as is the custom?"

Lasa's eyes never left the trees. "When last we hunted with the sun so low, darkness overtook us. Wolves found the child before the next dawn. The Goddess has shown you how to make wolves follow after you. My heart said the way of wisdom was to follow after the nose of the wolf." Lasa breathed a sigh as a small party came from the trees. The young mother nursed her child while Jack walked Frieda a comfortable distance from everyone.

"But my heart would have been happier if our eyes could have hunted with the wolf's nose. It is not easy for one person to tell the People to walk only one way, even if that person is She who Speaks for the Goddess." She wrapped her shawl around herself to ward off the cool air. "Come, let us join our men. We have much to feast about."

The people did celebrate that night. Or maybe they were just getting back to normal. River Bend's survivors were out of sight; a pot of stew had been taken to the camp. Launa suspected Antia liked keeping the troop to itself.

Launa watched the people go about their evening as they must have for the last hundred, maybe thousand, years. Change was thundering down on them in a cavalry charge, but they couldn't see it coming. Launa glanced at Lasa; that woman had been open to change, sending a tame wolf to find a child before the wild ones did. How could Launa reinforce that openness to change? Judith said these people would return gift for gift. *Let's see.*

During a break in the hunting stories, Launa stood up. "The Goddess has blessed our wolf. Soon she will give us cubs. If it pleases the Speaker for the Goddess, I will give two to the people of Tall Oaks."

Lasa stood, her eyes thoughtful as she silently polled the gathered people. "The Speaker for the Goddess would be happy to accept your gift to the People of Tall Oaks."

Launa sat down, wondering what she'd started. She glanced at Jack; he was grinning from ear to ear. *Don't get too happy, wild man. You and me still have to talk. I'm not trading the longbow for anything less than an army.*

The man whose granddaughter they had found was introduced as Samath, respected carpenter. He asked to see Jack's bow. Jack avoided Launa's eyes as he handed it to him. The woodworker examined the bow, then shook his head. "I know this wood. I have made bows from it and the arrows go no farther than any other. How is this done?"

"It is how you work the wood from the tree," Jack began. Launa got his attention by bouncing a rock off his skull. His "ouch" was louder than Launa had expected; maybe his head was still tender where the Kurgan had dented it. *Good.*

Samath and Kaul laughed. "We must let the women trade. Maybe tomorrow we will talk more after the women have."

Launa doubted it.

When the dancing began, Launa excused herself, with a sharp signal for Jack to follow. Kaul came too, carrying a torch. "Let me light your way."

Launa didn't let Kaul's presence keep her quiet. She just used English to lay into Jack. "This is the most stupid, shit-for-brains stunt you've pulled yet. The longbow is our one edge. We agreed no one would see us use it. Shit, you damn near offed those two kids just on the chance they might have."

Kaul led on with his torch, not even looking back at them.

"Launa, listen to me for a minute. Taelon considered us blessed of the goddess because we always brought home the beef. Kaul was already shrugging about the goddess turning her back on him today. These people really believe this stuff. Do you think we'll get them to follow us if the goddess has her back to us?"

Launa dearly wanted to take Jack's head off. He was going unilateral when she wanted cooperation. But, he had a point.

Launa needed three deep breaths before she trusted herself to say anything. "Jack, these people are next on the Kurgan hit list. You can see it coming. I can see it coming. They can't see a damn thing. They're sitting on their hands. We can't risk the Kurgans getting the longbow. Until these folks are ready to fight, I say we don't give them anything."

"Then why'd you just give away two puppies?" Jack shot back. "What do we do, Launa, abandon these folk and go upriver to the next village? What makes you think those people will be any easier to persuade? Antia had thirty people practicing when I stopped to get my bow. Think we can get that many next stop?"

Jack had her there. Why had she given away the pups? To start something.

Well, Jack probably wanted to start something too.

Their arrival among sleeping recruits saved her from having to answer. The camp had changed since the morning. Where there had been one fire last night, several now glowed. But the troops, survivors and recruits alike, were all sacked out.

Launa counted bedrolls, but gave up when she was well past twenty. So people had showed up to train with Antia, and stayed in camp. It wasn't the hundreds Launa wanted, but it was a start. Would they march upriver if she ordered them to? Launa doubted it.

Jack squatted down by a fire that had no bedrolls too close. After a second, Kaul settled across from him. That left Launa the only one standing. She slumped down. *Did everything have to be decided tonight?*

TWENTY-SEVEN

JACK KNEW HE'D done right and screwed up, all at the same time. Getting the longbow had been right. Every bone in his body told him he had to do it or risk losing everything to the jokers in Tall Oaks who looked to a full stomach for the goddess's guidance.

Would he have lost Kaul? Jack didn't know, but after a morning spent with the man, he didn't want to find out.

Of course, to do it, Jack had screwed up big-time where Launa was concerned. He had plenty of excuses. She hadn't been available to consult. They'd been too busy staying alive to plan contingencies. A soldier is supposed to improvise, seize the moment. *Yeah, but that trooper's supposed to earn his CO's respect first by following orders. Something you haven't been too good at since Launa took over the job.*

Jack settled down cross-legged and slowed his breathing. He was double-thinking himself. Kaul was here with him and Launa. That had to count for something. Jack centered himself on the moment, let his mind empty, and waited to see what would come next. His hand rested on his copper knife.

The three relaxed in the warmth of the fire for several minutes; Kaul seemed content. Jack waited for Launa to do something, but she just stared into the fire. As the minutes stretched, a thought came to Jack. Launa had given a gift.

Could he? He cleared his throat. "Among our people, a man may give another man a gift. How is it here?"

"It is done." Kaul's teeth showed white in the firelight as his face split in a wide grin. "And if She who Speaks for the Goddess should frown, well, from season to season there are days when we must remind these women that it is the Goddess who lights each dawn, not they." He turned to Launa. "Is that not so?"

Launa's eyes locked on Jack, demanding. *What are you up to now?* Still, Launa's answer to Kaul was carefully worded. "We come among you with no wisdom of your ways. Our hearts would be saddened if we were the cause of trouble beside your hearth." *There may be blood knee-deep around ours* was left unsaid.

Kaul laughed. "The gift of a wolf's nose in the hunt for a child and two cubs in time is already praised by my consort."

Jack reached for his copper knife. "My heart is led to give another gift." He took the blade from its sheath and glanced at Launa. At least he was giving her veto power. She'd given a knife to Nak the trader. God only knew where it was now. What had she started? Why not another knife?

Launa nodded slowly.

Jack offered the blade to Kaul hilt first.

The speaker looked at it for a long moment. Then, taking it in hand, he turned the knife over in the flickering firelight. "I have heard traders sing of such tools, but until you came among us, I had never seen such a blade. Never had I thought to touch one." He ran a finger along the sharp edge. "It is hard and straight, like you, Jack, whom I would call friend."

For several minutes, Kaul turned the blade slowly in his hand, his eyes reflecting back the play of the firelight along the blade. Then he got to his feet.

Jack stood to see him off. Launa followed suit. The hunter held the knife in front of himself for a moment longer, then reached for the stone knife that dangled from his belt. He replaced it with the new one. For several long breaths he fingered the finely worked leather of the hilt, the carvings of the pommel, and ran his thumb along the three-inch obsidian blade. Then he turned to Launa. "By your grant."

She bent her head.

"When I look at you, Jack, I see a man and a shadow. There is a strangeness about you, more than the twisting of your tongue at the People's words. My heart sees much need in you who give so freely of the power and wisdom that you have."

Jack shivered as he looked into Kaul's eyes. What did the speaker see that Jack did not?

Kaul held his blade out, hilt first, to Jack. "My father and his father before him wore this knife. How many sons have been given it are beyond knowing. Many Speakers for the Bull have carried this knife in their belt. With this knife comes the trust of our people. My heart knows you will wear it well, friend. Maybe you will need its spirit more than I."

As Jack took the knife, his breath caught in his throat. He felt the brush of an ancient strength. Gently he put the knife in the belt Taelon had given him. Jack reached to clasp Kaul on the shoulder, as he had seen his grandfather do, but as soon as his hands were off the dagger, Kaul pulled him into a powerful hug.

When Kaul finally broke away, Jack braced and turned to face his commanding officer. "Sir, how long do we play tourist? Antia saw me use the longbow. The secret is going to get out." Jack left it at that. He'd made the best case he could. It was up to her now.

Jack had learned to go with his gut in a fight, and trust his luck. Even when lives hung in the balance, sometimes all you could do was throw the dice and pray. *Had Launa learned that yet? You can analyze a problem forever and still be no closer to an "informed" decision. Come on, girl, do it.*

Launa worried her lips. Slowly she took in a deep breath, and just as slowly let it out. Her eyes darted from the copper knife in Kaul's belt to the stone one in Jack's.

"Okay, Captain, we'll play this one your way." She turned to Kaul. "With tomorrow's dawn, let the Speaker for the Goddess come to our camp to receive the gift of long-flying arrows. Bring the woodsmen of Tall Oaks that their hearts may hear the wisdom of our words."

Kaul nodded, reached for his torch, and walked the path to his town without looking back.

"I pray to God you're right, Jack," Launa whispered as Kaul passed out of sight.

"Amen," Jack answered, running his finger gently along the length of ancient black knife. He'd traded the knowledge of the longbow for a piece of stone. On the surface, it didn't look all that good a swap. But Jack remembered another guy who shared his name, and what he bought into when he traded a cow for a handful of beans.

TWENTY-EIGHT

LAUNA LAY AWAKE, trying to get a handle on her feelings. All her life she'd studied the great commanders, the generals who changed the world, and dreamed of the day she might be one. Well, she had her command, and her one subordinate was doing what he damn well pleased. She ought to slap the guy in the stockade.

That's one way of looking at it.

Damn it, what other way is there?

Analyze the situation, girl, the more rational part of her soul ordered. *What were you doing today?*

Hunting for ways to get these people formed up and moving out. Launa snapped at herself.

Did you?

Launa went over her morning and afternoon. She'd nudged Lasa with a comment here, a question there. Would Lasa have waited for the dog yesterday? Launa doubted it.

Would she have waited for the dog if Jack had come back empty-handed? Good question.

So how do we get a few answers?

Not easily. Not nearly as easy as reading history books where somebody else had done the research and made sure all the critical factors were there in black and white for the student. How many of her great generals had spent the night before those great battles, minds spinning, wondering what they'd missed, what they should have done differently? How many of those crucial factors the historians listed were obvious the night before?

Jack's last question had gotten her. "How long do we play tourist?" How much more did Launa have to see before she'd know what to do? Was she ready to let these people be slaughtered? *No!* It was time to start doing something. *Dear God, or Goddess, just give us enough people willing to fight.*

Next morning, there were no answers written in the dawn sky. Early light did show thirty-seven very earnest young people ready for P.T. and drill. Launa went through her morning workout with the troops and was just squaring off with Jack to show them some new moves with a staff when a small mob came down the path from Tall Oaks.

Launa knew why Lasa and Kaul were there. She spotted Samath surrounded by several men holding stone hammers, chisels, and other tools, but she wondered where the others came from. One or two older women Launa recognized from the longhouse—they had not been on her side. Several young people seemed to have joined, for lack of anything better to do. Antia eyed them like a one-woman press gang, hungry for recruits.

Lasa stepped forward. "The Speaker for the Bull says you wish to share with us the wisdom of the long-flying arrow."

"Yes." *We're committed now, kid.*

"That is a great wisdom from the Goddess." Lasa eyed her as if she were a used car salesman. "What do you ask in trade?"

Beside the speaker, the two women fidgeted. So that was it. They were here to check out the deal the speaker cut. Under their hawk gaze, Lasa couldn't swap the bow for the town's soul.

Jack pulled his bow from its scabbard. Young eyes followed it like those of high schoolers lusting after a Corvette. *What would these kids do to get their hands on a longbow?* If Launa couldn't draft folks, maybe she could entice enough good fighters to save Tall Oaks. When no one can tell another the path for her feet, why not recruit your army one trooper at a time?

Launa held up three fingers. "For every three bows the wise woodworkers of Tall Oaks make, two will go to those who follow after me and Antia." Launa spread her arms to take in all the troopers behind them. "Until all these, and those who join us, carry the longbow."

Launa hadn't finished talking before several kids were edging away from the townspeople and toward Antia's troop. Good.

One of the women at Lasa's side shook her fist, catching Launa's eye and probably the speaker's. Two fingers appeared.

Lasa frowned, her mouth working. Launa decided to save her the trouble. She held up one hand, five fingers spread. Then her second hand with three fingers up. "For every five bows, three come to us." *Hope these folks understand fractions.*

Lasa looked to either woman. No objections. "Let us walk that path with the Goddess," she said.

At that, the men got down to some serious technology transfer. Kaul stepped forward with Samath at his elbow. The man whose grandchild they had found last night was introduced as the wisest woodworker of Tall Oaks, able to see into the very heart of a tree and find in it the dream of the Goddess.

The carpenter stood silently through the formal introduction, then, without a word, held out his hand. Jack gave him the bow. Again, Samath examined the bow, even licking it, before handing it back to Jack. "I have made bows from this wood. The arrows fly no farther."

Jack started to say something, then shut his mouth. He let a breath out slowly before he spoke. "I too saw nothing in the wood, like you, but a wise old man of my people showed me the wisdom from the Goddess. Let my eyes see one of your bows."

Kaul handed Jack his. "Samath made me a good, strong one."

Jack examined the bow the same way Samath had, even licking it. He handed both bows back to Samath. "My eyes, my fingers, my tongue tell me that these are the same wood." Jack's admission drew a grunt from Samath. "But let your eyes see how differently these bows are cut from the tree." Kaul and Samath stepped closer as Jack held the two bows side by side. "Samath's bow is cut from a young tree—one no bigger around than two fingers."

"That is how all bows are made," Samath said.

"The wise man did not make this bow in that way." Jack used his thumbnail to highlight the line where the two types of wood met in his bow. "It is three fingers wide and cut from the heart of a great tree so that the skin of the tree is here, between the sinew of a deer and the heart of the tree." Jack's bow was two feet longer than Samath's, but it was the three layers that made it a composite bow and gave it its range.

Jack let the bow fall into Kaul's hands. "That is the power that the Goddess gives to you who know this tree and fashion a bow from its heart." Several woodsmen nodded. They passed Jack's bow among them as their conversation grew rapid.

After several minutes, Samath turned back to Jack. "It will gladden my heart to do this new work. It will be hard work to cut such a bow from the heart of so tough a tree, but if we cut a green tree, it can be done."

Jack shook his head. "You must work the wood when it is dry. If you work it when it is green, it will twist as it dries and the arrow may go . . ." Jack waved his hands around. The conversation took off again, getting quite animated.

Jack turned to Launa. "You getting any of this?"

Launa couldn't suppress a chuckle. Jack probably figured he was opening a can of worms for fish bait. She wondered how he felt about snakes. "They don't see how they can work seasoned hardwood, Jack. Have you checked out their tool kits?"

Jack scanned the woodsmen. Stone knives or axes hung from their belts. "These poor folks'll have a bear of a time doing the finishing work on a bow using stone tools on hardwood. They don't have the tools to make the bows." Jack turned to Launa and raised an eyebrow.

"Am I finally being consulted?"

She got an embarrassed grin for her answer.

Launa curtsied. "Why thank you, kind sir. Jack, I know you didn't bring all those copper tools for your own workshop. We're in for the dime, we might as well go for the dollar."

Jack seemed relieved at her reaction. Maybe he wasn't manipulating her. Maybe he was just like her, way behind the power curve on this mad slide down one bitch of an icy cliff.

Jack rummaged through their gear. He dropped several things into a sack and returned to Kaul.

"Will these help?" Jack handed the bag to the speaker.

Kaul looked into the sack, and his eyes grew wide. He drew out two copper chisels and passed them among the woodsmen. Next came two knives like the one that now swung from his belt, and, last of all, three adze heads. The woodsmen passed the bright metal tools from hand to hand, turning them over to let the sun dance on their fine edges. Respect and awe showed in their voices as their excitement grew.

Lasa cleared her throat. "Never have I seen such powerful tools. What can we offer in trade for such gifts?"

Exasperated, Launa remembered Kaul had never seen a knife like the one Jack gave him last night. *Here's another one we've let out of the bag. What is the metal technology here?* She'd seen jewelry made of beaten copper, but no large copper forging. *No time for that now.* Launa glanced around; what did her troops need that these people could make? Arrows.

Beside her, Jack whispered, "Arrows."

"I know, Jack," she snapped. Then, draining off her anger like the Colonel did, she turned to Lasa. She chose soft words, but put solid rock behind them. "We ask the people of Tall Oaks for arrows. For each bow, quivers with many arrows." Launa held both hands out, opening and closing her fingers twice; she hadn't learned the word for twenty.

They got the message; the women beside Lasa blanched. "How could anyone need so many arrows?" one demanded.

"A hunter has one, maybe two, but so many? No. One or two arrows. No more."

Launa would not give on this one. It was time people got an idea of what they were up against; they weren't hunting deer anymore. Putting on her game face, Launa took the voice Major Henderson used at West Point to matter-of-factly describe hell.

"You shoot at a deer. You miss. The deer runs away. You find the arrow and hunt for another deer. Yes?"

Heads nodded.

"You shoot at a horseman, riding at you with his lance aimed at your heart. You miss, there is no time to search for your arrow. You pull another arrow from your quiver and shoot again. You hit him, and still he rides at you. You hit him with two or three arrows, and maybe he falls from his horse. But you do not retrieve your arrows, for another horseman is riding with his lance aimed at your consort's heart. You will shoot many times until there are no more arrows or no more horsemen. May the Goddess grant that you find the last horseman before you find the last arrow. We will have this many arrows." Launa spread her hands twice.

Beside Lasa, the two women stood, eyes wide, mouths open, faces ashen. This time, the speaker did not look to either of them. "Those who follow after you will have that many arrows."

"Yes," Launa heard Antia hiss.

Samath grunted. "Now that the women have traded, let the carpenters do their work. Let us make handles for these axes. I know where one of these trees is. I girdled it two summers ago, but my young son was not chosen for a consort and I did not build him a house. Now I fear it would be too dry for me to cut and use for a roof beam. Let us see the bow it holds."

The woodsmen headed for their tree, but Kaul held back. "They will be busy today, but all must eat. Jack, let us hunt."

Jack passed that one right on. "Launa, would you like to do today's hunting?"

Maybe the turkey could learn. "Yes." *Let Jack hang around town today.* But then, maybe Lasa would treasure a chance to get out. Launa turned to the speaker. "Will you hunt with us?"

Lasa shook her head. "There are many who will want to talk on the trade we have made today. I must listen to the Goddess in their hearts, but my heart tells me you would rather be riding your great horses than sitting in the town square."

"Yes," Launa said with a laugh.

"Go with the Goddess," Lasa said.

"And know her ways," Kaul, Jack, and Launa answered.

Most of the people were headed back into town by now, and Lasa followed them. Jack rummaged up a spare bow. He glanced at Launa. "You mind if I loan Kaul a long bow?"

"Why not? You've given away the fort already. And we might as well do our hunting on horseback."

"Okay. Do you want to loan or give Kaul a horse?"

"We've given enough away today. Let's just loan him one."

Launa whistled in Star. Once mounted, she quickly collected Big Red and a spare mount for each of them to carry home their kills. "We'll see that there's plenty of meat in the stew tonight. Big smile from the goddess, right, Jack?"

Jack seemed too busy scrounging up a saddle blanket for Kaul to answer. It took a few minutes for Jack to help Kaul mount and get the hang of riding. Launa was glad that at least someone around here didn't take to a horse like he was born on it. The novelty didn't keep Kaul from grinning from ear to ear as he followed Jack's instructions. When Jack mounted Windrider, Kaul guided his horse to stand beside Launa. "Where shall we hunt?"

"Toward River Bend." That was, after all, the threat axis. Launa wanted to have a good look out that way. She led out at a walk.

As they approached the trees, they came upon the woodsmen. They had already lashed the copper adzes to handles and were just felling the tree. The ash was about a foot wide and had fifteen meters of straight stem before its dead limbs spread out. It groaned, cracked, and fell as they approached.

The woodsmen immediately scampered over the tree, lopping off limbs and topping it.

Samath put down his axe. "We will carry it back to our workshops soon. Will you show my eyes where your bow lives in this tree?"

"With a glad heart," Jack said as he swung his right leg over Windrider's neck and slid from his mount. He joined the carpenter at the foot of the log.

Launa and Kaul stayed on their mounts, she for a better view, he muttering, "If I get off, I will never get back on."

"Here is the hard heart of the tree." Jack tapped the center of the log. "It gives the bow power." He ran his finger along the outer ring. "Here is the gentle sap wood of the tree. It lets the bow bend. We split a large 'billet' "—Jack used the English word—"and then carve it down to the size of the bow we want."

Samath and the woodsmen around him nodded. As Jack remounted Windrider, the woodsmen turned to, hefting the log on their shoulders, while a young boy began a song. His high-pitched voice carried over their low grunts, giving a natural tempo to their labor.

Jack watched them go. "There will be hungry men tonight. Let us feed them."

They soon spotted their first herd, large red deer. They looked like Wyoming elk to Launa. Kaul pointed to them, but she shook her head.

"Let us hunt farther from Tall Oaks. These deer can be easily taken by those without horses."

They trotted on for an hour, passing up several herds. Launa decided they'd gone far enough as they approached a rise. "We will hunt in the next valley."

Which, of course, was empty. They had to cross a large prairie and another low ridge before they came upon a wide grassland with several herds. They paused long enough to string their bows, then rode slowly out onto the plain.

As they always did, they dismounted a half kilometer from the nearest herd and walked to within two hundred meters. Launa selected a medium-sized buck that was browsing somewhat apart from the rest. All three shot on her word.

Two arrows hit. The buck tried to run but dropped after several bounds.

"I missed," Kaul said, and his mouth hung open.

Launa suppressed a laugh. "Jack, get the horses. I'll tell Kaul what he's got to do different."

For the next several minutes, she explained the effect of wind and elevation on long-range shooting. Somehow she avoided mentioning gravity. Kaul used the deer carcass as a target. By the time Jack got back, there were four arrows in the dirt and a third arrow in the deer.

Kaul scratched his beard. "It will not be easy to use your bow. A hunter's eye will have to see the prey in a new way."

"Will you help me load the deer?" Jack asked.

As they walked to the deer, Kaul muttered softly. Jack signaled Launa to stand back a moment when they got there. Kaul knelt, touched the carcass, and spoke gently to it. It began to dawn on Launa just how heavy a thing it was for these people to take a life—any life, even an animal's. *How do you make people like Kaul into soldiers?*

Kaul didn't butcher the deer here. There was a sacred reason why everything went into the stew. In a few minutes, the deer was lashed to a packhorse and they were walking toward a second herd. This time an eight-point buck had three arrows in it when it looked up, then collapsed with a bellow.

The third deer was not so cooperative. Jack was pretty sure there were two arrows in it, but it took off for points unknown without a backward glance, never missing a bound.

They collected the arrow that missed and found blood.

"Now we track it," Jack said.

"Can't let a long arrow get away from us," Launa agreed.

Kaul seemed to take it as a matter of course that you did not leave a wounded animal to die alone.

The trail led across a stream and another stretch of grassland. Jack spotted a lone deer stumbling toward a tree line and they trotted after it.

The deer went down, and Launa and Jack galloped for it, Kaul trailing. It was their deer; two long arrows stuck from its hide. Kaul had just knelt when Launa lost interest in praying.

From somewhere came the pounding of horses' hooves. Several horses. Riding fast. Launa glanced around. The plain was empty. Jack pointed off to the right. The trees edged out onto the prairie not fifty meters from them. Dust rose on the other side of those trees.

Kaul stood. "What is it?"

"Horsemen," Launa answered.

"Shall we run for it?" Jack asked, slipping into English.

"Kaul can't outrun a horseman," Launa answered in the same language.

"Make for the trees?"

"Not enough time." Launa laid five arrows out in front of her. Jack took station to Launa's right and did the same.

Kaul's eyes went from one to the other. Launa felt them measuring her soul. What they did here would be reported to Lasa. *But only if we live first.*

"May I have arrows, too?" the speaker asked.

Launa pulled a handful from her quiver. Kaul spread four out in front of him and put another to his bow.

The horses were getting close. Launa expected to have a target any moment. Fifty meters to the trees. *Damn. I'm losing all the good of the longbow. That's just the way it goes, trooper.* She pulled an arrow back to her ear and waited.

A rider came in view. A second and third were right behind him. The wind was light. Launa aimed point-blank.

"Check fire! Check fire," Jack shouted.

"It is my old friend Taelon," Kaul shouted at the same moment. He relaxed his bow and stood. "Wise hunter, why do you ride horses?"

Launa's head swam as Tuam brought her horse to a halt before her. *I almost killed the only friends I've got here! Wasn't anything what she thought it was? Didn't things ever slow down around here?*

Taelon raised a hand in greeting. "I ride to the assembly of Tall Oaks. My brother was consort to a woman of River Bend. Does he live?"

TWENTY-NINE

JACK RODE BESIDE two men he hardly knew, but already called friends. Kaul and Taelon rode in silence, no words for how close one had come to killing the other or for what lay ahead.

Jack remembered quiet rides with his grandfather. At first, Jack had felt ignored when the Apache said nothing to him. Later he'd come to know that Grandfather was there for him, but also for the grass, the hills, the ancients who had ridden here before. Jack had the same feeling with these two. Their lack of words was not a wall, but a door that opened to all things and all time. And Jack was here to keep that door open.

Still, Jack wondered what the hunter and his woman would add to the babble at Tall Oaks.

The first stop was an urgent one. Kaul led his friend straight to the survivors. Taelon eyed each one, then shook his head. "Do any of you know of my brother, Hath, who took a consort from among you, or his children?"

"He went out to greet the horseriders." Antia's words were dry as summer grass. "I did not see him after that."

Taelon rubbed his eyes with fists. "Let us go to the Sanctuary of the Goddess, Kaul. I have words to speak."

Tuam slid from her horse to hug her man. For a long moment, the hunter stood, surrounded by his woman's arms,

out looking so alone. Then he turned his face to Jack. In a
voice so calm Taelon might have been talking about fishing,
he said, "There were dead horsemen in the valley where we
met."

Taken aback, Jack hesitated for a moment before nodding.

"Did they speak with you?"

"I do not speak their words," Jack answered.

"Yet five of them died."

Jack raised an eyebrow to Launa. *You're in charge of
diplomacy. How do you want to handle this?*

"Ten died." She cut her words from hard rock.

Taelon's eyes peered hard into Launa's. Jack waited for
the hunter to shout "murderers," knowing that would pronounce the end of their mission. How could he and Launa
explain to the fence-sitters the right of self-defense? Worse
yet, what words were there for that fine line between horsemen who killed, and he and Launa, who rode horses—and
killed?

But Taelon only grunted and turned toward the longhouse. There, it took only a moment to turn the deer over to
the cooks.

Word of Taelon's arrival must have swept through the
town, because elder women and men were walking in from
every direction. When Jack entered the sanctuary at Kaul's
elbow, the place was already packed. Women filled the
benches, then sat on the riser at the others' feet. Men were
wall to wall behind Kaul and edging into the women's half.
The youths were quiet in the back.

Lasa drew Tuam and Launa to her side with graceful signals; then she faced Taelon. "The sorrow of your heart for
your brother is ours. We mourn with you."

"If something truly has happened at River Bend," a
woman added as Lasa sat down.

That opened the floodgates. Everything that had been said
the day before was repeated, restated, rephrased, and re-
hashed. Jack wondered how long they could beat a dead
horse before it stank to high heaven. But these people
seemed in love with the sound of their own voices. The

noise went on for over an hour while Taelon sat, eyes peering intently at the floor. The man said he had something to say. Jack waited for him to say it.

Finally, the hunter stood, and the room fell silent as he did. He stroked his beard, letting the silence lengthen. Then he began.

> *"When I was a young man,*
> *I wanted to see many things.*
> *I wanted to hear many songs.*
> *I wanted to walk many paths.*
> *With Hath, our brother, we wandered far to the north,*
> *to the mountains that almost touch the sky.*
> *With Hath, our brother, we wandered far to the rising sun.*
> *We saw men with four legs,*
> *who fled across the grass like deer.*
> *Beside their fire, we saw four-legged men*
> *become a horse, and a man.*
> *For a winter, I hunted deer and lions with the horsemen.*
> *For a winter, I rode where the horsemen rode."*

Now Jack knew why Taelon had taken so quickly to their gift horse. The story told a lot about the hunter, and the horsemen. But that must have been fifteen, twenty years ago.

Taelon looked around at his listeners. "I have sung often that song of my youth. I have not sung of all we shared."

The hunter faced Lasa squarely. "I saw men say hot words. There was no woman among them who Spoke for the Goddess. Their hot words flowed until one buried his knife in the other's heart."

The sharp intake of breath around the room was the only noise. Jack's eyes found Launa's. *They've got to listen now.*

"I saw this many times in the seasons I shared with the horsemen. And I saw something stranger. Many horsemen rode to the hunt, but it was not deer or fish they hunted. It was other horsemen. On a spring day, I saw men hunt men, and kill them with bow, and lance, and knife."

The hunter's eyes dropped. Kaul patted his leg. "You never told me, old friend."

"Would you have believed me?"

Kaul seemed to have no answer; Taelon went on. "Last spring when the Hunting People gathered as is our custom, there were strange words. The families toward the dawn told of bands of hunters going forth, but none coming back. Two families told this story. In the hunt it happens that the Goddess may take a hunter. It may even be that a flood sweeps away an entire hunting band. But two bands in one season, with no one to come back and sing their song?" Taelon shook his head slowly.

"My heart is greatly troubled. I have seen the horsemen hunt horsemen. Now my heart fears the horsemen hunt the People."

Taelon turned slowly, measuring every person in the room. Some stared back; many looked away. The hunter sat down.

And Kaul whispered in Jack's ear, "Men who hunt men. Jack who rides a horse from where the sun sets, have you too heard of men who hunt men?"

Jack nodded.

"Are you a hunter of men?" The words were sharp.

Jack glanced at Launa. *Why aren't you getting the hard questions?* But Lasa sat her chair, listening to the talk bubble in the wake of Taelon's words, saying nothing to Launa and getting nothing in return. Kaul was asking the hard questions, and Jack would have to give answers just as hard.

"I hunt the hunters of men."

Kaul's body swayed as he tested Jack's words. "Is there a difference between men who hunt men and those who hunt such men?"

Jack took a deep breath; how would Brent answer? "A wolf hunts goats. A man hunts the wolf. Is there a difference?"

Kaul ran his hand along the smooth wood of his staff. "Yes. There is a difference."

With a grim frown, the speaker stood; talk slowly ceased. Jack breathed a prayer of thanks to two old scholars who insisted he and Launa learn all they could about Neolithic farmers.

Kaul took several breaths as the silence thickened. When

he spoke, his words were a whisper. "Oh Lady, our heart is saddened by the words we have heard. But more, our heart is saddened because we see the way of the Goddess shrouded with fog and the People do not know which way to walk. The story Antia brings is frightening, and some would have us protect our people as a shepherd does the flocks." He looked to Masin, who solemnly nodded.

"Others wonder at the story Antia brings to our ears. How could it be that people could wander so far from the way of the Goddess?" He bowed toward Bellda, who nodded in her turn.

"Some wonder how such a story could be true. Now, Taelon shares words that are very hard to hear." Kaul rested a hand on his friend's shoulder.

"I say we should see with our own eyes. Antia speaks to us with the scars on her body. Let eyes of our people look upon what she has seen and bring their given words to us. It is hard for our heart to hear such words. If they too speak such difficult words, then maybe some of the fog that confuses our eyes today will be lifted and we may see a path for our feet."

Jack's eyes widened. He'd heard this before. From an Army contract trainer giving them The Word on the latest and greatest way to make good decisions. First let the troops dialogue, get their raw opinions and feelings out, then gather more facts, examining them until you have agreement. That will be a decision everyone will support. The Army had taught Jack this, but he'd never seen a general actually do it. Here was Kaul, who couldn't read or write, going from dialogue to fact finding, using the best management techniques of the twenty-first century. *Judith said they weren't dumb.*

Taelon stood. "I would take my strong spear and see."

Lasa frowned. "Oh Speaker for the Bull, would you have us abandon our homes and crops to walk away to River Bend?"

"No, oh Lady, but our daughter's eyes could go for us."

Brege stood from among the serving youth. There was only a hint of tremble in her voice. "Mother, I would go and take my consort Merik at my side." A young man joined her.

Tuam stood up. "Taelon and I will go for our people."

Jack got to his feet. He didn't much like going back to Indian country with four green recruits, but nothing good would come if the rookies got picked off before they reported back. On the dais, Launa spoke as she too stood. "We will go with the people to the town that is no more."

Lasa seemed startled. "You have already seen. There is no need for you to go back."

"Yes, oh Lady, there is. Taelon spoke of hunters that did not return. It is in my heart to stand between your daughter and the horsemen. When she returns, all may see what now is hidden."

Lasa's glance went from Launa to Jack and settled on Kaul.

The shepherd cleared his throat. "When wolves stalk our sheep, we send the best hunters after them. Many young also go, but it is better for the wiser ones to meet the wolves for the kill. If not, the young may be surprised and hurt." Kaul rested his hand on Jack's shoulder. Jack felt the full weight of the burden he and Launa would carry for this man.

"My heart tells me Launa and Jack are wise in ways to guide people away from those who hunt them. Let them show Brege these ways. Let them take our daughter there and back unharmed."

Now Lasa stood and opened her arms to the assembly. "May the Goddess go with you, and may the dreams of those who await your return show us a path for our feet."

Jack accepted the blessing, but he was more interested in what Launa had in mind. She and Tuam headed like an arrow for the back of the room and Brege. Kaul, Taelon, and Jack attached themselves to the women as they went by. Lasa got hung up with several women at the head of the room.

"How soon do you want to leave?" Jack asked Launa before they got to the waiting youths.

"Soon," she shot back. "But not until I have some idea of what skills this crew has. I want this team as ready for a fight as I can make them. God only knows what's out there."

Jack could agree with her on that.

THIRTY

TYMAN, STRONG ARM of the Swift Arrow Band, sat his mount. He had spent most of a double hand of days on this or another of his horses. He would spend another hand of days there too. As asked, Tyman had ridden the boundaries with the weak woman Arakk—no Mighty Man he.

Arakk had fawned over Shokin, Mighty Man of the Stalwart Shield Clan, offering him soft words when fermented mares' milk was what the man wanted. Tyman made sure Shokin had much of that. He would long find Tyman's name easy on his lips. That was good.

Now, his face set as hard as the flat side of a dagger, Tyman waited as Arakk rode toward him. It would not be wise to let Arakk know the thoughts of his heart.

"You would still ride to the west?" Arakk asked as his horse settled in beside Tyman's own.

"Yes. My youngest son does not stand beside any of the Clan's fires. Neither do any who took the slaves for water that morning. That is one of the strange winds that blows the grass the wrong way."

Arakk grunted; Tyman did not need to remind him of Perto and the two hands of warriors who had not returned from their scout to the west. "How many lances will you take?"

Tyman raised his hand, opened and closed it four times.

and waited for Arakk to frown. Tyman was taking one warrior out of every five that rode with the Stormy Mountain Clan.

Instead, Arakk nodded. "Ride well, Strong Man of the Swift Arrow Band. Use the eyes of an eagle to see all there is to see so the Stormy Mountain Clan may strike in the spring like lightning from the Wide Sky." Then the Mighty Man kicked his horse and rode to join his own band.

Now Tyman could smile. *Ride far from me, weak woman.* Tyman had ridden the boundaries as he had been asked. He knew where his horses were supposed to graze this winter. He had seen it. It was too small. There was not enough grass there for his mares to grow fat and give him strong ponies in the spring. He would take more—to the west.

The women who strutted about their wooden tents could not stop a real man from taking what was his. Knife cuts, a few knife cuts were all warriors had to show for taking more heads than a man could count, and more slaves, too. What manner of two-legged rabbits were these animals who scratched in the dirt?

Tyman laughed. He would use eagle eyes to find the next nest of these weaklings. But when the weak woman of the Stormy Mountain Clan laid eyes on it, the totem of the Mighty Man of the Swift Arrow Band would be there. This Tyman swore. This Tyman would make so.

He called for his warriors. They rode swiftly to his side.

"We go," Tyman shouted.

They rode to the west.

THIRTY-ONE

THE HARSH RAT·A·TAT of a bird brought Launa awake well before dawn. Her heart pounded from the vague residue of a dream. She'd been lost, or chased, or facing the cold, unblinking eyes of the Colonel. Or was it Judith wearing her father's uniform? *God, trying to keep both of them happy is going to drive me around the bend.* One thing was sure; both of them would be pissed if she blew this next operation.

The morning was cool enough that Launa kept the blanket wrapped around her as she headed for the latrine. She let her mind rove over the basics: mission, economy of force, concentration, security for you, surprise for them. She weighed those basics against her six lonely people, and they didn't count for much. Patton had his Third Army; she had a squad—four of whom didn't know what they were up against.

Keep fretting like that and you'll be dead before you start. What would Major Henderson or any of your instructors say?

"Put on your game face and soldier," Launa answered aloud. Every minute of every day of her life, she'd been surrounded by soldiers. She could walk their walk, talk their talk. It was time to put it all on the line. It would take everything she knew to find a safe way through the deadly field problem ahead.

With shoulders back and a cadence to her step, Launa went to meet the day. The good feelings from her little pep talk lasted about fifteen seconds after her team joined up.

They were basically a good group. Brege and her consort could use a sling as well as a shepherd's staff. If there was anything Taelon couldn't do with a bow, it hadn't been invented by the twenty-first century, and he had some idea of using his spear for a quarterstaff too. Tuam had been using her sling to bring down squirrels and rabbits since she could walk. And there was plenty of enthusiasm for weapons drill. Some people might doubt Antia's word; the people headed for River Bend did not.

The problem wasn't basic weapons skills. It was doctrine.

"Brege, how fast can you sling?"

"Very fast." The young woman swung the leather thong until it hummed.

"No, no." Launa tried again. "How many stones can you sling at that tree fast?"

"I run fast," the confused woman said. "How do I throw the rock faster?"

Launa buried her face in her hands. How do you explain rate of fire to people who don't know how long a minute is? "Jack, get out there."

"By the target?"

Might not be a bad idea. "No. Over that way." Launa sent Jack running in the opposite direction. "Now, Brege, how often can you hit the target before Jack can reach you?"

"Ah, now my heart sees." Taelon nodded. "It is as if a bull charged you. If you have many arrows and rocks, you want to hit it many times. Kill it before it can touch you. I have faced a bull with my spear. I never thought to shoot at it."

"Yes," Launa said. "The deer you shoot once. When men hunt you, you shoot many times, as quickly as you can." With a dawning grasp of firepower, the slingers worked out with Launa while Jack took Taelon out to learn the fine points of long-range archery. That cost them the rest of the day.

Launa spent another sleepless night going over every option she could think of. There weren't that many, but that didn't keep her mind from spinning. *We're giving the team basic weapons skills, teaching them something about security on the march. Lasa would see that their minimum logistical needs were met. What am I forgetting?* Launa could think of nothing.

Next morning, she put her team through P.T. with Antia's recruits. The count was up to forty-five, but Launa wasn't sure any of the ones who'd been there the first day were still with them. Before starting exercises, Launa took a few minutes to organize the defense force into four squads of eleven each. Cleo and Soren got command of two. Bomel and a determined-looking woman from Tall Oaks, Kamini, took the others.

Taelon and Tuam took to the P.T. with a laugh. Brege and her consort Merik were not in as good shape as the older hunters.

"I thought we were going to ride to River Bend," Merik said between gasps.

"Have you ever ridden a horse?" Taelon asked.

"No."

"You may wish you could walk."

Taelon's humor drew smiles from people too low on oxygen to spare any for laughter.

After breakfast, it was time to introduce the team to the quarterstaff. "A pole is a very good way to stop a man with a knife from putting it in your belly," Launa began.

Taelon's eyes grew narrow. "There was a pole beside a dead horseman in the valley where I found you."

Launa let her face go slack, neither confirming or denying. The next move was Taelon's. What did he want?

"If a man comes at me with a knife, I would like to use a pole to keep him from scratching my belly," Taelon growled.

It seemed to Launa that everyone was especially attentive that morning.

In the afternoon, Launa got her first surprise of the mission. While Taelon and Jack trained the rest to ride, she headed into Tall Oaks to tie up the remaining loose ends. Antia fell in step beside her.

"I too will go with you to River Bend."

Launa came to an abrupt halt. So did the freed slave. For a long moment they eyed each other. Launa measured the benefits against the cost of another trooper on this recon. Antia was as solid in her decision as a granite boulder.

"Tall Oaks has chosen who will see with its eyes, speak with its tongue," Launa finally said.

Antia gave a brief nod. "I go to gather my mother's bones and present them to the Goddess. That is a daughter's duty."

Launa glanced to where the survivors trained with pugil-sticks. "Do not all of them have the same duty?"

"We have talked among ourselves. What we do here is good, but one of us must do a duty for all. She who Spoke for the Goddess in River Bend must be cared for as is our custom."

Launa knew too little to question custom, but the darkness behind Antia's eyes hinted at something more. *What are you not telling me?* Whatever it was, it hadn't been taught at the Point. Launa shrugged. "You will ride with us."

Once in town, Launa went through the logistics quickly. Her scout force would take only the horses they rode. Spare mounts would do them no good in a running fight against men born to a horse. If worse came to worst, they'd hole up in the woods and try to outsmart the bastards. The rest of the horses would be cared for by the growing defense forces of Tall Oaks.

Lasa promised dried food; hunting would not be necessary. Big Red would carry supplies. Both of the dogs had been pregnant when they came through time. Mist was heavy with her pups and would stay behind, but Frieda still looked able to travel. The dog would be their night security. Launa advised the speakers that the scouts would depart at dawn the next day.

Supper was subdued. Songs were limited to a few hymns to the goddess for guidance. Launa wasn't too sure anybody, God or goddess, knew what was going on here.

Kaul watched his daughter give one last wave as she and her six companions disappeared among the trees beside the river. Lasa's final "Go with the Goddess" still rang in his ears. He was sending their daughter to find the way of the Goddess for all of Tall Oaks. He might also be sending her to a terrible death.

Kaul knew what it was to face death. He had hunted wolves, lions, and bears to keep the flocks of Tall Oaks safe. He had found a lion only an eye blink before it would have leaped on a shepherd boy. Kaul had fought so the boy could live. Yes, Kaul knew death, but he had faced it himself, not sent his daughter in his stead. He shivered.

Beside him, Lasa started. "Do you See something?"

She knew he had the Sight; he must not worry her so. "No, no. It is cool this morning."

"It is not so cool that you would put something on, my goat." She stroked his neck. Despite the concerns of the going, he still felt the warm glow from their waking play this morning. *Would it be a good portent from the Goddess if we played here, now, before the People? It would be bad if we played and I failed the Bull.*

He kissed her cheek. "My sleep has been empty of dreams since these strangers came. I See nothing. And you, love, does the Goddess whisper anything?"

Lasa shook her head. "I hear nothing, and fear the silence is itself a word from the Goddess."

"Dreamless sleep is dreamless sleep, and silence is silence. Bellda told you that many springs ago."

"And now she tells me other things."

"Enough. Let us go apart for a while, soak in the warm waters from the womb of the Goddess, and wait upon Her."

"Yes!" Lasa yelped like a little girl. "You tell Bomel to look after his sisters for tonight. I will get a sack of food. The People will not fester if they must hold their little arguments for a day or two more. Let us, go."

Lasa almost skipped as she rushed toward town. Kaul smiled, remembering the young girl he had grown up with, flighty as a tiny bird until the heavy burden of Speaking the Words of the Goddess fell on her shoulders. It gladdened his heart, from time to time, to make her a bird once more

• • • •

Great, Launa thought. By the time she was sixteen, she'd memorized The Book for infantry, armor, special forces, and artillery operations. So here she was, leading a squad of horse troopers armed with slings and bows. Still, she'd go by The Book as much as she could. Her people were as well trained as she could make them, and they would train more.

She set her course across the steppe, direct for River Bend. The pace she set was as fast as her troops' rear ends would permit: one hour riding, half an hour walking, a five-minute break, then repeat the cycle. Without a watch, that wasn't as easy as it sounded. She'd read somewhere that she could throw in a half-hour run, but she didn't want to wear her troops out. *Conserve your forces.* She even spread the team out in line abreast to keep them out of each other's dust.

The men settled down together on the left, separated from the women by Big Red and the supplies. Taelon, Merik, and Jack talked and laughed among themselves—more of that male bonding that left Launa envious. Antia was no help; she rode alone about a stone's throw out on Launa's right flank. Resigned to letting her troops walk their own way, Launa waited for Brege or Tuam to start a conversation, waited to see what women here talked about when time was heavy, but both women rode in silence.

During the first walk, Brege came up beside Launa. "You and Jack are hard, like an arrowhead."

This was not what Launa had expected for trail chatter. She doubted talk like this would lead to friendly cama-raderie. *It is mission oriented,* she reminded herself. "Yes," Launa answered.

The young woman shook her head. "My heart cannot see the People hard as flint."

"When Taelon hunts a bear or wolves," Tuam said, "he takes the hardest point and straightest arrow and spear. When sharp teeth seek your throat, you do not want your spear to break."

"But what will become of the People if they become hard?"

That was a good question, and probably critical to the survival of these people. Launa thought she saw an alternative. "Maybe all will not have to walk the same way. If enough become hard and stand between the horsemen and Tall Oaks, the rest of the people can live as they do."

Brege was shaking her head even before Launa finished. "The People have always walked together. What you say would make us two people. That could not be the way of the Goddess."

Well, you better come up with something, Launa wanted to snap, even as she found herself agreeing. Oneness was the heart of this society. Could it survive with a warrior class? Launa didn't know, she just wanted an answer, and she wanted it now.

Take a deep breath and let these people find their own way, Launa heard Judith say. Give them time.

Time is something we don't have enough of, the commander in Launa shot back.

The women walked for a long time in silence. When Launa figured a half hour had passed, she hollered, "Let's ride."

As Tuam mounted, she turned to Brege. "The Badger People are of the People. We follow the path of hunting, not farming."

Brege settled herself on her horse. "Kaul hunts, and the Badger People have helped us get the seed in the fields. We share your songs and dances. We are the People."

As the women rode on, Launa prayed they were measuring their souls, hunting for that part, and that part alone, that made them whatever they meant by "the People." Launa didn't want them to give up any more than they had to for Tall Oaks' survival.

She pushed the troop forward, huddling under Maria's hat through the heat of the day. Just a glance at the hat had given Marbon enough to go on. They had started sprouting in Tall Oaks by the next day. All the scouts wore them. Launa wondered what Maria would think, her hats sheltering seven people so they could hurry toward death.

Two or three hours before sundown, Launa called a halt. While Jack made camp, the rest turned to weapons practice.

Brege went at Tuam during staff drill with growing skill. But that didn't answer Launa's nagging doubt. If Brege knocked a knife from a horseman's hand, could she kill him before he picked it up again? There was no question about Antia. Even during practice, her eyes would fill with anger. Then it would take all of Launa's skill to keep her blows at bay, until, inevitably, Antia would make a mistake and Launa would bring her down.

"Skill, not strength, is the soldier's edge," Launa said, offering a hand up. Antia only grunted.

The next day followed on the first with one important change. The other women began talking among themselves.

Tuam started it. Half to herself, she reminisced about the day Hath was named consort and all of River Bend celebrated. With a glance to make sure Taelon was out of earshot, the two women headed down a long trail of family memories, some shared, some different. Launa listened, a cold part of herself putting it all under the heading of social intelligence, mission critical. Her brain had a pigeonhole for it, even as she bled loneliness into a large, empty part of herself.

Launa stayed silent not because to share would have been to talk about things six thousand years away; she had nothing to say. She'd never been at uncles' weddings or a cousin's birth. Was it just part of growing up inside The Fortress, or was it another wall that the Colonel and his lady built around themselves? Launa had no answer.

Launa listened to the women talk about a place she'd never been—home. She hardly knew such places existed, but as the morning passed, Launa found herself desperately hungry for one.

They paused at midday in the cool shade beside a brook to let their horses drink. Launa tried to swallow her loneliness with the water. Taelon's soft whistle brought her head around. "Jack, look upon this."

The look on the hunter's face said more than his words.

Jack grabbed his bow before answering Taelon's signal. Around Launa, others reached for their spears and slings.

Launa strung her bow quickly, and, with an arrow nocked, headed for where Taelon and Jack stooped, heads together.

The hunter pointed at a half dozen hoofprints in the dark soil beside a bush. "These prints are not deer. They are horses, many horses."

Launa's head swiveled as she searched the glen. *Have I led my troops into an ambush?* She saw no threat; she did see horse droppings.

Jack stirred one with a stick. "Two, maybe three days old."

Taelon nodded agreement.

"How many?" Launa kept her voice low.

Jack glanced around. "Folks, let us spread out and see how far this goes."

Tuam and Merik obeyed, and were soon calling out as they spotted signs. Brege, no better at tracking than Launa, joined her in a continuous scan of their surroundings, searching the woods around them, the steppe before and behind, for any sign of a forming attack.

When the new reports of tracks slowed down, Launa again tossed Jack the question she'd been biting back. "How many?"

Taelon and Jack put their heads together. "Many hands of hands," the hunter said.

"Fifty to a hundred," Jack answered.

"Can't you get more specific?" Launa let her tension bite.

Jack gave her a shrug for an answer.

"Think there are more?"

Jack made a worried three-sixty. "When they took the horses out of River Bend, they broke them up into seven or eight smaller herds about this size. I think we ought to split up, some of us go up and the others downstream. See if we can find any more places where they crossed."

"I'll take Taelon and Tuam, and Antia. Meet us back here in about an hour." Launa's order was quick, economical, unambiguous—just like they taught her at the Point.

Jack waved as his three took off. Launa took hers in the opposite direction. Taelon took the lead, eyes on the ground.

Antia trailed them, her head swiveling nervously, trying to see everywhere at once.

"Do not fear," Launa called back to her. "Look for a cloud of dust. We will see the horsemen a long way off." Antia's anxious search seemed to slow.

Tuam dropped back to ride beside Launa. "What does this mean?" she asked softly.

Launa kept her eyes moving, meticulously scanning their environs, keeping the question at arm's length even as she answered it. "There are horsemen between us and Tall Oaks. How many, we do not know. If there is only one crossing, then a band has gone to see Tall Oaks even as we go to see River Bend. That is bad. If we find where more horses crossed, there are many on their way to hunt Tall Oaks as they did River Bend. That is very bad."

Tuam shaded her eyes and went back to studying the ground for tracks.

With Taelon and Tuam's eyes on the ground, Launa rode heads up, searching for any sign of dust, any threat. But in her heart she knew she had to look elsewhere as well.

This morning, she'd listened to the women talk about a way of life that Launa would risk her neck to save. Now she'd watched that way of life jump to its own defense. Taelon had spotted the threat with the eyes of a Neolithic hunter. Her team had hardly needed an order; each one of them knew what had to be done. In the moment of threat, they jelled as a fighting force.

All her worry, all her sleepless nights had not added one damn thing when the alarm went off. These people weren't the Colonel's troops and they did not need a hard-nosed bastard like him to lead them. Judith had been right. It was time to find a new way—and Lasa was probably the best example she could find.

They had found no more evidence of horse crossings when Launa felt a half hour was up. They raced back as fast as Tuam and Antia could manage.

With Brege trailing, Jack returned a short while later. "Nothing to report," he shouted as soon as they were within earshot.

Reining Windrider in beside Launa, Jack launched into an assessment. "Assuming each rider has two or three remounts, this looks like a small recon."

Launa didn't want to assume anything, but she couldn't argue with the basic estimate. "I want to backtrack their trail, find a camp."

"Shouldn't we return to Tall Oaks?" Out of breath, Brege had finally caught up. Her eyes flickered back to the west, toward home. A worried hand tugged at her ponytail.

Maybe there was a reason for never calling any place home. Maybe the Colonel wasn't so dumb after all.

Jack raised an eyebrow that had no advice in it. The call was hers.

Launa cycled quickly through what she knew. It was damn little. This force was nowhere near as big as the one that butchered River Bend. It was probably another recon team, reinforced after the one she and Jack ran into failed to return. It probably would not attack Tall Oaks on its own.

Launa winced at the "probablys." After the lack of opposition at River Bend, what were the odds some ambitious bastard might charge right in without support?

Damn! I should talk this through, let the team make the decision together. That's what Lasa and Judith would do.

This is a combat situation, Lieutenant. You start asking troops what they want to do in the face of the enemy and you'll have the longhouse all over again. Give them their orders.

That's the old way of doing things. We need something better. Old way or not, Launa would not turn a decision as important at this over to people who hardly understood the problem and had no idea of the tactical situation. This was her call to make. *Right, but will this bunch obey?*

You're wasting time dithering again, she could hear the Colonel say. *Let women tend to their knitting. Command, soldier, command.*

Launa rested a hand on Brege's shoulder. "I do not think they will attack Tall Oaks. They are too few. Lasa and Kaul sent us to see what we could and tell them. We must go."

Brege still looked toward home, her teeth gnawing her

lower lip. In the trembling of her neck and belly, Launa saw the price you pay for having one special place. *That's a price I can't afford today.*

Launa glanced around. The scouts stood, rooted. You've got your orders, Launa wanted to snap, now move. That's how they did it in the U.S. Army. But Launa commanded farmers and hunters raised where no one could tell another the path for her feet. She waited to see if her command would be countermanded.

Jack broke the tableau. As he turned for his mount, Taelon did too. Antia gave the shrug of one who had nothing left to lose and went for her horse. Tuam put a gentle hand to Brege's elbow. The townswoman shivered and let the woodswoman lead her. Beside her horse, Brege stooped to pick up several stones. She added them to her pouch, then mounted.

THIRTY-TWO

KAUL SOAKED IN the warm water as he rubbed the taut muscles of Lasa's back; she moaned softly. Never in all the years he had Spoken for the Bull had he found Lasa's back so tight with worry.

Kaul concentrated on each muscle as he worked it with his fingers. For himself, he emptied his mind, breathing slowly, measuring each breath against his own heart. Two beats, breathe in, *Dear Goddess.* Breathe out, four beats, *Show us a path.*

Lasa breathed with him. He knew from many springs with her that she breathed the same prayer.

The muscle knots loosened; Lasa's head lolled on her neck. It was time. Gently, so as not to bring her spirit back from where it walked, Kaul carried her to the bed of moss he had made. Laying her out, he covered her damp nakedness with a blanket. Himself he left uncovered. He sat, staring at the Speaker for the Goddess until his eyes lost their focus and his soul began its wandering. He journeyed forth, searching for a path the People might walk through this flood that threatened to wash them from the land of their mothers and fathers.

Tyman, Strong Arm of the Swift Arrow Band, stood with his arms folded across his chest, staring down at the abomination.

Like the other place, tents of wood and mud hid the animals. Beside Tyman, Givod stood, old eyes squinting. Alkon, who led the second double hand of warriors, joined them.

"The warriors await your command."

"Good." Tyman grinned. "Tell them to mount. We will ride among these animals and seize this herd for our slaves."

Givod's head turned quickly to face the Strong Arm. "Arakk sent us to see and bring words to him."

"And why should I share the hunt with him? At the other place, we brought many lances. There was no fight. Four hands of Swift Arrow warriors are strong enough to seize these rabbits. See, they are already out for the slaughter."

Givod and Alkon looked where Tyman pointed. Three double hands of people stood in rows. Givod shook his head. "Those do not look like the animals that came out to meet us at the other place. Look, there are knives in the hands of one line. The others face them with sticks."

"A stick against a knife." Alkon's voice dripped the sarcasm of one whose hand rested proudly on a long blade.

But his brows lowered as they watched the knife and stick people struggle, as in a fight. In a matter of heartbeats, the stick-wielders stood victorious over the knife-holders.

"And there is more." Before Tyman or Alkon could react to the first strange sight, Givod pointed to where four hands of people stood with slings hurling rocks at bundles of grass.

"Stones. What fear have warriors of pebbles?" Tyman snorted, but Alkon did not look so confident as he had.

Givod pointed again. "What is that?" More people came from the town. The two in front carried bows; others carried axes. "These are not the rabbits we slaughtered at the other place. What killed the four warriors of the water-gatherers, and where are those ten slaves? We must think on these things."

"We will make camp for the night," Tyman growled. "These animals will still be here at tomorrow's dawn."

"Yes," Alkon agreed. "Let us make camp far away from here."

Cleo grinned; Samath was bringing the first of the new bows for those who followed after the soldiers. With him came the woodsmen of Tall Oaks, eager to see the work of their hands. Cleo counted many; Antia would be glad. *If they all walked after us, no horseman would live to ride the streets of Tall Oaks.* Cleo jogged from staff practice to see what the archers would do with the new longbow.

Kaul awoke as Lasa cried out softly in her sleep. He went to his consort, took her hand, stroked her shoulder, tried to ease her back into sleep. Any dream that disturbed her so was not the one he wanted her to awake from.

"Thank you," Lasa said. "How were your dreams?"

"Full of horses and people and beasts—and much darkness." Kaul shook his head. There had been something else: Jack and Launa flying through the air. *No need to share that with Lasa.* "I awake no wiser than when I lay down. And you, little bird?"

She smiled at the memory of her childhood name. "The same. I wandered in the dark, and what light I saw gleamed from the teeth of wolves that hunted me. I fled until I fell exhausted." She paused. "There was one wolf that said it would help me."

"Did you let it?"

"No, I ran."

"What happened?"

"I awoke when the wolves were tearing at my flesh."

"All of them? Even the one who would help you?"

Lasa shook her head. "I do not know."

Kaul held her in his arms. The power of the Bull rose in him; they often celebrated dreams by playing in each other's arms. Today's dream did not feel like one to celebrate.

A sound drew Kaul's ears. It was not the usual noise of the woods. Lasa looked up, eyes wide. Kaul put a finger to her lips, then at a crouch moved downstream. He heard men's voices, and animals—horses. Carefully, he crept toward them.

Footsteps froze Kaul. As they came nearer, he rolled beneath a bush. The sun was setting, the light slowly fading. Hardly breathing, Kaul watched a horseman come down the path. At the bush Kaul hid under, the horseman pulled aside his breechcloth and made water, aiming at the ground not two hand-lengths from Kaul's head. Droplets splattered on Kaul's face.

Last full moon, Kaul would have walked forth from Tall Oaks, eager to greet anyone, hunter, farmer, trader, horseman. As the shadows lengthened, Kaul kept silent while a man pissed in his face. *Who is the wolf that would tear the flesh from Lasa's bones? Would I rise to greet that very wolf?*

Kaul's heart trembled even as every muscle in his body strove not to twitch.

Tyman hitched his breechcloth closed, rested his hand on his knife hilt, and turned to face his warriors. *No. Not warriors. Women, women in long skirts. No true warrior would fear to bury a lance in those mud-walkers. If I could get my hands on one of those rabbits, I would show my warriors some guts as I pulled them from the sliced belly of that rabbit one handful at a time.*

Tyman could almost feel his knife driving deep into the stomach of one of those animals, slashing its flesh open for his hands to grab what he would take. He could see the eyes of the rabbit grow wide with terror as it felt its life being taken from it. He had done it again and again at the other place.

He scowled; how to put heart back into the warriors of the Swift Arrow? They were like him. They lived and breathed for the days they carved human flesh or took a worthy head. He would call on their warrior blood. They would ride after him.

Without Launa issuing a command, Jack and Taelon took point and began backtracking the horsemen. The two led the team straight across the steppe. It also wasn't necessary for Launa to order people to keep alert. Heads swiveled constantly, searching for black dots on the next hill, dust between them and the horizon. The approach to each treed stream became a gut-wrencher.

The trail was easy to follow. When you're the only bastard doing unto others, who needs security? Once a large herd of cattle obliterated all evidence of the horses, but Jack picked up the trail on the other side.

The sun was low when they found signs of a night's camp—three fires, enough for fifteen to twenty-five riders. Further searching turned up nothing. By mutual agreement they did not camp there, but pushed on a few more miles to the next creek.

Practice that evening was determined. Without a word from its CO, the detachment trained until there was no more light. They ate their meal with exhausted hands and tumbled into bedrolls. Now, even more than before, Launa was grateful that Frieda was there for night security. Everyone seemed to fall asleep in a moment. Everyone but Launa.

"You wonder if you did right to press on, don't you?" Jack had stepped away to water a tree; now he appeared out of the twilight to squat beside her.

This trip, Launa had laid her bedroll on the opposite side of the camp from Jack's. It seemed wise to have one of them at each flank; it also kept them at the proper distance. For a moment, Launa wanted to take his head off, vent the tensions of the day at him for questioning her authority. But Jack had supported her when she needed it—and she needed to talk to someone.

"Yes, but what else could I do? They probably are only scouts, unless we missed more tracks. They could have come and gone before we raced back. Then we'd have nothing to show. Kaul is right. We need eyewitnesses. I just hope I did right."

Launa did not know why she was babbling like this. She had the command. The Colonel would tell her that if Jack agreed with her, it didn't matter. And if he didn't, well, that didn't matter either, did it?

"I think you did right. Remember that talk we had outside River Bend about luck? We've done our best, now we wait and see." Jack stood up and went to his bedroll.

The next day started before dawn. Launa pushed her team quickly through P.T. and drill. It was still early when they rode out with heads up. They spent most of the day on or walking their horses. Evening was more drill and exhausted bedrolls. Even Launa was feeling the effects next morning. Still, she began the cycle again as soon as the morning birds woke her.

Late the next day, Launa faced the hill where she had watched the pillaging of River Bend. She signaled the dismount.

Launa looked each of her tiny troop in the eye, one by one. "For two days we have seen no horsemen. We ride horses, but the horsemen will kill us. The townspeople, if they live, will kill us as horsemen." Awareness of the danger of their situation took only a moment to dawn. Putting arrow to bow, she finished. "We go, but like a deer that sniffs the hunter on the wind."

Jack nocked an arrow, as did Taelon. Those with slings loaded stones. Stealthfully, they led their horses up observer hill, Jack in the front. At the copse, Taelon and Jack searched the dust for signs, but Antia's woeful band of survivors had left the ground too confused.

Jack and Taelon stooped low as they jogged to the observation post. The others trailed after them, except Launa and Antia. Launa held the horses, her eyes sweeping behind them, searching their rear. She had seen enough of River Bend. Beside her Antia fidgeted, eyes locked on the crest of the ridge, her hands slowly fraying the rope reins in her hand. Launa reached out to touch the woman, provide some human comfort. Antia batted her hand away. Both of them stared at the others as the scouts got their first look at River Bend.

The gentle wind ruffling the pine trees was the only sound until Brege broke the silence. "What is that black pile, there, near the beginning of the street?"

"Heads." Jack's answer cut her no slack. There were no more questions. "I don't think anything has changed since we left. Launa, you want to check?"

"Yes." Launa gulped, pulled Maria's hat down firm on her head, and handed all the reins to Antia. Taelon said something to Tuam. She nodded and slipped downhill, giving

Launa an ashen smile as she split the horse-holding duty
with Antia. Brege made space for Launa beside Jack.

Launa took two long breaths, calling up memories she
had buried deep. Half the houses were charred ruins. Bodies
strewn about were dark and shrunken. Crows fought over
them. Scattered goats grazed on what was left of the crop.
She looked downhill to where the shepherds had been murdered.

"Jack. The shepherds. The girl. Their bodies are gone!"

"Shit! I hadn't noticed." Jack's eyes quickly searched the
valley from end to end. "Somebody buried them. We got
friendlies out there."

"Friendlies that won't be very friendly," Launa added
sourly. She explained the development to the rest.

"Someone lives!" Antia dropped the horse ropes and
dashed for the crest. Launa had to trip her to get her head
down. Antia's hand went to her knife hilt.

"We do not know who is in the valley, and who will kill
us before we speak a word," Launa hissed.

The scouts spent the hour until sunset beneath the tree,
scanning the valley for any evidence of life. Tuam and
Launa took the horses back to the copse and brought back
dried fish and hard bread for supper.

Toward sunset, Merik nudged Launa. "Could that be
smoke?"

Launa squinted at the patch of hill he indicated, upstream
from the town. Jack nodded assent when she looked to him.

"Merik, you may have found our lost friends," Launa
said.

"Or he may have found the horsemen," Taelon added
darkly.

Jack returned his arrow to the quiver and drew his knife.
"We go to look at that camp, but not to be seen or heard.
Taelon, will you come after me?"

The hunter grinned at the challenge to his woodcraft, and
put his bow away. The two men looked almost eager; they
also had not waited for orders. *But what other order could
you give?*

The sun set behind them; the valley darkened. Launa gave

the others their marching orders. "Follow us, but stay back. If they hear a twig break under your foot, they may greet us with arrows rather than hugs."

"And if arrows fly and we run back to you, please do not shoot us," Jack pleaded with a wry grin. The scouts traded understanding smiles.

Antia shook her head vigorously. "I will walk in front with Jack and Taelon."

Launa sighed and nodded. Jack scowled in her direction.

"You try giving orders," Launa snapped in English, "where not even the goddess can tell people what to do."

"Yeah," Jack said with a shrug. "We'll see."

And they did. Before five minutes had gone by, even Antia admitted that Taelon and Jack glided through the shadowing woods. She clopped. Shamefaced, she stood against a tree as the others passed her.

It took a solid hour to approach the camp. Jack and Taelon led the way, Frieda ghosting ahead and around them. Launa trailed them. Merik's talents as a shepherd served him well. He led the rear guard; somewhere behind him Tuam, Brege, and Antia stretched back.

Whoever tended the fire did so wisely. As the forest settled into darkness, few sparks showed when the fire was doused, but the wood smoldered. The last hundred meters, Launa homed on the smoke.

Jack signaled contact; Launa waved Merik to ground. He passed the signal along. The forest grew silent as death. Slowly, Launa worked forward to where Jack stood rigid as a tree. He pointed to Taelon ahead, then farther. Launa saw nothing but solid brush. She waited. The wind carried smoke to her from the thicket. She stooped low to see piles of something on the ground.

A muffled cry broke the silence; one mound sat up. Another reached out to comfort. Nightmares made it hard to keep cover.

Jack held up a rock. He waved it until Taelon nodded, then tossed it downhill. The stone's crashing flight set creatures scurrying. In camp, small forms rolled out of beds to grab clubs and what looked like two bows. There were whispered consultations. Huddled forms moved uphill. The two bows moved down.

Taelon put a tree between himself and the bows. Jack and Launa did likewise. Taelon's voice rang through the forest. "Are you of River Bend?"

A well-aimed arrow hit the tree that sheltered Taelon. Launa watched a dim figure draw a knife. Ammunition was short.

"Who calls to River Bend?" It was a woman's voice, questioning them from uphill. Launa knew a woman should answer, but not one with a twenty-first-century accent.

"Brege, daughter of Lasa who Speaks for the Goddess in Tall Oaks, calls to her sisters from River Bend." The young woman's voice rang out proud as crystal.

"Why are you in dark woods so far from Tall Oaks?" The question now was low, nearer a whisper, but it carried.

"Antia, daughter of She who Spoke for the Goddess in River Bend, came to my mother and asked what we would do for her people. I am sent to see with my eyes the work of the horsemen." Brege's answer was as soft as the wind through the trees.

"Approach our fire, friends. See what lives of River Bend."

They waited while the trailing women wound their way through the trees. The downhill survivors warily kept to their positions. In the dim moonlight, Launa made out three women coming back downhill toward them. Six small children clung to skirts.

Brege and Antia went to them. Only after the women embraced tearfully did others relax from where trees hid them. In a minute, two dozen survivors gathered around the smoldering fire.

Moonlight showed dirty boys and girls, small children, an old woman clutching a walking stick. Launa thought maybe six or eight of them were of draft age; it was a pathetic band.

"I am Taelon who leads the People of the Badger in the deep forest. My brother lived among the People of River Bend. Who can tell me of Hath?" The softly spoken question was urgent.

A young man, his arrow still nocked, stepped forward. "I am Tomas, son of Hath. Your brother went out to greet the horsemen on the day of their coming." The boy's voice was a flat monotone; he spoke of his father as one would a stranger. "You will find the body you seek before our town. His head is somewhere in the pile."

Taelon settled cross-legged where he stood. Tuam was quickly by his side, sharing his quiet tears.

Now it was Antia who stood beside the smoking embers. "You know me. My mother Spoke for the Goddess in River Bend." Quickly she told her tale of capture, rape, and escape. "Tonight, in Tall Oaks, hands of hands of us learn to hunt those who hunted their people. Come, join us until not one drop of blood flows in a horseman's arm."

A murmur went through the camp.

"That is not our way," the old woman croaked.

"What way have we left?" Angry sparks flew in Tomas's words.

"Let us sleep on this." It was Amatha, the young woman who had answered for the survivors who took the middle ground, and most followed her lead. The children settled back in their beds of leaves and moss. Tomas, however, sat with the scouts. Frieda plopped down between Jack and Tomas and, to Launa's surprise, let Tomas scratch behind her ears.

"How did these escape the fate of so many?" Brege asked.

Tomas gave the empty shrug of one who lived but did not know why—and no longer cared. "Some were in the fields and made it to the woods. Some hid in the river. I was hunting. When I returned, the horsemen were a dust cloud in the distance." He glanced at Launa. "How do I learn to kill horsemen?"

"To kill men and to hunt the killers of men is different." Launa waited for the boy's reaction.

Tomas stroked Frieda; she yawned. "The horsemen are dead at the hands of both. Is that not so?"

Launa shook her head. "A man may kill one or two. A hand of soldiers may kill hands and hands and hands of killers."

Tomas's grin held no humor. "How do I become a soldier?"

"It is a labor of many seasons to learn the wisdom to seek
and kill the killers."

"Let me start now."

"Have you seen horsemen since the day they left?" She
changed to a more immediate issue.

"Four, maybe five suns ago, this many came." He spread
his fingers four times. "They searched the river. There was
much shouting from far downstream."

"Let us sleep now." Launa needed time to think.

The scouts settled in where they could find room, but
Launa's mind was racing too much to sleep. The intelligence
was solid; somewhere out there were twenty bandits. *It took
all the luck in the world to kill ten. How're you going to face
twenty?*

One thing was clear. Her mission was to get the scouts to
River Bend and back. Nothing else mattered. Launa glanced
around the encampment and gritted her teeth. *Concentrate
on the mission.* But during the night when one child or another cried out, Launa came awake fast. She had not gotten
much sleep when dawn colored the eastern sky.

THIRTY-THREE

IN THE MORNING, while the survivors got the fire going again, Jack brought the horses over the hill and staked them out near the camp. Taelon took his longbow and slipped away with Tomas to hunt. They quickly returned with a deer. Excitement brimmed in Tomas's eyes, but he kept his thoughts to himself.

The hungry survivors hardly browned the venison before they devoured it. When everyone was fed, Launa approached Amatha.

"It is a ten-day walk to Tall Oaks. Do you know the way?"

"I have been there when my father saw his brother." Tomas's words were still hollow.

"Lasa will welcome you there," Brege offered.

Amatha looked slowly around the circle of grubby children. "We will go there." Her voice broke. "We have no place else."

It took only a moment for them to gather their few things. Tomas took the lead while Amatha encouraged the stragglers.

Launa went to the next item on the checklist she'd put together during her sleepless night. "Jack, see if Frieda will go with Tomas. They may need her warnings more than we."

"Right. Besides, I'm not sure how she'll take to that charnel house down there. Let's keep her out of that."

Taelon fidgeted as he watched the tiny band straggle out of camp. "They have no food and only two arrows. It is a long walk for bellies so empty."

"Yes." Launa let the word hang there, half statement, half question—as Judith said to do, as Lasa did.

"I would hunt for them this morning. The boys are strong enough to carry two or three deer if I shoot them."

Behind the hunter, Tuam signaled at Launa. *Do not let my man find his brother before I can prepare him for burial.*

"Go with them," Launa said, then turned to Antia. "Will you also go?" For a moment, Launa almost thought she would.

"I came to honor my mother's bones," Antia said slowly. "I will do what I have come to do."

The soldier in Launa would have given much to avoid the grief that lay ahead of this young woman, but since no order she might give would be obeyed, she merely nodded.

And now it was time to go. Launa rotated her shoulders to throw off some of the tension as she gave her orders for the day. "Let us get our horses and weapons. We will not be helpless rabbits in this place of death."

The scouts mounted up and rode slowly out of the protective trees into the open pastures of River Bend. Launa kept her eyes roving, searching for any sign of movement, any cloud of dust. Jack did the same. There was no movement, no sound except the birds. The stench of death rode the wind. Before they entered the town they found bodies, running people who had died with lances in their backs. Heads were missing.

The horses grew skittish at the stench; Launa ordered the dismount. They led their mounts into the ruins.

A body sprawled half outside a burned house. Half burned. Headless. Beside Launa, Antia stiffened. Tuam and Brege went pale.

A mother's body covered her child protectively. She had failed. Both were headless. A young man had died defending the door to his home. In its burned ruin, Launa saw the body of his beloved, sprawled on what was left of a bed.

How long had it taken her to die? Launa would not let her stomach revolt. She willed it to a cold, solid lump of hate.

She remembered the tight voice of Major Henderson. He wore the blue badge—Combat Infantryman. He had put into words the changings that make a human being into his country's professional killer. Launa had listened earnestly, tried to grasp the lesson. Now she experienced it. *She* was changing. Her eyes saw, but she no longer felt. It was better that way.

It was better that way when they entered the central plaza. Horsemen had made a bonfire here; burnt wood mixed with tiny skulls. Vomiting and choking, Brege, Tuam, and Merik fell to their knees, emptied their stomachs, then shook with dry heaves when there was nothing more to come up. Antia stood like a statue, eyes lost in the pit.

Launa too stared hard at the cold fire. She took it into her heart, hammered it, forged it into a weapon—a needle-sharp spear point. The two soldiers waited for the others to rise.

"How can you stand there? Do you feel nothing?" Brege gagged. Tears stained her cheeks.

Launa offered a hand to help the young witness to her feet. "I told you we are soldiers. We hunt the killers of these people."

"You have seen such as this so much that it does not move you, like a song heard too often?"

Launa shook her head. "I have heard stories told. Many stories. But never in my years have my eyes seen a sight like this." She took a step forward, checked the street they had walked, glanced down the other avenue they had yet to cover. *Stay alert. Don't let your guard down for a second.*

She turned back to Brege. "The wisdom of the soldier is to take what we see and feel here"—her fingers jabbed at her stomach—"and make it hard. To chip away at it like flint. To make it into a spear tip for the day when you will use it to cut the throats of those who did this."

Her case pleaded, Launa turned away, afraid to see the disgust she feared from these gentle people. It was a long moment before Brege rested a hand on her shoulder. Launa turned to face her, steeled for judgment.

Brege's eyes were glittering flint. "I do not know what we will do, but seeds such as these cannot be allowed to grow."

Launa's gaze swept the three. A change was starting. Judith's peaceful Old Europeans were gone. Launa did not know what stood in their place; time would answer that. She wanted to hug them all, for what they had lost, for what they gave her.

Jack's voice stopped her. He had walked past the fire and stared into the darkened longhouse. "People, I fear our eyes have not seen all they must."

With grave steps the five joined him. Launa started to take a deep breath; the stench clogged her throat. She looked to blue sky, green hills. She did not want to enter the dark maw of the longhouse. One of them must not. "Antia. Hold the horses."

Launa waited while each of them gave the woman their reins. All delay exhausted, discipline took her step by step into the longhouse. It took a moment for her eyes to adjust to the dim light. She wished they hadn't.

This sanctuary of the goddess was like the one at Tall Oaks. Raised platforms ran down the sides; a dais was at the far wall. The benches were gone, probably to feed the bonfire. Sprawled on the platforms were bodies, limbs spread wide. Clothes littered the floor. Only death had ended the rape. Launa grimaced. Maybe death only ended the agony. On the dais was . . . something.

Walking forward, Launa left behind the remains of her heart, anything in her that wasn't cold stone. Ahead of her lay the naked body of a woman. She was spread-eagled. If she had been raped, that had only been a beginning. Her chest had been hacked open, her ribs spread, her heart and lungs stretched out.

"Bloody Eagle offering." Jack choked on the words.

"What?" Launa asked without taking her eyes from the horror. Tuam ran for the door. Brege looked at Jack, Launa, the body, waiting for an answer.

Jack spoke, bending Old European words to a purpose they had never been meant to serve. "Killers of men we named Danes hunted a people we named English. They slaughtered many and sought to frighten the elders by killing the one who sat there." He pointed at the dais. "But they did not just kill that one. They made his death a blood offering to the one they worshiped. They called it the Bloody Eagle offering to their male goddess."

"Male Goddess?" Merik's voice cracked. "You mean the Bull."

"No. They worshiped a male they said was more powerful than the Goddess."

"How can that be?" Merik gagged.

Launa was losing it. The walls closed in; she had water for knees. Her tight emotional control was unraveling. "Can we hold this theology discussion outside? I need air." Launa took Brege's hand and drew her away from the body.

Brege came haltingly. "Will they do that to my mother?"

Launa gulped; Brege saw more than what lay there. She saw a future. The soldier wanted to run, but the buzzing of flies and the glint of white bone in a streak of light drew her eyes.

The body of what once had been a man lay on the floor. His arms were bound; his genitals cut off. They lay, smashed flat on the floor. His head was also gone, but not missing—at least not all of it. Flies swirled; the bottom of a skull gaped white.

"What have they done?" Brege's cry was strangled. Too many emotions struggled in her throat with air and words. They had found She who Spoke for the Goddess. Now they saw He who Spoke for the Bull.

"A drinking cup." Jack's whispered words could not hide the hard reality they conveyed. "They used the top of his skull for a cup to drink the blood of the ones they killed."

Launa had had it; she turned Brege for the door. But Antia blocked the exit. Tuam must have taken over the horses, freeing this poor woman to enter hell.

"Mother. Father." She spoke to fists that hid her mouth.

Launa quick-marched Brege up to Antia, then grabbed the other woman by the elbow and pulled them both out of there. The women came as children dragged by their mother.

The men followed. Tuam, standing with the horses, appeared grateful for the company.

Launa, Antia, and Brege stood, shoulder to shoulder, arms interlocked. None had strength to stand, but together they did not fall. Jack took the horses and walked them toward the river to drink. When they could, the women followed.

Launa waited for Antia to scream, to cry, to react. The woman moved like a sleepwalker. As they came to the trees by the stream, Antia stopped, leaned her face against one of them, and just stood there.

Launa stumbled on to collapse beside Brege at the stream. The soldier lay flat while she washed her face and neck. To cleanse the taste from her mouth, Launa lapped up a little water—nothing could cleanse the vision from her soul. Her knees too weak to stand, Launa crawled to an ancient elm and propped herself against its trunk.

Brege rolled over. Her eyes, gone old, fixed Launa with a question mark. *Why? What?* In the cool shade, with the sweet smell of water, earth, and living things, Launa dug in her gut for words to explain the sickness their eyes had seen. "The people honor the life-giving birth-blood of the Goddess."

"Yes," Brege answered.

"Those who killed these people honor the blood of death and offer it to the one they worship in place of the Goddess."

Merik shook his head as if trying to recover from a blow. Brege weakly waved a hand. "Speak more."

Launa took a deep breath. "You honor the blood of birth and life. They honor the blood of death and pain. That is just one of many paths you walk different from them. You give homage to the Goddess. They give homage to a male being they say is stronger than the Goddess. They will kill you or make you into animals to serve them until they hear no more of the Goddess." Launa paused.

Brege's whole body nodded. Merik paced back and forth, unable to sit. Tuam sat cross-legged, listening intently, then frowned. "This maleness they offer worship to. Is it not the Bull?"

Merik stopped, and nodded vehemently.

Launa hoped she remembered how Judith answered that question. "You speak of the Goddess as maiden, mother, and hag. Are they three different women?"

Brege snorted. "Even little girls know the Goddess is one."

"You show the Goddess as a bird or sheaves of grain?"

"But She is still the Great Goddess. She has many faces."

"And the Bull?" Launa asked.

"All life comes from the Goddess. It is female and male, as is the Goddess."

"The men we knew who offered the Bloody Eagle sacrifice to the one they honored said that all life came from men." Launa picked up a twig and held it in front of them. "They said that women only nourished the life men put in them and that a child born woman was broken—as useless as this stick." She snapped it in two, and laid the pieces in front of her.

The three Old Europeans stared at the testimony of the wood. Finally, Brege struggled to her feet. She stood, swaying, feet spread. "We cannot run with these people. Their hunting must end."

The others got to their feet and stood with Brege. She held out her right hand to them. Tuam and Launa put theirs on top of hers.

"Our People will hunt these beasts until they no longer come to our door. We will be soldiers." Brege made the pronouncement with the finality of a death sentence.

Launa swore it would not be their own.

THIRTY-FOUR

JACK PATTED WINDRIDER as the horse nervously nuzzled against him. The animals hadn't taken well to the slaughtered remains of River Bend. It hadn't been easy on the humans either. Jack had left the live people to Launa; he'd kept busy doing three-sixties, trying to look everywhere at once. River Bend did not need six more bodies—and with horsemen loose, Jack wouldn't let his guard down for a moment. They'd got out alive.

And with something more. Jack had never doubted Brege understood the problem. Now she'd seen it, breathed it in, vomited it out. Launa had found the words to turn a moment's anger into a lifetime of passion. Brege would never forget River Bend.

The mission was as close to impossible as any orders ever issued, but the new allies Launa had just recruited showed a lot more spunk than the traders she'd first tried to sign up. It made the grief she'd been sending his way almost worthwhile. *There's got to be some way for the two of us to get back on track.*

Jack came heads up at the sound of hooves—a single horse coming fast. He motioned the others to stay put as he trotted for the edge of the trees, staying low, following cover.

Taelon was heading for River Bend, riding a lot faster

than the old hunter had any right to. Jack drew an arrow and nocked it as he searched Taelon's six o'clock. Nothing was visible behind him. *What's got into the man?*

Jack stepped into the open, waving to get Taelon's attention. The rider turned straight for Jack. Only at the last moment did he rein his horse to a stop; Jack scampered out of the way, then rushed back to help Taelon as he fell from his only half controlled mount.

"What is wrong?"

"I have seen . . . the horsemen."

Trying to do a search scan, hold the hunter up, and keep a horse from stumbling all over them, Jack pulled horse and rider into the cover of the tree line. They collided with Launa and Brege.

"Say more," the townswoman demanded.

"I saw a dust cloud . . ." Taelon gasped for breath. "It is between us and Tall Oaks . . . Amatha and the children . . . are in danger."

"Merik, rub this horse down," Jack ordered. "Tuam, feed it some grain. Give it a little water, but not too much."

Brege grimaced. "Is this any time to worry about a horse?"

"The life of the one who rides that horse today may depend on how well we treat it." Jack knew he was snapping, but all their lives could depend on the tiredest horse if that one set the pace.

As the others headed for the stream, Launa shot him a glare that could have melted stone. *Yeah, I shouldn't be issuing orders, but is today the day for a trainee?* Jack kept his mouth shut. Launa did an about-face and hustled to catch up with Brege and Taelon.

"What did you see?" Launa asked.

"I went with the people . . . For most of the morning . . . I shot two deer. I told them to stay . . . In the shade of the trees by the river . . . To seek cover like you said, Jack. I left them one bend in the river away from here and crossed the plains to come back fast. At the top of a hill, I looked back. I did not see Amatha, but I did see a cloud of dust. It was far out on the plain, toward Tall Oaks. I fear the horsemen may water their horses where Tomas makes camp tonight." He looked from Jack to Brege. "I fear they have been stalking Tall Oaks."

Jack nudged Launa. "Looks like a good day for a battle."

She shook her head, scowling. "Our mission, soldier, is to observe and report, not kill something." She swallowed the rest of the sentence, but Jack heard it— "or get killed." He also heard the echo of his own words from the hill above River Bend.

He glanced at the five locals. "Do you think these folks will run away, let Amatha's kids get butchered? Do you want a team that spineless?"

Launa's eyes cycled between the scouts, the wreckage of the town, the plains that, somewhere, held the killers and their next victims. She said nothing.

"Launa, I want those bastards dead." Jack's hand clenched into a fist. "If there is any way we can do it, let's make it happen."

Launa wanted to scream, to burn Jack with the primal rage that tore at her gut. "I want them dead too, Jack." She bit the words out one at a time through taut lips that had forgotten how to move. "But seven against twenty, Jack! Remember the mission. Brege can rally Tall Oaks, and after today, she will. Do we risk this civilization, all of history, to save a few dozen half-dead civilians?"

Launa was tired, tired of the whiplash of emotions that had swept over her time after time this morning. First, terror at entering River Bend. Then, revulsion at what she saw. The challenge of searching out just the right words to get through to Brege and the other scouts had taken everything she had. The exhilaration of success had been an intoxicating—and brief—moment. Now she was back to terror—and fear. Fear to come this close and lose it all.

Jack's eyes were locked on her. "Seven can handle twenty easy. All we have to do is ambush them."

Launa snorted. "That's not jungle out there, Jack. How're you going to surprise twenty Kurgans on their own steppe?"

Jack didn't even blink. "It can be done. Let's at least try.

Launa, look at the team you've put together. You think they want to go back with their tails between their legs, alive because some more kids got their throats cut?"

One by one, Launa took the measure of her tiny task force. Every face was stone hard. Taelon had risked his neck, galloping back here to call them to arms, not run away. Brege's eyes glinted like sharpened flint in the sun. *I have created a weapon.* Now Jack wanted to wield it.

For a moment, Launa bridled, angry at Jack's presumption. Then she calmed herself. Somebody was going to die today. Her job was to make sure the right people bled. And Jack was the veteran here at organizing mayhem.

Launa took a deep breath. She'd had enough of being a guilty bystander. "Captain. Please assume tactical command of this meeting engagement. Your objective is to inflict maximum Kurgan casualties while keeping the risk to this force at an acceptable minimum." A predator's grin, hungry for meat, spread across Jack's face. Launa took it for her own. "These SOB's don't look the type to let a girl learn from her mistakes. I suspect there'll be a few battles for me later," she finished.

Jack came to attention. Slowly, his right hand came up the gig line neither of them would ever wear again. The stiff angles of his salute would pass the muster of any sergeant major. Launa raised her own hand in a salute just as precise.

"Yes, ma'am," Jack said.

Jack brought his hand down with a snap. Judith had said Launa was good. She'd been wrong; the kid was great. She knew when to push, and, more importantly, when to let experience take point. But now that he had the command, Jack had a few problems. *Just how do I set up an ambush on the open steppe? Do these gentle people have the stomach for cold-blooded killing? We'll take this one step at a time.*

Jack turned to his troops. He and Launa had spoken in English, but the symbolism didn't need translation. Every eye was on him. "Today we go hunting."

Four tight smiles were his reply. The look on Antia's face was orgasmic.

"Will you follow after me, walking in my footsteps?"

"It is wise for a man to lead the hunt," Brege answered.

"Today we hunt men." Jack made each word as hard as fire-tempered flint. "Your arrows will not be aimed at animals. Your spears will cut the flesh of people. Can you do that today?" *Let them taste what they intended here, in the cool of the trees. The heat of battle was not time for ethical qualms. Do you folks have murder in you?*

It looked like Jack had gotten through. Brege had no quick reply this time. Merik fidgeted and glanced away. Tuam looked up at her man, stroking his broad shoulders.

Taelon put his arm around his woman's waist. "Today you could die." His soft whisper filled the shady glen. Both shivered.

Brege's eyes focused on the flint tip of Jack's spear, as if seeing it already red with blood. When she spoke, it was half to herself. "I have seen what they have done. They will do to my mother what they did to Antia's mother. They will do to those who follow Amatha today what they did here. I would that I could walk a path without blood . . ." Brege choked on the last word. She swallowed hard and took a deep breath before going on. "But I have hunted squirrels and badgers. I have butchered sheep and goats. These hands have been red with the blood of animals before. Never would they cut the flesh of one of the People, but they *will* kill these animals that walk on two legs. Yes, Jack." She glanced at her comrades. Merik shuddered, but nodded agreement.

Tuam hugged her man. "Today is a good day to hunt."

Taelon grinned with the confidence of the old hunter. "Today we will follow after you, Jack."

"Yes," hissed Antia.

Now it was Jack's turn to swallow hard. Thousands of years of husbandry and peaceful hunting had formed these people. Today they were ready to follow him down a different path. *By tonight we'll know if they can do it. Assuming I don't get us all killed before noon by screwing up worse than Custer.*

Jack groped for the words he needed. "Launa told Antia it

takes many seasons to learn a soldier's way. Today, we go hunting before you have learned the wisdom Launa and I would share with you. I give you this one wisdom. Do as you are told. We have no breath for arguing. Will you do as I say, when I say?"

Six nodded—even Launa. Jack took a deep breath and gave his first orders. "The tired horse must rest, but we must travel now. Brege, your horse is the best. I need a bowman on it. Please share Tuam's horse until it recovers."

Brege seemed startled, and there was a deep frown on her face, but she quickly slipped from her pony. Launa helped Brege up to ride behind Tuam. Keeping his eyes peeled for any sign of the opposition, Jack led his fire team out at a fast trot.

Taelon kept up, but the rest quickly fell behind; Launa dropped back with them. As desperate as Jack was to establish contact with the enemy, it was still more critical to keep his troops together. He slowed the pace as they skirted the ruined town and headed for the ford.

Once across the river, Jack angled them out onto the plains. A trot brought them to the knoll where Taelon had seen the cloud. From its crest, he spotted a brown smear hanging in the air. Jack ordered a dismount to rest the horses, and to give himself some time to think. *There's not much roll to the ground, but it might be enough.*

"Could that be a herd of animals?" Launa asked.

Taelon shook his head. "It is many years since I have seen such a cloud, but I have seen horsemen make it."

Jack needed information. "Where was it when last you saw it?"

"Farther that way." The hunter pointed to the north.

"Where did Tomas say they would camp tonight?"

"There." Taelon indicated the northernmost bend in sight.

This was their last chance to run. Cross the next hill and they would put their head in the noose—and their bows between the bastards and Amatha's kids.

"Mount up. We ride for the next ridge. Brege, ride the tired horse if you will." Brege's face was a mask, but she moved to obey without a word.

Jack led the column off, but Launa quickly caught up with him. "Captain, you've got the command, and I won't question your tactics. But if raising this army is my job, you're making it tougher on me by riding a very important lady rather hard."

"Would you have asked Antia to trade horses?" Jack snapped.

"No. I'm just as scared as you must be about what'll happen when that woman snaps."

Jack nodded; Launa was not questioning his orders, just the way he was doing it. "You got a suggestion?"

"Talk to her. Tell her why you're bouncing her around like a ping-pong ball. We've told these people we'll teach them how to be soldiers. We've got a little time now. Do it. Besides, you could build up some IOU's. Knowing you, you'll need them later."

Jack sighed. "Do what Judith and Brent said, right?"

"And what Kaul or Lasa would do," Launa added, then paused. "You are right; today you should lead the fight. We've all got to come out of this alive. But we've got a long war ahead, and most of our troops will make hippies look like Prussian Grenadiers. We can't just be twenty-first-century soldiers stomping around the neolith. We've got to be something more."

Jack risked a raised eyebrow. "Like you've been the last couple of days?"

Launa laughed. "I know. While I'm telling Antia to find a new path, I'm strutting around just like my old man." Launa glanced over her shoulder. "These folks don't need the likes of the Colonel to do what needs to be done. We're both going to have to remember that. Now, would you please get back there and be diplomatic for a few minutes? I'll cover point."

Jack hated to leave Launa; she was acting like a human again. But she was right. There'd be time later. First they had to live. He slowed Windrider and joined the rear of the column with Tuam and Brege. They greeted him with silence.

"Brege, I value your following after me, using no breath questioning what I ask." He got a tight smile for his efforts.

"Soldiers must move fast. To find what they hunt, and sometimes to run away from what they find. Taelon's horse had run fast, and must be rested. You are the smallest and the easiest burden for a horse to carry. You have given it time to catch its breath. Because of you, it will be able to run fast again, if we must."

She nodded, brows still low in puzzlement. "I see."

There were other things Jack needed Brege to know. Things she'd have to do if matters got out of hand. "When we return to Tall Oaks, you must tell the story of what you saw. Your story must pass from mouth to ear and old to young. I may have to ride fast with Taelon and Launa to lead the horsemen away from you. You must live no matter who dies today."

Brege's eyes flashed. "I am a soldier. I walk to a soldier's fate."

"Yes, but the first fate of a soldier is to obey. You must sing the story of River Bend so all will hear. The horsemen have stalked Tall Oaks. If these horsemen return to their own and sing a song of Tall Oaks, your song may be all that stands between your people and the fate of River Bend."

Brege blanched. "I thank you for sharing your wisdom. What does this day hold?"

"If all happens as I foresee, many horsemen will die. Some of us may also die." Jack studied the women for a reaction.

"Birth and death are given by the Goddess." Brege's words sounded rote.

Jack grunted; life and death were his to give or take today—if he got it right. He kicked Windrider and trotted for the head of the column. It took less than a half hour to reach the next rise. They rested their horses while Jack studied the ground. *Can I win a battle here?*

A shallow valley lay in front of them. In its center, an ancient elm stood lone vigil, its leafy canopy offering the only shade. To their left lay the bend in the river that might well be the goal of both Amatha's exhausted band and the horsemen. Beyond the valley stretched another ridge. Dust and death rose beyond it. *Here's our last chance to run.*

Jack closed his eyes, let his vision soar above the ground, flow over it like water, following lines of force to where violence could be done and how. Accepting a cavalry charge with the extra momentum of a downhill ride wasn't smart. *Unless.*

He glanced at Launa. Her tongue worked its way around her open mouth, stopping to measure each tooth as it passed. "If they get unwound coming down that hill and go hard charging like someone else you know, Captain, we might have them before they knew what hit them. Yeah, we might just surprise them enough."

"My thought exactly."

Launa grinned. "Let's do it."

Jack gathered his troops and issued them their operation orders. "We will stand against the horsemen at that tree. Brege, Merik, Antia, and Tuam will stay there. Gather all the stones you can for your slings, but keep a watchful eye for horsemen. The rest will ride to that ridge. I want the horsemen to see us. Once the horsemen hunt us, we will join you. We will kill the horsemen in front of that tree. Have you any words for me?"

Jack studied his tiny band of warriors-to-be—he saw no second thoughts. They were committed; they wanted blood. Jack hoped his plan would flow with horsemen's blood—not their own.

In his gut, the old feeling was back. The fantasy of training and guessing what they might face was past. Now was real. Now it was time to act, not think. All the decisions were made. He would know soon enough who was right and who was wrong, who would live and who would die.

"Soldiers, let's ride."

THIRTY-FIVE

THE TEAM CAME to a halt in line abreast in front of the tree. Jack prayed they were as deadly as they looked. Brege's squad slid from their ponies. Jack also dismounted to rummage in the packs on Big Red for five bags.

Launa raised a quizzical eyebrow as he brought out bread, dried fish, and meat. "How can you eat at a time like this?"

Jack said nothing, but started walking, counting as he paced off the distance. Dropping a sack of meat at fifty paces, he grinned. "We don't have the Air Force to prepare our battlefield for us."

Launa's eyes lit with understanding. "You're putting out ranging markers."

"Yep. Their short bows will reach us if they get this far."

Launa and Taelon strode along beside him as he walked off more distance—one hundred, two hundred, and three hundred paces. At three hundred twenty-five, he opened the last sack; it held hard bread. He broke the loaf into thirds, shared out a hunk each to Launa and Taelon, then munched the third as he dropped the empty sack on the ground.

Finished with the bread, he leaped on Windrider and cantered for the ridge. Launa and Taelon followed. Ten minutes later, they crested the hill and got their first look at the enemy. Launa dismounted and pulled up handfuls of grass.

She gave Jack one and began calmly brushing Star's sweat-flecked hide.

Taelon chuckled and did the same for his horse. "You are true horsemen, always caring for your horse."

"Our horses may be our lives today," Jack answered, currying Windrider, his eyes never leaving the horsemen. "And it shows the horsemen we know no fear." Jack finished the rubdown and joined Launa. "I think they spotted us."

Launa dusted her hands. "Yes. They were going straight down the valley. A minute ago they started a swing in our direction."

Tyman edged his mount toward the three strange horsemen on the ridge. Since his warriors had balked at charging behind him into that new place, he had gnashed his teeth and followed behind them as they ran away. But these three horsemen were different. Weaklings, they led no spare mounts. Anyone who rode alone deserved to lose what little they had.

Alkon saw where he was leading and grinned. The clan had suffered too much in its long flight from its home where the Sun rose. They had endured. Now, let them take from another.

"Sly devils." Jack studied the oncoming horsemen as they slowly turned toward him. It was impossible to get a head count at six klicks, but they looked like twenty.

At four klicks, the troop angled straight for Jack.

"Okay folks, they took the bait." Jack turned to Taelon. "Ride for the tree. Tell the others we have visitors coming. Let us prepare a suitable greeting for them."

Taelon grinned. "I will use your words, but must I go now?"

Jack took his spare quiver from Windrider and handed it to Taelon. "You must go and prepare. Also, it is best that we wander about like grazing deer that do not know fear. Let the horsemen think we are as empty of a plan as a squirrel. That will make their surprise all the greater."

Taelon accepted the quiver and mounted. He trotted downhill and out of sight in a moment.

Jack turned back to the horsemen. "You scared?" he asked Launa.

"Shouldn't I be?"

"It's easier if you admit it to yourself."

"Well, I am, but I'm also where I want to be." She stood like a rock, watching the riders. A tight smile creased her lips. "Like the poet said, 'We stand between war's harm and our homes and hearths.' Maybe now I'll have a home."

Jack wondered what she meant. He'd ask her when the killing was done.

"What do you think our chances are?" she asked.

He licked his lips. "Pretty good. They look like the same light cavalry we've been running into." It was time to let her know. "Launa, I'm betting the farm that these SOB's don't have composite bows, just like the rest we killed. If things come apart, you and Brege have to make it back to Tall Oaks. Head out into the plains, skirt these bastards. I'll hold them off long enough for you two to make a run. Okay?"

"I'll follow your orders, Jack, but today their bill is due. We collect."

Jack liked what he heard. He wanted to say more, about starting over again when this was done, but the distance to the horsemen dictated his next words. "It's time to ride."

The horsemen had closed to two klicks as Jack swung onto Windrider. He could make out individuals now—no body armor except a few leather helmets. The bows were short, but there was no way to tell if they were horn-backed.

Jack turned his back on his enemy and followed Launa downhill at a fast trot. The slope was even; the soil packed— no ruts. It was good terrain for a cavalry charge. The tree was two klicks from the top of the ridge. The horsemen crested the hill before Jack and Launa rejoined their team. Instead of charging immediately, the Kurgans halted.

"Look at them!" Tyman shouted.

"Yes. Look!" Givod answered. "We saw three. Now there are seven."

"Four are women," Alkon sneered, "dressed for the taking."

"These are not Horse People. They dress like the others."
Givod shook his head. "Something strange rides the wind."

"We will take them like we did the others," Tyman
shouted.

"Yes!" the riders behind him screamed.

"I will spit them on my lance," Alkon bragged.

"Which one?" someone shouted from the rear, raising a
fisted hand, signaling to all that there were better lances for
women than those of wood.

"Will it matter?" another chortled.

"It will if he grabs one of the men."

Everyone roared at that.

Tyman sat his horse, laughing with his warriors. Their joy
for the coming battle was good. He relished the moment. Let
it continue as it should.

Jack gritted his teeth and kept Windrider to a comfortable
trot. It was better to spend a few extra minutes reaching the
tree than risk an accident. Behind him, he could hear deri-
sive laughter. *Go ahead, laugh. In a half hour, you'll be
doing it through a slit throat—I hope.*

As Jack neared the tree, he spared a glance over his shoulder. The raiders were still galloping back and forth on the
ridge, screaming battle cries and beating drums. Launa
slowed them to a walk as they approached the troops. *Right,
woman, let's look cool. No need to hurry.* As he slid from
Windrider, Merik took the reins and tied the horse to the tree
with the others. Jack shaded his eyes to study his enemy.

Brege came up beside him. "What are they doing?" Terror nibbled the edge of her question.

Jack put a steadying hand on her shoulder. "Even for
them, it is not easy to kill. They shout words to each other;
tell stories of what they have done and what they will do.
They will take time. Time we can use to plan their deaths."

Jack faced the scouts. "I want bows on the outside and
slings in the middle. Antia, you stand beside me; Merik,
Brege, Tuam, and Launa in a line. Taelon, you at the other
end." He paused for a moment. "Lay your quarterstaffs be-

side you in case they get close to us, but I hope to stop them with slings and arrows. Any questions?"

"Jack, I want a sling too." Launa leaned on her staff. "I've got an idea for some psychological warfare that might get them where we want them. Also, Taelon has your spare quiver and I'm at the other end of the line. Take a few arrows from my spare so you won't shoot yourself dry."

"Thanks." Jack was grateful for the polish Launa put on his plan. "Let's do it, soldiers." To screams and drumbeats from the ridge, they prepared to receive the charge. In a moment they stood in the tiny array Jack had chosen.

"People, we might as well sit in the shade and be comfortable." Jack settled down, trying to look like he hadn't a care in the world. Nobody knew how dry his mouth was.

The others sat or squatted as he folded his knees before him. From the corner of his eye, he took their measure. Antia's eyes never left the horsemen. She fingered a rock and waited. Merik was a different case. His breath came in rapid pants as his sling slipped through his hands over and over, faster and faster. Glazed eyes wandered over the plain before them, anywhere but the Kurgans on the hill. Still, every time the din from there took a sudden jump, Merik's gaze would snap back to them. Jack would have to watch him.

Brege was the opposite. She sat in a yoga pose, hands resting on folded knees, eyes half closed. Her lips moved. Jack hoped the Goddess was listening. He also hoped Brege wouldn't lock up when the fight got bloody.

Tuam wasn't praying. Like a bird, she turned first to the hill, then to Taelon. Her hands would check her sling, her spear, her knife, never stopping. She was another one Jack would have to look out for.

Launa and Taelon at the end of the line were a matching pair. Hunched down, they eyed the horsemen on the hill with a steady gaze, like cats waiting at a mouse hole. Jack's array had solid flanks. *Now if the center holds.*

Jack licked his own dry lips and tried to get a conversation going, something to drown out the raiders. "The horsemen were going to water. It is hot on that ridge. Let them sweat. Has anyone seen them drink?"

No one had.

Brege turned her face to Jack without breaking lotus. "While you were on the hill, we practiced with our slings. I now see the wisdom of the markers you put out. Our rocks can reach to the one by the clump of grass."

"Good." *Two hundred meters.* Jack had figured the slingers for that range. "Arrows can reach to the fourth. Launa and I will shoot when the horsemen reach the farthest marker. By the time our arrows fly to the fourth, the horsemen will be there."

Only Taelon's eyes moved as he measured the distances. "I will wait until the riders are at that bag," he said.

That said, the scouts grew quiet again; there was nothing more to say. Noise rolled over them from the ridge.

Tuam shivered. "Why do they wait? Why don't they come?"

Launa rested a hand on the woman's shoulder. "They wait so we will ask these questions. So our tongues will go dry in our mouths. So our bowels will knot in our guts. So we will know fear and run away. It is easy to kill someone who runs."

The woodswoman frowned. "You feel it, too?"

"Yes, Jack and I feel it, but our heart says we must stay, and we will."

Brege shook her head. "This is a strange way, a very strange way." She turned to Jack. "We have much to learn about this strange new way. Tell me, does your heart tell you how these animals will strike at us?"

"If I smell them right, one will come to show his strength and spirit. We must kill him, but not make it seem too easy."

"Jack, that's where I have an idea." Launa laughed. "Let the four women bring that one down with rocks."

"Yes," the other women hissed.

"We'll do it that way." Jack accepted the addition to his battle plan. "But Taelon and I will have arrows nocked."

They all shared in Launa's laugh. Jack tested its tone. There was a tremble here, a quiver there, but underneath was rock as solid as these people. They were as ready as any squad of green troops raised from birth to rule Britannia or put *Deutschland über alles.* Jack stood to face the hill from which would come their destiny—and a world's.

THIRTY-SIX

"THEY LAUGH AT us, Father. Give me the honor of first blood."

Tormiz hardly looked at Tyman as he set an arrow to his bow. The Strong Arm glanced at his warriors. They were almost ready. Why not let his oldest son avenge his youngest son's death by leading them? "Go, boy," he shouted.

Kicking his horse, Tormiz was off at a trot.

Tyman beamed.

"You have raised a good son," Givod said.

Those were the first wise words Tyman had heard from the old counselor in too many seasons. He waited to see who would taste the pain of his son's arrow.

Jack spotted the lone rider the second he broke from the pack. He held a bow in one hand, arrow nocked. The butt of his lance was in his boot. He did not use his free hand to guide his horse, but rested it on his hip.

The women were on their feet the moment they noticed the incoming. Launa called the four of them into a huddle that ended with a shouted "Yes." They strode from the shade and spread out to give themselves plenty of room to swing. Merik clutched his quarterstaff, knuckles white. He paced back and forth while Jack and Taelon stood, bow in one hand, arrow in the other.

One klick out, the horseman urged his mount to a gallop; at five hundred meters he kicked his horse to a dead run.

"Watch him." Jack realized he had been wrong to expect a straight-on charge. This guy was no romantic knight. "He'll turn so he can shoot sideways, not over his horse's head."

The women grunted and began to twirl their slings.

At three hundred meters, the horseman began to swerve, opening up the left side of his horse for his shot.

"He's going to pass to your left." Jack tried to keep his voice even. The women angled their line to face him.

"Wait until I say to let fly," Launa ordered and got grunts in reply.

"Remember, the horse will be closer when the stone hits it. Aim ahead." No sound answered Launa's last bit of advice.

"Let fly!"

A rock whizzed past Jack's head and bounced off the tree. Antia spun to face him, face going white.

"Don't worry," Jack called. "Load another stone."

With shaking hands, she did.

Three rocks arched out at the rider well before he got to the fifty-meter mark. One struck the horse, knocking it off stride. The others hit the rider, one square in the face. He tumbled from his mount. A loud crack resounded as he rolled like a rag doll in the dust, spending the energy of his charge. Then he lay still.

Three women, proud smiles on their faces, almost pranced as they came back to the men.

"The Goddess is gracious," prayed Brege as Merik came to her.

"We did it!" Tuam threw herself into Taelon's arms.

Launa tried to glower through her proud grin. "I thought you said we wouldn't have to worry about deflection shots."

Jack remembered his tactical assessment at the archery range a world and six thousand years away. "So I goofed."

Launa laughed, and he wanted to give her a hug and share in her laughter, but he had work to do.

Taking his spear, Jack jogged out to the fallen rider. Uninvited, Antia ran at his elbow. The stench from loosened bowels confirmed what he had expected to find.

"He is already dead." Antia sounded disappointed.

With his spear tip, Jack turned the raider over. The strange way the hips rolled before the shoulders told of a broken back. Empty eyes stared into the sky.

Jack pulled a long obsidian knife from the dead man's belt and used it to hack at the neck. Antia helped pull his head off.

"I will do this," Antia demanded, and Jack nodded.

Carrying the head by the beard, she took two quick steps and slung the head toward the ridge, where the riders were suddenly quiet. Jack let out a war whoop any Apache would be proud of, then turned his back on his enemy and walked with Antia to their own.

Launa grinned. Brege was puzzled. "Why did you do that?"

Jack glanced back at the horsemen. Screams and cries were starting up again. "They are thinking again about hunting us. I want them to come. They have seen Tall Oaks. They must not sing that song to their people."

"It is better they come soon?" Brege frowned at the ridge.

"Yes. We do not want them to make plans. Let them come angry."

Brege broke into a grin. "Let us go, sisters."

The other women followed her out onto the sun-browned plain. Brege said something. Jack missed it, but the women giggled. Twenty meters out, they turned, pulled down what little they were wearing, and mooned the ridge.

Tyman sat his mount, his mouth hanging slack in shock. Beside him, others watched as a man and woman used Tormiz's own knife to take his head, then tossed it back at them.

"The man has no honor," Givod breathed.

"Rocks," Tyman found his voice. "They used rocks to kill my son." Then Tyman lost his voice again. Four women were . . .

"No woman wags her ass in my face and keeps it," Alkon

screamed. "Come after me," he shouted as he threw down the rope to his spare mounts and set his lance.

Fear and relief washed over Jack as three riders broke for them, galloping in a V. Three more followed in a rough line. In a moment, the five on the left joined in, then the five on the right. Finally, the last four kicked their mounts to a gallop.

Jack brushed aside emotions; their time would come later. Now there was only time to do it. What seconds he had left, he used to weigh the situation. The Kurgans left no one to tend the spare horses, kept no reserve. They were coming whole hog—and stupid. Coldly, Jack calculated the arithmetic of death. At a full run these horses might make twenty klicks an hour, say three hundred thirty meters a minute. His team would have forty-five seconds when the riders were in their range but before the short bows were effective. But the raiders weren't charging in a body; there was a good two hundred meters between the leader and tag-end charlie.

He turned to Launa with a grin. She must have done the same math; she was grinning too. "Lieutenant, we get eight to ten shots each. Aim for the lungs. An arrow there will tear up a lot."

Jack turned back to the onrushing mob. They were over a klick out when the raiders broke into a run, spreading themselves out farther—some of those horses were tired. Several warriors brought their lances down. Not everyone had a bow.

"Those with lances will come straight at us. Slingers, aim for them. Archers, go for the bows." The first targets were near the most distant sack. "I'll take the leader. Launa, take the ones on the right. I've got the ones on the left."

It was time. He put an arrow in the sky and reached for the next one. This shot was for the last man of the approaching V. As he aimed, the first target went down with an arrow in his face. Next, Jack chose the leftmost of the three abreast. Their charge was losing formation. Jack lofted two more arrows toward the threesome. One of the first three was still coming. Before Jack could take aim, an arrow from Launa or Taelon took his mount. Rider and horse went down.

The two groups of five were in the killing zone now. Jack took the leftmost. Both groups were swerving toward him. Controlled targeting was becoming impossible; Jack selected targets from those still far out. "Taelon, shoot for any past the third sack."

"I do."

Suddenly, every horseman was past the third sack. There was no organization left among the ten that pushed on to the hundred-meter marker. Their speed slackened. They came to a halt, screaming at each other. One tried a shot. It fell short. Arrows or stones dropped four while they held at their high water mark, undecided. Then, as one, the six survivors turned to flee.

"I've got the left," Jack called.

"I'll get the right," Launa answered.

Taelon just shot.

"Ride, ride!" Tyman shouted. "Crush the strangers under your horses' hooves. Drive your lances through their hearts."

Tyman limped as he ran toward the animals, waving his lance, urging his warriors on. There was no time to think on why his horse had gone down, an arrow in its side at an impossible distance.

"Kill them all. Take their heads. Drink their blood." Tyman screamed, but his warriors were no longer galloping for the enemy. Now they galloped from them.

"Get me a horse," the Strong Arm yelled, waving his lance at Eddon. The boy swerved toward a stray mount, then tumbled from his own, an arrow in his back.

Tyman shrieked anger at the bright Sun that had abandoned him, then hobbled toward a horse.

Jack held his fire, an arrow to his ear. The last rider was down. None made it back to the fourth sack. Beside him, the scouts took a deep breath.

"We did it. We did it, dear Goddess." Brege hugged

Tuam. Merik danced a jig. Brege turned to Jack, beaming. "Their male Goddess thing is weak. That was easy!"

"Horsemen still live," Antia spat.

Jack had to agree with her; the battle was not over. Five dismounted raiders stared back at him. One ran after a horse. The others shouted and began to gather. Three more labored to stand on broken legs, walk with pierced lungs.

The battle was not over by a long shot. This was only a lull. Brege took a long look at Jack's face and grew quiet.

Jack took aim. The one who sought a new mount slowly stepped closer to a skittish pony. He presented a good target. Jack sent an arrow his way. The horse took it in the side, reared, crumpled in a heap. The man shook his lance, screamed something.

Jack sent a second arrow at the man. He dodged it. At two hundred meters, dodging was easy.

"We have a problem," Launa observed dryly.

Jack put down his bow and turned to his troops. "While they carried the attack to us, they were stupid and easy to kill. Now they have time to think and they grow smart. Now we must carry the attack to them. That will not be easy."

Launa nodded. The others looked worried.

Groans from the battlefield drew Jack's attention. "We also don't know who's dead, who's dying, and who will rise up to shoot an arrow in our backs."

Launa put down her bow and hefted her spear.

Another dismounted raider was edging off to snag a grazing horse. Merik sent a stone arching toward the animal. It took off as the pebble bounced past its nose. The man ran after it, then gave up and joined the others. Eight warriors, three of them walking wounded, began the slow trudge back up the hill they had ridden down so bravely.

How do we do this? Jack tried to total up the targets, assign a threat value to each one. "Brege, get the horses. The rest, take spears, bows, slings."

Brege froze. "Are we to charge them as they charged us?"

Jack bristled at the question, then remembered where he was. With a sigh, he turned to his troops. "We must kill the fallen. We must chase after those who walk, and kill them before they can mount the horses they left behind. Brege, we need our horses close so we can ride after the horsemen."

Brege's face had frozen before Jack finished talking. Now she stood, worrying her lower lip. Jack swallowed a scowl, keeping his face a stern mask. *We've hit the limit already!* Jack didn't know what he'd said that brought on this budding mutiny, or how he'd solve it, but it turned out he didn't have to.

Merik gave Brege a one-armed hug without taking his spear off guard. "A wounded bear is very bad. These men on the ground will die. They will suffer less Jack's way."

Brege sighed. "To kill those who need healing." She closed her eye for a moment, and Jack watched as a thousand years of nurturing struggled with what she had chosen to become today. Then she stepped off, obedient to his orders.

Launa watched Brege go. "Tough woman," she said as she turned back to Jack. "Now, how do we do this? Hand to hand?"

"Not with those bastards. They're too good. Don't give them a fair fight. If they look alive, use more arrows. If they look good and dead, put a spear through their neck or chest just to make sure. Never turn your back on one. Taelon, you keep an arrow nocked. Antia, protect Taelon with a spear. The rest of us, spread out and spear those we must."

Antia shook her head. "Let Tuam guard her man." Her lips curled into a cruel grin. "Let me kill horsemen."

Jack rubbed at his eyes, suddenly very tired. He had no energy to waste fighting his own people. "Do what you want, Antia."

The others did as they were ordered.

The first warrior Jack came to had broken his neck when he fell. That was the easiest of the day.

Somewhere off to his right, Antia had found one alive. His screams grew longer and louder. At least one horseman would not die quickly today.

As Jack approached his second wounded Kurgan, the man struggled to his knees. The arrow in his chest sucked air, spewing a bloody froth as he gasped for breath. The fall from his horse had ripped the wound wide open; two jaggedly broken ribs showed through the gore. Jack shook his head—then took a quick step back as the raider slashed out with a knife Jack hadn't seen. Unable to stand, the horseman still lunged from his knees.

Jack drove his spear between two prominent ribs. Blood spurted as he pierced the heart. The man fell, coughing, spitting, cursing. Jack stood over his enemy as the last ragged breath escaped him. What kind of men fought on even as death closed in? Was Antia's sport adding backbone, or were these guys always hard cases? Would Lasa's farmers ever fight as hard as this?

The next raider lay paralyzed with a broken back. Jack spoke to him. The warrior shouted something Jack didn't understand and held his knife to the sky. Jack slit his throat.

One tried to get an arrow off at Launa. She pinned him with a thrown spear. "These bastards don't know when to quit." A scream from Antia's victim drew their attention. They shook their heads.

Jack jogged over to where Brege held the horses. Mounting Windrider, he trotted for Antia. The woman was streaked with sweat, dirt, and blood. The man beneath her knife was a red pulp. Jack tried not to look too close as he drove the tip of his spear into the man's throat.

Antia snarled as she leaped up, then held her knife thrust as Jack's bloody spear point came up from the dead man's flesh to her belly.

"Walk with us," he ordered. *But would any of the others want to walk with her?*

With twelve Kurgans very dead, the soldiers rested on their bloody spears. Was it mere coincidence that all stood with their backs to Antia? Jack trotted for them as he studied the eight survivors making their way toward the ridge and horses. They were moving fast.

"Mount up," he ordered. "We must ride fast to stand between them and the crest. Then we close and shoot them down with arrows."

"The way the Persians did the Spartans at Thermopylae?" Launa shouted. "But no one will live to sing this story."

• • •

Tyman had never tasted defeat. He refused to drink of it now. "We will come back with more lances than the Great Sun can count," he yelled to those around him. "You will drink their blood from their own skulls."

No cheers answered him. "Swift Cazo, run. Get us horses while those fools loot the dying."

Cazo grunted and ran for the top of the ridge.

But now the animals were mounted. Cazo's run turned into a race. The boy dodged the first arrow that flew his way. He ran on even after the next arrow pierced him. Two more arrows hit him in the blink of an eye. He fell, crawled farther, then was still.

Tyman grabbed a bow from Daxon, nocked an arrow, and shot at one of the strangers. His arrow fell before it was halfway there.

"What manner of men have such bows?"

"The Stormy Mountain Clan must know of this," Givod whispered, then took off running for the horses. He dodged right, then left, then right again. Arrow after arrow flew at him, but he was gone when they came for him.

Tyman laughed. "Run, wise Givod, run."

A strange one lowered his lance and galloped for Givod. The counselor was almost to the horses. They shied from him, and he had to slow to coax them close. A lance took him in the back as his hand grasped the leads of one string. Groans were on every lip.

Then screams of pain as arrows pierced warriors. The other strangers had closed almost to within normal bow range while all eyes were on Givod.

Tyman saw the arrow coming, but it was too late to dodge. He tried to pull it from his flesh, but it was lodged in his side. Coughing blood, he waved his lance in defiance. A second arrow pierced his throat. He felt blood gush from his neck as he began his death scream. There would be nothing weak about him; even his death call would have power. He fell to his knees still calling on the Sun to blot this evil from the sacred grass.

• • •

Jack turned Windrider, circling back to retrieve his lance from the runner's back. As he did, the body rolled over. The guy had run and dodged like a kid; his face was lined and his hair streaked with gray. *Tough old son of a bitch. What made you tick?*

Downhill, the last raider fell to Launa's and Taelon's arrows. Jack rested a moment, letting the realization percolate through his gut. *I'm alive. I pulled it off. Us twenty-one, them nothing.* All he felt was tired.

Without a command, Launa and Merik started the grim business of going through the horsemen's last stand, making sure the dead were dead. Jack trotted downhill and slid from Windrider. *It's a dirty job, and you can't leave it to Antia.*

Still, Jack was tired of eyes that screamed hate as they closed forever. The last throat he cut was that of someone little more than a boy. That one shook Jack. *Will we have to kill even the kids?*

When he called the scouts to regroup, the administrative details left him no more time for questions. "Gather their horses, retrieve our long arrows, collect their knives and anything else we can use. Taelon, will you ride to find Amatha? Warn her that we will bring many horses to them this evening."

"It would not be kind to frighten them," the hunter said as he quickly mounted. Taelon had avenged his brother, killing horsemen with less compassion than he showed to the fish his tribe speared. Still, his face was ashen as his gaze took in what they'd done.

Antia was a different case. She grinned as she swung herself on a horse. "Now I go to honor my mother's bones." She waved her gory knife as she galloped for River Bend.

Jack wished he could be somewhere else, but there was work to finish. Launa and Merik trotted off to collect the horses. Launa went fully armed, but there were no surprises.

That left Jack with the butcher job. He picked up the empty sack he'd used as the three hundred twenty-five meter marker and went among the bodies. He tried to look on them as just dead meat, but he got the shakes anyway. An hour ago, they'd been screaming death at him. Now vultures

nd crows waited for him to finish. The birds would have
)een just as willing to feast on him and Launa.

Jack stopped at each body, cutting long arrows out of
:ooling flesh, putting bows, quivers, and knives in his sack,
ifting the bodies for their intelligence value. Once again, he
;ot the same answers. Bows were short; tactics were stupid.
[he same information gained the same hard way.

Near the three hundred meter marker, Brege knelt beside
ı sprawled body. An arrow had pierced its eye. The horse-
nan looked old, frail in death.

"This one led the hunt." Brege looked to where the first
)oeman lay. "Perhaps that was his son." She pulled at the
eather cord that hung at the man's neck. "What can you tell
ne of these?"

Jack stooped. One by one he fingered the stone and bone
:harms of the necklace. To him they were familiar; so many
varrior peoples had worn these or something very like them
or thousands of years. But for Brege, Jack knew they were
original. "The disk is the sun to which he sends prayers. The
:riangle is the holy mountain he climbs to be near his male
;oddess sun. The lightning bolt is the power of what he wor-
hips. The knife is his power to do that one's will." He
ooked down at the man. "See, it is repeated on his vest—
he sun above the mountain. The lightning bolt descends
rom the mountain to the dagger."

Brege grunted, removed the necklace, and rolled the body
)ut of the vest. She hesitated only a moment as new blood
;ushed. "I will take these to the People."

Vultures circled. Ravens hopped closer to the bodies,
eady for the feast. Jack wanted to leave the field to them.
_auna formed the horses up into one big herd. After round-
ng up the horses that survived the charge and slitting the
hroats of several that were lung-shot, they had eighty-seven
nore mounts, mostly mares. Brege and Merik took the
ight-hand side; Tuam kept them moving from the rear. That
eft him and Launa on the left as they headed out.

With most of the horses still tied in twos and threes, there
vas little straying. Launa trotted up beside him.

"We did it—our little band of goddess folk beat the bastards," she exulted. "I didn't think you could do it, set a trap on the wide-open steppe, but you did. Rommel would have been proud."

Jack accepted the pat on the back, and tried to keep his hand that held the reins from trembling too bad. He wasn't sure how much was skill—and how much dumb luck. Whichever it was, Launa deserved some of the credit too. "You didn't do too bad yourself. You gals bagging the first one with slings shocked the hell out of 'em, then Brege's idea. You got their blood up. Once they were in the killing ground, we didn't let them out alive."

"And they didn't lay a finger on us," Launa crowed.

Jack wanted to smile, but couldn't find one in him. He'd sounded that cocky the first night of the desert war. It was the next day that a rocket took apart his buddy's Bradley. "It happens that way when you've got the technical edge. At Agincourt, the English lost thirty men, the French knights eight or nine thousand. We had it in the desert, but it didn't always work."

"They just kept coming." Launa's gaze grew distant, her focus not on the steppe ahead, but on time an hour past. "I didn't know if we could stop them. Even though we were knocking them down, the rest kept right on coming."

"That's what we needed them to do."

"Yeah, and they were dumb enough to do it our way. That's a lesson I'll have to remember." Launa brought Star to a halt. Jack stopped, almost knee to knee with her. She reached out to touch his arm. "We did what we had to do," she whispered, "and so did Brege and the rest. We wondered if they could take a life. Well, when letting the bastards live means your death, and the death of everyone you love, they turned deadly enough. Charging down our throat, those SOB's were death come for us, and damn proud of it. Then when I went out there, killing them, I saw myself in their eyes—death come for them." She shivered. "Those bastards aren't going to turn Tall Oaks into a slaughterhouse like River Bend." Launa scanned the rolling land around them. "I've never had a home. Every two years I was somewhere else. Now, damn it, Tall Oaks is home, and nobody's

oing to take it away from me. Nobody." Launa's lips were
hard, straight line when she next looked Jack in the eye.

"Thank you. You were right to want to fight today. You
ere right to want the command." Launa glanced over the
ther scouts riding herd. "We're bringing back winners from
ne battle here at this tree. Now, I've got to figure out how
) make the most of it."

Launa kicked Star to a walk; Jack followed. He felt their
rivate moment slipping away, shoved into a corner of
auna's mind as the mission again took command of her
noughts. *When will there be time for us?*

The lieutenant turned her mount to face Jack. "I've got to
alk to Brege. Can you handle this side alone?"

Jack hardly had time to nod before Launa was galloping
or the daughter of she who spoke for the goddess in Tall
)aks.

Break's over, Bearman. Back to work.

Before long, Merik replaced Tuam in the trailer position
nd all three women had their heads together. An hour later,
s they approached the tree line, Taelon trotted out and
aved.

Amatha's band had made camp at the northernmost bend
a the river. People were very quiet that evening; the sur-
ivors seemed dazed by how close they'd again come to
eath. While Launa led Brege and Tuam on a long-range pa-
ol, Jack took kitchen detail, feeding and then bedding
own the troops. The sun had set before Launa's team rode
a. Jack took them steaks on skewers as they cared for their
orses.

"Thanks," Launa said, grabbing hers. "I'm starved and
og tired. Where do I sleep?"

To Jack she looked both exhausted and wired. He won-
ered if she could sleep, and what nightmares would come
or her when the night was the darkest. He wanted to be
nere for her, but he pointed at three bedrolls, laid out to-
ether close to where the horses were picketed.

"Where are the rest of you?" Launa asked.

"Taelon, Merik, and I will bed down each at a different
orner of the camp. I'll take the first two-hour watch. Taelon

says he'll be awake well before dawn. I don't see how we
can set up a full watch list yet."

"Sounds good. I want to get us back to Tall Oaks fast.
Think you can mount up the crew tomorrow?"

"Most of the kids can't wait to get their hands on a horse.
The old woman's a different situation. She can hardly walk,
but she won't even touch a horse."

"You'll think of something. Brege and I'll keep a long
range patrol out all day from now on. No more surprises."
She paused to finish off her dinner. "We're talking a lot.
Brege knows she's got a tough sales job ahead of her. We've
got to squeeze every drop of good we can from today's
win."

"If anybody can, the three of you will."

Launa smiled at the praise and headed for her bedroll.

Jack did several slow circuits of the camp; snores came
from the pallets of moss and ferns where the survivors slept.
Beside the glowing embers of the dinner fire, the old woman
sat, huddled in her shawl. Jack settled down across from her.

She stirred the coals as ruddy flames colored her flesh
red. "Where is the Goddess?" she muttered. "How can this
be?"

She glanced up at Jack. He could think of no answer for
someone who could not change. She was still there, mumbling to herself or her deity, when Jack called it a night and
went to his bedroll. The day had drained him; sleep came
quickly.

Launa and her team were already mounted the next morning
when Jack came awake. They trotted toward the coloring
dawn while Jack got breakfast started. He issued capture
bows to those who knew how to use them and cut rawhide
slings for others. *Launa was right last trip. These folks deserve a fighting chance.* Still, he allotted no time to weapon
drill but went immediately to the business of getting survivors mounted. It took several tries for a few of them to
stay on their horses.

Voices and spirits rose as young bodies warmed in the
sun. They were safe and fed and tackling a new challenge.

with all the gusto of young hearts. Those who caught on quickly taught the others. There was none of the "I can do it and you're dumb" that Jack remembered from his childhood. Tomas seemed the natural leader, yet his advice was usually "This is how I do it. Why not try something like it?" Several kids came up with better ways, and Tomas quickly adopted them with a laugh. Jack found himself in love with every one of them.

The old woman was another problem. She refused even to look at a horse. When the kids were ready to start, she stomped off in the direction of Tall Oaks—and crumbled after twenty paces. With Amatha and Tomas helping, Jack put together a two-horse ambulance, with her slung in a hammock between the horses. Being carried, she was able to keep the pace Jack set. Still, the old woman seemed to drift away, mumbling to herself and the goddess. Amatha stayed close to her, helplessness crowding her eyes.

"I'll get us to Tall Oaks as quickly as I can," Jack offered.

With everyone mounted, the smallest kids riding behind bigger ones of eight or nine, and the older ones riding hell-for-leather as perimeter guards, they made good speed. This didn't stop the adolescents from trying out their new skills. Tomas led a half dozen youths in a charge at a deer herd. The deer scattered, but one confused doe got close enough for Tomas to bring her down with his bow.

That night, Tomas proudly served steaks to Launa's team when she rode in. But he also saved back some of the tastier bits for one of the young women who took care of the little ones, when she wasn't riding like the wind beside Tomas.

"Sara and Tomas have been friends since they were naked babies making puddles," Amatha said as she came up beside Jack. Both of them watched the two young lovers, who were too intent on each other to notice the rest of the world. "Their mothers looked forward to celebrating the day when Sara would asked Tomas to be her first consort." Amatha wrapped her shawl tighter as the evening air cooled. "Now here is none left to come together in celebration, and we feast on only what we can gather."

While struggling to dig himself out of the hole Sandie and

Sam's death had put him in, Jack had read a lot on grief. He didn't want to reject Amatha's feelings; still, tomorrow lay before them.

"My first consort and our son will never feast with me," Jack whispered. "While I breathe, they live in my heart. I celebrate each day I live. And do what I must to keep my heart in my chest, and not on some horseman's lance."

Amatha sighed her agreement, and hastened off to find out why a child was crying.

The fourth day after the battle, the ground started looking familiar; they were near Tall Oaks. He dropped down the line to tell Amatha. He found her beside the ambulance, folding the arms of the old one into final repose.

"We are there," Jack said.

"It is just as well." Amatha's words were soft, as for a child. "Her heart could not bear what she saw coming." Amatha quickly mounted. "Let us see what Tall Oaks holds."

Jack let his gaze drift over the horses to the hill that hid Tall Oaks. Launa and Brege would be coming in soon; he wanted to be at their side when Brege reported in.

THIRTY-SEVEN

HE BATTLE AT the Tree had surprised Launa. After her first combat, she expected the worst initiation was over. But standing there watching the horsemen, waiting for what would happen next, had torn a new hole in her gut, maybe her soul. *And that's what most battles will be like.*

Would you have been so quick to volunteer if you'd known you'd be spending the rest of your life looking over your shoulder, waiting for someone to try to kill you?

It really didn't matter. She was alive; the rest of the twenty-first century was dead. *Forget this, kid. It's show time again.*

At least today all she had to face was Tall Oaks. No one would be trying to kill her. And she and Brege had spent the last four days hunting for words, stalking them like Kaul or Taelon hunting deer. *Judith swore we could do it. Now we find out.*

Beside her, Brege and Tuam rode abreast, the speaker's daughter in the middle. Antia had not rejoined; Launa had no time to worry about her. Jack, Taelon, and Merik galloped up, extending the line to the left. The hunter took the middle slot there. Like her, Jack rode the outer flank.

The six of them led the troop. Bringing this many horses in, Launa had suggested they have friendly faces up front for all to see. Brege had agreed with a grim nod.

No crowd came out to greet them. The people tilling the fields had vanished, too. Launa signaled the troop to a halt well out of normal bow range. She'd spotted archers lurking in the shadows of the first houses.

"It's Brege," a woman shouted, and the scene changed. Kaul stepped from a nearby house. For a staff, he held a bow, the arrow now in his other hand. A moment later, Lasa came in view behind her consort. The order had been reversed the first time Launa entered Tall Oaks. People were learning.

Thirty or forty youths with spears rushed toward them, laughing now at their pointless fears. Launa allowed herself a half smile; it was a poor deployment for shock infantry, but Cleo's heart was in the right place. If the scouts had been horsemen, they would have paid for their sport.

A glance into town showed people going about their business as usual. Launa rubbed the palms of her hands into suddenly tired eyes. *What will it take to open these people's eyes? Dear God or Gracious Goddess, I hope Brege and I have found the right words.*

Brege slid from her horse and ran to her mother; the women embraced. Launa saw worry lines on Lasa's face that hadn't been there before. The speaker had paid a price for sending her daughter in harm's way. Kaul joined in the hug.

Launa watched the family scene with a growing lump in her throat. As daughter to the Colonel and his lady, she'd grown up to a cool, civilized way. *Or had they just been too afraid to touch?* Launa glanced at Jack. *What do I want for me, ten, twenty years from now?* Launa wished she knew.

Brege broke from the hug. From the look on Lasa's face it was too soon for the mother. Brege returned to her mount, tossed onto her shoulders the bags her horse had carried, and turned to face the crowd. Her voice rose above the babble.

"Let the horses be taken to graze. Let the People gather at the plaza." Brege's voice was strong, her shoulders thrown back. The shy young woman who had listened quietly from the back of the longhouse was gone.

Kaul called for horse wranglers, and Soren dashed for

ward. The survivors of River Bend seemed to sense this council was not for them. From where he sat his horse, Tomas shouted to Soren. Soon both young men were mounted and herding the beasts, one with a quarterstaff, the other with a captured lariat.

As the two groups separated, Jack came to Launa's side, a questioning eyebrow raised. *Where do we belong?*

The separation of the two groups was not something Launa and Brege had talked about, but the only way Launa would be kept out of this decision was if they tossed her out bodily. True, these people had to choose their own path, but Launa wouldn't let them head down the wrong one without giving it one hell of a fight. She and Jack joined the mob following the scouts.

At the central plaza, the four witnesses stood in front of the longhouse, facing the people, Lasa and Kaul on their right. Brege scanned the crowd, smiled when she caught sight of Launa, and signaled the two soldiers to her side.

Teeth gritted as tight as when she faced the horsemen's charge, Launa joined the witnesses before the people of Tall Oaks. Brege slipped over to stand beside Launa, squeezed the soldier's arm, and whispered, "You are one of us."

One of us! Emotions swept over Launa, clogging her throat, rimming her eyes with moisture. She tasted, for the first time, just how much she had wanted, through all the transfers, to belong to one place, one sacred place. *Here* was *her* place. God or goddess help them all. She wanted them as much as they needed her.

Then Brege stepped forward, and Launa prepared to fight a war for the life of her new people—and their souls.

"You sent us to see with our own eyes
the deeds done at River Bend.
You sent us to see with our own eyes
what the horsemen did to our kith and kin.
You sent us to open our hearts
to what no heart had seen.
Our hearts found kith and kin
hiding in the woods like hunted animals.

Our hearts found kith and kin
slaughtered by their hearths.
Our hearts found sisters slaughtered and . . ."

Brege faltered. There was no word for murder in the
tongue. There was no word for rape. Brege's eyes fell to the
ground. No one moved to interrupt her. Finally Brege spoke
to the dust of the plaza, but her words echoed to every ear.

"Our hearts found sister taken,
Sisters taken not in playfulness, not by arms that caressed,
Sisters taken by arms that held them down,
took their life."

Dismay widened eyes around the plaza. People who had
held to dreams of what the world should be, even in the face
of Antia's words, now came up hard against Brege's echo of
the same horror. *Open your ears, people.* Launa saw other
heads nod slowly; some had believed Antia.

Brege took several deep breaths and began again.

"Harken to my words.
Let my words pass from ear to heart.
Let my words pass from old to young forever.
The horsemen came to River Bend
and slaughtered our kith and kin,
The horsemen came to Tall Oaks
to look upon us for slaughter."

Heads came up. Shock was universal. No, not quite.
Launa watched Lasa's and Kaul's faces go impassive. She
studied them, but their rigid stance told her nothing—or
maybe everything.

"The horsemen returning from Tall Oaks
hunted the women and children that fled from River Bend.
But the horsemen hunted unaware
that they were hunted themselves.
For soldiers hunted those
who had done slaughter at River Bend.
For soldiers hunted those
who stalked Tall Oaks for slaughter.

For soldiers put themselves between the killers
and those they would slaughter.
First the soldiers drew the wisdom
from the killers' hearts.
Then the soldiers lured the killers to their death.
The soldiers lured the eyes of the killers
so they did not see their death
until it was too late to flee it."

Brege pulled the vest from the bag. Throwing the sack at her feet, she waved the bloody garment.

"Here is the shirt of him who hunted the People.
See his life blood on it.
With these hands,
I let that life blood out of his veins.
We standing here before you
let that life blood out of all the horsemen
who would hunt our People and slaughter us."

Brege stepped into the empty space between the witnesses and the People, then pivoted to face her mother. "Lasa who Speaks for the Goddess, let us meet in council, for this shirt tells many stories and our hearts must hear them all."

Lasa seemed taken aback by her daughter's formal address, but in a blink she had recovered and led the way into the longhouse. Brege took Tuam and Launa in hand and led them toward the high dais. "Stand here beside me, my sisters."

My sisters. The word sent a tremble through Launa. Emotion threatened to rise again as she found herself with Brege to one side, Lasa to the other. *I am home. I am really home.*

Now to keep home safe.

A shudder rocked Brege as women filed in to take their seats on the benches. Launa looked down into eyes gone hollow. She squeezed Brege's hand. She, too, could see another longhouse.

Not with my people, they won't, Launa swore to herself.

The men gathered in their place. Kaul sat cross-legged

with Merik, Taelon, and Jack around him. It took several minutes for all to find their places. There were no refreshments today; the youngsters were gone. When all were seated, Brege stepped forward and held up the vest.

> *"Let all eyes see this shirt.*
> *Let all hearts harken to the story it tells*
> *for the story it tells*
> *says much about the heart that wore it.*
> *See above all the sun and the mountain.*
> *See from them the lightning bolt and the blade.*
> *See nothing here that is sacred to the Goddess."*

Brege raised high the chain with its charms.

> *"See here again the sun and mountain, bolt and blade.*
> *My eyes saw hands of hands of horsemen*
> *that we had slain.*
> *My eyes saw many of these*
> *but nothing sacred to the Goddess."*

Brege discarded the vest and necklace, dropping them on the floor as she turned to old Bellda who had once spoken for the goddess. "You ask how someone who followed the way of the Goddess could do the deeds you have heard. I say these men follow another way, a way that knows nothing of the Goddess." With that Brege sat, and all hell broke loose.

For the next hour Launa listened as shocked voices questioned how anyone could follow any other way than that of the goddess. Others still could not believe that anyone of the goddess could do what the scouts had seen. One man even went so far as to question whether Brege had seen what she had said.

God damn it! What's it going to take, a horseman driving a lance through your heart?

Brege rested a restraining hand on Launa, held her in place before she could leap up and give voice to her thoughts. "Peace, sister. Everyone must Speak the Words the Goddess puts in their heart. How else will we know Her ways?" Brege paused, glanced at the man. "At least that was what my mother taught me."

Launa took a deep breath. She wasn't here just to win a war, but to save the soul of her people.

Right. But what do you save, everything? That was the problem. What do you change? What do you leave alone? And what little bit of change today is a monster tomorrow? *Maybe facing horsemen at three-to-one odds is the easy part of this job.*

At one point Jack looked ready to stalk out. *So even the Indian has a limit to his patience.* Launa swallowed a grin while Kaul swung his staff around to rest it in Jack's lap.

But Kaul was not silent. While Lasa listened intently to every word spoken, Kaul whispered to those around him: first Taelon, then Jack, later Masin. *What's he up to?*

Finally, Kaul got to his feet. He leaned on his shepherd's staff while talks lowly died around him.

"The wolf and bear live by sharp tooth and claw.
Like us, the wolf and bear are children of the Goddess.
Only in dreams can I ask the wolf and the bear
what they know of the way of the Goddess.
For the Goddess has not put words on the tongues
of the wolf and the bear.
The horsemen's tongue does not speak our words.
Even in dreams I have not asked them
what they know of the way of the Goddess."

Kaul stopped, and frowned thoughtfully. "Maybe a day will come when I do ask them face to face, but that is not a question for today." He straightened his shoulders and continued.

"The wolf and the bear fill their bellies
by sharp tooth and claw.
The wolf and the bear fill their bellies with deer and fish.
But if the wolf and the bear fill their bellies
with goats of my herd,
I do not ask them how they follow the way of the Goddess.
I do not ask but drive them away.
If they do not go, I kill them.
Listen to these words from my heart and my strong arm.

Let the horsemen follow the way that they must.
Let us follow the way that we must.
He who would slaughter the goats that I shepherd
must be driven away or I will kill him.
These are my words.
Soldiers stood between death and my daughter.
Let us hear how they would stand between death and us
*   all."*

Kaul leaned on his staff as his eyes swept the room. So Jack was right. Kaul was telling them, "We've dialogued. We've discussed. Now it's time for a decision." Launa checked out the sanctuary. Heads nodded, some vigorously, some slightly; several shook in disagreement. Way too many for Launa's likes met his gaze evenly, not yet agreeing, if not in opposition. Kaul sat.

Beside Launa, Lasa rose from her chair. Slowly, she opened her mouth. The moment of decision had come to these people.

"Mommy, Mommy." A little girl of four or five ran into the assembly and made a beeline straight for Lasa. The speaker swallowed her words and stooped to sweep the child into her arms.

Launa remembered a downsized version of herself bursting into her mother's bridge group. Something had been very important to Launa that morning. She had been swatted and sent back out to play. Today, the entire town waited while Lasa soothed her youngest daughter.

"What troubles your brow, little Blossom?"

"Titi hit me and Mamma Hammem told me I shouldn't have hit her and told me to say I was sorry and I'm not and she can't make me and I didn't mean to hit her first but she had my favorite doll and . . ."

"Shush, shush, now my little one." Lasa hugged the child, rocking her gently. Around the room, hands covered knowing smiles.

These people are unbelievable! This meeting, as important as the cabinet meeting she had watched on a TV monitor, was on hold for a child's momentary tragedy. Then Launa had to hide her own smile. God knows, somebody should have stopped that twenty-first-century meeting.

After a moment, Lasa pushed her daughter out to arm's length. "Now, Blossom. You know that hitting never solved any trouble. I have told you that since you were a little baby. You're a big girl now, learning the way of the Goddess. Does that way mean hitting?"

Little crushed curls began to shake back and forth. Tiny lips formed a pout.

"Now you go back to Mamma Hammem and tell her you are sorry for disturbing the tranquility of her home and that you are ready to play nicely with Titi. Go."

Small feet padded their way from the room.

With a trembling chin, Lasa watched the child go. "I tell my daughter that hitting never changes things." Lasa spoke half to herself, but the entire room listened. "Mother spoke those words to me. But today . . ." Lasa shivered—and Launa felt the cold as the speaker for the goddess turned to her. "Let us hear how you would stand between the horsemen and our deaths."

As Launa got to her feet, Brege rested an encouraging hand on her arm. At the men's end of the sanctuary, Jack made a fist, punched air. *Go for it, partner.*

Launa had studied the grand words that marched people off to war. She'd shared them with Brege on the ride back; they'd meant nothing to her. Launa rested her eyes on the door the little girl had disappeared through. How do you answer a mother's wisdom, guiding her daughter in the way of peace and harmony? Launa had to find words for peace and harmony—and war.

Her fingers touched Maria's hat. Launa took it off, ran its wide brim through her hands. Its feel calmed her, like rosary beads, worry beads. *What words would Maria give these people?* Words from the heart. Words of their own. Judith and all her knowledge had brought Launa to this point, but it would be the soldier's ability to inspire that would win today.

Lasa must have seen the doubt in Launa. She leaned forward. "Do not fear us, stranger. Our ears are open to your words. It is the Goddess's way to change. Does she not change the seasons? At least that is what I tell myself."

Launa nodded a thank-you and stepped forward to plead her case. "Forgive my simple words. For many years I listened to the wisdom of those who would stand between their people and the slaughter. Only since coming among you have I heard the art of your storytellers." Launa's thoughts wandered over all she had seen and done among these people.

"The first day I walked among you, I learned how you build fences to keep the pigs from feasting on your gardens. I have followed after your hunters to learn their wisdom. The wisdom of those who stand between their people and slaughter is much like your own wisdom. If we could, we would keep the horsemen from our people as you keep the pigs from peas." *Who can argue against a fence?*

"But if the beasts will not stay away from the people, we must lure the killers where we can kill them." Launa had said it the best way she knew. Several women and men nodded.

"To keep the hunters from our door, I would build a wall around the town. It would tell the wise horsemen to keep out. Only if they did not, would we kill them. For that I would ask many of you to stand with Antia to learn the wisdom of the long spear. With these and arrows, we would slaughter horsemen who lacked the wisdom to leave us in peace."

"How would you do that?" One man asked.

"That is not simple. I will look with a hunter's eye at Tall Oaks to create a trap. Also, much would come from what the horsemen did on the day they rode upon us. As Brege saw, the horsemen laid their plans to slaughter us. They did not change their plans when they fell into our trap. They died for that. You who have hunted the bear and wolf know that you must have a plan, but you may need to change it very quickly."

There were wry grins and nods among the men. One held up a scarred arm, and the nods increased.

"If you build a wall around our town, how will we get to the fields?" A woman asked the practical question.

"You leave a gate to enter your garden. We will leave a hole in the wall."

"It will take us more time to bring water."

"When you trade to gain something, you must give up something." That got more nods. The assembly grew silent. *You're winning them, kid.*

Then Samath stood up. "My consort Hanna sits with a woman in childbirth, so I will speak her words. I ask that I may grasp the full worth of what you ask us to trade. My heart knows what you offer, but I am not sure of the value we will lose."

Launa waited, her back knotting. Samath's words were pleasant. There were no used car salesmen here, so why did he sound like one?

"You want us to build a wall around our town. What will we use to make the wall?"

Launa relaxed a tad; technical questions were no problem. "We will dig a ditch and use the dirt to make the wall. Thus, the earth will serve us twice. What we dig from the ditch will keep the horsemen away as will the dirt we pile up in the wall."

Samath nodded. "Is earth all we will need for the wall?"

"No, wooden poles and split planks will also be needed."

"And where will you get this wood?" the woodsman snapped like a trap closing. "The woodlot is only so big."

"I do not know. You have the wisdom of the forest here. Are there trees up the river that could be cut and rafted down?" Jack gave her a thumbs-up on that answer, but Launa's nerves were tight again. There was something more behind Samath's questions than curiosity. *But what?*

"I did not see that. We have never done it, but yes. Wood could be floated down. Good." The carpenter stroked his beard. He plucked a wood chip from it and absently tossed it aside.

"My heart is deeply troubled by this next question. When I was young, my heart set its eyes for a woman, the most beautiful woman. I went to my father and I asked him, 'How do I make her want me for her consort? What must I do, Father?' He smiled at me, the way old men do when they speak to young men. He told me, 'Son, believe that you are hers. When you walk with her, believe that you are hers. When you talk with her, believe that you are hers. Believe, my son, and it will happen, and for my part, I will believe that you are hers and your mother will also. Believe, my son, believe.' " Samath looked around the room. From the looks on the faces of many women and men, Launa suspected many mothers and fathers had given and received this advice. She waited to see where Samath was leading.

The woodsman smiled. "And that beautiful woman chose me for her consort. We have lived together twenty happy springs. When I go to a tree, I ask, 'Where is the chair I want from you?' and I believe the chair is in it while I work, and lo, the chair is there. When my son works with me, we both believe and lo, it comes to pass." Samath's eyes swept the assembly.

"Now you say work every waking hour of every day preparing for the horsemen. I say if we believe and work for it, it will come to pass. We have better things to believe in and bring to pass. I say that our fears will bring our dread to us." He looked straight at Launa. "I say we send these people away. These killers of men came and the horsemen came to kill men. Is it not their belief that has brought this upon us?"

The meeting was bedlam. Launa glanced at Brege; the woman stared straight ahead. She'd never told Launa anything like this. *Thinking about something can make it happen!* What meant nothing to Launa swept around the longhouse like a fire.

Lasa touched Launa's leg, motioned her to sit. Launa collapsed into her place, flattened by a truck she didn't know existed. *Just like these people will be flattened by a war they can't see coming.* There was irony here, but Launa was too overwhelmed by what had happened to appreciate it.

Long minutes went by as the roar of talk filled the room. Launa had never heard the longhouse so noisy. On the dais, everyone was silent. In the end, it was Taelon who stood.

"I too remember believing that the woman of my heart would be mine, and she was. As a young man, I wanted to wear a wolf's pelt about my loins to impress that woman and draw her eye to me. All my belief and longing brought no wolf to our woods that year. I had to win her heart in rabbit skins." He gave the assembly a toothy grin as they laughed with him.

"In all the years I have hunted deer and bear, wolf and rabbit, I have never known the comings and goings of those of claw and fang to pay any attention to my belief in what they would do. Yes." He held up a hand. "When they are here, I ask the Goddess and she gives them over to my spear or arrow, but"—he shook his head decisively—"they go where they will. They stalk where they will, and the horsemen do the same." He looked Samath straight in the eye. "I say we stalk them if they come here, stalk them and kill them. My people will not be slaughtered as my brother's were." The hunter sat down. The room was silent. The silence grew.

Finally, Lasa leaned forward in her chair. "Have all the Words in our hearts been Spoken before the Goddess?" Many women and men nodded solemnly.

Lasa rose; her soft voice brought everyone forward in their seats, straining to hear. Yet, there was a solidness beneath her words that transcended all the others spoken here. "Let all hear the wisdom of the Goddess. Let no one tell another where to walk, what to believe in her heart. Let those who would follow after the soldiers do so. Let those who would keep their mind clear do so. Let all walk together in harmony along the way of the Goddess." The room's silence held as Lasa sat.

Then the room exploded with noise as everyone began talking at once. Launa kept her seat, locking her face down rigid to hide the emptiness inside. Lasa sounded just like the Colonel and his lady, hedging a bet by doing both. In the end, it hadn't worked in her parents' lives. Would it work here any better?

THIRTY-EIGHT

LAUNA HAD BEEN seven years old when the Colonel's lady informed her daughter that "It is time you become a lady." Being a "lady" meant ballet lessons, learning to sew, and a dozen other things. Yet the Colonel was just as adamant. "A leader of men"—it was always men—"must be the toughest man in his command." That meant archery, shooting, riding, and soccer—"You must know victory and defeat." What he meant was you've got to win, because defeat meant hell around the house for three days until you won the next game.

Launa did what she had to do to keep peace in the house. She did what the Colonel wanted, and his lady. She did it for seven crammed years, giving her folks every waking moment of her life. On her fourteenth birthday, she'd had enough. "I'm going to West Point," she told her folks, and managed not to add *and you can go to hell.* She knew what she wanted, and it was clear by then that nothing she did could save her parents' marriage.

Four years later Launa left for the Point. There, they put into words what she had learned as a kid: know your objective, concentrate your mass where you need it, and economize where you don't. Launa doubted her folks ever figured out what they needed. Had Lasa?

Jack came up beside her. "You did good."

"I didn't do shit," Launa snapped, then did what she should have done before she said anything: let out a long breath. "I just don't get it. What was Samath talking about?"

"Not something they covered at the Point, that's for sure." Jack fidgeted for a moment, enough that he had Launa's full attention. "Sandie showed me an article in a magazine once. I think the word they used was 'imaging.' If you keep telling yourself you're dumb and can't do it, you will be. If you visualize yourself as capable, you will be." Then Jack got one of his lopsided grins. " 'Course, visualizing yourself winning the lottery doesn't work all that well."

Launa glanced around. Maybe these people weren't so strange. Maybe she'd just been run over by another part of the education she missed because the Colonel and his lady saw no use for it. *Okay, concentrate on the mission.* "Did we win anything today? Certainly not the whole jackpot."

"We may have won more than you think. There were a lot of men nodding right along with you."

"Did you get a head count?"

Jack shrugged. "Maybe twenty-five."

"We'll need a lot more than that."

"Yeah, but remember, these are the old folks. It gets harder to change as you get used to the way things have been. Let's give the younger people a chance. There looked to be over fifty drilling with Cleo when we rode in."

Launa nodded; for better or worse, she was committed to Tall Oaks. This fortress town would be the keystone of a defense that would shield Europe from the first Kurgan onslaught. If they held them off here and now, they could buy Europe a thousand years of peaceful, cooperative development. The next time the horsemen got restless, they'd fine Europe a much tougher and more advanced nut to crack.

Launa headed for the speaker for the bull. He was surrounded by men his own age or younger. Kaul greeted her. "Your words spoke to many hearts. The men understand the hunt and many will run with you." Kaul's confidence took a bite out of Launa's doubts.

"Samath doesn't sound as if he will."

"Samath has a big heart," Kaul said with a sigh. "I wish

his head were as big. There is much wisdom in what he says, but true wisdom knows when to draw from the old and when to seek the new."

Other men said much the same. But Launa noted that few of them actually volunteered to join her at drill. Every few moments, Kaul would glance toward Lasa huddled with her own group of elders, both women and men.

As minutes stretched, Launa got edgy. "What is happening?"

"There are those who still must talk on what has been said," Kaul answered. "If they can, they will fill Lasa's ears until the night is old."

Launa's gut knotted tighter. Hanna had come in, joining her consort. Was even the half decision subject to change? Kaul took her elbow. "Let us wait outside."

On the veranda, Hass stopped Launa. Hanna's son, he was also father of the two-year-old Frieda had found their second night here. "I do not care what others say. I will follow after you. I and many others will build the wall that will keep the horsemen away from those we love. I have seen into your heart. What you call us to follow is from the Goddess. Show us the new path for our feet and we will walk it with you."

With Hass were other young men and women. Too young to be in the assembly, they must have held their own meeting out here, listening as the older heads decided their fate. But if no one could tell another the path for her feet, then these young people had a right to choose for themselves. Launa glanced around the plaza. There were over a hundred men and women. Some were leaving, walking their own way, but over fifty were staying and more were trotting in, talking with the leavers and the stayers—and making up their own mind.

"Will you drill with us in the morning?" Launa asked Hass.

" I spend many hours with my father making bows. I also must work the fields on the days that are mine, but yes. I will be with Antia at tomorrow's dawn."

"Thank you," Launa said, feeling the first budding of

hope since Jack, six thousand years from now, had told her exactly what she'd volunteered for.

"Not a bad commitment from a National Guard type," Jack whispered beside her.

"No, not bad at all," Launa agreed. "We came here to save a people. God willing, we can save their lives and the way they live them."

At last Lasa came out; Kaul hugged her, whispering something that Launa missed. The speaker for the goddess sighed and turned to Launa. "There will be more talk, but now there are words I must say to you."

But she said nothing. Kaul, grinning like a fox who owned the henhouse, led off, and the others followed him. With each step, Lasa seemed to shuffle off the burden of the longhouse. By the edge of town, she too was grinning.

"The winter is coming. Kaul and I wondered what we could give to the strangers who brought us the bow. We do not know where you come from, or where you are going, but we do know that you cannot reach there before the first snow. While you were gone, the People built this."

Kaul stopped, opened his arms wide, and pointed to a house. The air held the scent of newly worked wood. Lasa's voice was solemn as she went on. "You brought our daughter home through much. That was a great gift."

The speaker's arms engulfed Launa in a mother's hug. After the fighting and the killing, the worry and the terror, Launa let herself drift in its warmth and protection. Maria's hugs were like that. *Have I done enough, Maria? I'm trying.*

Lasa held the soldier out at arm's length. "This house is yours."

"My house." Launa whispered the words, half a prayer.

Lasa nodded. "We could not have you living under a tree. You have given us so much. Our hearts had to give something in return. Come, look upon what is here." Kaul drew aside the deerskin door, and Lasa preceded him in.

Launa stopped at the door, but only for a moment. *My first home, and nobody to carry me across the threshold. Damn!* Inside, she slowly took in her house, even as her mind heard Brent catalogue its contents. "Four meters wide by eight long. Wooden beams support a thatch roof. A stone and clay hearth about half a meter off the floor to the right, a bed for the man across from the fireplace. At the far end, a large bed for the woman." There was no way for the old archaeologist to know about the basket at the bed's foot or the pile of sticks beside the fire. Clay pots, wooden tongs, spoons, and jars brimming with grain filled out the inventory. Launa flew to hug Lasa.

"This is beautiful. This is wonderful. I have a home." Tears fled down Launa's cheeks, falling on the speaker's shoulders. *You're overreacting, girl.*

Damn it, I've got a right to lose it now. I've done all I can for one day.

Lasa seemed taken aback. "Such tears for a gift as common as a house?"

"Among our people"—Launa struggled to get the words out—"soldiers do not have houses of their own."

Kaul shook his head. "Such a way is not good. Here you will always have a home." Launa's embrace expanded to include Kaul and Jack. For several moments, Launa swayed back and forth with them, lost and found. When the two couples broke apart, Kaul held Lasa. Jack's arm was a bit tentative on Launa's shoulder as she spoke her heart. "Thank you for my home. Thank you for making me one with the People."

Lasa gave Launa a motherly kiss, then turned to Kaul. "Let us leave these two to themselves." She stooped to pass through the door.

Kaul looked back before he dropped the deerskin flap. "I will see that the horses are cared for tonight. Thank you for what you have brought to us and for what you bring us in yourselves."

THIRTY-NINE

LAUNA AWOKE NEXT morning in her own bed in her own home. Birds chirped and soft light trickled through the rafters.

Last night, wrung empty from the emotional roller coaster of the last week, she had collapsed into bed almost as soon as Lasa and Kaul left.

Maybe it wasn't exhaustion, Maybe I was just feeling safe for the first time since I left the Point. Or maybe both. She'd been asleep before her head hit the blankets.

This morning she woke slowly, letting herself luxuriate in one thought. *I'm home. I have a home.*

Jack rolled over in his bed across from the hearth. *Is it time to go back to where we were before the damn dog growled?*

She stretched. *I'm alive, and all the SOB's who wanted different aren't.* Every muscle of her body luxuriated in the power of life. It flowed through her, gathering into a hunger centered well below her stomach. It was a good morning to start the rest of her life.

"Jack?"

His head came up sleepily.

Launa lifted the covers, inviting. Jack came, not even trying to hide what he was coming for.

Launa grinned, threw the covers back, not caring as they

tumbled off the bed, and reached for what she wanted. Jack slid into bed, put his arms around her, and kissed her. She kissed back with all the power of someone who had seen death and lived to celebrate life.

There was a sound at the door. Before Launa could say or do anything, Brege and Merik drew the skin aside and walked in. "It is a beautiful day to be alive," Brege called. Then, seeing Launa and Jack, she beamed. "The Goddess is truly gracious."

Launa grabbed for blankets. Nothing was in reach. Jack sat up, his manhood doing likewise. Launa faltered, feeling her face flush, seeing the red of her embarrassment as far as her breasts. She couldn't decide whether to cover herself from Merik's gaze, or stand between Jack and Brege's. Brege looked Jack up and down and grinned at Launa. "The Goddess is truly gracious to some of her sisters. The soldier has many implements besides his bow."

Launa gave up. The icy modesty her mother had demanded puddled at her feet, unable to survive the open warmth of these people. Launa sat back on her bed and put a proprietary arm around Jack.

"What brings you to us as the sun rises?" Two could play that game. A sunbeam from the ceiling lit the two visitors. Neither wore anything. Merik lacked a belt. Even Brege's hair flowed free without a ribbon to restrain it.

The townspeople settled onto the spare bed. Brege took a moment before answering Launa's question. When she did, it was with a small voice. "After my mother and father left you last night, they talked with other elders. Hanna joined them, and the talk went long into the night. Many were disturbed by what we had done." Brege's eyes lost their focus. Launa could almost smell the tree again, hear the shouts. *How bad were the nightmares, sister?*

Brege shivered; Merik put an arm around her shoulder, one Launa suspected had been there a long time last night. Brege gave her consort a wan smile for a thank-you and continued. "We have come back to the People smelling of death. What could clean us of that stench? After much talk about learning the leadings of the Goddess and how we could do such terrible deeds in her way, a woman remembered a field of winter grain that needed planting. We will spend today in the arms of the Goddess." Now Brege did smile, a penitent sure that blessing awaited her.

Launa wasn't so sure. With no clothes to fumble for, she fumbled for words. "I had thought to spend the day with Kaul outlining the wall and ditch."

"Oh, no." Brege shook her head. "People need a sign of the Goddess's favor. If the field is fruitful, that is good. If our bellies are fruitful, that is even better."

"Let me guess," Jack whispered in Launa's ear. "The uniform of the day, isn't."

Launa shrugged. She had her own problems. With the implants in her arm, her belly wasn't likely to do any swelling.

Jack scowled down at his swelling problem. "A boy got ribbed something terrible about a boner in the locker room. Now I'm supposed to parade this down main street."

Launa gave one more thought to all her mission-related problems. They weren't going to happen today; her new people had their own agenda. One glance at Jack's baleful face, and Launa had to struggle to stifle a laugh. Tossing her soldier's duty in a cocked hat for today, she bounced out of bed, then offered Jack a hand up.

"Jack is truly in the embrace of the Goddess. We go with a good omen already." If that was what Brege and everyone else thought, that was fine by Launa. But the red on Jack's neck told her he wasn't adjusting so easily.

Toward town, someone had left several sacks of grain. Jack picked two up, Merik the others. As they made their way to the field, passersby called and waved. Jack's manliness brought high praise from both sexes.

"Damn, won't this thing ever go down?" Jack mumbled as Launa bit her lip to keep from laughing.

"Well, Captain, I could drop right here and let you do some push-ups over me. Would that solve your problem?" Then she did laugh as her suggestion only added to the source of his discomfort.

"Damn you." He grew redder; then his eyes twinkled and

he leered. "Come, my modest Lieutenant. I accept your offer."

Launa thought better of the idea on second review. She danced easily away from his lunge, slowed as he was by the sacks he carried. Both women ran ahead of their men, putting some distance between them and Jack's condition, which now proved to be contagious. Merik, however, was quite pleased with himself.

"My father told me I was born from just such a field plowing as we go to today. He plowed the field and it was fertile. He plowed mother, and here I am." He shrugged and grinned.

Both women laughed, and Merik joined in. Finally, even Jack did, but the women kept a healthy lead on their men the rest of the hike out.

The length and width of the field was marked with short sticks. A wooden plow lay at the beginning of the first furrow. A tree stood nearby. From one of its branches hung a water bag. A sack lay against the trunk.

"Shall we plow a few furrows before we eat?" Brege asked.

"Yours?" Merik gave her a cheerful leer.

"The field's." Brege's scowl had too much smile in it, but she pointed sternly at the traces on the plow pole and Merik went to one side, offering Jack the other. Brege stood the plow up, its handles firm in her grasp. Launa shouldered a bag of seed, wondering how she was supposed to spread it. Brege saw her confusion.

"When they have broken the ground, drop a few seeds in and brush the earth back over them. The seed must be planted deep." Since this last was aimed at the men and drew a cheerful grunt and playful hip thrust from Merik, Launa didn't know how important depth really was.

Brege glanced back at Launa frequently as she and the men cut the first furrow. Brege seemed satisfied with how Launa dropped the seed.

The sun warmed Launa. It was hot and dusty work, but it was real work. As a child, Launa had been shushed for pointing at cows and saying "Big Macs." Mother had insisted on a world without sources, without causes and effects. The Colonel and his lady lived in a world created by their own minds.

Under the beating sun, Launa felt rooted to the real. What she did would put food in the mouths of her people. There was nothing artificial here. Seed and work meant full bellies and life. If, Launa reminded herself, luck held and the goddess smiled with rain and sun in the proper proportion.

She remembered the Oklahoma farmers around Fort Sill. They had lived by work and seed and weather, just like these people. She had thought little about them. Now these people were all she had and all she ever wanted.

After five furrows, Brege called a rest. The men doused their thirst while Launa and Brege rummaged in the sack. There was bread and dried fish, nuts, berries, and four apples. Brege put half back for later and divided the remainder into two small bags. She gave one to Launa and kept the other. Launa was prepared to wolf down the meal and get on with the work, but Brege stopped her. "We feed our men first. Didn't you tell me that a rider must first care for her mount?"

Warmth shot through Launa's thighs; her breasts tingled. There was more to feed today than just their mouths.

A reclining Merik held out his arms to Brege, and she went to her man. Bestride him, she bent to receive his kiss. The embrace was long enough that Launa began to suspect all thought of food had fled, but no. Brege pulled herself up and, still astride Merik, began to again divide the meal. She'd feed a piece of bread or fish to Merik, then one to herself. Occasionally Merik would wiggle beneath her. She would smile and adjust herself. Never did Merik quite manage to find the sheath he so earnestly sought.

After a while, Brege looked up at where Jack and Launa were still standing. "Don't you know how to play?"

Jack ran his tongue along tight lips, yet his eyes did not hold her to the morning's promise now that they were here, in a public—what would her mother have said—orgy. From Jack came only a question, open, undemanding, but pulsating with a need that must be as strong as her own.

"Yes, we do," Launa breathed. Jack slowly sat, then rolled onto his back. She stood over him, admiring the soft tremble of his lips, the ripple of his muscles, the pulsing of his manhood. What made this vision so horrible to look at? She'd seen ugly enough pictures in public: savagery, brutality, loneliness.

Those belonged to a dead world; she belonged to this one. Could she play this new game as well as the senseless games she had been born to? She had learned a lot in her life. Softly she smiled down at Jack, the realization dawning of how much she loved that man. She would play by Lasa and Brege's rules.

She fed Jack, piece by piece, as his manhood tapped ever more demandingly at her yearning cleft. How could Brege hold back? Yet the woman did. Each nut, each berry, was slowly, languidly shared out between them.

Time and again, Launa found herself watching the other couple. Was she part of a wild orgy like her mother condemned? What was it she saw that made her look again and again? Was it two naked people having sex that drew her eye? Or was there something they had that she lacked?

Certainly it wasn't technique. They hadn't shown Launa anything she hadn't picked up in the back seat of a car in high school. But they had something; something she couldn't grasp.

There was an innocence about them. They were totally involved in each other. Naked to the sky and open to anyone's view, still they were unencumbered by guilt, control, power, ownership—obscenities that had never been far from the sexuality Launa learned at her mother's knee.

The distractions of thinking could not overpower the rising tide of Launa's hunger. She struggled for breath, the demands of her loins drawing her back, pulling her deep within herself. Her yearning to be filled mocked the food in her mouth. Finally, after an eternity of aching, Brege pulled out the apple. Laughing, she rolled over until Merik towered above her. With the apple in her mouth, she used her eyes to beckon her man to come and eat. Merik thrust for her fruit as they bit into the apple in her mouth. Juice sprayed, dripping down lips and cheek and throat.

Launa looked in her sack; several berries remained. She reached for the apple and tried rolling over without losing touch with Jack. She had never done that before; both groaned as they rolled apart.

In a moment Jack was back. Breathing a deep sigh, she emptied herself of so much that had come with her through time. Opening herself to him, she opened her soul. Still trying to play the new game to the fullest, she reached for the apple. The damn thing rolled beyond her grasp. But Jack needed no juice to lure his lips to hers. Feverishly, her mouth traveled down the lines of his throat. He tasted of salt and earth. Today she hungered for that.

She felt him gather himself. She arched, waiting for his plunge into her. But when he came to her, it was not with a thrust, but gently, slowly. It only served to inflame her need.

"Where is the Bull?" She threw her hips up at him, demanding he hasten. And he did. With each thrust, he grew more powerful. He was the Bull, she the Goddess. Then the universe exploded and they were separate no more.

An eon later, Launa heard Brege calling them. "We have more furrows to plow."

"Can't you see? She's broken his plow." Merik laughed.

"I'll break your head." But Brege's scowl had too much mirth to make the threat believable. "Up, you lazy men. There's more seed to be sown beside your own."

With good-natured grumbling, those who spoke for the Bull took their place at the plow. It was Launa's turn to do the tilling. Her furrows wandered far from the straight. Merik insisted it was all Jack's fault. He had seen how Launa's knees had gone weak. She didn't care. The seed was being put in the ground.

Often Launa glanced back at Brege. She wore a contented smile. Once or twice Launa caught her moistening the seed in her hand with the juices of her and Merik's play. Part of Launa felt revulsion, instilled by the Colonel's lady in cool, crisp, air-conditioned quarters. Another part could hear Lasa telling her daughter, "Let all the power of the Goddess be in you and your seed." Home was no longer with the Colonel's lady, if it ever had been. Home was here. Launa smiled at the thought of how she would spread the seed next time.

After ten more furrows, they stopped again for water and food. This time Merik took the lead. He fed Brege and let his hands wander where they would between bites. Launa suspected food was left in both sacks when one hunger overtook another.

Launa felt the change. Now when her eyes wandered to the other couple, it was to pay respect for the skillful way Merik played Brege. He a concert violinist, she responding like a Stradivarius.

Launa had been taught to value the cool, the calm. That brittle world was in the grave now. She had chosen a new one. This gentle playfulness was a part of that choice. She surrendered herself to play, to Jack, to new life. In the warmth of the afternoon, she discovered her new soul in the wild, abandoned passion of Jack's arms.

When finally she could form words again, embarrassed, she apologized. "I, I'm sorry Jack, if I took and didn't give back. I . . . I just got lost in myself."

Jack's grin was not that of someone who had suffered a loss. "I never knew making someone feel so good"—a hand languidly wandered from breast to belly—"could make me feel so fantastic myself. Just watching you was an orgasm."

Five more rows finished the field. The couples went together to wash in the river. Brege slowly let the men pull ahead of them. She frowned, seeming to have a question but lacked the words to ask it.

"Yes?" Launa encouraged her.

"You never learned the play between woman and man, the sport of lovers?"

"You have taught me much today I never knew."

Brege worried her lip. "You spoke of listening for many years to the wisdom of those who would hunt the killers of women."

Launa nodded.

"Yet you have been told nothing of the play of joy."

Launa sighed and nodded again.

Brege shook her head slowly. "Yours is a strange world, to sing songs of killing, and none of loving."

The soldier looked ahead, seeing more than trees and river. "There is more wisdom in your words, Brege, than you know."

Launa wanted no more of dark thoughts on this day of life in the Goddess. "Run with me to the river." There was no way to say "Race you to see who gets to the river first" in the tongue of the People. Today, Launa was glad of that.

In an instant they dashed past the men. With a shout, the men were in hot pursuit. Four splashed into the water too evenly for even an Olympic judge to declare a winner.

Launa would have thought that Jack was spent for the day, but the cool summer water refreshed more than their spirits. Each couple found its own piece of leaf-shaded moss. They were quite late when finally they joined the People for supper.

Launa gave no thought to her or Jack's nakedness before these people, her people. When the evening songs were sung and Jack's hand moved to caress leg and thigh and breast, she sought no deeper shadow than any other couple as the Bull again spoke to the Goddess.

Later that night, as they walked back to their home, Launa did not stop at her door, but strolled on to the first field. The engineer in her marked out where with tomorrow's dawn they would build a wall—the first fortification in Europe. She turned back to watch Tall Oaks as it slumbered under the full moon.

She'd come through time almost as naked as the day she was born, but her soul had dragged the heavy baggage of twenty years of careful teachings. She'd fought the horsemen for her life, but she'd had to fight the Colonel and his wife for her soul. Not just them, but Judith and Brent too. Each of them had given her what they thought she needed to know, but none of them could have guessed what she needed for life here, among the People.

Launa clinched her hands in the soft light. Tomorrow would be the first dawn of a new life for her—and a new future. She would live it, here, in this town. She had sweated and bled and killed for Tall Oaks. It belonged to her just as she belonged to it. Whatever future there was for either of them—or the world—they would weave together.

She glanced up at the moon. It was virgin once more, untrod by Earth's children. Someday, people again would walk its face, not at the end of a race that one side won and the other lost, but because it was there. This she swore. With her life's blood, this she would make true.

She hugged Jack on the doorstep of their home. Without a word, he picked her up and carried her across the threshold. Launa laughed, and offered a prayer that Judith and Brent found their new future as wonderful as she found the past. Maybe even that poor little dog they tested the time transport on, Muffin, would find a good home.

EPILOGUE

SCHOLAR JUDITH LEE, wise woman of ancient cultures, cut the power on her electrocycle and let it roll to a stop in the parking lot of the Lady Livermore Laboratory for the Study of Energy. She dismounted and glanced at her watch, fifteen minutes early to pick up her daughter. Judith relaxed, spreading her arms to the sky. She loved the warmth of the California sun, the smell of the soil.

The feelings and smells of these visits to her daughter brought back memories of the first digs she had gone on, nice memories for a woman at her age. Before she lost herself in reveries, she remembered to spread out the solar cells on her cycle. Every minute's feed was a few extra watts to the battery.

Her eyes roved the horizon. The hills to the west were still green from the April rains. New windmills were being added to the row upon row that danced up them. The windmills jarred the scene. No matter how hard modern society tried to stay in harmony with nature, there was no way to make a propeller or eggbeater look like something natural.

Still, Judith would not complain. She had seen the belching smokestacks of some of the alternative energy sources that were being experimented with. The gaping holes in the earth from the new open pit coal mines did not look to Judith like a proper way to treat Our Mother Earth. It was almost enough to drive Judith from the Progressive Party. Almost, but not quite. As a student of the past, she knew the future was not there.

Another windmill began to turn, and she smiled. It was the wind that brought the windmills here and the windmills that brought the Center. Here was one of the few places on earth with extra electricity for study. And the Center brought her daughter, and her daughter was the reason Judith could make her too few, but oh so wonderful visits. Such were the strange cycles of modern life.

A door opened behind her. Judith turned to see Tanya walking across the grass leading a dog on a makeshift leash. "What have you got there, first-born daughter of mine?"

"I don't really know, Mom." Her daughter's face was a puzzle. "This morning we had more wind than we expected. We actually had nearly twenty megawatts to work with, the most ever. As soon as Lady Harrison and scholar Milo stabilized the field they wanted, there was a pop and this little gal was sitting on the floor. We don't know where she came from."

Judith stooped to pick up the dog. She didn't look like any sort of breed Judith was familiar with. "What are you calling her?"

"The tags say Muffin, but look at it."

Tanya held the dog so Judith could read it. They both stared at each other.

"Where is the City of Los Angeles?" Tanya asked.